JILTED

SU MATTIE

Published by I_AM Self-Publishing, 2017.

ISBN 978-1-912145-82-9

I AM SELF-PUBLISHING

@iamselfpub
www.iamselfpublishing.com

Contents

PART 1

Chapter 1 9
Chapter 2 20
Chapter 3 26
Chapter 4 38
Chapter 5 49
Chapter 6 61
Chapter 7 68
Chapter 8 77
Chapter 9 92
Chapter 10 100
Chapter 11 103
Chapter 12 117
Chapter 13 124
Chapter 14 129
Chapter 15 134
Chapter 16 139
Chapter 17 146
Chapter 18 153

Chapter 19 159
Chapter 20 169
Chapter 21 177
Chapter 22 187
Chapter 23 201
Chapter 24 211

PART 2

Chapter 1 223
Chapter 2 237
Chapter 3 251
Chapter 4 258
Chapter 5 262
Chapter 6 273
Chapter 7 278
Chapter 8 288
Chapter 9 307
Chapter 10 325
Chapter 11 334

About the Author 344

"I have brought you the rose of love and you have crowned me in these dark hours with their thorns."

Kristian Goldmund Aumann

Part 1

Chapter 1

On Friday evenings, when she finished her shift at the hairdressers, Kalyani parked her red Clio two doors away from her own house, in the off-street parking space in front of Fat Fred's house. She knew that Fred would then have to park further down and walk uphill. It was a bonus that his shifts at B&Q finished late, so it was unlikely that she would ever come face to face with him. Everyone on the street knew who Fat Fred was, because his cholesterol collections were displayed so flamboyantly; they hung and swung more majestically than anyone else's.

'I am doing him a favour,' she told herself. 'He needs the exercise or he'll end up dead years before his time.'

There was a reason for this bizarre routine. On Saturday mornings, arriving on the morning train from Swindon, was Raffa. Dapper, geeky Raffa, with an appealing CV for a dating ad – 'tall, fair IT consultant from England, only son and heir…'

Except that he and his family worshipped at the local mosque, twice a week, while her family went to the Hindu temple in Dudley, about three times a year. Kalyani never paused to analyse the consequences of this disparity. Surely, in this day and age, such a minor inconvenience would not be an obstacle to love.

And in love she was! The sort of love that made her get out of bed at this godforsaken hour on a cold February morning, before her family, and leave the house quietly. Neither of which came naturally to her. All her life, her parents and teachers took it upon themselves to inform her that she was a 'noisy so and so', and that she was 'giving them a headache', because she bumped into tables, tripped on rugs, rattled crockery, dropped cutlery, and often banged her head when she retrieved it. *Oops, ouch, sorry, ow…* Now, borne out of necessity, she learned very quickly to avoid stepping on the creaky third step on the staircase, to lift the kitchen door by a few millimetres when she opened it to stop it from squeaking, and to duck the wind chimes swinging in the breeze. She had oiled the hinges of the metal gate at the bottom of their small garden with liberal squirts of WD-40, on an afternoon when her family was visiting friends. She carried her soft moccasins in her hands until she was out of the kitchen door and tiptoed out to her car, parked a few doors away. Although the likelihood of Fat Fred hearing her start the car above the noise of his snoring was miniscule, she avoided slamming her car door, and did not switch on her headlights until she moved away.

She drove past Raffa's house, pleased that its residents were still asleep, and paused at the crossroads, where her headlights picked up the street sign. Under the green graffiti, it said 'London Road', as if its migrant and Asian residents needed reminding that they lived in England.

The streets around the train station, normally bustling with humans and traffic, were deserted, and no one honked at her bad driving. At the station, she was spoilt for choice for a parking space, but she chose to drive up the ramp to the first level. From here, she could see the train approaching over the bridge and disappear from view as it entered the station. A queue of taxis formed at the entrance, waiting for the groggy passengers to emerge, yawning behind their gloves, their stale breath misting the air, shoving their tickets and passes back into their handbags or pockets, dragging their luggage noisily behind them.

She spotted Raffa breaking away from the masses and moving towards the stairs to the first level. She knew she would lose sight of him for a few minutes while he walked up. Just enough time to glance at the mirror on her sun visor, fluff up her hair, and pinch her lips. Then he was at the top of the stairs, striding purposefully towards her. Her heart was beating with a rhythm of its own, and her lips couldn't stop smiling. He opened the Clio's door and eased his hulk of muscles into the front seat. He gave her a lop-sided smile.

'Hey sexy.'

They had learned the hard way not to touch each other. The rotund, grey-haired parking attendant was on the lookout, since the morning he had caught them in a compromising position in her car. She put the car in gear and, after stalling a couple of times, she roared out of the car park, took a couple of left turns, drove over a roundabout into an industrial estate, abandoned for the weekend, and screeched to a halt behind an articulated lorry. She clutched nervously at the steering wheel and waited for one of his usual comments.

'How long have you been driving?' or 'Where did you get your licence again?'

Today, he said, 'I am just checking to see if I am still in one piece.'

'Do you want me to help?' She fluttered her eyes at him.

'Don't mind,' he said, as they both climbed into the back seat. The magic started almost immediately and soon exploded like a Skittles advert on TV. If anybody noticed the car swaying wildly because of the two writhing bodies joined at the hips and lips, they didn't bother investigating.

Later, they sat side by side, wrapped in each other's arms. 'When they give you a pay rise, Kals, please could you buy a bigger car?' he requested, moving his head to release a crick in his neck.

‘Fat chance of that.’ She reached out to massage his neck. ‘How about you renting a van and driving up instead?’

‘A very plausible solution,’ Raffa agreed. He got out of the car, tucked his shirt in, and zipped up the essential parts of his wardrobe.

‘You are the only man who wears a tie to bed,’ she teased, coming out to stand beside him.

On the horizon, the new day streaked the sky with pink and turquoise hues. Around them, the dark shapes hidden by the night lost their mystery and the dawn chorus rent the air. He turned towards her, and watched her watching the sunrise; her caramel skin glowing, eyes dancing with joy, her hair black and sleek like a river at midnight, even after the rough and tumble in the back seat of her car.

He had chosen well. This one was a keeper.

*

It was past 7a.m. when Kalyani sneaked back into her parents’ three-bed semi. She had dropped Rafik off at the bus stop at the top of the street, from where he would walk to his family home, pretending to have arrived by bus. Most of the street was still asleep, the houses dark and silent, apart from the soft, orange light seeping through the odd window.

In the kitchen, the boiler, which was set on auto timer, had started rattling and buzzing, masking any noise she made when she let herself in and tiptoed back to bed. She stifled a giggle as she passed her parents’ room; her mother was muttering in her sleep, and her dad was answering back with a loud snore, followed by a soft honk.

As she crept under her duvet, Minna stirred in her bed on the other side of the room they shared.

'Where did you go, Kals?' she mumbled, her words thick with sleep.

Kalyani stiffened. 'Only to the loo.'

'Yeah right!' Minna now peered through half-open eyes at her. 'I heard the back door.'

'Why don't you stop imagining things and go back to sleep? Or go down and check if a burglar has broken in,' Kalyani chided, relieved when her sister grunted and pulled her duvet over her head. *Phew!* That was a narrow escape. She should invent another excuse for her early morning perambulation. Maybe she could say she had taken up jogging. They'd never believe her. Pigs would fly before she woke up early to exercise.

Kalyani hoped Minna would have forgotten the conversation by the time she woke up. She watched her sister's rhythmic breathing, her long hair fanning over the pillow. With only a year between them, they were close, but they couldn't be more different. Nineteen-year-old Kalyani was dark like her father; she had sharp features and a restless energy about her. Minakshi, on the other hand, was fair like her mother. She had a soft beauty and an aura of control around her. Minna was intense, pernickety; she gave well over a hundred per cent in everything she did. She spent hours over her homework, ripping up her work if she made a tiny mistake, sulked endlessly if she missed out on top grades, and planned everything methodically. Kalyani, on the other hand, was a dreamer; a whirlwind of ideas buzzed like a swarm of bees in her head constantly, most of which never saw the light of day. She lived for the 'here and now'.

Kalyani made heads turn when she walked into a room, if only because she had tripped over the rug and bumped into the coffee machine, or squealed with delight at meeting someone unexpectedly. Minakshi blended in quietly and gracefully, gravitated towards familiar acquaintances.

'Minna could get away with murder,' her mother always said. 'She will leave no evidence at the scene of crime.' Fair comment. Minna kept her side of the room immaculate, her pastel frocks neatly arranged in colour-coordinated rows, while her sister distributed her eye-wateringly bright couture between her bed and the floor; scrambling like a dog in search of a buried bone when she wanted to find any particular item.

They wanted different things from life. Kalyani wanted romance, and a family, while Minna wanted to be an academic. The only feature that linked them both was their long, sleek hair, inherited from their mother.

By the time the house stirred itself awake, Kalyani was fast asleep. Minna crept downstairs, fixed her breakfast, and went out for a jog. Shekar, her father, was catching up with the morning news, and Nimmi, her mother, was writing lists. No one expected Kalyani to come downstairs until half the morning had ticked away – just in time for her shift at the hairdressers in the afternoon.

*

'Kals, are you doing the tea orders today?' Karen called out to her. Saturdays were busy at the Hair Express, and the girls were always parched due to the heat of hair dryers and constant prattling. Low down on the pecking order meant she was in charge of keeping them well hydrated.

'In a minute,' Kalyani called back, hurriedly sweeping the last of the hair off the floor and dusting off her apron. She had already washed umpteen heads of greasy hair, discussed the weather, the offers on the high street, and the latest episode of *Emmerdale*. She had scooped up all types and colours of hair off the shiny floor. *Gee! Working as a dogsbody sucked.*

It wasn't as if she wanted to be a hairdresser for the rest of her life. She grabbed the little notepad and prepared to write down their tea orders.

'The usual for me!' said Janice, the chief stylist.

Karen snorted. 'Doubt she knows what that means.'

It was a standing joke that Kalyani could never remember the tea orders or the staff preferences.

'Why don't you have a list on the wall of the kitchenette?' she had suggested.

'No point. We may want to drink something different. There is only so much tea a person can drink,' Guy had whined. Guy was now looking at her in a judgemental way. He was a senior hairdresser who charged around as though he owned the place. He had given up colouring his own hair, and the distinguished looking greys on his temples made him look the part.

'Maybe he will retire when he goes bald,' Karen had once commented, when he was out of ear shot. Guy was the only male member of staff, but he whined and bitched as much as the other girls, and was accepted as one of them.

'Tea, no milk,' he said.

The girls shouted out their orders.

'Coffee, white. Two sugars.'

'Just hot water'

'Earl Grey tea. Tiny drop of milk.'

'Decaff. Tin is on the side by the kettle.'

'Oh. Can I have coffee instead? Actually, Pam, can I borrow your decaff?'

Kalyani scribbled as fast as she could. Back in the kitchenette, she filled the kettle and switched it on, lined up the cups, cross that she had to wash some of them, and distributed the tea bags, coffee and sugar, cross- checking with her notepad. As she poured the boiling water into the cups, the phone she had secreted in her jeans pocket vibrated. Phones were not allowed at work. Guy would be annoyed if he found out. *Raffa!* As she reached for the phone with her left hand, her right hand, which had been pouring hot water into the cups, wandered. By the time she realised this, she had deposited a stream of water on the notepad, and it had soaked through the paper, erasing the pencil marks. Annoyingly, the phone stopped ringing and the caller showed up as unknown. She shoved it back into her jeans and squinted at the wet notepad, trying to make out her writing. Besides, she had forgotten which cups she had added sugar to.

If she didn't get the sack today, she promised to light three candles at the Dudley temple, learn the 'drinks list' by rote, and permanently switch her phone off at work. She could not afford to get distracted. But distracted she was. Ever since they met, nearly a year ago, she could not get Raffa out of her head; the memory of his smile, his touch, and his gregarious eyes, sent electric shocks down to her groin, and made her nipples tingle. If this was love, may it last forever. If this wasn't love, she was at a loss to know what else it could be.

As usual, her thoughts strayed into her future with Raffa. She pictured them in a three-storey townhouse in the leafy suburbs. Raffa tapped away at his computer at the oak kitchen table, while she cooked dinner, and they caught up on the events of each other's days. Then he would race her to the bedroom, undressing her on the stairs. She had already thought of what she would call their children. Mira, if it was a girl, and Dara, if it was a boy...

'This is *not* tea!'

'Mine has a lot of sugar.'

'Mine has none.'

'Milk makes me sick.'

'Sorry. Sorry,' Kalyani apologised, blood rushing to her face. In a small voice, she tried to explain what had happened, leaving out the bit about the phone, and offered to do the teas again, but no one was interested. She quietly removed the offending drinks, avoiding eye contact with everybody, and tried to lock herself in the unisex bathroom for the rest of the day, foiled by Guy, who ordered her back to broom duty.

At least Raffa would pick her up later, when her shift ended, in his dad's silver Mercedes, she consoled herself. A part of her wanted Raffa to drive right up to the tatty salon and hold the car door open for her. That would show the girls! But for now, they were going to keep their affair under wraps.

As far as his parents were concerned, he was visiting them regularly because he missed them. His mother, Shahida, spent Friday nights cooking his favourite meals, and his father, Ashraf, loaned him the use of his silver Mercedes with a full tank of petrol, so he could meet up with his friends and enjoy himself, no questions asked. After all, he had a demanding job and worked very hard all week. One day, they would find him a wife, a demure beauty, who would keep him happy in every possible way. Allah forbid he fell head over heels for a headstrong, white girl from his office who will tower over them, and leave blonde hairs in the bath. Not in their wildest dream did they see their son falling for a dark Hindu girl who worked at the hairdressers and lived on the same street.

At the end of her shift, Raffa pulled up at the bus stop, tapping impatiently on the steering wheel. She barely had time to close the door before he accelerated away.

'I thought I recognised the old man getting off the bus. There will be embarrassing questions at home if he reported seeing us.' He made her wind up the tinted windows until they left the city.

'You are such a fuss pot,' she complained.

Over the months, they had established a routine. They would meet up, away from familiar streets and prying eyes, eat pizza in the car, and decide to watch some obscure movie, during which his hands would probe shamelessly over her body, making it tingle with pleasure. Neither of them ever recalled the details of the movie.

Some days, Raffa took her to his friend's flat in the suburbs, when he was away visiting his family up north. Other days, he booked a room at an out of the way B&B. She wouldn't have cared if it was a tin shack with an outside loo.

That night, Raffa's hands were fumbling at her shirt buttons. 'Let's go away,' he whispered in her ears, hot with desire. 'A dirty weekend in Paris.'

'And have my parents launch a police search?'

'The police don't start searching for twenty-four hours. Time for me to get bored with you and dump you,' he teased, toying with her long, dark hair. Kalyani slapped his arm playfully.

'Would you?'

'Take you to Paris? Yes!'

'No. Dump me?'

'Depends on how you perform in Paris!' he smiled, gently tugging at her tresses and bringing her head down. Before she could slap him again, he planted his lips on hers.

'Not in twenty-four hours. Not in twenty-four days,' he muttered, as he moved over her.

He always brought her back home before midnight, a little tipsy and radiant. He dropped her a few feet away from her house, waiting until she reached her doorstep and let herself in. He then drove around the block before arriving at his own house.

A strategist, my Raffa, she thought to herself proudly. Her parents did not wait up or ask questions, because those were the nights her friend, Helen, covered for her. 'Yes, Mrs Sinner, Kals is with me. Yes, thank you, we are having a good time. Yes, my mum will pick us up.'

Helen found it difficult to pronounce 'Sinha', despite Kalyani's tuition.

'Well,' Kalyani conceded defeat, 'after all, I am a "sinner", lying to my mother.'

Chapter 2

Helen and Kalyani had known each other for yonks. Ever since their parents stood anxiously outside the red brick building of the primary school on the first day, waiting for their daughters to toddle out, their uniforms askew, their bags trailing behind them. Helen had blindly followed Kalyani, her thumb in her mouth, her fair hair tumbling over her face.

'I have a *fyend*,' Kalyani shouted, holding Helen's chubby hand up like a trophy. She struggled extra hard to pronounce the R in 'friend' and made it sound like 'fiend'.

'Fiend means devil,' Scott, a fat boy with deep-set, mean eyes had teased.

'No! Fyend!' Kalyani yelled at him, her hands balled into fists, nearly in tears.

The adults had quickly moved in to separate them. As easily as she had found her best friend, she also found her nemesis. Fortunately for her, Scott soon moved to a different school, leaving Helen and herself in peace. Over the years, they had fallen in and out of friendship a dozen times, drifted in and out of each other's rooms a hundred times. They read Roald Dahl together, tutting when one of them was slower than the other, spent warm summer evenings jumping on the trampoline, and raiding the kitchen for cookies and lemonade. They spent several nights stacked beside each other in bed, their hair fanning out on the pillow, black and blonde. Soon, they grew out of the confines of their rooms and sought adventure elsewhere, in town, house parties, teen gigs and secret nooks.

*

'You are not listening, Kals,' Helen complained, chewing on her cereal bar.

Kalyani looked up from her phone. 'I am. You were saying…'

'Never mind!' Helen shrugged impatiently. 'Who is messaging you now?'

'Raffa,' Kalyani grinned.

'Should have guessed. Anyway, let's pack up here and go see a movie. There's a thriller showing at the Gallery, "Murder Tonight".'

Helen and Kalyani were lounging on the wrought-iron bench in the park in their coats. Despite the cold, they had opted to meet there because Helen's house was taken over by her brother and his friends, who wanted to watch football on Sky Sports in the living room. Their mother had retired to the small kitchen-diner to have a rant over the phone to her sister, between puffs on her cigarette.

Kalyani's house, on the other hand, was too quiet, and they had to keep their voices down to avoid being overheard. Her mother would insist on making polite conversation and plying them with snacks – too healthy for Helen's liking.

Kalyani would have preferred a rom-com, but it was Helen's turn to choose. She texted Raffa, 'Going to see "Murder Tonight" with Helen. Not my choice.'

While Kalyani queued for the tickets, Helen agonised over which flavour of popcorn to buy – the extra-large tub of the butterscotch or the twenty per cent off the toffee. She did not mind sharing it with Kals. Her slim friend was a nibbler, and never made any significant dent in the quantity of food. She added a large iced coke with two straws to her order and impatiently waited for the doors to open. They chose an empty row, away from the aisle. The matinee show had not attracted huge crowds, and their row of seats remained empty.

Almost immediately, Helen handed the coke to Kalyani, and scooped a fistful of popped corn into her mouth and crunched. Kalyani nudged her. 'That's loud,' she whispered.

Helen shrugged and looked around. 'No one is noticing anyway,' she whispered back. That was true. The handful of people around them were either talking to each other or on their phones, or chomping their own popcorn.

Kalyani sipped her coke and checked her phone for messages again. She also periodically swivelled around in her seat every time the door opened.

'Stop fidgeting,' Helen hissed. 'Who are you looking for?'

'Just looking to see if there is anyone we know.'

As the movie started, someone slipped into the seat next to Kalyani. It was a woman wearing a hijab, covering her lower face. Her eyes were hidden behind dark glasses. Even stranger, she nodded off to sleep within the first quarter of the hour. Kalyani ignored her, or tried to, but the woman kept slumping onto her shoulder.

'Hey!' she whispered, pushing her away. In response, the woman leant across her and reached into the popcorn tub that Helen was clutching, proprietarily. Kalyani drew back into her seat and was about to scream, when she noticed the designer watch on the woman's hairy wrist. She recognised the watch, and she recognised the musky perfume the woman wore. Hand cupping her mouth to stifle her giggles, she turned towards the hijab-clad figure.

'Raffa?' she whispered

She couldn't see the face behind the veil and the dark glasses, but she could feel him laughing. She giggled, very inappropriately, considering the murder victim was being carried out in a body bag on screen, while the spouse cried inconsolably. Helen was holding a tissue to her dribbling nose, briefly forgetting to carry the popcorn to her mouth.

When she turned back, the woman in the hijab was leaving, crouching low to avoid obstructing the screen. Hastily, Kalyani placed the drink under the seat and got up to follow the woman.

'Where are you going?' sobbed Helen.

'To the loo,' Kalyani whispered.

'But you just got here!'

'I know. It's all that coke I drank.'

Helen let her go. She did not want to miss the forensic investigation.

The foyer was deserted and the sunlight blinded her as she hurried out. The hijab was nowhere to be seen. There were a couple of them outside with kids trailing behind them, hailing a taxi – they were definitely women. She was looking for a man in a hijab.

'Boo!' The hijab-clad figure dragged her into the shadows behind heavy, red drapes. Within seconds, the hijab was lifted and thrown over her. Alarmed that she was being kidnapped, she struggled to free herself and ended up popping out at the top, her face close to Raffa's grinning mouth. He smoothed the hair off her face and bent down to kiss her. Trapped in the hijab, she could do nothing but return the kiss.

'What on earth did you tell your parents?' she gasped when he finally let go of her lips. Sunday afternoons were dedicated to the company of his parents.

'I offered to get some milk.'

She giggled. 'And what are you wearing?'

'Borrowed it from Grandma's wardrobe.'

'We better be careful not to tear it.'

'It is time she bought a new one anyway.'

His phone rang. He took off the hijab. 'Got to go.'

'Don't forget the milk,' she reminded him.

'Do you want to drive around with me?'

'Yes, but I can't abandon Helen. We drove down in my car.'

'She can take the bus, can't she?'

Kalyani hesitated. 'No. It does not feel right.'

Raffa shrugged and tapped her nose with his index finger. 'OK.'

She watched him go, already regretting her decision. She should have really gone with him. Sighing, she went back to join Helen.

'Where the hell did you go?' Helen demanded.

'Oh, there was a queue for the toilets,' Kalyani lied.

Helen scowled. 'You missed half the story. Now you won't understand the second half!'

'Doesn't matter. It won't kill me! Eat your popcorn and shut up.'

She knew from Helen's silence that she was pissed off with her. They had a habit of dissecting every movie afterwards, and it wasn't going to work if Kalyani had not watched the important scenes.

She texted Raffa. 'Sorry. See you next week?'

The movie was nearly over before he replied. 'About that. I am busy next weekend. That is why I came to spend extra time with you today. Hope you enjoyed the movie with your friend.'

Kalyani burned with guilt. He had come to spend time with her and she had turned him down. Now, she wouldn't see him for two whole weeks, because she hadn't sacrificed a movie and her popcorn-guzzling friend for love. She directed her anger towards Helen by maintaining a sullen silence on the drive back, for which she would have to make amends later. Helen was her best friend, and right now, she couldn't afford not to have her on her side.

From the confines of her bedroom, Kals rang Raffa several times without success; he had either switched off his phone or wasn't going to reply. She could hardly blame him. She wanted to see him, to apologise, but she couldn't just march up to his parents' house and demand that their son speak to her. Neither could she live without knowing that he had forgiven her. Miserably, she curled up on top of her clothes with her pillow between her knees, ignoring her mother's summons to dinner, until his message arrived hours later.

'See you in two weeks.'

She felt the weight on her chest shift, great gulps of air filled her lungs, and her eyes prickled with tears.

'Never again,' she promised herself, 'will I reject him.'

Chapter 3.

Winter, with its long, dark nights and bare-branched trees, faded away, ushering in the tender buds of spring. Cherry blossom flashed their colours shamelessly before the wind, and early April showers plucked them off and strew them on the pavements.

The sisters were each happy in their own way. Kals revelled in her romance with Raffa, while Minna chose her favourite universities, listed them in order of choice, and sweated over her mocks. Easter holidays not only brought some respite from the mundane, but also an invite to Rita's wedding.

Rita's family lived a couple of streets away. Rita's mother, Hana, and Nimmi had met at a school charity cake sale and bonded over a gingerbread house that kept collapsing – the left wall first, followed by the roof, then the right wall. Hana and Nimmi had desperately tried to hold it together, but in the end, amongst a great deal of giggling and laughter, gave the masonry away for free. Of course, theirs was the first stall to sell out.

All Hana's children, three daughters, and Romesh, her son, went to the same school as Kals and Minna, and were constantly in and out of each other's houses. Romesh, or Romy, as they called him, was a couple of years older than Kals. Hana was a gregarious woman. She met life with her loud, infectious laugh every morning. When her husband died on the M25, in a multi-vehicle accident, Hana dragged herself out of bed on the third day, prepared breakfast, and packed the children off to school. She had a funeral to organise and a new life to build for her children.

Rita was the last of her three daughters to find her Mr Right. She was easily the flightiest of the siblings;

she changed jobs like she would her clothes, and she changed boyfriends twice a year because she was bored. Neil, her husband to be, had lasted longer than the rest of them. His parents, however, did not think Rita to be 'wife material', and in return, Rita declined to acknowledge them as her in-laws. In a bid to get as far away from them as possible, she flushed her prospects of becoming a junior executive down the drain, and started a new career in the US of A, leaving Neil no choice other than to follow her there. Hana had alternately laughed and cried for hours when Rita announced their decision to tie the knot. Taking advantage of her mother's good mood, Rita called the shots.

She wanted a quick wedding. She was coming for the Easter weekend to get wed. The ceremony would be at the registry office, with a couple of witnesses in attendance. Hana would be given a free hand in arranging the wedding lunch. Rita was going to be civil to her in-laws during the wedding, if they attended, and include them on her Christmas card list.

'Wonder what their long-term plans are? Would Rita convince her husband to settle in the States? Or would Neil bring her back to the UK?' Kals switched on the hair tongs.

'Depends on who wears the trousers, I suppose.'

'Oh. That is definitely Rita. Romy does not think Rita would want to be on the same side of the planet as her in-laws.'

'Why?'

'Dunno.' Minna inspected the tips of her hair. 'Maybe Neil's parents are snobs. Maybe they believed that he deserved better. A homely beauty, who would cook and clean and bear a brood of healthy children... You could hardly call Rita "homely"! She is a tomboy and a bit of a feminist. And hardly a beauty.'

'You can say that again. What girl in her right mind gives two weeks' notice for her wedding? Two weeks! Poor Hana and Romy have run themselves ragged to make the arrangements.' Kals leaned closer into the mirror to apply mascara.

'They are a close-knit family, always looking out for each other. Mummy says it is going to be a small crowd and the food is catered locally.' Minna now had possession of the hair tongs. She glided them through her long hair, satisfied with the healthy shine. 'With all the sisters married off, Romy is going to feel left out.'

Kals pulled a sad face. 'How dreary for him.'

Minna raised an eyebrow. 'Why the sudden interest in Romy, Kals?'

Kals did not rise to the bait. 'Nothing really. I am not interested in Romy's dreariness!'

'He is not dreary! He is actually quite funny,' Minna insisted. 'Not bad looking either. He plays cricket, and the guitar. He works as a freelance journalist. And he has a thing for you.'

'No, he hasn't!' Kals protested. 'Don't be silly, Minna.'

'Come on, sis. He is like a puppy dog around you.'

'If he is such a good catch, why don't you marry him?'

'Me? I am not going to get married for the next ten years, thank you very much! My degree doesn't study by itself, you know!'

'Thanks for pointing out that I don't have a degree,' Kals said.

'But that is your choice! You are the romanticist. You want love and I want an education.' Minna opened her wardrobe to choose her outfit, and her back was turned towards Kals. In a low voice, she asked, 'What is with all the comings and goings in the early hours of the morning, Kals? You haven't exactly taken up jogging all of a sudden, have you?'

Minna could not see her sister flushing a bright pink, but felt her discomfort.

'I... don't know what you are on about!' Spoken way too fast; the lie detector was screaming.

'Oh, come on, sis, we share a same room, in case you forgot. I notice you leave at an unearthly hour on Saturday mornings, and coming back smelling of aftershave and peppermint. I am going to be a law student. You don't expect me to ignore it, do you?'

Kals could still tell her to mind her own business and stop making things up, but she realised she actually wanted to discuss this with her sister.

'It is not jogging... or Romy,' she said quietly.

'Well? Are you going to tell me who?'

'Rafik.' Her sister's voice was barely above a whisper, too quiet for Minna to have heard. 'I meet Rafik.' Louder this time.

Minna betrayed her shock by dropping the wooden hanger, heavy with clothes, on the floor with a clatter. Ignoring it, she turned to face her sister.

'Rafik? The Posho from number forty-seven, who went to Henry VIII?'

The fact that Rafik went to an independent school because his parents had the money to pay for it, while the girls went to the local state school, had always been a bone of contention with green-eyed Minna and her friends, who called the boys in their smart suits, 'Poshos'.

'Yes. That one.' There was a hint of defiance in Kals' voice now.

Minna grappled with the possibility of the 'Posho' from number forty-seven becoming her brother-in-law; something that would give cause for banter amongst her friends. But another fact surfaced like a corpse from a bog.

'He is a Muslim... boy.'

Kals felt an electric shock shoot up her spine. She felt like a little girl who was caught red-handed stealing cookies.

'Is that a problem for you?'

'Not for me.' Minna rolled her eyes at the door, indicating the rest of the family. 'Mum, Dad, and the rest of the world.'

Kalyani gulped. She wasn't unaware of the resistance her family were likely to put up, but had conveniently pushed it under the carpet. When they were younger, they often sat around the dinner table, savouring their mother's fusion cooking, and playing the 'what if' game. *What if I had a wart on my lip? What if I walked down to school without trousers? What if I told you I am a lesbian? What if I had a boyfriend? What if I came home drunk?*

Their parents were liberal in a lot of respects. They allowed Minna and Kalyani to stay out late, as long as they answered their phones by the fifth ring; allowed them a drink or two at parties, as long as they could still balance themselves on high heels and recite their address backwards; allowed them to invite friends of both sexes over, as long as sex was not on the agenda. They were tolerant of all lifestyles and religions, as long as it did not cross their threshold. They had an 'open house' policy; the girls could discuss anything at any time.

The 'what if' game, seemingly benign, served a dual purpose. The parents were able to keep tabs on what went on in their daughters' brains, and the girls were reminded subtly where the boundary lines were drawn. The possibility of being a lesbian was met with shocked silence; then their dad shrugged his shoulders. 'If you are one, you are one. Nothing anyone can do. Are you?' They were secretly relieved when the girls dissolved into embarrassed giggles.

'What if I had a boyfriend?' This had been met with amusement.

'Ooh! Is he handsome? Does he know how much it costs to keep you?'

'What if my boyfriend was white?' Kalyani challenged. Mummy shrugged.

'What if he was black?'

Naniji, their grandmother, who was visiting at the time, and had observed mutely thus far, had quipped, 'Any boy but a Muslim.' Surprisingly, their parents nodded in agreement. Kalyani could understand her grandmother's old-fashioned views about inter-religious marriages, but she was dismayed that her more forward-thinking parents had not contradicted Naniji's views. After all, one or two of their close friends had married into another religion, and her parents had not treated them differently. Why weren't they saying, 'Mummyji, that is an old-fashioned thought? Look at so and so, who are happily married with two beautiful children; everybody is doing it nowadays.' Were they just pretending to be open-minded, as long as it didn't affect them? At that time, Kalyani was not having an affair with Rafik, but now that she was in a full-blown relationship with him, she was apprehensive about her parents' reaction to her choice.

The Mahmoods were outwardly no different from the rest of the residents on their street. Number forty-seven was a three-bed semi with two functional cars on their driveway, one of which was the Asian man's all-time favourite – a C-Class Mercedes. They had nine to five jobs, went shopping at the local market, and smiled when they passed by. They had probably paid off their mortgage, had a healthy bank account, and a modest stash of gold in their safe. They wore Western clothes and spoke English with only a slight accent. Rafik's mother, Shahida, did not always wear a veil, and his father, Ashraf, sported a stylishly trimmed goatee.

Minna was still probing. 'Are you in it for the long haul or just for the fun?'

'Hey! What do you take me for?' Kals protested.

'Well?' her sister persisted.

'I hadn't thought about it like that. Certainly not just for the fun. I am in love, I think.'

'What about Rafik? Does he feel the same?'

'Of course. We make a good couple, I think.'

'OK,' Minna said. 'In that case, are you planning to get married?'

'Probably. Possibly. I don't know!'

'You don't know? Is he like... a religious Muslim? Staunch? Is he willing to marry outside his religion? If not, will he ask you to convert into his religion? What religion would your kids belong to?' Minna fired questions at her sister like a machine gun.

Kalyani gave a small laugh. She felt cornered, foolish that she hadn't contemplated these issues.

'Goodness, Minna! You will make a very good lawyer. When you fall in love, you ask him all these questions first, and while you are at it, find out about his gene pool and test him for STDs!'

'I will certainly do a bit more homework,' Minna retorted.

'We will see.' Kalyani nibbled gently at her lacquered nails. 'Me and Raffa, we don't really talk about those sorts of minor things.'

She thought to herself: we don't really talk. When she was with Raffa, their passion for each other ignited and burned. She was in 'Raffa mode'. There was no need for insipid conversations; the world conducted its business elsewhere. Logic and practicality were trivialities, something to be mocked, and used only to make plans to meet up safely and secretly. If there was any talking, she did most of it, gabbling on about her day, her bitchy colleagues, and how unfair the world had been to her that week.

'Kalyani! Minakshi!' their mother called from downstairs. 'We are going to be late for this wedding if you don't come down *now*.'

The girls were galvanised into action. If they didn't hurry up, their mum would stomp upstairs and yank their door open. She would not be pleased that between them, they had mascaraed three eyes, and only one of them had changed out of their pyjamas. There was no time for any more conversation. Each thinking their own thoughts, they hastened to get themselves presentable.

But as Minna collected her handbag, Kals whispered to her, 'You won't tell, will you?'

'Not me. *You* have to tell them. This is serious,' Minna whispered back, before holding up her sequinned skirts and descending the carpeted stairs to join their waiting parents.

The wedding day that Rita and Neil had chosen dawned true to British tradition – grey and drizzly. The hurriedly chosen venue was not exactly adventurous. It was the community hall in the middle of the market place, heaving with market day shoppers and vendors unpacking their wares, jostling for parking spaces. The wedding guests attracted a few wolf whistles because they stood out in their colourful silks and chunky jewellery, as they made their way up the steps. Inside, the spacious hall was packed. Hana had used fairy lights and seasonal flowers abundantly to decorate the pillars. Friends greeted each other across the hall, and with exaggerated grace, waded through the crowd, eager to catch up on the latest gossip. They remarked on how beautiful the bride looked ('This is a vast improvement on how she really looks.'), how elegant the hall looked ('See what you can do on a shoe string budget?'), and what the groom's family thought about the bride (nothing complimentary). Little girls in frilly frocks and boys in tuxedos chased each other through the aisles, their laughter and squeals ricocheting around the hall; others sat on an adult's knee, squirming in their itchy outfits. A fusion of old and new music blared in the background, as caterers offered canapés and cheap fizz. The newlyweds glowed happily as they greeted and thanked their guests for their presence and their generous cash contributions; they had requested cash only as practically, they would not be able to transport toasters, pasta makers, champagne glasses and mini chocolate fountains to the USA. While the cameraman captured timeless images of the happy couple, a queue formed, moving towards the dining hall upstairs.

'Please have something to eat,' Hana urged, as she hugged Nimmi. She looked tired – happy tired.

Romesh gave Kalyani an admiring glance. 'All looking good!' he complimented the whole group, not wanting to single her out, but his eyes dwelt only on her. Minna nudged her, and Kals blushed, uncomfortably. She glared at her sister as they joined the queue for food. Nimmi and Shekar had spotted some long-lost friends, and lingered behind to talk to them.

The gorgeous smells of the wedding feast, rich, creamy casseroles, pastry stuffed with fried nuts and spun sugar, wafted down to them. From her place in the queue, Minna could see the fondant cakes, delicately decorated with icing and edible glitter. 'Mmm. I am starving,' she declared, loud enough for others in their vicinity to hear. Her fellow sufferers smiled at her and nodded in agreement.

Kalyani had been looking forward to the meal too, but even as she opened her mouth to reply to her sister, her stomach contracted; its contents rushed up into her throat. Sweat broke out under her carefully applied make-up. The faces around her appeared to dissolve and reform, only to dissolve again, their voices hollow, as if they were travelling from afar. They were all around her, suffocating, stifling. She needed air and space. She tugged at her silk clothes, which were tailored to cling to every curve of her body, and were therefore unyielding.

'I don't feel very well,' she whispered to Minna, clutching her arm. Minna looked at her, at first with irritation, and then with concern. Her sister had turned green under her dark skin, sweat had sprouted over her brow, and her eyes were hooded and unfocussed. She was starting to lean heavily on her.

'Do you need to sit down?' she whispered, trying not to attract attention.

'I... think I need air. Too... hot.' The words were slurred, thick.

Minna looked around them. Behind them, more hungry people had joined the queue. Pushing past them would be futile. She spotted a fire door behind the caterers, and pulled Kalyani towards the door.

One of the caterers, a young Jamaican with hair sculpted into spikes, smiled politely. 'There is a queue.'

'My sister is sick. She needs some air. Can we go out through there?' Minna pointed to the fire door.

The lad took one look at Kalyani clinging to Minna, and he opened the fire door. He preceded them down the service stairs, and held the door to the outside open. Minna thanked him. 'Save some cakes for us,' she called out, as he returned to his catering duties.

The noise of the market and the damp drizzle enveloped them. Kalyani sat on the wet steps, breathing in the cool air, until her vision cleared and the queasiness passed. The contents of her stomach decided to stay put. Minna sat down beside her thinking that they would both end up with damp stains on their silky butts, and frizzy hair, by the time they went back in. She toyed with her phone, wondering whether she should ring her parents.

Five minutes later, Kals whispered, 'I feel better now. Go back if you want.'

'How about you?'

'I will just sit here for a while longer.'

Minna hesitated, but the thought of all the lovely food she was not eating clinched her decision. 'I will find Mum. Is there anything I can get you?'

'Mum will only worry. I feel better now. I wouldn't mind a glass of water though.'

The fire door had closed behind them. Minna walked round to the front entrance of the hall and bumped into Romy. 'Ah! Romy, have you seen my parents? Kals is not feeling very well.'

Romesh became concerned. At Minna's request, he soon returned with some squash. 'Why don't you go and find your mum? I will take this to Kals.' Minna nodded gratefully, and after directing him to where she had left her sister, she headed towards the dining hall.

By the time she found her parents, Kalyani had already texted them. 'Romy with me. I feel better.'

Romy, Rita, Kals and Minna had practically grown up together. During school holidays, their mothers dragged them to activity clubs and coffee mornings. When they were bored, they escaped to play silly games, or chitchat. Minna and Rita were hot-headed and opinionated, and liked to argue, whereas Romy and Kals were as flexible as the tall grass in the flower beds, swaying in the breeze. Together, they set the world to rights.

Kals found being with Romy felt comfortable, except for Minna's earlier observation that he had a soft spot for her. Kalyani knew it was true. She remembered the time Rita caught a butterfly. 'That looks like the one in your collection box, Romy,' she said.

Much to his embarrassment, Minna and Kals were intrigued by this secret collection box. He had stayed silent at the time, but a few weeks later, he allowed Kals to have a peek into his collection of items reminding him of important events of his life. A scoop of mud from his visit to Glastonbury, turf from The Oval, his dad's cuff links, a lock of his baby hair, and a broken guitar string.

'Why is the guitar string special?' she had enquired.

'Let's say there was someone special in the audience that day.'

Kals blushed as she remembered Romy's guitar string breaking with a twang mid performance with his band. 'You are so sweet,' she had said, giving him a peck on his cheek.

She had a lot of affection for Romy, and was grateful that despite his busy schedule, he sat with her, talking about random stuff. It helped take her mind off her queasy guts. Soon, she was laughing at his dry humour. He led her back into the hall, sat her down, and fetched a plate, laden with food. Grateful that she didn't have to stand in the queue again on shaky legs, she accepted it, smiling sweetly.

'Such a lovely man,' Nimmi commended on the way home. 'He is always so helpful.'

The next episode of nausea hit her at work. This one was not as forgiving, and she had thrown up her entire breakfast and got sent home. By the time she reached home, she felt fine.

Chapter 4

Helen texted Kals as soon as she returned from visiting her dad. 'Care to go for a drive?'

Helen was always in a mood after these visits. Her parents separated just before her tenth birthday, and in her mind, she blamed her mother for not trying harder to save her marriage. So she usually avoided her mother for a couple of days on her return. Kals had been there for her during those difficult times. On the surface, Helen and her family seemed to pull through, but something changed deep inside her friend. She seemed to grow up overnight.

They all grew up over the years. While Kals grew tall and slender, and her brown skin, long, black hair, and pretty face turned heads wherever she went, Helen was the opposite. Everything about Helen was big. Despite being a foodie, Helen was not fat; she was just big-boned. She had big lips and big teeth, big eyes, the colour of cornflowers in summer. She had a big, beatific smile, which created deep dimples on her cheeks, when she deigned to smile, that is. While Kalyani made friends easily and moved through a room full of strangers at any party like a hot knife through butter, Helen studied the plants plonked in brass pots in the corner of the room or scratched abstract art into the armrests of the sofa with her fork.

Of course, things became more complex when the opposite sex started to matter. Everybody was constantly talking about boobs and pecs, designer jeans, hairstyles, and each other's beds. Kals found her Prince Charming, literally the boy next door. Helen, at first, stood on the sidelines, firmly believing that the whole process was a waste of time, besides being disgusting. After all, she didn't lack male companionship; she had brothers at home with their multitude of friends, and was well aware of their boyish graces or disgraces; their sweaty T-shirts, cheesy feet, muddy trainers and crass jokes; not exactly an endorsement of their species.

Her hormones and peer pressure finally won. She took the bull by the horns and waded in. She practised being coy and experimented with make-up for hours in front of her own or Kalyani's mirror. It all seemed so unnatural to her, not befitting Helen. So, she decided to create a new person altogether; a popular princess, who rocked at parties and was every boy's wet dream. She called herself Helena, and although she wasn't as glamorous as her namesake in *A Midsummer Night's Dream*, her love life was just as messy.

As Helena, she sampled the boys in her vicinity as frequently as she changed her pants: long, short, squat, lanky, dysmorphic… she went through them all. There was Jams Jimmy, who had earned his name by once sucking the jam out of all the donuts at a birthday party when he was nine years old. Jams really didn't care who he went out with, or if he went out with anyone. He was easy, bordering on lazy. Pizza and chips, lager and sci-fi movies, a sofa to snore on, was fine by him. Helen soon decided it was more interesting to watch football with her brothers.

Then there was Scaredy Callum, who hid behind her when he saw boys in hoodies; braided Tristan, who spent more time in front of the mirror than with her.

She hit jackpot when she hooked Sporty Tommy, an athletic, popular boy, who was in between affairs. That Tommy and Helena were an item had not gone down well with the other girls. That summer, Helena had her share of hate mail. The affair lasted the entire summer, longer than any of the others had, until he finally gave in to the relentless chase from a pink-nippled, blonde bombshell, who had no qualms about flashing her bosom at him, at every opportunity, and parted from Helena. But they remained friends.

One day, well into her first year of her art course, someone walked into her life and turned it into a kaleidoscope. They had an amazing time together, in a condo on the sandy beach, singing along with Anastasia and David Bowie, dancing to Arabian music, eating bizarre combinations, like peanut butter and horseradish sandwiches and fish fried in marmalade. They spent all day in bed and all night on the beach, throwing beer bottles into the waves and chasing after crabs. Helen had never been happier than with fair-haired, long-legged Lola. She posted vivid pictures on social media that left no doubt about her sexuality.

As if they had a pact, that same year, Sporty Tommy declared his sexuality too, much to the disgust of the blonde with pink nipples, who had spread mouth-watering stories of their lovelife. The girls were not surprised about Helen. 'Always knew she was a weirdo,' they said, and sent her more hate mail. They rallied around Blondie, pretending to help her get over her shock, all the while sniggering behind her back.

Lola had gone away for the holiday, and Helen dedicated some time for her old friend, Kals. As they sipped lattes and shared sticky buns at the coffee shop, Kals told her about being sick.

'Do you think it is a bug?'

'I don't know. I throw up once and I feel fine afterwards. If it was a bug, shouldn't I be puking every few minutes? Or having diarrhoea or something. This has been going on for two weeks.'

After a while, Helen asked, 'What about your monthlies? Missed any?'

Kals paused to think. The last time she remembered having her period was when Raffa told her that he was going to Germany for a week of training – something to do with his latest project. That was in February. She racked her brains to remember if she had one in March.

'So you could have missed one… or two? They can be irregular. Mine comes whenever. I don't even keep tabs,' Helen said to reassure her.

'Mine are regular as clockwork. Not missed the blasted thing once,' Kals moaned.

'Could you be… you know?'

'I don't know!' Kalyani wailed in panic. 'I… don't want to be!'

'Did you use any prevention, when you umm…'

'I might have forgotten to take the pill a couple of times. He did… or he said he would when he needed to. He said he knew when to stop. I am not sure he always did…' Under Helen's scrutiny, Kalyani started to wilt; she looked past her friend, up at the sky, and then at her Ugg boots. Helen did not have to say it aloud: *How stupid can you be, Kals?*

'OK. You know what we should do,' she said finally.

Miserably, Kalyani nodded. Helen did what any good friend is expected to do; she went into the local chemist to buy pregnancy test kits, two different types to be sure, annoyed that they cost so much. She took Kalyani to her house, which thankfully, was abandoned temporarily by her mother and brothers, stood outside the loo while Kalyani peed on both the sticks, and sat with her, watching the display window for the result.

It was the longest two minutes of their lives. Kals munched her nails and muttered 'Please God' repeatedly, her eyes full of panic. Helen held her friend's hand and prayed that God was listening.

'It will be OK, Kals. Don't worry,' she repeated every few seconds. The faint beep from the kit startled them.

'You go first. Please God…' Kals whispered.

Helen hesitantly reached out for the nearest one. 'Oh no!'

'No?'

'No. I meant …'

Unable to wait any longer, Kals looked at hers. The silence that followed said it all. Kalyani was 'up the duff', 'bun in the oven', or whatever else it was called.

'My mother will kill herself!' Kalyani wept, holding her head in her hands. She couldn't hear herself because her heart was pounding in her ears, like a power drill. 'Then she will kill me.'

'That doesn't make sense. I mean she should kill you first…' Helen was shaking too. She frowned. 'It is Posho's, isn't it?'

'Unless I was artificially inseminated by someone else when I was asleep.' Kalyani rolled her eyes up at Helen.

'Sorry Kals, dumb question. What are you going to do?'

'I don't know!' Kals whined, kneading her lips with her fingers.

With trembling hands, Helen wrapped the incriminating evidence in newspaper, took it downstairs, and deposited it in the rubbish bin outside, shoving it under last night's fish and chips bag. Thank god, it is bin day tomorrow, she thought to herself. By the time she returned, Kalyani had tottered to bed on jelly legs. Helen got into bed and lay down beside her. For a while, they stared at each other despondently.

They discussed possibilities. Could the pregnancy test be wrong? Surely, Raffa had used an industrial grade condom.

Then they discussed plans. Eating a hot curry, hot cups on the tummy, rhubarb tea… clinics…

'Or do nothing,' Helen shrugged. 'Do you want to keep it?'

Kalyani covered her face with her hands, pressing the tips of her manicured fingers over her eyelids. Waves of dread washed over her. She shook her head. 'I don't know.'

Helen switched on her phone to google options. Her fingers tapped 'What do you do if you are pregnant?' She then texted her girlfriend, Lola, the same question, phrased differently: 'What do you do if your friend is pregnant?'

While Kals drank her rhubarb tea and munched on ginger biscuits Helen had fetched from the kitchen, her friend paced around the room, having a conversation with Lola, who had called back almost immediately. First, Lola needed reassurance that it was Helen's friend who was pregnant, not Helen. Then she made sure they had bought good pregnancy kits to test, not something from Poundland. Lola then proceeded to list options. Helen listened carefully before approaching Kals. She sat on the bed, the stubble on her long legs rubbing on Kalyani's arm like sandpaper.

'OK. These are the options.' Her tone was measured, but soft. 'You tell Posho he is going to be a dad. You tell your parents. Together, you decide if you want to keep… it. Or you tell nobody and have an abortion. Either way, you will have to go and see the doctor.'

'I am going to kill myself!' Kalyani sobbed into Helen's pink pillow. Alarmed, Helen brushed the hair off her friend's face, and spoke softly. 'Listen Kals. No one is going to die. We will get through this. I will be with you, do you understand? Promise you wont do anything silly.' Kals sniffed and nodded. Relieved, Helen went down to the kitchen for more food, and returned with cheese sandwiches and a jug of very sweet hot chocolate, and packets of crisps. She insisted on Kals eating some of the food. By the time she took the plates and cups down, loaded them in the dishwasher, her mother pulled into the driveway with groceries.

Helen helped put them away. 'Kals is staying over tonight. We have had something to eat.'

'Oh. Great, give her my love.' her mother said.

Kals was fast asleep when Helen returned to her room, her body rolled into a ball, her hands tucked between her thighs, her long lashes damp against her cheeks.

Helen felt sorry for her guileless friend. She called 'Mrs Sinner', Kalyani's mother, to inform her that her daughter was staying the night with her, and couldn't come to the phone as she was asleep. For once, it was the truth.

*

In the morning, Kalyani tried to wish it all away. Perhaps if she stayed under the duvet, and held her breath for long enough, she might starve herself of oxygen and get rid of the alien in the basement of her body. If she slept all day, the nightmare may pass. She and Helen would paint the town red, stuff their face with cake and wine, and laugh it all off. *Remember the time you had that horrible stomach bug and thought you were pregnant? Haha!*

None of the above happened. As soon as she rose from the bed, bile rushed to her throat with an urgency that made her run to the bathroom, tripping on the trailing sheets. After she had thrown up, she sat on the tiled floor, trying to clutch at straws, searching for something that could tell her that yesterday never happened. The pregnancy test stick with her pee on it. She looked around Helen's tiny bathroom; the bin was empty. There was no evidence. Where was the evidence? It was only a dream. A wicked… wicked dream.

Helen was not in the best of moods after spending the night sleeping on the floor, and being woken up at five in the morning by Kals throwing up in the loo. She was not feeling benevolent. Leaning against her wardrobe, she yawned and rubbed her eyes, trying to ward off the vestiges of sleep. Her matted locks fell over her face as she shook her head at her friend.

'You have to face it, Kals, it is not going to go away.' She pointed to Kalyani's tummy, where 'it' was happily cooking. 'Go home, now, and talk to Raffa. I need my bed.'

Despite the sound advice from Helen, Kalyani spent the next few days in denial. She called work to say she had a lingering gastric bug, and did not want to distribute it to her dear colleagues. For once, she was glad that Raffa was not coming that weekend, because he had a project to complete. She texted him and told him she was ill.

'Oh? Damn! Better stay away then. Do not want to catch the bug,' he replied, and switched his phone off, as if he was scared of her infection travelling down the phone to him. He could have said 'I will miss you' or 'get well soon'. But Raffa never said such things. He liked being told that she had missed him though. Must be a man thing. And her dearest Raffa was every bit a man. The thought made her smile.

Anyhow, she needed time to deal with the arrival of 'it' on the scene. She mooched around in her room, nibbling her nails, keeping tabs on where everybody was. Her mother was downstairs doing 'mummy jobs', Dad was at work and Minna at college. She would have to tell them all soon. She had waited to see if her periods arrived that month.

Second month no show from the regular unwelcome visitor.

Who should she confide in first? Her parents? Minna? Raffa?

Her parents would go ballistic. Missiles would fly, tears would fall like a sprinkler putting out a fire, the army would be despatched to start negotiations with the boy's family, and the blame game would start as to who had seduced who. Or they would march her to the family planning clinic, demanding that the 'it' was exorcised away into the ether it arrived from. Would they ever trust her again? Would they ever again think that their daughter was an intelligent girl with 'potential'? That is what her school records had said every year. 'Kalyani has potential, but does not always apply herself.' Well, this girl had exhausted her potential. She had no degree, no career, no marriage, no virginity, no USP. The only potential she had shown was her capacity to make babies. What a loser their daughter was! She wouldn't blame them if they gave up on her and transferred all their love and expectations to their second daughter, Minna. Minna would be their new potential.

And what would his parents say? Call her a slut, question her family values and intentions? Accuse them of being gold diggers, who encouraged their daughter to ensnare the highly-paid, eligible bachelor next door? They might decide to lock their son away, refuse to allow them to meet, while they arranged a beautiful, rich Muslim girl from Pakistan to marry him.

Maybe she should tell Raffa first. How would he take the news? She had no doubt that after the initial shock, he would be overjoyed. He would take the day off, wine and dine her (no wine for her); they would then make fabulous love, after which he would conjure up a ring and propose to her. He would present her proudly to his parents, his arm around her waist, adamant that she was his life partner.

She grinned to herself, excitedly, caught up in a dream in which she was standing with Raffa in the baby's nursery, decorated baby blue with clouds for a boy or princess pink with angels for a girl. From the cradle, bonny limbs jerked to the tune of *Rock-A-Bye Baby* from the wound-up mobile. Raffa tucked a lock of hair behind her ears and whispered, 'Let's go and make some more "its".' Her bliss was complete.

Standing in the path of their bliss was his family, and their religion. They could be heading into a storm, wherein one or both of them was about to be fried by lightning.

She placed her hand over her abdomen. What did she herself feel about 'it'? How does one feel about someone who barges in, uninvited to a party, and poops it? She wished that 'it' had knocked on her door and requested permission to enter. She wished she had the chance to talk to 'it', and explain why waiting for a more opportune moment might be a good idea.

Cloistered in the bathroom, she googled images on her smartphone. Foetus. At nine weeks, it looked no different from that of a chick or a rodent. Difficult to fall in love with something that looked like that. She had loved holding her cousin's baby last year, and playing with her tiny pink toes, but she was taken aback at how loudly a hungry baby could cry, and was only too happy to hand her over. She had felt the same love when she watched videos of fluffy kittens.

Helen had asked her if she wanted to keep it. Or putting it crudely, did she want to get rid of it? If she did, she would be no different from the boy on the news who drowned kittens in the river. What would Raffa think of a woman who wants to get rid of her firstborn? Unfit mother. Unfit wife.

She could never drown kittens, or strangle a chick or kill a baby. She had no choice but to welcome her baby into her life.

She imagined various scenarios of breaking the news to her parents. Over Friday night cocktails, when they were a bit tipsy and 'gung ho.' Or on a Saturday, when they were entertaining friends, or on Monday, when they are in a rush. She sighed; either way, she was going to be shot down in flames.

Chapter 5

As events would have it, the news came out sooner than she intended. A week later, on Sunday morning. It was a lazy, late morning when everybody was still in their pyjamas, Shekar reading *The Guardian*, dropping sections he wasn't interested in onto the laminate floor, where Minna sat cross-legged, checking messages on her phone. Her cup of tea was within reach on the coffee table. *Sky News* was on repeat on TV, and Nimmi was nibbling on toast and brewing her third cup of jasmine tea, loudly bandying ideas for lunch. Curry with rice or curry with roti? Shekar was grunting incomprehensible replies, and Minna was shrugging her shoulders as if to say 'whatever', while giggling at her phone messages.

Kalyani came down, looking flushed from throwing up.

'You are still ill, hmm? Better get that checked up,' Nimmi commented, a concerned look on her face. 'Shall I book an appointment with the GP tomorrow?'

'Not "Yoda",' Minna quipped, gesturing the quote-unquote with her fingers. It was true that the wizened, small doctor with hooded eyes and prominent ears resembled Yoda, the legendary Jedi from *Star Wars*. Nimmi frowned at Minna.

'Tea?' she asked Kalyani.

'Yes, please. Can I have some toast as well?'

Nimmi put the slices of bread into the toaster and poured hot water on a tea bag.

'This bug has been going on for a while, hasn't it? It must be at least two weeks.'

Three *actually*. 'I know.'

'But you never get sick. Where did you get the infection from?'

'You better not give me the infection!' Minna cried. 'I have my uni interview on Wednesday.'

'Is it from work? Some people don't wash their hands after… What is the manager at the hairdressers saying?' Nimmi asked, spreading peanut butter on the slices of crispy brown toast. She handed one to her daughter and bit into the other. 'Surely they are not going to withhold pay for the time you were sick?'

Kalyani shrugged her petite shoulders. 'Guy told me not to come in until I am clear. I suppose they don't want to get the infection either!'

'I don't think anyone wants to be puking for weeks,' Minna said, getting agitated. 'Can you move into the spare room or something? I am always so careful not to get these horrid infections. Kals, don't you wash your hands when you come home?'

'Ha! Always been a problem for Kalyani. Remember how we used to shout at her all morning to have a shower!' Nimmi directed this to Shekar. Shekar smiled, without looking up from his newspaper.

The suggestion that she was unclean irritated Kalyani. Although her father had said nothing, his lack of support left her seething. Without pausing to think, she burst out, 'Well. You lot can all shut up about my hygiene! It is not an infection!'

'What else can it be?' both her mother and sister spoke in chorus, rolling their eyes.

'You don't really need old "Yoda" to tell you it is an infection!' Minna's tone was mocking.

'It is not infection. I am pregnant!' Kalyani blurted out. The word sounded louder than the stroke of Big Ben inside its belfry. Time stopped in the Sinha household. Nimmi's hand froze midway between plate and mouth, her toast depositing crumbs on the countertop, her mouth open. Shekar nearly broke his glasses, which he had been polishing using the corner of his cotton shirt.

He squinted myopically at his family gathered around the breakfast bar, wondering which of them had said they were pregnant. Minna knocked her cup over, and it stayed suspended three inches above the wooden floor, its contents ready to spill over. *Tic toc. Tic toc* said the clock on the mantelpiece, beside the family photographs, taken a decade ago, in which Minna's eyes were shiny from crying because she had been told off for misbehaving, and Kalyani's shone in triumph.

The moment passed.

The cup smashed on the floor, tea spraying the magnolia walls. The toast slipped from Nimmi's hand, bounced off the plate and fell butter side down on the tiled floor.

They all stared at Kals, waiting for the curtain to rise on the second scene in act one, where she would jump up and say, 'Got you! Joke!' But she stared right back at them, wishing the earth would open beneath her and swallow her alive.

From somewhere, a tiny, whiny voice said, 'What?' Kalyani didn't wait to find out whose voice it was. She turned tail and ran upstairs, slamming her door to her room harder than she intended to. The impact caused the mirror on the landing wall to jolt out of the hook and crash. Breaking a mirror brought seven years of bad luck, her mother would say, her frowning face reflected in the broken shards. Well, bad luck had preceded the breaking of the mirror. Doom was already in the house.

Downstairs, while Minna picked up the pieces of her smashed cup with shaky hands, her mother wiped the peanut butter off the floor, and threw the toast into the bin. No one spoke. Nimmi avoided eye contact with her husband. She did not want to deal with his opinion before she had time to process what she had heard. She dried her hands and followed her daughter upstairs.

On the landing, she stood over the broken mirror, her chest heaving. She was tempted to retreat into her own room, slam the door to shut out the world, but she tiptoed around the broken glass and scratched half-heartedly at Kalyani's door. Nothing happened. Nothing stirred. She hoped it had been a bad dream. That in reality, Kalyani was at work. Her GP had given her the all clear, saying, 'Half the town has a vomiting bug.'

She was just about to turn away when, with a flurry, Kalyani threw the door open and flung herself into her mother's arms, sobbing loudly. Nimmi held her tight, caressing her long, silky tresses, and murmuring soothing things, which she did not feel. She sighed at the mess on Kalyani's bed, and the floor. The sunlight filtering through the voile curtains at the window reflected off the trinkets on the bedside table and splattered into pieces of rainbow.

'Do you know who the father is?' As soon as she said it, Nimmi knew it was the wrong thing to say. Her daughter stiffened in her arms.

'Of course I know who it is. Did you think I sleep around?' she wailed.

'Shh. Baby. Shh,' Nimmi soothed. 'I did not mean that at all.' But what had she meant? Was she pleased with her daughter because she hadn't slept around or was she displeased with her for sleeping with the father of this child?

By sundown, the story of Kalyani and Raffa had been repeated several times, and examined from all angles, as if it was a piece of abstract art that needed definition. From every angle, it spelt disaster. Kalyani was only nineteen. She was pregnant; yes, she had confirmed it two times. She was unmarried. The father was a Muslim boy. The family lived a few houses away.

Their intelligent daughter had made a humongous error in judgement. Her close-knit family had been oblivious to what was going on right under their noses, smug in the belief that these things only happened to the world outside.

'Are you keeping it?' Minna whispered into the darkness on Kalyani's side of the room. They had all crept into their beds, too shocked, too tired, too close to harsh words and tears. The house was too quiet, though they were all awake in bed, staring into the black depths of the night, too afraid to be left alone with their thoughts, too afraid to lay them out in the open.

'I… don't know,' the darkness whispered back. Minna clung to the hesitation in her sister's voice. Was there hope? Could her sister be persuaded to get rid of the evidence, before the crime is discovered by the outside world?

Minna propped her head up with her hands. 'How far gone are you?'

'I… am not sure. Nearly three months.'

'So there is still time… Have you told Raffa?'

Silence.

'Will he stick by you?'

'Yes.'

'Really?'

'I… am not sure. I… think he will.'

Minna made an exasperated noise. Truly, her sister was dumb. 'What are you sure of?'

Her tone was harsher than she wished it to be. Her sister turned away from her in a huff. The conversation had ended.

*

Nimmi sat on the wooden bench, damp with the aftermath of spring rain, confident that her long coat would keep the wet away from soaking into her pants. They were well into spring, but the temperature was anything between a miserable ten degrees to a healthy fifteen. She could have sheltered from the rain in the café, but she did not want to bump into anyone she knew. Her family had been in an inordinate hurry to leave the house that morning, while she pretended to be asleep. She could have stayed dry and warm in the kitchen, watching the antics of the grey squirrel trying to steal from the bird feeder out in the garden. But the events from the day before hung around like the smell of stale curry, and Nimmi wanted some fresh air. She tore a hunk of bread from the loaf she had bought at Tesco, wrapped it in yesterday's newspaper – the date that their world had been turned upside down – and walked to the duck pond.

This was her favourite spot, under the weeping willow. The sky was thick with grey clouds, but the park felt fresh, as if the rain had cleansed it. In summer, it buzzed with squealing children and barking dogs. The inclement weather on a weekday morning kept visitors away. Only a couple of hardy joggers and a mother walking home with her frisky toddler after dropping her older children off at school graced the area.

She wanted some time alone, to get some clarity around what was happening. Instead, she found herself reminiscing her own childhood. As a Hindu girl, educated in a girls' convent run by nuns, whose Catholic principles were woven into the fabric of school life, she was pulled between two different religious lifestyles. At home, her mother dedicated an entire room to Hindu family deities, of which they were many, each with a legend attached to them, portraying great power, romance and feminism. Nimmi believed in them as much as she believed in Jesus. She trusted in the quick fix of crossing herself in the 'name of the God, the son and the Holy Spirit, Amen', or dabbing sacred ash on her forehead, just as she believed in avoiding stepping on cracks in the pavement and counting the number of black ravens to predict her day. But somewhere along the line, in between Retreat, Vespians, and Confessions that her Catholic friends attended, and Poojas, Vrithams and Bajans that her Hindu family did, she realised that despite their friendship, deep down, they were fundamentally different. She could not bring the Gita to them, nor could she take the Bible home. Just as it would be for Kalyani and Rafik.

Her thoughts shifted to Shekar. Being an only child, with a paucity of male cousins in the extended family, and educated in a girls only school, Nimmi's exposure to the opposite sex was limited. She approached them with awe, and even with a degree of suspicion, as her mother's voice rang in her ears: 'Beware of the boys, Nimmi.' An Indian girl, in her era, was not under any pressure to find her own life partner. Her parents would arrange a marriage for her. After careful screening, they shortlisted applicants for her to meet and rubber stamp. Her first encounter with Shekar in her parents' living room had made her tremble so badly that the cups of tea rattled loudly on the tray she carried, and spilt over the samosas. She could not remember Shekar's face, or what he had said, if indeed he had said anything, but the fragrance of fried onions, milky tea, sweet jasmine flowers woven into her braid, and the metallic thread of her aunt's silk saree entrenched itself deep in her brain. She remembered the dull shine of Shekar's expensive jacket with mother-of-pearl cuff links, his perfume of musk and masculinity, and his aura of confidence and security. She was told that he was a good-looking guy and that she was lucky.

Lucky was Nimmi's second name. Lucky to have got into a good school, lucky to have graduated with good grades, lucky to have such a good husband, lucky to settle abroad, lucky to have two beautiful daughters... Somewhere along the line, her lucky streak had fizzled out.

Behind the façade of a happy family, Nimmi buried her insecurities and uncertainties. She took refuge in the clockwork routine of life – Shekar, school, homework, mealtimes, budget holidays, bills... She accepted her position as a housewife; she accepted that she was not a career woman. She did not dwell on her role, and did not seek feedback on how well she did her job, not because she was confident of her performance, but because she didn't wish to be reminded of her failures. She knew that she had been too tolerant, too indulgent with the girls, because it was easier. Easier not to argue over outdated rules and boundaries of a society they did not live in. In the process, she had failed to instil a sense of belonging, and pride in their faith; failed to pass on the vital message from her own mother. 'Beware of the boys.' She had failed to prevent this catastrophe. As a stay-at-home mother, Shekar would have expected her to be vigilant at all times. How had she missed the signs?

What was he thinking about her now? Was he blaming her? Was he regretting his marriage with her?

Nimmi put her head in her hands and broke into sobs. She cried softly until the ducks got tired of waiting for more crumbs and moved away, quacking and grumbling. The wind picked up and shook raindrops and yellow laburnum blossom over her. Finally, spent, she blew her nose on some tissue she found in her bag, and dragged her bedraggled self home.

After a warm bath and some hot porridge, she told herself to pull her socks up. She was an adult, a parent, and a wife; she had to take control. All day yesterday and today, she and her husband had avoided each other. As if by doing so, the problem would just disappear. But she had to know what he was thinking. If he held her to account, she wanted it laid out in the open. Tonight.

She set about preparing the battlefield. She texted Minna and Kalyani, asking them to stay over with friends. Neither of them protested, only too eager to stay clear of the ticking time-bomb at home. When Shekar came home, Nimmi heated up leftovers from the supper no one had eaten last night. They dined in silence. Shekar brought his iPad to the table, and seemed more interested in the antics of Westminster.

He seemed oblivious to the noise Nimmi was making on purpose as she loaded the dishwasher. After that, she brought the bottle of wine chilling in the fridge and banged it on the table, grateful it hadn't broken. Unfazed, Shekar rose to get the wine glasses.

'We need to talk,' he said, stealing the thunder from the speech she had fastidiously prepared. She nodded, annoyed at the lump that had risen in her throat. Maybe it was best she allowed him to take over, but he didn't. He waited for her. She took a big sip of her wine, forgot her script, and instead, in a small voice, she started.

'I don't know what to do. I don't know what went wrong. One minute, she is this good, little girl who is enjoying life, and then she drops this bombshell.'

Shekar grunted and emptied his glass.

'Well?' Nimmi prompted.

'Yes. Yes. The problem is clear. The solution is not.'

'It is complicated,' she sighed. 'She is too young for any of this. I want her to get rid of it!' There! It was out! Poor, naïve, sweet Nimmi was actually a wicked witch, who killed unborn babies.

Shekar tapped his teeth with his spectacles, his eyes narrow, expression stony.

Say something, for God's sake! Nimmi screamed to herself.

'Is that what she wants?'

Nimmi gulped several times, trying to shift the lump in her throat. 'She doesn't know what she wants! She has her whole life in front of her! She cannot be burdened with a baby!'

'Her baby.' Shekar moved to the drinks cabinet to choose something stronger than wine.

'What?'

'*Her* baby,' he said, choosing a bottle of cognac. 'Her baby. Her decision. We have to ask her what she wants.'

'But... what if she wants to keep it? I can't imagine... the shame of it all!' The annoying lump leapt out, uncorking the bottled-up tears. 'I can't bear it, anymore...'

Alarmed at her wailing, Shekar abandoned the cork he had been prising out of the cognac bottle and strode over to her. He gathered her against his chest, at the same time, casting his eyes around the room to ensure that the windows were closed. He did not want the neighbours rushing in, wondering if one of them had died. 'Shh... shh... shh.' Her body was a tight coil of anxiety and worry. It shuddered and writhed in his arms, until it exhausted itself with a sigh. He sat her down on the sofa and switched the kettle on. Two minutes later, he placed a mug of sweet, hot tea in front of her and removed the half-empty glass of wine.

'You could never keep a drink down,' he joked, as he sat next to her with his glass of cognac. In spite of herself, she smiled. The battle was not between her and Shekar. They were on the same side.

'Let us look at the positives.' Shekar was in familiar territory. He did this for a living as a management consultant, solving other people's problems. 'She is not exactly a child. She knows who the father of her baby is. She tells us they have been seeing each other for a year.

He is a well-educated man, holding down a good job – not a bad catch.'

Nimmi watched his fingers, counting off the points.

'Haven't you forgotten the biggest stumbling block? He is a Muslim! If she marries him, she will have to convert into Islam.' The tremor was back in her voice. Shekar pushed the tea towards her, and waited until she took a few sips, blowing on it to cool it down each time.

'You missed a step,' he said, his voice low and steady. 'He has to agree to marry her. If that is what she wants.'

Nimmi hadn't considered that, at least not yet. The bottleneck of her worries shifted from the baby to the father. Would Rafik refuse to marry her daughter? What if he dumped gentle, sensitive Kals like discarding a used tissue? Her whole world would collapse around her. Was her daughter strong enough to cope?

As her mother, it was her duty to support her daughter. To stop her from hurting. To be strong for her. Nimmi finished her tea, blew her nose long and hard, just as the doorbell rang. Kalyani stood outside, raindrops shining on her furry hood like gems.

'Forgot your keys?' Shekar asked, closing the door behind her.

'Err… yes. I just wanted to be sure you both are OK.' She saw that her mother had been crying, and her father had been drinking. She rushed into her mother's arms, and the tears started all over again.

'Shh… baby. It will be alright. You will see.'

'We are there for you, Kalyani,' Shekar said, and she turned and fell into his arms. He held her at arm's length, before hugging her. 'But the decision should be yours… and your boyfriend's. You have to talk to him. Have you?'

Kalyani nodded to agree that she had to talk with her boyfriend and then shook her head to indicate that she had not done it yet. It dawned on her that her parents were not opposing the relationship; she had passed one hurdle.

Next stop was Raffa's. Unlike her parents, she had no doubt about Raffa's response.

Chapter 6

The restaurant that Raffa chose was a converted barn, set in acres of forest, with views to die for; layers of pine and birch trees housing wildlife – squirrels, hedgehogs, badgers, and if you are lucky, a stag or a peacock strutting through. The renovation was rustic, and blended seamlessly with the surroundings. Inside was a mish-mash of country and contemporary: large, stone fireplaces with copper and brass pans suspended over them, dark nooks with chunky, wooden furniture and white, plastic windows and skylights. Even the paintings were a combination of Constable and Andy Warhol. But strangely, it worked. The tables were arranged carefully to offer privacy to the diners.

It was a new concern, well-advertised in corporate circles. The food was neither inexpensive nor extraordinary, but the experience was magical. Raffa had organised a big Christmas dinner for the office there, and in return for the promise of a repeat this year, the owners had thrown in a meal for two, on the house.

When, out of the blue, Kals phoned him to say that she was travelling down to meet him at his office, he decided to use the free meal tickets. The place was tucked away in the woods, and it was unlikely they would meet anyone who knew them. It was mid-week and normally, Raffa would have tetchily refused to entertain anything that would disrupt his work schedule. But he was in an upbeat mood; he had finally submitted the blueprint for his project, and preliminary feedback from his boss was positive. In lieu of the hours of overtime he had put in, he took an hour off and drove down to the restaurant. As he pulled into the gravelled car park, the sun was an orange orb, inching towards the horizon. He had suggested that Kals took a taxi from the train station to save time. He had a few minutes before she arrived, enough time to choose their table and preview the menu.

The same orange orb of the sinking sun played hide and seek with the tree trunks as Kalyani's taxi sped along the country lanes. She hadn't seen Raffa for a whole month now; they had both been busy. A few times, in the last couple of weeks, she had nearly blurted out the news over the phone to him, but refrained because she wanted to be there when she told him about the baby, to share his happiness, and his excitement… and to dissipate any doubts he would have. The knot of nerves in her middle, however, promptly disappeared when she saw Raffa, smart and confident in his white shirt and grey chinos, his grey jacket wrapped around the back of his chair. On the table for two, a large glass of iced orange juice waited for her. Obviously, he had come straight from the office. Her heart warmed towards him – her Raffa was a hard worker. He rose as she approached and gave her a peck on her cheek, and pulled her chair back for her to sit. The dying sun changed the glass on the floor to roof window into liquid amber. Outside, the woods stretched for miles. 'What a view!' she exclaimed.

'Spectacular. I know,' he acknowledged. For a moment, they watched the orange and purple streaks trooping across the skies. A plump squirrel balancing on an overhanging branch nibbled on a pine cone, its bushy, grey tail tucked neatly behind it.

'Let us eat. I am starving.' Raffa hooked a finger at a hovering waiter and placed the order. Seafood linguini and salad. The chef's special, Raffa explained. At the best of times, Kals would have avoided seafood on any menu; the thought of it now brought a rush of bile up her throat, which fortunately, she was able to control.

'Can I have a side order of chips, please? And ketchup.' She smiled sweetly at the waiter, while Raffa frowned from the other side of the table.

'Why the special request to see me?' he teased.

'Isn't a girl allowed to visit her boyfriend? That is what happens if you miss several dates with me,' she teased back.

'OK. I told you how busy I was. What have you been up to? Anything special?'

'I did do something special, yes. But I want to tell you later. Tell me about your project.'

'You really want to know?'

'Yes,' Kalyani nodded, suddenly feeling grown up. She would have to listen to his projects all the time when they were married, like a good wife.

Raffa launched into a description of the project and his part in it. Kals dutifully listened, her chin resting on her palms, eyes wide open with interest. After the first five minutes, especially when logistics and the economics crept in, her attention drifted. Raffa could have talked Greek and Latin, for all she cared. All that mattered was they were together – all three of them.

The pasta arrived, pale as puke and smelling fishy. She tried to ignore the smell and concentrated on her salad and chips. They were delicious once she coated them with ketchup and aioli. So as to not upset Raffa, she ate a bit of pasta that wasn't coated with the sauce.

'Sorry Raffa. Haven't been right lately – you know, with the tummy bug and everything.'

'Oh? I forgot to ask. How are you now?'

'Better. Here, you eat my share if you want.'

'After you infected it?'

'Oh no. I am not infectious. I only took a bit from this side.'

Raffa grinned and helped himself to the pasta from the other side. 'I am truly starving.'

'Well. They aren't exactly big portions, are they?'

Raffa allowed her to choose her pudding and he opted for coffee. A lull fell on the conversation. If Kalyani hadn't shoved a spoonful of her sticky, gooey pudding into her mouth, she could have used the moment to spill her news. Raffa claimed it with more dreary details of his beloved project.

Pudding and coffee over, Raffa reached for his jacket. She had an hour before she had to catch the train back home.

'Now, what do you want to do?'

'I have to tell you something.'

'So have I,' he said. 'Let us take a walk. There is a brook somewhere here.'

The brook was not easy to miss. The gentle tinkle of water guided them. The banks were overgrown with reeds, the ducks were having a last swim before retiring for the night, and an early owl hooted short, hollow notes. They found a stone seat beside a massive oak, its trunks calloused and gnarled with age. The seat must have been designed for small people or lovers. As they squeezed beside each other, his arms brushed against her oversensitive nipples. Her breath caught in her throat.

'I see you have missed me!' he grinned, his eyes glinting with desire. He brought his lips down on hers. She yielded helplessly as he moved over her, the growing bulge in his pelvis grinding into her, his fingers burning her skin, wherever they touched.

When he let go of her lips and nibbled at her slender neck instead, she said, 'It is time we stopped missing each other. Don't you think?'

Raffa was breathing in the scent of her raven-black hair. 'Um... hmm?' he mumbled.

'We have to.' Kals continued, as he breathed heavily into her ear. 'Now that I am pregnant.'

A split second later, the breathing in her ear stopped, his fumbling hand stilled, and his organ withered.

'What?'

'I am pregnant.'

'What?'

Kalyani nodded. He nodded back, his eyes vacant, his mouth gasping like a fish out of water. He slid down from the seat onto the wet grass, forgetting to protect his chinos from mud stains. Kalyani sat down beside him, her hair on one side tangled up in her dangling earring. She cupped his face in her hands and turned it towards her.

'Raffa. Think. Our child.'

'What?'

'We will be mummy and daddy. In six months, you will have to build a cradle and brush up on your lullaby.' She glowed like an entrepreneur selling the dream to her most important investor.

Raffa had stopped repeating 'what'. Instead, he was staring at the horizon, black against the twilight. What was this gossamer dream she was busy spinning around him? Round and round, like a crafty spider weaving its web.

'But first.' The spider was talking. He watched her lips moving, spellbound, mesmerised. 'First, Raffa, we should get married. I am not having our first born out of wedlock. You should tell your parents. Before I swell up like a giant peach.'

Round and round, the sticky, silvery threads wound around him; taking its time, confident that her prey couldn't escape. He was a trapped butterfly, fluttering his lustrous wings one last time, before succumbing to his fate. Soon, the spider's luscious lips would stop spewing its web, and she would move in for the kill, the strings of the web twanging in discord as she approached. His life flashed before him – the eligible bachelor with a highly sought-after CV turned into a delectable morsel, laced with pricey seafood sauce. The world around him flickered and plunged into a cavernous blackness.

When he came to, he was lying on his back, staring up at the canopy of leaves. Somehow, the spider hadn't eaten him. She had retreated; watching him with her head cocked to one side. The moon had risen and its light glowed on her beautiful face. He found he could move his hands and his legs and his body. He sprang up quickly to his feet, afraid she would catch him again.

'I know it is a shock, Raffa. It took me weeks to get used to it.'

He cupped his palms over his mouth, stemming his panic. He hadn't accidentally flown into the web this woman had spun. She had arrived with a plan. *A premeditated entrapment!*

'But you must get used to it. Soon.' She was still talking earnestly. She hugged him from behind, her painted talons resting over his heart. She kissed the back of his neck, tiny, short pecks. 'I love you. But I need to go now, or I will miss my train. Promise me you will think about what I said. Right away.'

Shakily but obediently, he nodded, and followed her back to the barn. The cosy building lit by warm amber light no longer held magic for him. He remembered to stay in the shadows because of the green and brown stains on his shirt and chinos, as they walked back to the restaurant car park.

Kalyani turned to him. 'Oh! What did you want to tell me?'

'Me?'

'You said you had something to tell me too.'

Raffa tried to recollect what he had wanted to tell her. His memory was suddenly fuzzy. Was he pregnant too? A sign on a billboard, advertising Finlandia Vodka, jogged his memory.

'I was going to say that I have been promoted. They were pleased with my project.'

'Wow! Raffa. A double promotion – a dad and a super IT... man!'

'There is a downside. I have to go to Finland for further training... for a year.' A year apart from the... situation may slow down the pace of events, allowing them to think rationally. But Kals only needed a split second to turn it to her advantage.

'Oh Raffa!' she gabbled excitedly. 'We should get married before you leave, and then I could come with you! Finland will be our honeymoon! I have heard Finland has a good health service too.' The cab that she had pre-ordered pulled up in front of the softly glowing restaurant, its motor running.

'When do you have to leave?'

'In a couple of weeks!'

'What?' Raffa could almost see the cogs in her brain moving. 'Never mind. You will just have to take time off for the wedding later, like my friend Rita did. Anyway, first you have to tell your parents. Good luck.' She waved at him, and blew kisses out of the window as the cab pulled away.

As he followed the disappearing tail lights of the taxi with his eyes, his breath came in long, wheezy sighs. All evening, he had assumed he was in control: he had chosen the venue, the seat, the menu; but in reality, she had held the reins. Just as she would all his life once they were married. He felt as if he was bound with massive iron chains, and left to sink slowly into quicksand.

Chapter 7

It was soon apparent that no one had a choice in the matter. Neither Raffa nor her parents. Kalyani was a force unto her own, a mini hurricane, who swept people along with her excitement. Her passion was compulsive, bordering on obsessive. Her mind was made up and there would be no negotiation.

1. She was going to be a ravishing, beautiful bride.
2. She was not going to look like a giant peach on her wedding day.
3. She was moving to Finland for a year with her husband.

That meant she only had a few weeks to plan a wedding. She stood sideways in front of the full-length mirror and pulled her nightie tight over her waist. Her pregnancy wasn't showing, yet. If she planned a wedding in two or three months and dressed cleverly, she may get away with it. Did she say 'a' wedding? Think again. There was no way that her parents or his would settle for just a Hindu or a Muslim wedding. He was an only son and she was a first child. Their families would insist on a grand wedding, in accordance with their own religions. They would have to have two weddings – a Nikah according to Islamic traditions and a Shaadi for the Hindu tradition. Instead of terrifying her, the idea served only to boost her excitement. However, doing it all single-handedly was out of the question. Helen and Minna pledged their support, but they were both busy with coursework and exams. The only definitive thing she did was to hand in her notice to Guy at the Hair Express.

Romy's mum, Hana proved to be an unexpected source of help. Having married off three daughters, the last one in record time, she was a self-professed guru, but when she heard Kalyani's idea of arranging two weddings in less than three months, she decided it was more than even she could handle.

'How about a wedding planner?' she suggested.

After trawling through the Internet for an entire day for Asian wedding planners with any star rating, Kalyani shortlisted a handful of companies with seemingly reputable websites. Most of them were booked up for at least three months. One dropped her phone in shock when she heard the plan. Another was more tolerant, and fired questions at her over the phone: 'What religion are you? Would you like a Hindu, Islam or English wedding? Are you planning separate weddings or a fusion? Are you planning to have it at home, in a hall, in a hotel or in a converted barn? Is it going to be a summer, winter, autumn or spring wedding... or a monsoon wedding, like in the Bollywood movie? How many guests will be invited? What is your budget? Have you decided on the menu and the dress code?' By the time the call was terminated by the voice, which was coated with pity and scorn, Kalyani's head was reeling. In panic, she fished out everything she owned that mentioned 'wedding'. Hana, who dropped in a short while later to say hi to Nimmi, found her waist-deep in wedding magazines, paper cuttings and cups of chamomile tea. Nimmi had gone to stock up on groceries, and the front door had been left unlocked.

'Oh. Sorry. I thought Nimmi was in,' she smiled.

'No worries, Mum won't be long. Would you like some tea? I am parched.'

Hana was about to decline but felt that the girl needed a break. 'How's it going?' she asked, as Kalyani poured hot water onto tea bags.

Kalyani gave a snort of laughter. 'As you see, it is not really going anywhere. I keep going around in circles. I don't know where to start.'

Hana nodded, smiling. 'It is a difficult task. Why don't you start by making a list? On paper,' she added, when Kalyani fished out her phone to make the list. Obligingly, Kalyani pulled out a notepad from under the debris and drew a dividing line down the centre. In one column, she wrote Hindu wedding, and in the other, Islamic wedding. 'This is where I get stuck.' She tapped on the second column with her biro.

'Why?'

'Because Raffa hasn't told me what he wants.'

Hana blinked, genuinely confused. 'Haven't you asked him?'

'Yes. Yes, but he is busy. He hasn't told his parents yet.'

'OK.' Hana took a long breath. 'Do you know when he intends to tell them?'

'He wants to discuss it with them in person. Not over the phone. He is coming down this weekend.' Kalyani had worried when Raffa hadn't rung her for a couple of days. She knew Raffa hated being disturbed at work, so instead of ringing, she sent him a carefully worded text message.

'My olds are planning to meet yours this Sunday. Hope you have told them by then. Good luck. Talk soon. XXXX.'

He had rung later that day. 'Sorry for not ringing, Kals. Of course I am excited. But there is so much to think about. My presentation. My transfer. Listen, you have to wait until I speak to my parents. Don't go rushing in there, all guns blazing.'

'OK. Do you think it will be alright?'

'Dunno. We will have to see.'

'Ah! You have to pin him down then,' Hana was advising, when Nimmi's arrival interrupted them. Hana left Kalyani with her paper cuttings and joined Nimmi in the kitchen as she put away the groceries.

'You do realise your daughter is trying to arrange two weddings in less than three months and the groom hasn't even told his parents!' Hana whispered harshly to Nimmi.

Nimmi shrugged her shoulders. 'She thinks she knows best.'

'OK. Let us stick with the Shaadi. Have you any thoughts about the type of wedding you want for her?' Hana asked.

Nimmi's eyes took on a faraway look. Of course, she had dreamt of Kalyani's wedding. A fairy-tale venue, decorated with garlands of imported flowers, muted lighting, faux mist. The bride and groom would sit on swings, decked with sweet-smelling roses. At least three dress changes, plenty of jewellery, at least a couple of hundred guests, delicious catered food from Curry Dreams, no less, and bhangra dancing. Her eyes misted, and Hana sighed. Like her daughter, Nimmi was a dreamer, not a doer. At the other end of the room, the daughter was having her own visions.

She imagined Raffa breaking the news to his parents. Gale force winds predicted at number forty-seven, due to Hurricane Raffa! Maybe the high-speed winds will blow Raffa right out of his home to hers, screaming, 'To hell with my parents! Let us elope!' She giggled at the thought. Maybe she should keep a small bag packed with essentials ready, just in case. She didn't want to be in Gretna Green without her foundation and her favourite lipstick, or her smartphone for selfies.

The sooner Raffa spoke to his parents, the sooner she could get on with her plans, which would include any bowing and scraping that was necessary to obtain their blessings. Would they insist that she converted to Islam? Kalyani did not have a staunch religious upbringing. To her, one religion was as good as the other; his God was as good as hers. She would look no less fetching as an Islamic bride.

She had to warn her parents to be ready to visit the Mahmoods at short notice – as soon as Raffa gave her the green light. She would have to wait for an opportune moment. Her dad was not going to be happy if she barged in as soon as he arrived from his office, proclaiming that she had organised their weekend for them, and planned a potentially unpleasant meeting with the Mahmoods from number forty-seven.

But they had no choice; she had no choice. The microscopic mound of specialised cells nestling in her womb was calling the shots. 'It' was dividing and multiplying, cell by cell, forming a heart, brain, face, using genetic material from mummy and daddy. 'It' was not going to procrastinate or wait for opportune moments. Six months from now, he or she would become a reality with flailing limbs and feeding mouth.

It was high time they all pulled their heads out of the sand and moved forward.

*

Rafik Mahmood was in a meeting, scheduled to discuss the impact of his project on the global markets. He felt confident and pumped up with adrenaline. He listened intently to the speaker on the podium, Adam Watts. In exactly fifteen minutes, Rafik would be up there, tearing Adam's ideas to pieces and replacing them with his own. He would seek eye contact from each and every person in the small audience around the table, especially from the Finnish team, who had chosen him for advanced training prior to promotion. He would pump his fists and use his laser pointer to emphasise the key points of his presentation. He should remember to speak slowly so that the Finns could follow what he was saying. He rifled through his papers to clarify his data.

That was when his phone buzzed to alert him of a text message. Normally, he would have switched off his mobile phone, but his statistician, Linda, had phoned in that morning to say that her son was ill, and she had to work from home. 'I will be at the end of the phone, Rafik. I will keep the data sheets open on the home computer, so just text me if you want any clarification,' she had promised.

Rafik fished the gadget out, to check if it was Linda messaging him. What popped up instead was the message from Kals, informing him of the coup she had organised. 'My olds are planning to meet yours this Sunday…' His heart skipped a few beats, causing him to break out into a sweat. He hoped the cheese and onion bagel he had wolfed down for breakfast that morning did not ooze out of his armpits. A picture of the Sinhas marching up the street dressed in their Sunday best to meet his parents with a marriage proposal played itself before his eyes. He could see the faces of his parents as they reacted to the Sinhas. Shock. Bewilderment. Amusement. Would they laugh into the Sinhas' faces, show them the door and fling their proposal and their gifts behind them, shouting abuse? The whole street would witness this fiasco. His name would be mud, and the wrath of Kalyani would descend on him; chase him to the edge of the nearest cliff, where she would leave him hanging for his life, from the tips of his manicured nails. He could feel the pain surging through his fingers, making him scream until his vocal cords dried up, their capacity reduced to the production of inefficient crackles and squeaks.

Someone from his team prodded him in his ribs. Startled, he looked up from his phone, straight into his boss's frowning face. *Shit*. The chair had already called for him twice. He squeaked 'yes'. He lumbered to the podium, cleared his throat, and reached for the glass of water. His hands shook, spilling water. *Damn*!

'Sorry,' he mumbled. Then, to his horror, he dropped his papers. He followed their path as they oscillated, spun around a few times, shifted out of place, and hit the wooden floor with a soft crash, which to him sounded like Mount Vesuvius erupting. His audience moved restlessly in their chairs, coughing politely, and looking away to hide their embarrassment. A few left their seats to visit the loo. Hastily, the chair called for an early coffee break, allowing their star speaker to collect his thoughts.

Rafik walked briskly back to his office, where behind closed doors, he banged his fist on the walnut veneer table top, making the metal stationery stand jump and spill its contents on the floor. His secretary slipped in with a cup of double-strength coffee and discreetly withdrew. Rafik opened drawers and rummaged until he found the round, smooth pillbox. He tipped a couple into his sweaty palm and swallowed them with the scalding liquid. In the bathroom, he ran cold water into the sink, splashed handfuls of it on his face, and smoothed down his hair with wet hands several times. While he stood in front of the mirror, rearranging his alarmed face, he made two decisions.

1. He would sparkle with his presentation, as he was expected to.
2. He would take the bull by its horns and sort the marriage situation out with his parents, once and for all.

When he returned to the podium, he was focussed and confident; he had rearranged his notes and left his phone under the files in his drawer.

*

Saturday couldn't have come sooner for Kalyani, but Raffa would rather it never came. He did not relish the conversation with his parents. He wished he could find an underworld in his mattress and bury himself in there with the dust mites. Yesterday, he had finally salvaged his presentation, and by sheer dint of the passion he had poured into the project, received a standing ovation. During the dinner afterwards, no one reminded him of the earlier attack of nerves. Now, as the white light of morning pierced through the voile panels, he knew he had no more excuses. Time had run out.

He decided to drive up. Saturday morning traffic was always much lighter. If he kept to the slow lane, he could think things through without wandering into the path of other road users; also, having his own car on his parents' driveway will prove handy if he had to beat a hasty retreat.

Kalyani did not feel as nervous as Rafik. She had given her parents time to think of her plan. They were in agreement that meeting with the in- laws as soon as possible was crucial. If her pregnancy didn't show, they did not have to explain the bump to their nosy friends and relatives. Besides, apart from the small inconvenience of religion, there was nothing more either party could ask for. Handsome groom, beautiful bride, budding career, baby on the way...

Kalyani messaged Helen. 'Waiting in the wings. R to tell his parents today. Hope their roof is screwed on tight. Keeping everything crossed.'

Chapter 8

As ever, the unsuspecting Shahida and Ashraf greeted their son with warmth and love and a sumptuous breakfast. It would be followed by an equally elaborate lunch and dinner. Shahida was a good cook, but when her son was not at home, she was not motivated to drum up the energy to cook complex meals after a gruelling nursing shift. Her husband joked that he only got fed when his son visited.

Raffa dutifully praised his mother's parathas and accepted another perfectly rounded flatbread stuffed with spicy potatoes. No one made it like mummy dear.

'I will miss all this,' he said nonchalantly between mouthfuls.

'What do you mean?'

Raffa grinned cheekily, his cheeks bunched up, creating attractive dimples, a feature that melted his mother's heart every time. 'Got a promotion at work.'

'Wow. That is good... great news!' both his parents congratulated him.

'There is a downside to it though.'

'Is there?'

'Mmm hm. I have to go abroad to train. Finland for a year.'

'What?'

Rafik gave his parents some time to absorb the news. Shahida made several starts to say something, then decided against it.

'What did you decide? Have you accepted it?' his dad asked.

'Really, nothing to decide. I would be a fool not to take this opportunity. It is only across the Channel, a few hours away. I will miss this though,' he said, holding a paratha up. 'Maybe I will pack you in my suitcase, mummee.'

Shahida smiled, evidently pleased that her son would miss her.

'I am too old for all that now. Seriously, what you need is a wife!'

Raffa knew it was spoken in jest, as it had been several times before, but it was the best opening he could have hoped for.

'Oh! I have taken care of that too,' he said, trying to sound casual.

Shahida paused in the middle of clearing the table and Ashraf stopped tapping the table with his spoon. The silence was deafening. They were obviously waiting for him to carry on.

'Have you?'

'Yes.'

'Really?'

'Really!'

'You have chosen a... girl to marry?' Shahida was aware of a worrying flutter in her chest. This was the moment she both looked forward to and dreaded. What was her favourite cat going to drag into her kitchen? She hoped it was a girl (Allah forbid it was a boy). A girl who would fit seamlessly into their lives was all she hoped for.

'You have probably seen her several times, even said "hello" to her.'

'OK.' Shahida quickly trawled through a mental list of who she had said 'hello' to. The plump girl buying cigarettes at the newsagents, the older woman at the post office counter, the single mother with face piercings walking her baby...

'Kalyani Sinha. From number thirty-five.'

Ashraf dropped his spoon and dived under the table to retrieve it. The creases at the root of Shahida's nose deepened into a frown. She remained lost for words for several minutes. Rafik wondered if he could take advantage of this silence and sneak away, but he decided to remain seated.

Finally, she spluttered. 'But… they are… not… Muslim.'

Despite himself, Raffa felt irritated, not exactly because he promoted intercultural marriages, but because his judgement was being challenged. 'So?'

'Have you thought this through?' his father asked, at the same time as his mother said, 'Have you lost your mind?'

Even as the questions left their lips, his parents knew those were the wrong words to say. Rafik's features rearranged themselves into stubbornness. His eyes became hooded and his jaws clamped down, a vein stood out on the side of his temple, and the left corner of his mouth twitched. Like it always did as a child when his parents refused his choice of PlayStation games or took away his toys. From nearly three decades of living with his wife, Ashraf knew exactly where his son had got that behaviour from. Shahida could be equally stubborn, but after a battle of wills, she was the one who always gave in to her son. She made excuses: *all his friends have the same PC game, I don't want Rafik to feel left out*, or *the designer trainers he wants are worth the extra money.*

Ashraf was a patient man when he had to be, and learnt to stay out of the skirmishes, finding quiet pleasure in watching his wife fall on her sword. But today was different. This was something else entirely; other people were involved. There were eggshells all around the issue. He raised his brow at his wife, and gave a small shake of his head in warning.

Shahida swallowed several times before speaking, in an attempt to stop fire exploding out of her mouth like a dragon when she opened it. Her voice still carried an edge to it.

'Have you been having an affair?'

'Yes.'

'Oh my God! How long?' She ignored her husband, banging his plate with his spoon. 'How long?'

'A year.'

'A year! Behind my back!' The spoon banged. She turned to Ashraf and snarled. 'What?' And to her son, she said. 'OK, so you had an affair. It does not have to end in a marriage. These inter-religion marriages are difficult to maintain. So often... they don't last. You do know that. The best thing to do is to end the affair and find somebody more suitable.'

Rafik winced. He was in his mid-twenties. His mother was making him feel like a nine year old being told off. Humiliating, undermining, pulling rank. He had hated it then and certainly disliked it now. With some relish, he said, 'She is pregnant.'

His mother lost it. 'What? How can you be so... stupid?' She scraped her chair back with a horrible grating noise and rose. She paced around the kitchen like a tigress in a cage. For a while, Ashraf and Rafik kept her in their sights, fearing for their safety.

'Rafeek!' she growled. 'Is this baby even yours? I mean girls... can often... well... sleep around.'

She had finally stuffed her foot in her mouth! The air around them became dense. So dense, it was settling around them like concrete. If they didn't move, they would be trapped in it forever. Ashraf rose from the table, putting a warning hand out towards his wife. 'Shahida!'

Rafik flung his napkin on the table and glared at his mother. 'Get a grip, mummee. The Sinhas are coming around tomorrow. 3p.m.'

His parents could only stare helplessly at Rafik's receding back, his shoulders hunched in anger.

*

My. My. Never say life was boring. The weekend was dishing out adventure by the spadeful – not all good ones. Shahida dragged herself out of bed and splashed cold water on her face. She caught her reflection in the mirror. For her age, early fifties, she was in good nick. Her skin still glowed, no wrinkles crinkled around her eyes or mouth. People had told her she looked like her mother. She disagreed. The features that made her mother look aristocratic and regal looked harsh on her. Her nose was too beakish, her lips too thin, and that small, pale scar on the inside of her left eyebrow gave her a permanent frown. She did not have any childhood photographs without that scar; she might as well have been born with it. The scar somehow reminded her of all the pain and uncertainty of her troubled childhood; and when life threw wobblies at her, the scar hurt – an uncomfortable burn. Like Harry Potter's scar, she thought wryly. All of yesterday, the scar had burnt.

Her son had shut himself in his room, and after spending hours trying to make her see sense, Ashraf had opted instead to spend the evening at a friend's house. This morning, father and son had both left for morning prayers at the mosque, leaving her to sulk in bed. Last night, exasperated, Ashraf had shouted at her, 'if you want to drive a wedge between us and Rafik, you are doing everything right. If you want him to stop this affair, you are doing everything wrong!'

Unfortunately, he was right. By opposing her son's decisions, she was ruffling his feathers. If the marriage went ahead, without her blessings, the couple was likely to break off all ties with her. Is that what she wanted? But she did not want to be the first one to back down. Not before she had pointed out all the flaws in the situation. It was her duty as a mother.

Rafik had not given her much time. Silly boy. He didn't know what he was getting into. At the best of times, marriage was not a bed of roses. To marry someone who had no understanding of their culture and religion and did not share the same beliefs was an invitation to lie on a bed of thorns. The community would always view them as outsiders – over polite, outwardly approving, but inwardly reluctant to invite them home, lest they contaminate the minds of their own children. In fact, they would not fully belong to either religion. There will only be isolation and misery for them and for this wretched child they were planning to bring into this world.

She desperately wished she could speak to somebody. Someone who would not judge her. Someone who did not have emotions and ego vested. She knew who she always turned to: Fawzia, her sister-in-law in Pakistan. Three-thousand miles away, with a four-and-a-half-hour time difference, her family would have just had lunch and would be preparing for their siesta.

Fawzia was the second wife of Alam, the brother who was closest to her. Alam was eight years older than her, but Fawzia was of a similar age to her. They had always got on well with each other and shared similar views on various issues. Alam's sons from his first marriage now lived in the US. Fawzia and Alam visited their children often, and on the way, spent a few days with Shahida and Ashraf in the UK too. Alam himself had worked in the UK for a few years, before moving back home to Pakistan.

Shahida made herself a cup of coffee and dialled the number. It was good to hear Fawzia's delighted voice from the other end. After initial pleasantries and enquiries, Shahida brought up Rafik's choice of partner, avoiding any mention of the bride being pregnant. That would cast her son in a bad light. Some things had to remain a secret, even from favourite relatives.

'What did you expect?' Fawzia asked. 'Temptation is all around the poor chap. In the form of tall, white, golden- haired beauties.'

'In an odd way, I would understand that. After all, he must meet them regularly in the office. But he has chosen a dark, short Hindu girl.'

'Are they in love?' Begum Alam asked, after making sympathetic noises in response to the news.

'Rafik thinks he is.'

'You don't know for sure?'

'Rafik has shut himself in his room all day. I… we might have said the wrong things to him yesterday.'

'Why?'

'I don't know. It was all very sudden. A shock to the system. I just felt he was being silly or immature.'

'Shahida!' Fawzia laughed; it sounded like the tinkling of small bells. 'My Alam is nearly sixty. He is still immature! Have you met this girl?'

'They are arriving today. From two houses down the road.'

'Haha. Be nice to them. Nowadays, the choice of our children is not in our hands. We have no choice but to accept. If Rafik is bent on marrying her, you and I can do nothing to stop it. Be mindful that you do not start off on the wrong foot with the possible daughter-in-law.'

'We are entertaining the future in-laws this evening. Rafik sprung it on us yesterday! What do I do?'

'It is a bit unusual – the girl coming to the boy's parents to ask for his hand in marriage. But these are modern times; we have to oblige. Keep it simple. Tidy house. Tea and snacks. Talk less; listen more. Is the girl willing to convert to Islam?'

'I guess I have to ask her.'

'That is a must. Anyway, it is necessary that she has an understanding of her husband's religion and culture. At least, she should have read the Qur'an. Look at it as a test of her love for him. If she agrees to convert, it would mean she loves him a lot.'

'Or she loves her own religion less,' Shahida muttered to herself.

'Relax,' Fawzia reassured her. 'I know a few people who have married into a different religion. Some long and happy marriages, and others short and sad. Like any other marriage these days, it all depends on their ability to look past the differences, and let their love for each other carry them through. Support from the extended families helps too. Must be the same in the UK, no?'

Shahida had no other option but to agree.

'How about the Dragon? Does she know?' Shahida winced at the prospect of discussing it with her mother-in-law, who was stuck in her traditional beliefs; it would be difficult to convince her. The Dragon and her daughters would have a field day dragging Shahida's name through the mud.

'Not yet. Sooner or later, I will have to tell her.'

'Maybe she will be more agreeable if the girl agrees to convert to Islam.'

When she finished the call, Shahida felt happier and more in control. She had less than two hours to prepare to meet this girl and her family.

*

At 3:05p.m, the doorbell rang. Five minutes late! It wasn't as if they were delayed by traffic, thought Shahida, uncharitably. Beside her, Ashraf was tense. He wasn't sure which way this meeting would head.

Shahida discerned three anxious faces on the other side of the door, distorted by the lens on the door peep-hole. If they sprouted antennae from their heads, they would resemble bugs in the cartoons.

'Open the door,' hissed Ashraf. She obeyed him. A bunch of chrysanthemums and a box of garishly -coloured sweets exchanged hands, as introductions were made. Awkward shuffling and exchanges of faux kisses and handshakes ensued.

'And this is Kalyani,' Nimmi said, as if she was introducing a celebrity. The scar on Shahida's forehead tingled, making her frown, despite herself.

'Come in. Come in,' said Ashraf, leading them into the living room. In the silence that followed, both parties surreptitiously appraised each other.

'Tea?' Ashraf offered. His wife bridled. She wasn't going to offer them anything, willingly. She had spent the two hours after chatting to Fawzia plumping up cushions and removing last week's free edition newspapers. She had rummaged through her snack cupboard and freezer for food to entertain with. She dumped the frozen pakoras in the oven, and debated what to serve tea in. Should she use her pale blue china or stick to mugs? Her heart said mugs, but her brain said, 'Set an example. You don't want your future daughter-in-law to think that she can get away with being slovenly.' She had then debated on what to wear. Should she portray herself as the modern woman, who believed in integration, or the traditional Pakistani wife?

'Where is Raffa?' Kalyani asked, craning her neck as if it would help her see through walls.

'Oh. He had to go down to the travel agent to confirm his flight to Finland,' Shahida said, moving the bunch of chrysanthemums up the kitchen counter, closer to the bin.

'Finland? Is he planning a holiday?' Nimmi asked, hoping she wasn't probing.

Shahida frowned some more. So Little Miss Muffet hadn't mentioned Rafik's transfer to Finland to her parents. Or she wasn't aware of it.

'He has a promotion to the Finland office – for a whole year.'

'Yes!' the girl gave a squeak. 'Sorry. Forgot to tell you. I am going with him.'

Uncomfortable silence, before Shahida broke it. 'I have to find a vase for those flowers. Excuse me. Did you say you take tea?'

'Tea would be fine, thank you,' Nimmi said. Ashraf followed his wife to the kitchen, and Nimmi glared at her daughter. 'Is there anything else you haven't told us?' she hissed.

Kalyani, cheerfully pretended to tick off an imaginary list of things on her fingers: 'Boyfriend, wedding, two weddings, Finland, baby… No. Nothing else.'

Before her parents could react, Ashraf returned with plates laden with pakoras, his wife following close behind with a tray of tea.

'Homemade pakoras? My favourite!' Kalyani exclaimed, biting into one.

'Shahida is a good cook,' Ashraf claimed.

'Nimmi makes some mean puddings,' Shekar retaliated. Shahida felt irritated. This wasn't about mothers' and in-laws' cooking skills.

'What about you?' she addressed Kalyani.

'Oh! I can learn. And the supermarkets sell these things anyway. Raffa and I can decide on who… I mean on a meal plan.'

Embarrassed laughter.

'Of course. I can see that you have made a lot of decisions,' Shahida said with ill-concealed scorn.

More awkward laughter.

'I know!' Kalyani exclaimed, ignoring the sarcasm. 'All we need now is your blessing. I thought Raffa would be here too. He must have got the time wrong. I will just ring him, shall I?'

'He knows you are here at 3p.m. He will come.' Shahida's voice had a hint of triumph. 'I mean, he might be driving when you call.'

'That is true,' Kalyani agreed

Shahida regarded the girl. She was petite and pretty. There was something alluring and fragile about her that boys might find attractive. She had taken care to look good; the peach-coloured outfit made her glow seductively, and the matching pearl earrings dangled enticingly. She was radiating positivity and naive confidence. As if she had a right to walk in and claim what was rightfully hers. A part of her wished that Kalyani was swarthy with acne and buck teeth, and talked with a stammer. She wished that the pregnancy story was a lie, intended to entrap her son into marriage. She had discreetly searched for a bump. The pregnancy was not showing yet, but there was a puffy glow to the girl's face, which supported it.

Nimmi interrupted, clearing her throat. 'We are not sure as to how to proceed here. The children appear to have taken the decision to marry. We are just here to iron out any tangles… er… wrangles? Tangles?'

Shahida now turned her attention to the mother. There was no question where the daughter had acquired her looks from. Nimmi had aged well, if the customary, age-related gain around the waist was ignored. The girl's parents were nervous. Naturally, as they had more to lose. Their daughter was young and pregnant.

'There are many tangles. Our religion does not encourage a Mussalman marrying a non-Muslim. Our cultures are so different.'

'I think Kalyani understands that. She has been brought up in a Hindu lifestyle, but we have always been open and receptive to other religions,' Shekar contributed. 'At the end of the day, they will have to live in the religious lifestyle they mutually choose.'

Shahida worried at her nail for a few seconds, and then nodded. 'Our religion is not just a lifestyle. We live by the scriptures and teaching of the Qur'an. Any member of a Muslim family should be familiar with the holy book.'

'Reading any holy book is only good for the soul,' Nimmi conceded. 'Kalyani here is already planning for a Muslim wedding – the Nikah.'

Shahida snorted derisively. 'A Nikah is only for Muslims. If your daughter is arranging a Nikah, she must become a Muslim! It is a basic requirement.' *How naïve are these people?*

Shekar felt the atmosphere become rancid. Using a calm tone, he clarified what he had heard. 'So if they want a Nikah, Kalyani should convert into Islam?'

Using an equally calm tone, Shahida affirmed.

Shekar turned to his daughter. 'Something for you to think about, eh?'

Both Kalyani and her parents had expected this outcome. What riled Shekar was that the 'would be' groom hadn't deigned to make an appearance and participate in these discussions. Kalyani would not change her religion for her in-laws, unless the groom wished her to. What did the boy want?

'I think we should ask Rafik for his opinion too. The decision should be theirs. Isn't that right?'

Shahida inclined her head and Ashraf remained noncommittally silent.

The Sinhas left soon after, promising to consider the suggestions the Mahmoods had made. Once outside, Nimmi placed a restraining hand on her husband's arm. It felt like a tightly-coiled spring.

Although her dad had not said anything to her, Kalyani was not impervious to his silent rage. Once home, she shot upstairs to her room. Her only thought was to vent her frustration on Raffa. Why hadn't he been there?

Raffa had the good manners to apologise. 'Sorry Kals. Took a long time at the travel agents. He turned out to be the brother of my classmate. So we chatted a while. Then got stuck in traffic because of some demonstration for gay rights.'

'Why didn't you ring? Anyone would think you were afraid of your parents.'

'Oh! Don't be silly, babe. Forgot my charger, and my phone is running low on battery. How did it go anyway?'

'Well, the pakoras were nice.'

'Mummee's pakoras are nice.'

'She wanted to know if I can cook!'

'Can you?'

'You think it is a joke?'

'But you need to cook, don't you?'

'Never mind that! Your mother wants me to convert.'

'Into what?'

Kals ignored his attempts at keeping it light hearted. 'Into Islam!'

'Oh?'

'Indeed oh.'

'So? What did you say?'

'What did you want me to say? Ask your son to convert to my religion?'

'You didn't!'

'No. But I could have. In fact, why don't I suggest it now?'

'Look. You knew about this before. I am a Muslim. Your religion does not require that I convert. But mine does.' Kals was at a loss for words, and Raffa took advantage. 'Look, my battery is too low. Consider what I said and we will talk further. Apologies to your parents.'

Kals wasn't sure if he had rung off or the battery had finally given up. She sighed. 'If I didn't love you as much as I do, Raffa, I would gladly strangle you.'

*

Downstairs, the topic of discussion was the same, but the tone angrier. Nimmi had quickly poured Shekar a stiff drink and planted it into his fist. She understood that her husband's anger stemmed from a feeling of helplessness. Shekar was a proud man, who did not ever want to be indebted to anyone. He lived within his means, worked hard and paid his taxes. He was just and loyal. Now, he was caught between his daughter's welfare and his principles. It was not as if Shekar and Nimmi could not string an apt reply to the Mahmoods, when they laid down the law. An unimaginative 'stuff you and your religion' would have sufficed. Where would that leave Kalyani, their most precious possession? She and the baby would be the ultimate losers. Her current and future happiness depended on how sensitively they handled the situation. But the injustice of it all sat like an ugly tumour in his chest, hurting like hell.

Nimmi busied herself with making some strong tea, absent-mindedly mashing the tea bag. Outside, the clouds darkened with the threat of rain, reflecting her dark mood. There would be no spectacular sunset today, nor would there be stars twinkling at night. The clouds will hide it all; the day would draw quietly to a close, but its legacy would stay on forever. She wished she could put all the different emotions chaotically traversing through her into neat piles. Anger, guilt, blame, desolation, despair, shame, pride, and above all love. If the love between Rafik and Kalyani was strong, it would certainly win. She hoped there was enough love. The first drops of rain crashed onto the glass pane, distorting her view of the garden.

Chapter 9

Twenty-four hours later, the mood on either side stayed grim, with no forecast for a white flag. Raffa had gone back to work and the countdown for his move to Finland had commenced. Ten more days. His mother laboriously prepared and packed spice mixtures, and his dad looked up details of affordable accommodation near his son's Finland office.

Kalyani, loathe to waste any more precious time, roped Helen into browsing Asian wedding magazines. After hours of imagining themselves in costumes and jewellery, they decided to take a break. The two friends rolled on to their backs, and stared at the George Clooney poster on Helen's ceiling.

'That needs to come down. He is married to a gorgeous chick now. Bet he had the best wedding planner on the job,' said Kals, munching on the penultimate Rolo from the packet Helen had fished out of her handbag.

'Listen up, Kals. You know you cannot make plans until you are sure that there is definitely going to be a wedding. Is there gonna be one?'

'Has to be one. No way out of that. Too late to do anything with this one now.' Kals touched her tummy.

Helen laid her hand on Kalyani's tummy as well. 'Can you feel it moving?'

'Not yet.'

'Have you seen a doc yet? You will need a scan.'

Kals sat up. 'You are right! None of us thought about it. What with all this going on. Who do I go to?'

'An obsess-tician person. You said his mother is a nurse. Does she know a reputable obsess-tician?' Helen lisped on the word obstetrician.

'No way I'm asking the monster-in-law. She will ask me to convert if I need to see a Muslim doc.'

'Did you speak to Raffa again?'

'Nope. Can't call him at work. He has sort of left the ball in my court.'

'In what way?

Kalyani squirmed uncomfortably. 'Convert or don't marry.'

'In this day and age?'

'He only wants to keep his parents sweet. It may not matter once we are married.'

Helen gave her friend a sidelong glance. She had a few choice words – the best of English slang to describe this lover boy, but knew from experience that they would only serve to awaken the protective tigress in Kals. Instead, she reached over and helped herself to the last Rolo.

*

Kalyani soon forgot the cold gel over her abdomen, and the desperate need to pee. She had drunk as much water as possible before her scan and tried her best to relax when instructed to. Beside her, her mother sat holding her hand. She would have preferred some drama around her first antenatal scan: Raffa holding her hand, staring excitedly at the monitor for the very first glimpse of their baby, with the monster-in-law trying unsuccessfully to have a look in.

Acting on Helen's advice, she had made an appointment with "Yoda", who had not been entirely happy that she had taken so long to start antenatal checks. She was lucky to have got a cancellation slot for the scan on the same day. The next available slot was a month later on the NHS. Under the circumstances, her mother drove her down in a hurry. She did not have time to inform Raffa or anybody else.

Unravelling on the screen in front of her in 3D was the grainy image of a mystic creation, floating serenely, the perfect head and a snub nose, stubby fingers and toes, and a beating heart. As she watched, the stubby hand seemed to wave to her. 'Hi Mum!' Her eyes welled up. Beside her, Nimmi sniffed and blew her nose. Kalyani extended her own hand towards the screen, disappointed when the angle of the scan changed and she was looking at some other part of the baby's anatomy.

'All fine,' Katya, the Polish sonographer smiled at them. She gave her a wad of tissues to clean up the goo on her tummy. The machine whirred and she placed two copies of the scan in Kalyani's hands.

Kalyani brought the image to her lips and kissed the snub nose. 'You may pee now,' said Katya, as if on cue.

As her mother drove out of the car park, Kalyani took photographs of the scan on her phone, selected the cutest one, and posted it to Raffa. Then to Minna, and Helen, and her dad. At her request, her mother dropped her off at the post office near their house, which housed an ancient photocopier, tucked away behind shelves of assorted greeting cards. She photocopied the image, enlarging it to an A5 size, placed it in an envelope and sealed it. On the way home, she posted it through the Mahmoods' letterbox.

'Work your magic, sweet pea,' she said, as the envelope passed through and landed on the other side with a soft thud.

*

Raffa's phone pinged, as he stood behind Marina's chair and reached across her chest to point out the corrections he wanted her to make in the notes on her desk. On the way there, he had made sure that his palm brushed against her small breast buds. He felt a pleasurable tingle. Marina was a sweet, fresh-faced apprentice with very kissable lips. She was so keen to please the boss that she either did not notice his unhealthy interest in her, or preferred to ignore it. He wondered how long it would take her to get into bed with him.

He had a pretty good track record with the ladies. OK, he wasn't beating them off with a stick; a steady trickle was all could manage in his busy schedule. Last month, he had Marjella from Bulgaria or Romania, he couldn't remember. She was between affairs, resolute that she wasn't going to get involved with the opposite sex ever again. Her resolution had lasted a week.

Then there was Sophie, who had cheated on her boyfriend with him. That had made him feel good.

Before her was Liski from up north, who seemed to be having a race of her own. 'This month has been dismal!' she had complained after their night together. 'You are only my tenth man.'

He had raised his glass of coke and toasted to that. 'Happy to be your tenth, ma'am.' She raised her bottle of beer, and raised her eyebrow at his choice of drink.

'Muslim. We don't drink,' he said proudly.

'Oh man! I bow to thy self-control. I couldn't last a day without the booze.'

Truth be told, he had tasted alcohol once or twice in his rebellious teen years, and had intensely disliked it.

Then there was Kals. He had actually been disappointed with Kals. He had expected her to play hard to get. A good parent abiding girl that she was. But within an hour of meeting him for the first time, she had offered him a ride in her Clio, and by the end of the month, she had allowed him to ride her.

The ringing phone startled him. He pulled back his hand to answer his phone, brushing against her breast again.

'Sorry,' he said, as he stabbed the buttons to retrieve the message. He stared uncomprehending at the grainy photograph in front of him. There was no accompanying message, but it was from Kals. He looked at it from a few different directions, enlarged it a few times, before it dawned on him. An ultrasound scan of his mistake; their mistake. Here was the evidence of his lust – the one that would either link two families together or separate them apart forever. The cold enormity of it all squeezed his heart dry, and a few inches below, his organ that had reacted to Marina's nipples withered with a sigh.

*

Ashraf found his wife in the kitchen, still in her nurse's uniform. There was something disturbing about the stillness with which she sat, her hands clasped together on her knees. On the kitchen table was the evidence that she had drunk her evening cup of tea and eaten at least one of the two biscuits she had placed on the small, gold-rimmed saucer. Crumbs stuck to the corner of her lips and on the paper in front of her. She was usually careful to brush the crumbs away when she finished. He moved to her side, his gaze bypassing her vacantly staring eyes, to the blown-up photograph on the table.

'What… in Allah's name…?' he muttered. This time, their eyes met and lingered.

'Our first grandchild,' she whispered. He could smell tea and biscuits on her breath. He reached out and touched the scan with the reverence it deserved. The reverence that only someone who had endured heartache and despair in order to conceive would feel. The same reverence and gratitude that they had felt when they held the result of the pregnancy test that confirmed Rafik's conception, twenty-four years ago. She pre-empted what Ashraf was going to say. It echoed her own thoughts.

'Shahida,' he said, his voice soft and gentle. 'If we don't do the right thing, we will lose our first grandchild, and our son. We will never forgive ourselves.'

Leaning on his arm, she nodded, her tears leaving wet stains on his polycotton shirt.

*

Kalyani lounged on the sofa, browsing through the messages on her phone. Congratulations from Shekar, Minna and Helen, and her other friends, kisses in the form of three x's from Raffa. None from the monster-in-laws.

For the umpteenth time, she studied the photo of the scan, proud that she was responsible for this little life. Raffa was coming on Friday, to say goodbye before flying to Finland. She felt happy, loved and complete. She would soon be everything a girl would ever want to be – wife, mother, daughter-in-law (if she played her cards right), daughter and sister.

The phone rang. Damn, it was the house phone. The house phone only rang when the mis-sold PPI chasers or a double-glazing salesman wanted to hassle. Only her parents answered the house phone, cursing if it took them to an automated recording. She shuffled on the sofa, hoping it would stop. It did for a while, as if recuperating, before attacking again. Kalyani tutted.

Maybe it was her mother ringing to say she had forgotten to switch off the stove… Sighing, she got up to pick up the phone handset. 'Hello?'

A hesitant voice said, 'Mrs Sinha?'

'No. It is her daughter, Kalyani. Can I help?'

'I… oh, I actually wanted to speak to you. It is Shahida, Rafik's mother.'

'Oh. So did I. Want to speak to you… I mean.' Kals felt lightheaded all of a sudden. She groped around for the sofa and plonked onto it.

'Thank you for the scan. He… she is beautiful.'

'Your grandchild.'

'Yes. Rafik's… and your child.' There was a hint of awe and longing in her voice.

'I have been thinking,' Kalyani said, choosing her words with some care, 'for the sake of this unborn child, and with deference to the wishes of my future husband's family, I shall convert to Islam. I shall read the Qur'an, and try to understand it. I will accept Allah as my God.' She heard Shahida's sharp intake of breath. But before she could say anything, Kalyani took a deep breath and hurried on. 'But… I will not change my first name, nor will I wear a hijab, unless I choose to, or if it is necessary for religious reasons. I shall continue to share important religious festival days with my parents, when I can, and continue to believe in the Gods that I have been brought up with.'

By the time she finished, she was shaking like a leaf. The silence at the other end was not absolute. She could hear Shahida breathing hard, intercepted by clicks of static. Just as Kalyani thought that her offer was not going to be accepted, and she would have to go to plan B, if only there was a plan B, Shahida spoke. Her voice sounded small and distant.

'I cannot ask for more.' Both Shahida and Kalyani knew who held the cards now. At least for the moment.

'Can I help with the Nikah?' Kalyani could almost hear the *Shehnai* trumpets, equivalent of wedding bells, blaring out the wedding music. She could almost feel the crackle of Raffa's wedding outfit next to hers.

'Only if my parents help with the Shaadi,' she said triumphantly.

Kalyani was still dancing when her mother walked in with the groceries. When she heard the news, Nimmi danced with her.

Chapter 10

The flow of traffic between number thirty-five and forty-seven had never been so hectic. Kals walked up at the crack of dawn in her pyjamas under her jacket to ensure that everybody in number forty-seven was awake and awaiting Raffa's arrival. Did Shahida need any help? She walked back home when Shahida reassured her that everything was in hand. She walked back up again within the hour, still in her pyjamas, could she please have a shirt from Raffa's wardrobe, so she could get the correct size to the tailors for his wedding suit? Shahida promised to look in the wardrobe, and Kalyani left. Shahida sent Ashraf down to Number thirty-five with the shirt. Shekar asked Ashraf if he knew of any good workmen, who could give the house a face-lift in time for the wedding. Ashraf suggested they employed the man who painted the windows at number forty-three; he could introduce Shekar to them. Shekar tucked his shirt in and they both walked to number forty-three. Nimmi took a sample of her casserole up, and Shahida returned the saucepan with a sample of the dessert she had made. Of course, some of these transactions could have been made over the phone, but the two families used every excuse to bond.

Raffa arrived; Raffa packed; Raffa left. Raffa hid his anxiety well, but he was hyper-vigilant, and somewhere over the clamped muscles of his jaw, a nerve jumped and ticked. He was immensely relieved both the families were getting on quite well with each other and he did not have to witness or referee shouting and slanging matches between them. Through the afternoon, he lightened up and even enjoyed his mother's cooking. If his parents were prepared to accept a Hindu girl as their daughter-in-law, and were willing to convince their extended family that it was the right thing to do, he had no objection to offer. Kals was easy-going, pretty, a homemaker. She loved him enough to forgive him his trespasses. Better the devil he knew…

In the hour Kals spent with him, as he packed for Finland, she spoke without pause. She quoted word for word everything the sonographer had said about their little baby: how perfect everything was, how alert he or she was, kicking like a football player, how cute the little fingers and toes were. The discussions she had with his parents, and her parents; everything they planned to do in the next couple of months. The Hindu wedding, Shaadi first, the Islamic wedding, Nikah next; note the immense sacrifice she was making by converting to Islam. All because of her love for him, which he could return with interest on their honeymoon. Spoken in jest, of course. Then, she had launched into her vision of their married life as Mr and Mrs Rafik Mahmood in the land of snow-peaked mountains and forests of silver birch. She had already thought of the type of house they would rent – a three-storey townhouse with horizontal wood cladding on the outside. She didn't mind a flat if it came with a view. Imagine waking up to blue skies and woods, and reindeer nibbling at moss. Imagine sitting around a real wood fire, them and the baby. They could enrol for ski classes, and she could learn some Finnish cuisine… blah… blah… blah. He congratulated himself on making all the right gestures, and saying all the right things, even bringing some passion into the goodbye kiss he planted on her soft lips.

After she left, Raffa listened some more to his mother and his father. Dress warm, cook fresh food, get a good night's sleep, remember to change to snow tyres, careful with the passport… thankfully steering away from the subject of marriage.

Kals returned to say her final goodbye, with a green scarf of hers, which she stuffed into his bag. 'To remind you of me. It will keep you from falling for those tall, blonde Finnish damsels,' she said.

He finally found peace on the flight. As the plane ascended, he felt the layers of atmosphere lifting off him, like an onion being peeled. He found himself smiling, not the rictus grin he had been putting on for people at home all evening, but a glowing smile of happiness. F for Finland; F for freedom. He smiled at the blonde air stewardess, who was handing him the headphones. He smiled at the obese man sat next to him, who would probably snore all night. He smiled at the six-year-old hyperactive child behind him, who would probably kick the back of his seat for the majority of the flight.

In his briefcase, stashed in the luggage compartment above his head, was the official document confirming the details of his new post. It had arrived at the last minute, yesterday. When the pilot switched off the 'fasten your seatbelt' sign, he stood up and fished out the file, and opened it with reverence. He studied his contract with the Finnish company. There were photographs of the office, and the team he would be working with. The office was sparse and minimalist, his team middle-aged and pleasant, in a business sort of way. No blonde bombshells that he would have to ward off with Kalyani's green scarf.

He had spent countless hours working towards this promotion. Now, the power he held lit him from within. He had everything... youth, success, riches... understanding parents, pending marriage, and a child. What else could a man ask for?

He had not been in a hurry to marry or become a father. He wasn't sure he would ever be. He wasn't sure how his life would change. Right now, he would simply savour his freedom.

Chapter 11

Two months. Two weddings. Travel abroad. Joining a new religion. Being pregnant. Enough to drive anyone to distraction.

After a couple of weeks, wasting time, money and effort, bandying ideas, arguing, rejecting, and sulking, Minna, who was fed up of being hassled and set up as the 'fall guy' – let's see what Minna says, and if things go tits up, we can blame her – insisted they hired a wedding planner.

Kalyani hired Raeba Bose, founder and owner of Regal Weddings. They literally stumbled upon each other in an Asian clothes shop. Kalyani had crouched down to inspect the trinkets displayed on the lower shelves, and Raeba tripped over her. One thing led to another, and ended in Nimmi, Kalyani and Raeba squeezing into a tiny office at the back of the shop. Raeba's family owned the shop, and she was in the process of setting up her business – weddings. Kalyani and Nimmi were more or less her first clients. It was soon evident that Raeba did not work from the claustrophobic confines of the tiny room. Her products and ideas were scattered all over the shop. Mannequins dressed in sequinned silk and costume jewellery, wedding magazines and her business cards seemingly casually left on the counters, rows of fabric in all shades of bright. Raeba herself was a petite, buxom girl, probably in her late twenties; she walked with a confident stride, her passion oozing from every pore. She smiled often, showing small, even teeth, but behind the façade was a steely businesswoman.

She clapped her small hands in delight when she heard it was an inter-religious marriage, hoping she could have a free rein planning a fusion wedding, and was disappointed that it wasn't.

'Only the Hindu wedding from our side. The Muslim version will be arranged by the groom's family,' Nimmi explained

'We still have plenty to do.' She clapped her hands again. The next few hours flew by in a flurry of catalogue browsing, fabric sampling, FAQs, copious note taking, and more clapping. After she allowed them to leaf through her collection of catalogues, full of beautiful models wearing awe-striking wedding attires, posing in front of castles and expensive hotels, she asked the most important question: how much were they willing to cough up for their first daughter's wedding.

Raeba cleverly masked her reaction to the amount quoted, but with a sleight of hand, replaced the shiny, beautiful models on glossy paper with a budget model of brides on her computer screen. Before the Sinha family chastised themselves, she drummed up their enthusiasm again by printing off a formatted spreadsheet. Number of guests, the venue, the food, the music and entertainment, the theme/décor, the flowers, the photographer… Two months, on a shoestring budget, for two weddings!

She thrust the list at them and sent them away to think long and hard. On the amount they were willing to spend, they were going to have to do a lot of the work themselves. From the moment they submitted their answer and deposited half her fees, she would become their lord, master, and fairy godmother rolled into one. 'You have three days to complete that list. Three whole days.'

At first, Kalyani tried to rope Raffa in by sending him photographs and ideas. Would he prefer the red, spangled jacket or the glitter-coated, puce one; would he prefer a three-tier Victoria sponge with plastic bride and groom figurines on top, or a chocolate and marzipan leaning tower of Pisa; would he prefer purple-tinged, electric-blue lighting or colour-changing stripes of light chasing around the stage? Cabaret dancers from the local club, or wedding singers off the Internet? Fusion music by a DJ, or a selection of nostalgic songs on the MP3 player? At first, Raffa responded, then he texted that he was too busy, and she should decide. When she persisted, he switched his phone off during office hours, and conveniently forgot to switch it back on. With Raeba breathing down her neck, she wished she had paid more attention to his likes and dislikes. She felt inadequate; surely, after months of dating Raffa, she should know his preferences, just like her mother knew her dad's.

'Your dad likes his toast golden and his coffee bitter; blue shirts, but not blue on the walls...' Nimmi could write an essay on Shekar's likes and dislikes. Kalyani tried to remember the colour Raffa frequently wore, the food he ordered at the restaurants, and the perfumes he chose. How does one transfer seafood linguini to an Asian wedding feast, or a striped, blue shirt to a sequinned turban?

She could ask his mother, but she couldn't bear the triumphant, mocking look on Shahida's face, as if to say, you mean you don't know? In the end, she pretended that she had discussed it with Raffa, and made the choices, using her dad and Romy as her male models. Of course, their physique was different. No one was as handsome as her Raffa – not even her dad!

Infected by her enthusiasm, both the families spent the next few days in feverish frenzy, their carpets littered with paper cuttings, adverts, visiting cards, guest lists, and their brains buzzing with things they had to remember, things that they should have remembered, and things that they would now never remember.

The parents spent sleepless nights planning crucial conversations with friends and relatives, to explain their child's choice of partner. To the older relatives back in India and Pakistan, they apologised for their children marrying out of religion. To those in America or the UK, they bragged about their forward-thinking children, and how very much in love they were. The wedding was being arranged in a hurry because the groom was moving to Europe. Neither side mentioned the baby.

Their lives were vaulted into a cycle of shopping, 'spring cleaning', and more shopping to replace the items that they had thrown away, answering phone calls at odd times of the night, and plying layers of foundation and lipstick to look good on Skype, when conversing with far away family and friends. Shekar, Ashraf and even Romy were cajoled into ferrying them to every hotel, garden, barn and village hall, in search of a suitable venue.

Slowly, out of the chaos, a plan emerged. The preliminary number of wedding guests, a draft menu and final ideas for the wedding costumes were drawn up. Challenged to start earning her fee, Raeba gave them the earliest tailoring slots possible; after all, it was a family business. She found a rundown hotel, being revamped, out in the sticks. The owners had a cashflow situation, therefore agreed to hire out a part of the building at short notice.

Shekar and Nimmi had stared aghast at the scaffolding and blue plastic around the building, the churned-up, sticky mud foaming on the ground, and builders' tools blocking the front door.

'Our guests would have to wear wellies,' Shekar prophesied.

'And helmets,' Nimmi added.

But Kalyani only saw the beauty of the place. They were in the middle of nowhere. The hall had a simple charm, and was an open canvas. Outside, the bramble-ridden garden led into the woods, replete with a trickling stream, rickety bridge, hopping bunnies, and a family of red foxes. A few wooden seats, desperate for a lick of paint, loomed out of tall grass. The whole atmosphere reminded her of the barn converted to a restaurant Raffa had taken her to.

'Look at those photo opportunities!' she exclaimed, rushing to pose in front of gnarled and knotted trunks, and the dry, moss-ridden fountain, clapping her hands in glee when a couple of alarmed bunnies, flushed out of the wilderness, fled into the unruly hedgerows.

When the owners agreed to lay paving slabs to enable the guests to access the hall, mow some of the grass, get rid of the brambles from the parts of the woods chosen for photographs, and offered a tempting discount, Shekar paid the deposit. It wasn't as if they had a choice. Most of the venues were booked years ahead, and the other pathetic excuses available were much more expensive and uncompromising.

The family soon learnt to rein in their wild ideas, and not to change their minds so often. After patiently listening to Minna's suggestion that they choose a *Star Wars* theme, Helen's choice of heavy metal music, Nimmi's desire to import peacocks and black swans, and Kalyani's dream of a helicopter dropping glittering confetti, Raeba sweetly, but sternly, reminded them to keep it simple. Shekar was flummoxed at how much this simplicity was costing him. None of his cheques were for anything less than a thousand pounds.

The invitees soon sent their RSVPs. Despite the short notice, and a few disparaging remarks, most accepted.

While Shekar frantically went over his accounts again, hoping he had made a mistake about the number of zeros in the final amount, Shahida appeared not to mind adding them to hers. Only the best would do for her only son's wedding. She sent Kalyani a constant stream of YouTube videos, featuring grand Islamic weddings. She sent her photographs of the final shortlist of costumes for the Nikah, sent to her by Fawzia in Pakistan. They took Kalyani's breath away. The quantity of metallic embroidery and gems woven into the silk should make the costume weigh a ton. She would probably be crawling around the floor on her hands and knees by the end of the ceremony.

'I will get it tailored in Pakistan. Fawzia will bring it with her, when she comes for the wedding,' Shahida said, her eyes looking pointedly at Kalyani's waist, wondering how much bigger it would grow over the weeks. 'My sister-in-law is a dab hand at sewing; I am sure we can make some last-minute alterations, if needed,' she reassured her.

'Are you not having an engagement party before the wedding? Or a hen night?' Raeba asked, quick to stress that this was not included in the existing budget. 'You could have a small one at home. A *mehendi* ceremony, perhaps? Mehendi is a plant-based dye used to decorate the palms of the bride and the groom and anyone else who is interested. My sister is good at it.'

Of course, another source of income to the family, thought Shekar.

Raeba was drumming up a vision from across the table. 'You could have a joint one with the groom's family. Rafik can have his palms decorated too, if he wishes.'

'Raffa is only coming on Thursday. His dress rehearsal is on Friday, the day before the Shaadi,' Kalyani informed her. 'Nikah is arranged a week later, after my conversion to Islam. He won't be able to take any more time off work.'

'Well, you can have *mehendi* on Thursday evening. Mind you, it will put you out of action for most of the evening.' Kalyani wasn't sure she could sit still for an entire evening, waiting for the dye to stain her palms and feet, but it would set the festivities off to a good start.

'Yes. Let us! I will invite Rafik's family too. Rafik can join us as soon as he arrives home.'

*

Minna came bearing gifts. With a generous donation from Nimmi and Shekar, she had done some serious shopping. She lifted her designer bags high, and stepped gingerly over people and things on the floor, trying not to upend bowls of food or mehendi to reach her sister. They hugged without hands, as Minna carried bags in hers and Kalyani's hands were being prepared for the mehendi. Raeba and her sister resembled pretty witches as they stirred a pot of orange-green goo. They had prepared the mehendi in accordance with a special family recipe, and were scooping globs of it into special applicators with a nozzle. A print-out of patterns had been passed around the ladies, some of whom were having a hard time choosing. Kalyani had chosen an intricate pattern of peacocks and flowers, which would make the sign of a heart when she brought her palms together, and a similar one for her feet. Raeba's sister stencilled the pattern in ink on her hand.

Minna chose a single peacock, and Nimmi chose a floral pattern for one hand, so she could keep her other hand free for chores. Shahida went for an Islamic style, involving arches, domes and turrets.

The sisters evaluated each other. Minna looked slimmer, angular, and somehow older in a grown-up sort of way.

'I can see a halo of knowledge around your head,' Kals teased.

'And you have a bridal glow... and a maternal glow. In short, you are positively glowing, sis.'

'Is your boyfriend coming? He is invited, you know.' Kals was teasing again, but was surprised at the faint blush spreading across her sister's cheeks. 'Hey! You have news? Go on, spill!'

Minna tried in vain to deny it. 'Look. It is only in the early stages, OK? Only an attraction.' She moved her free right hand in an undulating gesture to emphasise this. Her left hand was being decorated with the mehendi. Kals did not let it go so easily and made Minna divulge more. 'Matty attends some of my classes. He wants to specialise in European law. He is driven, intelligent...'

'Handsome?'

'Not striking. But I think he is. No. I don't have a picture of him. And no! I am not telling Mum about it.'

'Watch and learn then, sis. See how my wedding is planned.'

'Oh, I will have a lot more time to plan!' Minna waved her right hand in dismissal. For a moment, they watched Raeba and her sister pump a thin string of the dye over the pattern, with great precision.

'By the way, where is *your* boyfriend? Posho?'

'Hey! Show some respect! He is your brother-in-law,' Kals admonished. 'He is due anytime now.'

Kals had checked her phone for messages from Raffa, before submitting to the mehendi torture. She had been regularly sending updates to Raffa. 'Can't wait to see you again, and then we never have to be apart ever again!'

Raffa had messaged her back a couple of weeks ago. 'Yes Kals. If I do not finish the allocated work here, I may not have enough time to spend on the honeymoon. Just be patient.'

And patient she had been, waiting for this day. A week ago, he had sent another text to say he was still very busy. And ditto to her messages of love. There had been no message that day to say that he had boarded the flight, not unusual where Raffa was concerned.

Over the next few hours, aunts, uncles, and cousins streamed in, their young children ran around, squealing, while their mothers cautioned them not to jostle the adults who were having their hands adorned. Nimmi and Shekar received them with joy, and made sure they were wined and dined. Nimmi fed her daughter rotis. 'Just like when you were five years old! You and Minna used to watch TV, and I shoved the food into your tiny mouths, reminding you to chew before swallowing.'

'Mum! You are so embarrassing!' both her daughters protested.

Three hours from ETA. No Raffa. She had requested Nimmi and Minna to discreetly check her phone for messages from him. Perhaps he had been in a hurry, and forgotten to charge his phone. Or he simply did not think to send a message. Men don't work that way, she reminded herself. She finally confronted Shahida, keeping her voice low. 'I thought Raffa was arriving at 6p.m. Has he rung you to say he was delayed?'

Shahida shook her head, but did not seem worried. 'He might have dropped into his Swindon office on the way.'

'OK. Thanks. Wish he had rung me to say so.'

Shahida smiled knowingly. Kalyani felt irritated. If only you had brought him up to be punctual, she thought to herself.

For the rest of the night, she kept one eye on the door, her heart lurching expectantly every time it was opened.

'Would you like me to ring Posho? Ask him if he has cold feet?' Minna saw the hint of worry in her sister's eyes, and quickly backtracked. 'He probably missed his flight, and is running around trying to find another one. In his rush, he dropped his phone and it shattered to a thousand pieces! Clumsy Posho! Don't worry!'

'Are you sure you sent him the right date and time?' Helen whispered.

'Men!' Hana shook her head disapproving.

*

Kalyani slept fitfully. Last night, after the dried paste had been washed away from her hands, and the reddish-orange patterns it had left were praised by the guests, she had retired to her room and called Raffa. His phone was switched off. Nevertheless, she texted him several messages. The first few were angry, the next ones worried, the last ones pleading.

'Missed you, Raffa. Please, please let me know you are safe and are on your way home.'

The morning did not bring a flurry of apologetic replies from him. No 'sorry I missed my flight' or 'sorry, misplaced my phone'. He had not rung home either.

Unlike Kalyani, Shahida was used to his telephone silences, and therefore maintained calm. The day before the marriage stretched over twenty-four hours, enough time for a man to arrive, and scrub up for the altar. But he was cutting it fine.

By the afternoon, the bride and her family were frantic, and she was running out of excuses. They barged en masse into her kitchen and settled at her dining table.

'Why don't you check with the company? See if he has been delayed because of last minute work commitments or something,' Nimmi urged Shahida.

'I don't think I have his company contact details. We always contacted each other via the mobile. Or email,' she apologised. 'I have tried contacting him by them.'

'What about his Swindon office? If he was going to drop by, they might know where he is, or at least if he arrived in the UK.'

'We will only embarrass him. What should I ask? Have you seen a missing bridegroom?' Shahida protested. 'He must have a good reason for the delay.'

'It is Friday afternoon. In a couple of hours, everything will close down for the weekend. We should ring now.'

'There is a wedding at stake here,' Nimmi squeaked. 'I need to know if Rafik will be there for his own wedding.'

Shekar moved protectively towards his wife.

'Here, let me.' Ashraf took the phone from his wife's trembling hands and dialled the Swindon office.

'Can I speak to Rafik Mahmood please? He asked me to call him here, regarding some data he was collecting. He was... is in the IT sector, something to do with security.'

The ruse worked, and Ashraf was connected to Rafik's previous colleague, Tom. Tom confirmed that Rafik worked for their Finnish associates now. No, he hadn't seen him since he left for Finland, not last night, no phone calls either. Tom obligingly gave them the number of the Finnish company. 'Hope you get your data.'

Meanwhile, Shekar checked with the airline. At first, they refused to run a check, unless they had all the details. 'I don't have his PNR number,' Shekar told the attendant. 'He was due to arrive at Heathrow at 4p.m. UK time yesterday. From Finland. You can understand our anxiety that he has not reached?'

Static crackled on the line. 'There is no one with that name booked into the flight, sir.' 'I am sorry, sir, we cannot check all airlines from Finland without further authority.' 'I am sorry, sir, a missing person enquiry is a police matter.' Shekar was unable to make any further headway.

'No reservation in that name. No cancellations. They cannot check all flights,' he repeated for his family's benefit.

'But they have to! What if he had caught a later flight? What if…?'

Shekar stared back at Kalyani. He had no answer. There were a lot of what ifs. There was also the possibility that Rafik could still walk in the door, with a sheepish grin.

'Have you checked your email and Facebook?' Minna asked her sister.

Kals nodded miserably. 'He is not a regular Facebook user.'

'I know someone who works at Heathrow,' Shekar said. 'I could ask him to check the other flights. I must have his number somewhere.' He scrolled through the contact numbers on his phone.

No one noticed Ashraf sneaking back into the room. He touched his wife's elbow lightly; it sent a shiver down her spine. She turned around and looked at her husband. There was pain and confusion in his eyes. She raised her eyebrow in a query. Although his hand was touching his wife, it was Shekar that Ashraf addressed.

'No need for that.' His voice sounded hollow. The people in the room froze and turned to him in unison. 'I spoke to his company in Finland. Rafik left last week. He tendered his resignation with a month's notice.'

It was quiet enough to hear a pin drop. The first sound that broke the silence was a nervous squeak from Kalyani.

'What… does that mean?' She swayed on her mehendi-adorned feet; the room whirled around her. Shekar steadied her and led her to the sofa. He sat beside her and stared at the floor in front of him.

'It means that he had been planning to leave his job for a whole month. He left a week ago.' He looked up at Ashraf. 'Did he leave a forwarding address?'

'Not that they know of.'

Kalyani fixed her eyes on Shahida. 'Did you know about this?'

'So where did he go?' Nimmi asked, tears springing into her eyes.

Shahida was mute and still like a statue. It annoyed Kalyani.

'You knew about this!' she pointed at Shahida and shrieked. 'You must have known about it!'

Nimmi flew to her daughter's side. 'Did you?' she asked Shahida.

Shahida said nothing. Kalyani continued to screech like a demented woman. 'You must have known! You are his mother! How can you not know?'

'We didn't know,' Ashraf said, trying to calm the situation.

'She did! She never wanted us to marry! You knew! She knew!' Kalyani sobbed on her mother's shoulders.

Nimmi hushed her and led her away from the room. 'Stay calm. Remember your baby.'

With his daughter gone, Shekar turned to the Mahmoods, his anger barely sheathed. 'What about the marriage tomorrow? Will your son come? Do we wait? Do we cancel?'

Ashraf shook his head despondently. 'I truly do not know. Rafik did not tell us. My wife does not keep secrets from me.'

Shahida's silence crept under Shekar's skin. He clenched his fists and felt his head fill with a rush of blood. A vein pulsed on the side of his neck.

'You do understand that you are playing with my daughter's life? She is carrying Rafik's child. She trusted you. She loved him. You understand?' Shekar himself was surprised by the calm grit in his voice. ‘I will not cancel the wedding. I will wait with my daughter at the altar tomorrow. I expect you to find your son and bring him to his own wedding. You have exactly eighteen hours from now.’

Chapter 12

Autumn flew in almost overnight, turning trees to copper and gold. Sporadic patches of sunlight filtered past the overgrown apple tree in the garden, and cast wavering shadows on the magnolia walls. The lawn was peppered with weeds, and the shrubs were straggly with invading brambles. No one had tended them this season, and it showed.

Kalyani sat at the kitchen table. She held her hands out in front of her. With the eye of faith, she could recreate the pattern left by the mehendi, a peacock on either hand, which held side by side created the shape of a heart, now reduced to pale, orange streaks. Beneath them, her bump was prominent, more so because the rest of her body had become gaunt.

Ten weeks ago, this place had buzzed with happy voices, squeals of delight, and gentle teasing. It was filled with hope and love. Except for one missing piece of the puzzle – the most important one. Rafik. They had left the doors to their house open all day for the missing piece to walk in.

At 7a.m. wedding day, Ashraf rang Shekar.

'I couldn't trace Rafik's whereabouts. You have to believe us when we say we did not plan this. We do not know where Rafik is. You have to cancel the wedding. Do not subject your daughter to the shame of being jilted at the altar. Please cancel the Shaadi, while we investigate.'

Shekar had not slept all night. His eyes were red-rimmed and his face haggard. He had paced most of the night, while his exhausted family finally succumbed to sleep. His anger spilled over. 'You bastards! Do you know what your bastard son has done to my family? Do you?'

If Ashraf had banged the phone down on his side, Shekar would have understood. The fact that Ashraf didn't cut him off made him a better man than Shekar wanted him to be.

'Shekar. I understand your anger. You have to realise that there is something more inconvenient than the cancellation of a wedding. I... we are also concerned about Rafik. I do not know where he is. Shahida is beside herself. We are all suffering.'

'Ashraf could have said he was sorry,' Shekar mumbled to himself several times, after he hung up. 'They are not sorry,' he said to his wife, who, disturbed by his shouting, hurried to join him.

'We have to cancel the wedding,' she told him quietly. Together, they had called Raeba, requesting that she cancel the venue, the florists, the catering, and anyone else who were due to deliver on the day. Raeba warned them that it was too late to ask for refunds. The hall had been decked, and the caterers were already on their way. Kalyani's parents and Minna rang the guests, hoping to stall them before they left their houses or hotels. Shekar and one of the other relatives stood outside the venue to personally apologise to anyone who did turn up. The food was donated to a charity.

Kalyani did not remember how her non-wedding day had passed. She had slumped down at the foot of her bed, staring at the beige-painted corner of the room, on which the cherry tree cast shadows as it swayed in the gentle breeze, until it was too dark for shadows. As if she had drifted out of her body, she watched people come in to speak to her, their voices hollow and distant, unrecognisable, their touch remote, superfluous. They came, they stared, they shook their heads and left. Her body alternately sobbed, shuddered, giggled and slept, but her soul waited for him, not daring to move, lest he took flight and disappeared forever. Over the next few days, she felt as if her brain cleft in two – one that protectively shut down, and another that drummed up a destructive rhythm meant to maim and hurt.

Jilted. Jilted. Jilted.

Days turned to weeks, shock faded to anger, concern escalated to fear, unhappiness changed to grief. The Sinha household hunkered down for the rest of the year, shuttered itself from the outside world of scandal and gossip, and went into graveyard mode, where the only thing that ticked were their hearts and the clock on the kitchen wall. The cracked pavement between number thirty-five and number forty-seven was smeared with blood and gore, and the air thick with cannon smoke and battle cries.

Living like a recluse under her parents' roof, Kalyani was struck with an identity crisis. She would soon be a mother, but not a wife. Was she a bride-in-waiting or a widow-to-be?

More questions than answers. Where was Raffa? Had he left Finland, with the intention of coming home early to surprise her? If so, why had he not arrived? What happened to him en route? Was he hurt or lying unconscious in a hospital ward? Or wandering around with amnesia? The Mahmoods had reported him as a missing person, but the police found no evidence of foul play. His exit was planned. He had not bought flight tickets to any destination in the UK from Finland. He had withdrawn all his savings before his departure. He had given notice to his landlord in Finland, and checked out a week ago, without a forwarding address. The consensus opinion was that he had run away from his impending marriage.

A runaway groom. His bride must be a witch.

So where had he gone? He seemed to have disappeared off the face of the Earth.

Around her, her relationship with the people she knew changed rapidly. Her dad was no longer a hero, who specialised in fixing things; her mother had turned into a cursing witch, casting spells; and Minna had changed to a raging virago, who blamed her sister for this whole situation.

By week two of the non-wedding day, everybody was tired and fractious. They tutted and yelled at each other. Their tolerance for Kalyani's prolonged sulks fell to an all-time low. Finally, Minna laid into her.

'Did you not see the signs? He did not give you any answers to your wedding-related questions. He had not sent you pictures of quaint houses in Finland. His last text to you was a week ago. Are you dumb?'

'Raffa is a hard worker,' Kalyani defended herself. 'He was taking a whole week off for the wedding. So I did not want to disturb him.'

'You pushed him too hard. Here's your wife, here's your baby, build the nest, fight with your parents and your religion… too much for poor Posho. I always told you he was wrong for us. You never listen!'

'Wrong for *us*? I was the one marrying him, not all of us!'

'Exactly what I said! You did not think of the repercussions to us, if you married a Muslim. I mean… no Hindu worth his salt is going to seek a bride from this family any more, are they? You did not think of the difficulties your baby will have in the future – he or she would belong to neither religion and neither community. And our parents will be the talking point wherever they go. You only thought of yourself, and look what happened! That… Posho… only went and dumped you!'

'At least I am not a heartless bitch that you have become!' Kalyani screamed at her.

Appalled at their own vicious language, they stopped, but did not kiss and make up. The atmosphere between them continued to crackle and fizz. Minna cleared out the small box room and moved her bed into it.

Kalyani overheard her parents discuss their finances, one night, when she had crept down for a snack.

'That is a lot of money to lose, Shekar,' Nimmi was saying.

Her father sighed. 'A good chunk of our savings. We cancelled too late. We could not salvage anything to speak of.'

'Well. If there is another marriage on the cards, we will have to borrow.'

'What about if she decides to go to university? It will be difficult to support both of them.'

'I wish I had worked as well. We could have saved more for our children,' Nimmi lamented.

'Oh, I don't think so. We saved on childcare. Children are expensive,' Shekar generously consoled his wife.

Kalyani retreated to her room, and sat in the dark, her hand over her growing bump, feeling very alone and very vulnerable, and so very stupid. She relived the passion and tenderness between her and Raffa over and over. There could be nothing but love there. Why then should he run away? Couples broke up all the time, marriages put on hold because the bride or groom got cold feet. She would have understood… given time. She would have understood, if he had explained.

*

In late November, Minna rang home to say she had returned from her weekend in Spain, the stray cat that had wandered into their garden had kittens, and Kalyani delivered a seven pound, two ounce baby boy, who came out kicking and screaming. He brought colour back to the house, a smile on grandma Nimmi's face, a pat from grandpa Shekar, and a cry of 'OMG! I am an aunty!' from Aunty Minna.

Days later, when Shahida and Ashraf heard about it through the grapevine, they sent congratulatory cards in the post. The family had thus far stayed well out of each other's paths.

For Kalyani, the delivery had been long and difficult; the pain had been out of this world, each hour competing with the previous one on the scale of agony; she felt violated at every stage, bared, prodded, pushed and shoved. In the face of escalating electronic beeps from the machines monitoring her baby's heartbeat, indicating impending distress for her baby, they tore and gouged into her in their urgency to get the baby out. She felt as valued as an errant carrier pigeon, shot down in order to retrieve the all-important message it was carrying.

Throughout her ordeal, she desperately wished for Raffa to be at her side, holding her hand, smiling encouragement. Then the nurses wouldn't have cast judgemental glances at her, and been critical about her poor performance on the delivery table, nearly resulting in disaster for her baby. Scarred emotionally and physically, she rebelled. She was too tired to feed the baby, too sore to get out of bed. Yes, she was opting for bottle feeds. Pushed for beds, the midwives allowed her to bottle feed and discharged her into care in the community.

Her family gave her some space to rest and heal. They were thrilled at the opportunity to feed and cuddle the newcomer. He belonged to Nimmi in the morning, Shekar, when he returned from work, Minna over the phone when she called, and his mother at night. Minna started a countdown to Christmas holidays, when she could visit.

'Seven sleeps to Christmas! Seven sleeps before Aunty Minna sees you again!'

'He is like a ray of sunshine,' said Nimmi to Kalyani one morning. Kalyani sipped her honeyed tea and watched her son flail his tiny limbs, enjoying the rare sun filtering through the glass windows. Nimmi laughed at his excitement. 'Look at the faces he pulls!'

'Ray of sunshine! Kiran. Let us call him Kiran – ray of sunshine in Hindi,' Kalyani suggested.

'That is a brilliant name. We should have a naming ceremony,' Nimmi suggested.

'No. No more ceremonies, Mother.'

Nimmi was not in the mood for elaborate ceremonies either, but she could not let tradition go. She lit an oil lamp in front of the deity of Ganesh, the elephant-headed god, and whispered the baby's chosen name three times into his tiny ear.

'There! Now we should let the world know his name.' Nimmi whipped out her phone and texted Shekar and Minna, Hana and Romesh. Her finger hovered over the number for Shahida and Ashraf. Feeling mellow, she photographed her grandson and typed 'Kiran' beneath it. What was Kiran's surname? Was he a Mahmood or was he a Sinha? She shrugged her dainty shoulders. He was Kiran, just Kiran. She pressed the send button, and sent the photograph to the Mahmoods.

'I will text Raffa!' said Kalyani, picking up her phone and going to her room.

Nimmi looked at her daughter, startled. Had she heard right? 'Huh?'

Kalyani appeared not to hear. She walked past, leaving her baby in her mother's care. Nimmi watched her daughter climb the stairs to her room, her spine tingling. What did she mean by texting Raffa? Had he contacted her? Kiran was starting to grizzle, distracting her. Feed and nap time.

Chapter 13

'How much milk does a baby need?' exclaimed Minna, with a yawn.

The smaller room she had moved into was right next to her sister's and the partition wall was not soundproof. Through the night, Minna was disturbed by noises from her sister's room – creaking of floorboards, banging of shelves, squeaking of windows, crackle of plastic bags, and the hum of conversation. It made her feel tired and grumpy.

Her mother was replying to her question. 'A lot. Some want frequent feeds, like Kiran here.' Minna watched the baby feed hungrily from the bottle Nimmi was offering, making gurgling noises, milk dripping out of the corner of his mouth. His fists were clenched and body trembling, as if he had been starving for days.

'Do they feed all night? Don't they stop when they are a few months old?'

'Sometimes. Every baby is different. Maybe he snacks on the breast for comfort all night.' After the initial reluctance to start breastfeeding, Kalyani had been persuaded to try it at night.

'That explains why she is up all night!' Minna said, screwing her face in disgust. Breastfeeding was yuck.

'He will soon wean to solids. That will settle him.' Nimmi gently rocked the infant, rubbing his back to wind him. Minna did have a point. Why was the baby ravenous in the morning if he had been fed all night? There was no doubt Kalyani was exhausted in the mornings, bleary-eyed and incoherent, as she handed her screaming son over for bottle feeds. Was she running out of milk? She made a mental note to ask Kalyani, or perhaps leave a bottle of prepared formula for the night with her. Her thoughts miles away, Nimmi wasn't paying attention to Minna.

'Sorry. What did you say?'

Minna watched as her mother now busied herself with changing the baby's dirty nappy. She shrugged. 'Never mind. I might see if I can catch up on an hour's sleep.'

Minna, in spite of herself, was annoyed. She came home expecting some home comforts: her favourite meals to be cooked and her laundry to be washed and ironed, while she caught up with her friends, but the baby had taken over her mother's time. Nimmi fed the baby, Nimmi bathed the baby, Nimmi washed the baby's clothes three times a day. And Kalyani was nowhere to be seen. Her sister had never been an early riser, but now, she slept until the afternoon, and when she came down, she slumped around, grunted at everyone, nibbled at the food, refused to take the baby out for some fresh air. Then she crept back to her room, leaving the baby with his doting, but tired, grandparents.

'Your mother was a total grump when you were born. Oh boy! I took refuge in the garage most of the time,' Shekar had joked, when Minna brought up the subject.

'My second one was like that for the first two months,' Hana had commented when Nimmi discussed it with her. 'She was sore, uncomfortable, tired, and wanted to catch up on sleep all the time. Don't worry, Kalyani will come around.'

If Minna wasn't still so angry with the thoughtless choices Kalyani had made, she would have noticed that her sister was not her normal self. But Minna was furious that Kalyani was still managing to get away with not accepting the consequences of her actions. With no further education, no money, no job, no fiancé, and no husband, her sister was selfishly and shamelessly using the bank of Mum and Dad. Minna also felt guilty for harbouring these thoughts, which irritated her even more. After all, she loved her sister too.

*

While her sister checked out the new restaurant that had opened in town with her friends, Kalyani lay awake in bed.

Last night, like every other night for the past couple of months, she had dreamt of Raffa. He walked up the street, his feet not touching the ground, he opened the garden gate, floated up to her bedroom, and knocked on her window. She had let him in, urging him to be quiet. He took her in his strong arms, brushed his lips on her burning skin, and called her beautiful names. They paced the room together, talked about everything under the sun, laughed at funny jokes, and made wild love.

When the noise woke their baby, who whimpered and rooted for a feed, they giggled and shushed each other like naughty school kids, and waited until the infant stuck his fist into his mouth in an attempt to soothe himself back to sleep. The kid had learnt quickly that feeding him at night was not on his mum's agenda.

She wished to wake up with Raffa beside her in the morning, their feet intertwined, their naked bodies stuck with a thin veneer of sweat, but he always left at the crack of dawn. Sometimes, he climbed back out of the window, sometimes through the door, sometimes just faded away in front of her eyes. He beckoned to her to follow, and in her panic to keep up with him, she tripped on the rattle, stepped on the squeaky toy, and bumped into cot sides. In despair, she called out to him, and searched all around the room for him. In the end, exhausted, she succumbed to a restless sleep. For weeks, her Raffa had wandered freely in and out of her body and mind, playing her like a violin. She could not or would not close the chapter on that part of her life.

*

Minna gave up working on her presentation. The lack of sleep made it difficult for her to concentrate and her head was starting to ache. What a waste of a morning. Idly, she checked her emails and then her Facebook page. There was a time when this would have been a routine occurrence, but since starting her law course at university, she had fallen out of the habit, and nearly forgotten her password. Some of her friends were still active on Facebook, and for a while, she checked the photographs of Christmas get-togethers around champagne-laden tables, New Year's resolutions in Lycra suits and holiday photos – 'Eating fish and chips, Turkey style, haha', or 'Skiing in the Swiss Alps, Leicester style, haha'. She noticed that Kals had not been on it either. There were no pictures of the baby on her sister's home page. The last photograph she had uploaded was of the wedding invitation. 'Kals and Raffa are proud to invite you to their wedding on…'

Minna scrolled down the rest of the photos. Kals and herself holding up designer shopping bags; Kals drinking a blue cocktail, decorated with little paper umbrellas and a sparkler; Kals pouting seductively; Kals at Rita's wedding, posing with the newlyweds; Kals hand wrestling with Romy; Kals and Helen, baring their thighs for the camera at a hen party, clearly tipsy. Kals looked so carefree and full of the joys of life.

Helen! That is what Kals needed – some 'me time' with her friends, away from the baby. She had been cooped up in her room like a milch cow in its shed, looking fat and shabby, greasy hair in a messy clip, lips chapped and nails chipped. She needed a makeover – manicure, pedicure, hair styling, and a harvester to mow months of hair growth on her legs. But, with the stubbornness of a mule, Kals had ignored any advice or suggestions made by her well-wishers. Well, time for the mountain to come to Muhammad.

Some time ago, when they were all one happy community, Minna had befriended Helen on Facebook. She clicked on Helen's page now, happy to note that she had changed her status only a week ago. Minna sent her a private message, asking if she could visit Kals if she was around. Nothing to do now but wait. She logged off and decided to have a nap.

Chapter 14

Helen arrived at the Sinha's doorstep two days later, with Lola in tow. It was at once apparent that inviting her over may not have been the best decision Minna had made. The pair of them were dressed in odd, shapeless clothes that revealed more than they covered; their faces were caked with make-up, as if they had applied another layer over the previous one, and they smelt of stale smoke and booze. They were unnaturally cheerful, giggling and prodding each other. Lola's eyes were shiny, her pupils small. Nimmi wished Helen had rung to ask if it was convenient before visiting and bringing her lesbian friend along.

Nevertheless, Kalyani seemed happy to see them, and Nimmi hoped the visit would cheer her daughter up. The two of them made such an exaggerated fuss over the baby, cooing loudly and jiggling him rapidly, that he vomited his entire bottle of milk. Nimmi retrieved him, claiming he needed a nap, and took him downstairs. Kals sat cross-legged on her unmade bed, strewn with sweaty, breast milk stained T-shirts and baby toys. Helen cleared a space amidst them to sit down. Lola curled up on the wicker chair at the foot of the bed.

Helen reached across and tugged her friend's tangled hair. 'Goodness, Kals, motherhood suits you. But you need some major pampering, gal!'

'She already is – Pampered,' Lola smirked, holding up the Pampers nappy packet.

'Ignore her. She had too much sugar in her tea for brekkie.'

'Yep. Brown sugar!' Lola conceded.

'Atta girl. What say we book a joint makeover session and then go to the cinema or something? Like old times,' Helen suggested.

'Joint? Yes please, I say!' Lola grinned.

The word 'cinema' took Kalyani back to the time when Raffa had hijacked her from the movie, wearing a hijab. A waft of misery washed over her and her eyes brimmed with tears. Helen turned to Lola and hissed, 'Shut up, Lola!'

Lola pouted and withdrew into her chair to sulk.

'Are you alright, Kals?' Helen squinted at her.

'I am OK, I think. Why did you have to bring her?' Kalyani whispered, pointing to Lola with her eyes.

'We are an item now. Moved in together. She is actually a smashing girl, when you get to know her, and she is not high as a kite.'

'I can hear you!' sang Lola. Kals and Helen ignored her.

'Oh? Sorry, I wasn't aware' said Kals.

Helen nodded happily. 'You have been busy with your own stuff, haven't you? Too busy to notice the world go by. I tried calling, you know.'

'I suppose.'

'Have you heard from him?' Helen queried.

'Raffa? No, not really.'

'Do his parents visit? Does his mother know where he is?'

'They have a couple of times. Don't think they know where he is.'

A few days after receiving Kiran's photo, Shahida had asked to see her grandson. After initially resisting, Nimmi yielded and invited her over.

'That is bad! He is a naughty boy. How do you feel about it all?'

'He is not a bad man!' Kals shrugged her shoulders. 'Maybe he is stuck in something he cannot get out of. I am more... worried.'

Helen looked sceptical.

'He comes to me every night to tell me he loves me,' Kals confided, as if to restore Raffa's credibility.

'You mean, he comes to you in your dreams?' Helen asked.

'It feels real. I can feel him. Sometimes, he asks me to follow him.'

'Follow him to where?'

Kals pointed to the window. Helen followed her finger and then looked at her closest friend with concern.

'So what do you do?'

'I... try... to follow. He is always too quick.' Kals flapped her hands in frustration.

Helen leaned forward to take her hand. 'Kals, your room is on the first floor. You can't follow him out the window. You do know that, don't you?'

'Yes. Yes! I haven't...'

'Lost your marbles?' Lola completed the sentence.

Both Kals and Helen shouted to her to shut up.

'But she has the loonies,' Lola insisted. '*Baby loonies. Blue as the sky. Dark shades of grey*,' she sang tunelessly under her breath.

Helen turned to her. 'How do you know?'

'I had it with mine. For a whole bloody year!'

Helen stared at her lover, not knowing how to react to this news. 'Sweetie, you never said. What happened to the baby?'

'Oh! There was no baby. I mean it didn't get to live. But I still had the blues pretty bad.'

'You poor thing!' said Helen, moving quickly to Lola's side. 'How did you deal with all that stuff?'

'They only went and dosed me up to my eyeballs, didn't they? Will be the same for you, unless you find your marbles, dearie,' Lola shook her head at Kalyani. Kalyani was by now distressed. She was wringing her hands and rocking on the bed.

'No! No! No, no! It won't! Get out!'

Helen rushed to her friend's side. 'Kals, calm down. Lola is not in her right mind today... I shouldn't have brought her here today. Sorry. But she might have a point. Have you considered the fact that you might have the baby blues?'

'Yes! Yes! She does!' Lola pouted. 'If she doesn't get help, I am afraid she will be locked up.'

Helen and Lola beat a hasty retreat to the door as Kals rushed at them with her table lamp. Helen tried to apologise, but Kals pushed her into the stairwell.

'Don't come back, you lezzie, and don't bring that druggie with you!' Kals yelled down the stairwell behind them, just as Shahida, who was visiting her grandson, entered the living room, downstairs. She looked startled as the words 'lezzie' and 'druggie' floated down, and even more when she saw Lola trying to get a piggy back on Helen as they left.

Nimmi, alarmed at the turn of events, called up to her daughter. 'What is all this shouting about, Kalyani?'

'That horrible woman tells me I am mad and need to be in the mental asylum. Cheeky mare!'

'Okay! Don't swear! We have company.'

Kalyani did not care about the company.

'F... the company!' she shrieked, as she rushed back into her room and slammed the door. But the damage had been done. Shahida was staring at them with horror.

'Nimmi, you have *mental* health problems in your family?' she asked, her voice low, stressing on the word mental. Before Nimmi could deny the allegation, Shahida continued. 'Mental health problems could be passed onto their children, you know!' She looked at the baby in her arms with suspicion. Nimmi gently took Kiran from her, and held him close to her bosom, protectively.

'I have to go and see how Kalyani is doing. Upstairs. Could you… er… come back later?'

Shahida did not need persuasion to leave. She did not want to be in a mad house longer than necessary.

*

That evening, in her oak kitchen, Shahida prepared dinner. Her mother-in-law, who was visiting, sat at the table, rolling out the dough for chapattis, while Shahida cooked them on non-stick pan. In a rare moment of womanly bonding, Shahida recounted the day's events. After all, what woman resisted gossip? The older woman raised her bushy, white eyebrows.

'Her friend told her she was mad?'

'I heard her say she should be in a… you know… mental home.'

'No wonder Rafik left her. He must have known!'

'Is it true? That mental illness runs in families?'

'Of course! I know of whole families affected by it. Allah be my witness.'

'How soon can we get the baby tested for inherited madness?'

'We must keep this quiet. At least until we know that the baby is sane of mind. Otherwise, Rafik… our family, will get blamed. The girls in our family will never get good offers for marriage.'

Shahida called Nimmi the next day to convey her mother-in-law's warning. 'Keep this shame quiet, Nimmi. What will Rafik think? He might decide never to return, even if he could. Think also of your second daughter. Who will marry her, if news of family insanity gets out?'

Chapter 15

Nimmi felt very alone. She wanted to talk things through with Team Kalyani. Her husband, Shekar, was in India, on business, and staying with family. With the time zone difference, Nimmi never got it right, and often rang him when he was in a meeting or when he was asleep. Shekar was forgiving, but couldn't always mask his irritation. Besides, Kalyani was not an easy subject to discuss at the best of times. Not with his relatives trying to eavesdrop.

She could call Minna, but Nimmi was aware of the animosity that had crept between the sisters, and did not feel comfortable discussing one sister's problems with the other. Kalyani might feel betrayed. What did Minna know about motherhood, baby care, and Asian culture anyway? She didn't even know how to make decent roti.

Nimmi felt like Hercules, weighed down by the number of secrets she had to keep. The pregnancy, and now the threat of insanity. The Sinhas had become worthy of gossip, when Kalyani's marriage with a Muslim guy was announced, and then when she was jilted at the altar. Nimmi had told herself that she didn't care. Besides, she was busy waging war with the Mahmoods.

Abuse was freely exchanged between the families on the day of the wedding that didn't happen; Rafik's family accused Kalyani of using witchcraft to snare their eligible son, and then making him disappear; Nimmi retaliated by calling Rafik a coward and a cheat. In the cold light of a new day, they took a mutual decision to stay out of each other's lives. If and when Rafik returned to claim his bride, truce and reunion would be negotiated between the families.

Things changed when the baby arrived. Shahida relented when she knew she had a grandson. She had come bearing gifts, and waving the proverbial white flag. Nimmi, who could not hold a grudge against anyone, talked herself into allowing Rafik's parents back into her daughter's life. Ashraf and Shahida were grandparents for the first time too. It would be cruel to deny them the right to spend time with their grandson. She invited them home, but kept their visits short and formal. Shahida did not protest. She was not the maternal type who wanted to cuddle and kiss and shake rattles in front of the baby's face to make him laugh. She held him for a few minutes, scrutinised his features, analysed his development, and handed him back if he cried or needed a nappy change.

At best, the relationship with the Mahmoods was as fragile as the overwintered, rotten twigs in her garden. Shahida accusing Kalyani of being mentally ill was like chopping the whole tree down. Nimmi itched to gouge Shahida's eyes out. She was definitely not inviting that woman to her home again.

But what was up with Kalyani? Kiran was almost four months old, past the passive poo-pee-eat-sleep stage, and was demanding attention from everyone with his cooing and dimpled smiles. He was receiving it in bucket loads from every one, apart from his mother.

Was she depressed? Nimmi had hinted to Kalyani that she should see her GP that morning, to which she had responded with a torrent of verbal abuse that would put a Tourette's syndrome sufferer to shame. 'You are all on the same side. You think I am mad too?' she screamed, then abandoned her baby and stormed upstairs.

Nimmi was close to tears. In desperation, she texted Minna. 'Not urgent. Ring if you are free.'

Minna texted back within the hour. 'In lectures all day, then going out for drinks. Coming home tomorrow for the weekend. Can it wait?'

Well, Nimmi couldn't ask for more. As a reward, she decided to cook a batch of Minna's favourite meals.

Poor Minna was being side-lined and overshadowed by Kalyani's constant drama.

*

Kalyani put her head in her hands and compressed her eyes with the heel of her palms. A centrifuge of emotions whirred in her head – none of them healthy. Ever since her arrival, Minna had sat in conference with her mother at the kitchen table, no doubt discussing her mad sister.

Her mother had not thought to include her in the conversation, nor had she brought Kiran up to her all day. Obviously, she was no longer thought to be capable of having a conversation or of looking after her own baby! Now they were talking behind her back, scheming and planning.

Since shouting at her mother yesterday, she had shut herself in the room, sneaking down in the dark at midnight to stock up on food and drink. The fridge was stocked with Minna's favourite dishes. Minna, the model daughter – the ambitious and sensible one. Minna would never lose her groom before her wedding day. (She would have tied him to the lectern the previous day.) She felt a new emotion towards her sister, besides anger and annoyance – jealousy. Minna had everything to look forward to, while she had right royally screwed up.

And doubt. Had Minna invited Helen home on purpose, to abuse her and poke fun at her? Why wasn't it obvious to her mother that Minna was playing games? Damn her interfering relatives. The whole lot could jump into the river for all she cared, and they could take the blooming baby with them. Kiran did not need his mother anymore; her breast milk was drying up anyway.

She was done. She curled up into a foetal position under her duvet and cried herself to sleep. A few more hours to go before Raffa came knocking, and listened patiently to her rant about this latest injustice in her life.

Downstairs, oblivious to the green-eyed monster stirring in her sister's mind, Minna purred appreciatively over the lovely meal her mother had slaved over. The baby was asleep in his rocker, dreaming of his next bottle, his lips making sucking movements. Her mother was explaining the latest drama to afflict the Sinha household.

'I can understand where Shahida is coming from, when she says I should keep her condition secret, but Kalyani is my priority. Right?'

'Ignore Shahida!' Minna flapped her hand impatiently. 'Who cares what that woman thinks?'

'Kals needs help, but I don't know what to do or who to turn to. I cannot physically drag her to see a doctor.'

'Do you think she is depressed? Baby blues, like Helen said?'

'It was the other one who said it. Helen's friend,' her mother clarified. 'I don't understand these blues or greens. I felt fantastic after I had you two. Besides, I was too busy to indulge in fancy feelings. Between us, your father and I did it all... taking turns to feed and change, wake up at night.'

'It is months after the birth. Surely, baby blues is something you would expect soon after birth. Why now?'

'What if she had been depressed all along and we haven't noticed. We kept making excuses for her – she was tired after a difficult birth, or after night feeds. She is still missing Rafik...'

Minna could see that her mother was beating herself up about it. She patted her arm to reassure. 'Why don't we call Kiran's health visitor, Debbie? She would know what to do.'

With a bit of rummaging, they found the baby book with the health visitor's contact details. The answerphone kicked in after the third ring, informing them that all their staff were out on visits, and their call will be returned as soon as possible. Nimmi left a message for Debbie to ring back.

It was nearly the end of the day when someone from the health visitor's office rang back. It wasn't Debbie – she was on holiday until Monday. Could it wait until after the weekend?

By then, Nimmi was feeling calmer. The talk with Minna had helped. She had also spoken to Shekar, who confirmed that he would return home early next week. Whatever was the matter with Kalyani, it had been going on for months. There was no urgency. She agreed that Debbie arranged a visit for Monday.

'Did you not tell them what you suspect?' Minna asked when she rang off.

'Well. It is not exactly something one would discuss over the phone, is it? You never know who else is listening.'

Chapter 16

The house was dark and quiet when Kalyani woke up. Too dark, too quiet. The same dream had woken her. The one in which her baby dies. One minute, his cries were echoing off the four walls, piercing and pounding into her head, and then silence, which was even more terrifying. What had she done to him? Where was the baby? Everything around her was a blur as if she was in a fog. Kiran was not in his cot. Not in her bed. She pulled down all her bedding and then her mattress. Definitely not tangled in the sheets. Not under the bed, behind the headboard, in the drawers or in the wardrobe. No! No! The answer was always no! She wanted him gone, and now he was gone.

She stood in the middle of the room pulling her hair. The bathroom. She must have left him in the bath to drown. She ran into the bathroom, trying to be quiet. If she had killed him, she did not want anyone to find out. She did not want to go to prison. Raffa would never find her if she got locked away. Kiran was not in the bath, bloated and blue in death. Had she flushed him down the drain? She opened the bath taps to wash away any evidence then reached over for a towel and in the process, knocked the ceramic vase down. She watched it fall, tracking its path in slow motion. It bounced on the edge of the bath, landed on the tiles, and shattered into three neat pieces. That was the vase her mother's friend bought her for her fortieth birthday; mummy's special vase. She dropped to her knees, frantically grappling with the pieces, trying to put them together. She did not feel the jagged edges cut into her hands and was bewildered to see blood everywhere.

It must have come from her baby. She must have cut him to pieces and left him to bleed to death – drop by bloody drop. He must be empty by now, lying somewhere white as a sheet. She must put all this blood back into him. She must find his bottle, fill it with all this blood and feed him.

She rose and caught her reflection in the mirror, which was misted over from the hot water running in the bath. Translucent. Mysterious. From beyond the mist, Raffa beckoned. She reached to touch him, smearing the mirror with her blood.

'I have killed him, Raffa. Finally, I have killed our son. I am free now. I am free to come with you,' she whispered.

Raffa smiled from his world inside the mirror, a world that she couldn't enter with her body. She was not free yet. She had to free herself from her body. She looked around, frantic. The bath had stopped draining, and was filling up. The plug must have shifted, and blocked the drain hole. She fumbled around in the grey haze for the taps and turned them off. The lukewarm, rippling water invited her in, to drown her sorrows. She glanced at the mirror to see if Raffa was still waiting for her. Like she had waited for him at the train station every Saturday morning. He was, but he was receding, walking away in the mist. Soon there would be nothing but smoke and mirrors.

'Wait. Raffa, don't go away,' she gasped. On impulse, she selected a jagged piece of broken vase, and drew it across her wrist, deeper and deeper, until the dark-red blood bubbled out like a fountain. It spilled all over her hands, down her knees to the floor, warm and smelling like the iron tablets she had to take throughout her pregnancy. What a mess she was making. Her mother won't be pleased at all. Clumsy Kalyani. Can't get anything right. Not even in death. It would be better if she got into the bath. The water would wash it all off.

*

That is how they found her, her nightie swirling around her midriff, her hair floating like seaweed in the bloody bath.

Earlier, Minna had persuaded her mother to get out for some fresh air, because she had been cooped up in the house with her gloomy thoughts. She had peeped into her sister's room to ask if she wanted to come too, but Kals was fast asleep.

'We will be back in half an hour. Don't worry. Sleep is good for her,' she assured her mother.

'I will take a tray up to her when we return.' Nimmi agreed. 'She must be hungry.'

They slipped Kiran into his coat. Unusual for March, but not unheard of, the temperature had dropped sharply, and rain and sleet made the roads slippery. Not a pleasant night to be driving around in.

'Nice for Dad, he must be enjoying the hot sun in India!'

The half hour extended to an hour because Nimmi wanted to stock up on food. On the way back, they passed Hana's house; the warm light from their lounge window spilt on to the pavement like an invitation.

'Can we say a quick hello?' Nimmi wondered.

'Of course.'

The quick hello stretched to a cuppa, over which Nimmi shared her worry with Hana and Romy.

'She just needs some cheering up. Go on a holiday perhaps,' Hana wondered.

'The long winter does not help,' Romy added. 'Maybe she has S-A-D, Seasonal Affective Disorder.'

'She has gone M-A-D over that loser, Rafik!' Minna grumbled. For once, her mother did not shush her. Romy and Helen had tried to ring Kals and visit her, but her sister had resolutely ignored them both.

When it was time to go home, Hana and Romy decided to go with them and cheer Kalyani up.

'I am good at cracking bad jokes,' Romy told them.

They called out to Kalyani when they returned home, as they hung up their jackets and bags, and parked the baby's buggy. Kiran was still fast asleep, having nodded off within the first few minutes of being wheeled around.

'Typical man!' Minna quipped. 'Let's leave him there while I check on Kals,' she said as she went up the stairs. The light was on in her sister's room, but her sister wasn't in. A sliver of light showed under the bathroom door.

'Kals?' she called, as she knocked on the bathroom door, expecting her sister to shout at her for interrupting her bath. No noise from the other side of the door. There was something not right about the silence. It was not the empty silence from an unoccupied room, but a leaded one: a drip, a trickle, a rustle of blinds blowing in the wind, and something ominous.

'Kals?' she whispered, as she opened the door a few inches. Blood, water, and pieces of broken vase led her eyes to the bath, in which Kals lay still and white in the bloody water, her head wedged into the corner of the bath, at an awkward angle. Her eyes were half open, her damp hair plastered to her head, dripping. The water was lapping at her lips, and the skin of her face glistened with a mixture of water and clammy sweat

Minna's screams brought her mother running up, Romy and Hana at her heels

'I need the phone.' Minna squeezed past them on the stairs as she rushed down to retrieve her phone from her handbag, which she had left downstairs.

'Why? Whaa—' Nimmi reached upstairs, not knowing what to expect. She glanced into Kalyani's room first, just as Minna had done, and then in the bathroom.

'Oh my God! Kalyani! What have you done?' She hurtled towards her daughter, slipping on the wet floor. She hit her knee on the edge of the bath with a crunch, but barely noticed the pain. She leaned over to her daughter, her voice dying in her throat as terror seized her. She slapped the girl's cold cheeks.

'Wake up, Kalyani. *Wake up!*'

Minna's tremulous voice floated up through the stairwell, as she made the 999 call. 'Ambulance. Police. Help.'

The calm, professional voice on the other side of the phone urged her to take a deep breath and listen, before answering their questions.

What was the address... her phone number... was her sister alive?

'Is she alive?' Minna called out to her mother.

'I... don't know!' Her mother's voice was pitched high with panic.

'We are not sure,' Minna relayed to the person on the phone. She was then asked to describe the scene. Yes – she could have slipped and hit her head. Her head is at a funny angle. Yes, the bath is full. So? Maybe she drowned? No, she did not know where the blood came from. After reconfirming details of her address and phone number, Minna hurried upstairs, past Hana, who was standing outside the bathroom, paralysed with shock.

'We have to get her out.' Romy was kneeling beside the bath, talking to Nimmi. 'She is cold. Icy.'

Minna tried to help Romy move the body, but Kals was a dead weight. In the tight space, it was difficult to manoeuvre, and apart from shifting her by a few inches either way, they couldn't lift her out. At least her face was now well above the water.

'Let's drain the water.' Romy suggested. Minna reached under the cold body, feeling for the plug. Grunting and tugging against the pressure of the water and the body, Minna started sweating, but finally managed to dislodge it. The water squelched and gurgled as it drained away.

'Get something warm!' she shouted to her mother, but the older woman just sat there gaping. Hana woke up from her trance, pulled off the duvet and blankets off Kalyani's bed, and handed them to Minna, who tried her best to wrap them around her sister's body. She held her damp hand under her sister's nose, but it shook so badly that she couldn't discern if Kals was breathing. She gently prised the hand from under her body to feel her pulse, gasping at the bloody, gaping cut on her wrist, still oozing pink, watery blood. Her sister hadn't accidentally slipped in the bath or drowned; she had tried to kill herself! Tears welled up in her eyes, as with trembling hands, she held the hand up and wrapped it with a corner of the bedspread, applying pressure.

'Where is that effing ambulance?'

As if in answer to her question, she heard the approaching siren coming to a stop outside their house with a whoop. Loud banging, unfamiliar voices entered the lounge, and tromped upstairs. Swirling lights lit up the house like a discotheque. The baby woke up screaming. Nimmi was galvanised into action. She limped downstairs, leaving the paramedics with Minna and Romy in the bathroom. Once downstairs, she undid the clips on the buggy and lifted Kiran out, and removed his coat. The damp from her wet clothes soaked into his Babygro, making him squirm. She bounced him up and down, too roughly, and instead of calming down, he cried louder, as if knew that his mummy was in distress… dying… dead.

'Here, let me,' said Hana, who had also come downstairs to give the paramedics more space. Nodding vigorously, Nimmi handed the baby over, and moved to the foot of the stairs. From there, she could see Minna standing on the landing, the light from the bathroom highlighting the contours of her face. She seemed to be talking, either to herself or in response to questions from the paramedics. Nimmi could not hear what she was saying, what with the baby crying, and radio crackling from the emergency vehicles outside.

'There is only an emergency car outside,' Hana noted. 'No ambulance.'

Nimmi turned to her friend, shaking like a leaf. 'Why? Have they given up on Kalyani? Is she dead?'

Only the piercing cries of the baby answered her – echoing into the night, fearful, alone.

Chapter 17

The paramedic stood before Nimmi. Mesmerised by the rhythmic play of colours on his face, reflected from the plethora of emergency vehicles outside, she couldn't make up her mind as to whether he was a god or an alien monster. His eyes were red with worry and his face was lined with tiredness. He was still wearing latex gloves and a flimsy, plastic apron, which fluttered in the draught from the open door. He was saying something and gesturing. Nimmi stared at him, uncomprehending. Minna was kneeling on one side of her, holding her hand tightly, and Hana sat on the other side, holding Kiran, who she had managed to rock back to sleep. Romy stood by the door, looking wretched.

A few minutes ago, Kalyani was carried away in a stretcher, a barely visible bundle, wrapped in silver foil like a Christmas turkey, amidst all the equipment around her. She was loaded into the ambulance, which had arrived later, and blue-lighted to the nearest hospital; only the muddy, wet footprints from the ambulance crew on the wooden floor remained to tell the story. A keening wail rent the air. Nimmi suddenly realised it came from her own mouth.

The paramedic who had arrived in the Rapid Response car stayed behind to explain the situation to the family. He was a tall man in his forties, who spoke with a heavy Scottish accent. He apologised that the family hadn't been given the opportunity to say goodbye, before Kalyani was whisked away.

'The patient needs urgent medical care. There is not much more we can do until she is in hospital. She has clearly lost a lot of blood; therefore, she is in shock, and very cold. She is unconscious, but is breathing on her own. We are giving her fluids and oxygen, and keeping her warm in the ambulance. I am afraid there is not much else I can say at this point in time. The ambulance has taken her to the Leicester Royal Accident and Emergency. Would one of you like to drive down there with us? Or take a taxi? You shouldn't drive after such a shock.' He paused to allow the family to absorb the information. 'Is there anything else I can do?' At Hana's request, he checked Nimmi's knee, which she had knocked against the edge of the bath when she slipped.

'Only a bruise, nothing that a pain killer won't help,' he reassured them. 'But you are all in shock. Get out of those wet clothes and drink lots of hot, sugary tea,' he advised before leaving.

'I will stay with your mother, and the baby,' Hana addressed Minna. 'You should go to the hospital. Romy can drive. Get changed out of those wet clothes first.' Hana took charge as Nimmi stared vacantly, her mouth opening and closing like a goldfish gasping for air.

'She is dead. She is dead,' she chanted. Minna bent over her, gripping her arm. 'No, Mum. She is alive. Kals is alive. She is just very poorly. I'll update you every fifteen minutes from the hospital.'

Nimmi's initial relief soon became pockmarked with doubts. How bad was she? If she was alive, why did they need an ambulance? If she was in shock, wouldn't a cup of tea with three sugars, and a thermal blanket suffice? Was she going to die?

Though grateful that Romy was driving her, Minna wished her dad were there with them. But he was thousands of miles away in a different time zone. Waking him up at 2a.m. and giving him a heart attack was not going to help. Besides, he wouldn't be able to help from there. Later. She would ring him later, when she had more information. She scrolled down her contacts on her phone to see if there was anyone else she should ring. Shahida? No way! Not if she was the last human on Earth! Helen was probably with Lola, who was dosed up to her eyeballs. She did not want to call any of her own friends and tell them her mad sister had attempted suicide.

'What do you think happened?' Romy asked Minna, when she put her phone away.

'I… don't know, Romy. She must have been more depressed than we thought she was. She was asleep when we left home. If we had known this would happen, we would have stayed at home.' *On suicide watch.*

Just as Romesh dropped her off in front of A&E and went to park the car, her phone vibrated. *Daddy*! Had he sensed that something had gone wrong? His voice sounded far away, crackly and hollow, but she could tell that he knew. Her mother must have rung him soon after they left. And he was not going to have a heart attack.

Minna told him what she knew, which was very little. She did not mention the gash on the wrist.

'Don't worry,' her father said. 'Kalyani is strong. She will pull through. I am heading for the airport and will catch the first flight home.' His voice crackled and faded, but she felt the pressure lift off her shoulders. Her dad would move Heaven and Earth to be here as soon as possible. Until then, she was still in charge.

With Romy next to her, she entered the resuscitation area to be by her sister's side. While the medics swarmed around her sister – stabbing, prodding, shouting into her ear, asking if she could hear them, or feel them, or smell them – she gripped her sister's bandaged hand under the thermal blanket, unsure as to who was reassuring whom. She ran her thumb over the bandages on the wrist with the ugly gash.

'Why Kals?' she whispered under her breath. Her parents would be distraught. As soon as she had seen the gash, Minna had wrapped the wrist with the blanket, to stem the flow of blood. The paramedics thankfully hadn't mentioned it. With luck, no one would know about the suicide.

*

The night stretched long and dark and unending. Under Hana's insistence, Nimmi changed into dry clothes, wondering if she should dress to go to bed, or to rush to the hospital at short notice. Hana brought her strong, sweet cups of tea and a packet of all-butter shortbread, and stood over her until she had drunk half her tea and eaten at least one of the biscuits. She then thrust a couple of oblong pills at her. 'Paracetamol, for your knee. It will hurt really badly later. If you tell me where the ibuprofen is, I will get some for you.'

Nimmi told her where the medicine cabinet was, and Hana trudged up the stairs, the floorboards creaking loudly under her weight.

Nimmi cradled the phone in her hand, checking every few minutes in case she missed any messages. The baby was sleeping on a cushion on the floor, his fingers in his mouth. *He can't be hungry after guzzling down an entire bottle of formula. He must be missing his mother, poor tot.* Nimmi bent down and ruffled his curly, black hair. Then she dialled Shekar's number.

Unlike Minna, Nimmi did not have any qualms about waking Shekar up from his dreams. He had no right to paradise while his family were in the throes of terror. She trialled a few opening phrases in her head, as she listened to the burring of his phone. 'Are you sitting down, Shekar?' Silly – as he would actually be lying down in bed. 'Don't panic. All will be well.' When she had no idea if all was going to be well.

When her husband's sleepy voice, gruff and otherworldly, came on, Nimmi dissolved into a blubbering idiot, and a wailing waif. Hana, who had returned, triumphantly holding a pack of painkillers, gently took the phone off her, and explained the situation to Shekar.

'Minna is at the hospital. She will let us know what is happening. Romy is with her.' She finished and handed the phone back to his wife. She then retreated into the kitchen to give Nimmi some privacy, and to raid the snack cupboard. They had all missed supper and she was starting to feel peckish. When she returned to the lounge with a stack of toast and jam, Nimmi was staring at the rug under the coffee table.

The rug had a faint brown stain, an inch long, half an inch wide, tear-shaped, like someone had splashed tea on it. It was an old stain. She hadn't noticed it before – another thing that stupid Nimmi hadn't noticed. Feeling lightheaded, but buoyed with the empty calories in her tea and biscuits, she wanted to do something, to keep her from throwing the coffee table at the TV screen, or shouting at Hana to stop crunching the biscuits. She collected a mop and a bucket, and ignoring Hana's protests, climbed resolutely to the messy bathroom. After mopping the floor several times, she scrubbed the bath until it shone. She sprayed the area with bleach and scrubbed some more, until the smell of blood was only a memory in her head.

All the while, she kept an eye and an ear out for her phone to ring; a cluster of prayers played in her head like a broken record. *Oh God, let Kalyani live, let Kiran have a mother, let Shekar come home safely, let Minna be strong for her sister...* She wondered if she should leave Kiran with Hana and drive down to the hospital. She set herself time limits – if there was no news from the hospital by the end of the hour, she would go. Until then, she would sit on the top stair in semi-darkness and torture herself.

A few miles away, a couple of hours since they arrived, Minna chomped on a mini Mars bar, and downed coffee that smelt and tasted of sodden cardboard. Romy paced nearby, trying to accost anyone in uniform wandering out of the emergency room. The doctors and nurses were handing over care of their patients to the night shift, and visitors had been politely turfed out to wait in the reception area. Minna rang her mother, reassuring her that Kals was still alive.

The reception was buzzing with walking wounded, and their relatives – some dazed and confused, some trying to fill the hours of waiting by browsing through the tattered magazines, or watching the tiny TV screen installed in a corner. Others stared, mesmerised, at the digital messages running over the reception desk, informing them of the current waiting time, and what they could or couldn't do about it. Go back to your GP on Monday, which you should have done in the first place, if you were organised enough; approach the receptionist glued to the phone on her desk to warn her that you are fast approaching death; but whatever you do, for God's sake, abstain from violence – desist from pulling out firearms or blades of any description, or make fist-shaped gestures, because it will result in the waiting times going up exponentially.

Finally, they were called in by the doctor.

'Do you want me to come?' Romesh asked Minna. His eyes betrayed his anxiety, his thumbs tapped restlessly on his phone, but he wasn't family.

'If you don't mind, I would like to go by myself. I will let you know.' Minna squeezed his hand.

Fifteen minutes later, Minna tried to recollect and make sense of the conversation she had with the doctor in the tiny, sterile room. Shock, blood, fluids, oxygen, sutures, injuries, stable, pain, X-rays, scans… whizzed around in her brain. As she sat by the bedside, holding her sister's hand, Romy standing next to her, the nurse patiently explained it all again. Kals had lost a lot of blood and was in a state of shock. She also had hypothermia, having sat in a cold bath. She had been given several pints of fluid and blood through her veins. She was now in a stable condition. They had sutured the cut on her wrist, and she would have a scan of her head, after which, she would be monitored on the High Dependency Unit. She was sedated, not in a coma, and they would know more in the morning.

'There is nothing more you can do by staying. Try to rest and come back in the morning. We will call you if anything changes,' the nurse told them.

'What should I do?' she asked Romy. He placed his hands on her shoulders and looked into her eyes.

'You heard them. Kals is in good hands. They will ring us if anything changes. I will sleep at yours and will drive you back at any time if necessary. Now, you should go home and rest.'

Minna started to thank him, but what gushed out was a frantic wail. She leaned on his shoulder and sobbed uncontrollably.

'Hey! Hey, everything is OK. You heard them: she had a shock and is on the mend. Shh. Shh, now!' He hugged her tight until she stopped, spent and tired. 'You be strong, now, for your mother.'

Chapter 18

Forty-eight hours later. Forty-eight hours, spent in an endless conundrum of restless napping, unhealthy snacking, changing baby nappies, driving, and sitting beside the hospital bed later, Kalyani was declared out of danger. The dragon nurse had literally dragged her out of the hospital bed, insisting that she needed some exercise. The first time she attempted it, the room swam around her, taking Raffa with it. She was walking on a giant feather pillow towards him; he kept circling away, making her spin around, faster and faster, and she swayed and stumbled in her haste. During the last forty-eight hours, she had drifted in and out of terrifying nightmares. Sometimes, she was being attacked by blue-green forms with masks on their faces; they drove lancets and swords into her; at other times, the forms took on the identity of her parents and Minna, who held her down on the bed.

*

At the end of the week, the nurse led Minna and her parents into a private visitors' room. This one had embroidered cushions on the fabric sofa and fibre optic lights that changed colour – pink, blue, yellow… pink, blue, yellow. It was already occupied by someone scribbling notes in a file. She half rose from her seat and introduced herself.

'I am Dr Blick, Amanda Blick, psychiatrist.' She was a good inch taller than Shekar, thin and bony; hunched a little, as though she was conscious of her 'above average for a woman' height. She wore red-rimmed glasses in the latest style, and her hair was cut in a razor-sharp bob, which framed her bony cheekbones, and swung to and fro when she nodded her head. They squeezed into the sofas around a low table, on which brochures explaining the flu jab and help for domestic violence were arranged in a fan.

Dr Blick swivelled her chair around to face them and fixed them with her blue eyes. The trio blinked back at her. She cleared her throat loudly, making the three of them jump. 'It is a routine procedure in cases like this – where the patient attempts to self-harm – that the psychiatrist is involved. We assess the risk of the patient attempting suicide again.'

They nodded at her in agreement, like keen students trying to score points with their professor. Nimmi and Shekar had known for the last twenty-four hours that Kalyani had tried to kill herself, but were still coming to terms with it.

'Can she come home?' Nimmi asked in her soft voice.

'Your daughter Kaal… yeni.' Dr Blick had difficulty pronouncing her name. 'She is physically doing quite well, and will make a quick recovery. But there is another far more serious problem. Mentally, she is very sick.'

The trio on the other side of the table continued to blink at her like idiots. Dr Blick was apparently used to dealing with idiots. She softened her tone and simplified her language. 'Your daughter has a form of depression – postnatal depression.'

'But… but… she has been a mother for four months!'

'Postnatal depression can last for a long time. She has probably been depressed for some time. You might have noticed her feeling low, spending a lot of time sleeping, not showing much interest in looking after the baby…'

'Are you saying that we should have noticed? That we ignored these... things?' Nimmi's voice rose by an octave. Shekar took his wife's hand in his, and squeezed it, with the intention of keeping her quiet, rather than comforting her.

'On the contrary,' Dr Blick smiled slightly. 'I was going to say, these signs are often recollected in retrospect. They can be subtle.'

'So, you can start her on treatment?' Minna asked.

'I can indeed start her on antidepressants.'

'And, she can come home?' Nimmi asked again.

Dr Blick paused for effect. 'It is not as simple as that. Ms Sinha has a rare form of postnatal depression. A psychosis. It is called puerperal or post-partum psychosis. A condition caused by the birth of a baby.'

'Er... what is this "purple syco-sis"?' Nimmi wrinkled her nose in disgust at the condition.

Dr Blick took out a leaflet from her file marked: Post-Partum Psychosis.

'Usually, it starts within a few weeks. The mother feels low, irritable, mood swings, paranoid, has hallucinations and delusions...' She handed over the leaflet to them. 'This explains it further.'

'We can look after her at home. She needs lots of rest, food, family around her...' Nimmi argued.

Dr Blick's expression seemed to say, *been there, got the T-shirt. Didn't work.*

'What delusions?' Minna asked.

'Of killing her baby. Of running away,' Dr Blick revealed cautiously. 'The baby therefore is at risk. She is also at risk to herself. She needs to be in hospital, until she is safe.'

'How long would that be?' Shekar queried.

'I cannot say. A few weeks; a few months. Depends on how the patient responds.' She paused a while, before delving further. 'Often, this sort of psychosis happens because of previous history of mental illness or a family history. Does Ms Sinha have such a history?'

'No! No!' Nimmi was quick to deny this. 'No one in our family has... that.'

Dr Blick nodded, understanding. The reaction from the Sinha family was not unusual in Asian families. Mental illness was a stigma. She decided to end the conversation. For the time being, at least.

*

Nimmi jumped every time the doorbell rang. The police wanting statements, nosy neighbours, even the local rag, which had temporarily run out of news to report, seemed to want to have a go at ringing it. The ring tone of the doorbell resembled birds chirping, but now it was starting to grate on her nerves. When all this was over, she promised herself she would pull the doorbell out of the wall and bin it. It rang again now. She did not want it to wake Kiran, who had just dozed off, so she hurriedly pulled her dressing gown together and opened the door. A burly, black woman with obviously fake hair extensions stood outside, her painted nail hovering over the doorbell switch. She held up the badge hanging around her neck.

'Nancy Obe, from the department of Social Care.'

'What? The Social? You must have the wrong house. Try the one across the road, two doors to the left. They are always swearing and throwing things across the fence.'

Nancy stuck her foot in the door. 'We are at the correct house, Mrs... er, Sinha. Maybe we should talk inside, not on the doorstep.'

Nimmi noticed curtains twitching next door, and agreed with Nancy; the only thing they would agree upon that morning.

Nancy took her time going down the list of 'who's who' in the house, ignoring Nimmi hopping and flapping impatiently. 'Mrs Sinha, Kiran's health visitor referred him to us. Non-engagement with health services, she says.'

'What non-engagement? We haven't seen this health visitor at all. Even when we called for help. It just goes to answerphone while they are... sat around drinking cups of tea and chatting, no doubt.'

Nancy read out the referral from Debbie. In January, when baby was six weeks old she had sent a letter inviting Ms K Sinha for a weighing of her baby. This was followed by a telephone call.' Nancy tapped her bright talons on the paper as she went down the list. Baby K was seen but not gaining weight... Baby K losing weight... Baby K not brought for another weighing. Ms Sinha not answering her phone. Ms Sinha not answering the door. Ms Sinha...'

Nimmi sat frozen to the seat. She had known nothing of this. Her daughter had not responded to the health visitor's calls. Kiran was losing weight, and she had not taken action. She had not taken him for his repeat vaccinations.

'You do know that she... Kalyani, has been severely depressed. Postnatal depression. Why didn't this health visitor spot that?'

'She cannot do that if she cannot gain access to the house, or reach the mother by phone. Which is the reason she contacted us.'

'I... we were not aware of this. But Kiran is with me now. I am looking after him, while his mother is in hospital,' Nimmi said, defiantly sticking her chin out.

'I understand. I still have to do an initial assessment, to make sure the baby's needs are met. Until such time that they are met, we have to keep him under our surveillance. You may be required to attend conferences to reassure the authorities that you can prioritise Kiran's welfare.'

Nimmi pinched herself discreetly under the coffee table and jumped as the pain registered. This wasn't a dream. Nancy Obe with her fake hair was still sitting in front of her, writing copious notes with her left hand.

'Or what?' she voiced.

Nancy looked up startled; it was obvious she had forgotten about the grandmother in the shocking-pink dressing gown. 'Sorry?'

Nimmi graciously repeated her question. 'What happens if we refuse? I mean, you come into our home and accuse us of not looking after our grandchild. We are law-abiding, tax-paying citizens. My husband is a well-paid and well respected consultant, and... and my younger daughter is studying law at uni. We have rights.'

Nancy did not flinch. Instead, she packed up her papers, and seemed to puff up like a dragon.

'Not when a child is involved, Mrs Sinha. If you do not co-operate with us, we will have to remove the baby from your care. The baby has rights too.'

As if on cue, Kiran woke up and bawled. Under Nancy's scrutiny, Nimmi crawled up to the baby, not trusting her trembling knees to hold her up, and gathered him to her bosom. Over the top of his head, she watched Nancy Obe exiting her house.

Chapter 19

The exhausted family gathered around in the living room. The past few weeks had been a pandemonium of hospital visits to see Kalyani, visits to the doctors for Kiran's vaccination and the dieticians for his weight, and attending meetings at the Social Care centre to reassure the authorities that his needs were being met.

This was the first Sunday morning in weeks that their diaries were clear. As if on auto-pilot, Nimmi prepared a breakfast of toast, crispy for Shekar, and soft in the middle for Minna; coffee for Shekar and tea for the ladies. Shekar opened the newspaper, and Minna switched on the TV. No one was really interested in any of the morning's obligatory functions, but they were desperate for some normality.

They blamed Dr Blick, the hospital, and the entire health system for Kalyani's problems. Blaming the baby or the mother was taboo. Blaming themselves was unproductive. But it was the elephant in the room.

How could they not have known? The girl had been withdrawn for months. She slept all day. She ate rubbish. She neglected the way she looked. She was irritable. She did not want to talk. Her baby spent the entire day being looked after by Nimmi. The baby was always ravenous in the morning, which meant he was not fed at night. As if the clues were not enough, Helen's drugged friend had mentioned it. Shahida had irritated them with it.

Something had been wrong for months – right under their noses – and they had ignored it. They hadn't sought medical help. They wanted to cover it all up – to maintain normality; to maintain a façade of coping; of playing happy families. They preferred to worry about their own puny problems – Shekar about the money they had flushed down the gutters, Minna about the number of classes she was missing, Nimmi about scoring points over the Mahmoods...

They should hold up their hands and accept the blame.

'I blame that boy, Rafik,' Nimmi said all of a sudden, venom in her voice. Shekar and Minna bit urgently into their toast, as if the impending storm was about to destroy breakfast. 'And Shahida! Their whole family is trouble. Nothing but trouble. They should be locked up.'

Nimmi was a gentle soul, a kind person. Friends sought her out because she was a good listener, and made them feel good. The venom she was now spewing was disconcerting.

'What did my poor daughter do to them? She fell in love. She believed in making a family. But they just treat her like a *pariah*, an untouchable,' she sniffed. Shekar and Minna looked up in alarm. 'They never came to see her. They came to see their grandchild. But not her. They made her feel rotten. And we let them.'

Minna went over to sit by her mother.

'Mum, don't...'

'Don't what?' Nimmi was now shedding hot, angry tears. 'Don't cry? Don't talk nonsense? Don't have an opinion...? What about her friends? Why did they not come around to see her? She must have been so... lonely... so depressed.'

'Her friends tried calling her, but she did not reply. We know now that the health visitors tried to call her, and she had ignored them,' Minna tried to reassure her mother.

'Besides, Rafik's family have also lost out, haven't they?' Shekar ventured, withering under his wife's glare.

'I think Dad is right. Despite all that bravado she is putting on, Shahida is probably a broken soul. Her only son left her; walked out on his bride-to-be and his child. He chucked his lucrative job away. All that private school education gone to bloody waste! If I were his mother, I would be mortified.'

'Maybe they should publicly disown him; throw him out!' Nimmi was still having a rant.

Minna considered this. 'Would you have disowned us, if we did something that stupid? You didn't disown Kals because she got pregnant out of wedlock. You didn't throw her out when she decided to convert to Islam. Just saying.'

'So! You are all on Shahida's side! Supporting her and that snake, Rafik!' her mother sobbed.

'Not at all, Nimmi.' Shekar's calm voice was like a damp blanket over fire. 'I think we should stop finding someone to blame. Least of all that little baby. He did not ask to be born amongst all this... chaos. We are all suffering. We should concentrate on what we should do from here on. Redefine our priorities.'

Nimmi responded to her husband's soothing tone. She reached for tissues and blew her nose.

'Our priorities are with our daughters. Kalyani's health and Minakshi's education.' Shekar was making a whole lot of sense. Nimmi hugged her younger daughter tightly, wishing she could do the same to the older one too. Shekar came over and hugged both of them. The baby whimpered and cooed.

'Yes. And you too,' Nimmi laughed through her tears.

A new normality was establishing itself in the Sinha household.

*

The dining table was strewn with things, none of which had anything to do with dining. Clothes that needed to be ironed: Minna's dresses, Shekar's button-down shirts, the change of clothes Kalyani had requested from the hospital. Kiran had grown a mile with all that extra milk and solid food he was on, and none of his clothes fitted anymore; they needed sorting and taken to Oxfam. Laptops, old newspapers, supermarket brochures and gardening catalogues jostled for space amidst baby lotions and fresh nappies.

Nimmi ritualistically stirred the cauldrons cooking on all five burners of the stove – bland meals for the baby to be blended and frozen food for Minna to take to her halls, and Kalyani's favourite curries. She was shouting orders to everybody and to nobody in particular, not concerned that they went unheeded. Shekar was walking around, looking for his wallet, and Minna was searching for her phone charger.

'Have you packed the train tickets and the keys to your room?' Nimmi asked her again, for the third time.

'Yes!' Minna replied testily. She had obviously not done so, because they were still lying on the table amidst her T-shirts and underwear. They were going to visit Kalyani that afternoon, so Minna could say goodbye. It would be a fortnight or more before she came home again.

Finally, Nimmi brought some order; she lined up Tupperware containers, filled with her prepared meals. Minna had pressed most of her clothes and packed them away. Shekar had stopped pacing around. She would give the baby a bath before showering herself, and they would be on their way. Being busy suited her. The less she thought, the better it was. She made lists every morning, and worked through them, until, tired and aching, she would crawl into bed, asleep before her head hit the pillow. Her oven gleamed, her wardrobes were colour coordinated, her garden weeded. Maybe she should take up knitting as well – the baby would need winter gear in a few months' time.

Kiran had been their saviour in many ways. He was a joy to watch; his expansive smiles and his will to keep trying, if he didn't succeed at first, was endearing. It was a shame that his mother was missing out on his early days.

Nimmi avoided taking Kiran to hospital with her on her visits. Hospitals were not healthy places for a little child – full of germs. Besides, Kalyani showed no interest in her baby's progress. *Nice. Good. Thanks for looking after him* were the type of responses she gave; her tone polite but flat. She seemed happy to see them; pleased to sample the food, and watch videos of Kiran on her mother's phone, but within the hour, she tired of them fussing, and wanted them gone. Please could they visit another day? She seemed unable to make a decision, or even a simple choice. She stared blankly in front of her, and said things like, *don't mind, dunno, you decide...* She couldn't remember what she had for breakfast, sometimes even what she had done in the last hour. She did not laugh, or cry or scream. Nimmi often came out of her room, feeling desolate and irate. Her daughter had been turned into a zombie. The daily bulletin from the nurses ranged from, 'Ms Sinha had a good week – she did not try to flush her head in the loo', and 'It was a bad one, she refused to get out of bed to go to the loo.'

She discussed this with Dr Blick at their fortnightly appointments. Amongst her grocery lists, she had a list of questions she planned to ask the good doctor.

Dr Amanda Blick had not changed very much in a month. Her bob was still severe and her eyes still a piercing blue behind her glasses. 'She is on three different types of medication,' she explained. 'She is tolerating her medicines and experiencing no side effects. Progress is slow. This is not unusual. It may take several days before we notice any big change, but she is no longer psychotic.'

'But she is so flat. She has no interest in anything. I can't see my daughter anywhere in that… zombie.'

'The medication can do that. And she is still depressed. We will, over the next few days, adjust the dose of the tablets. That may help with her delusions as well.'

'What delusions?'

'I am told that she talks to herself, often in the night. There seems to be a consistent pattern to it. She gets out of bed, with her hands held out, as if she is following someone, only she can see. Someone called Affa or Raffa?'

Shekar interrupted his wife, as she began to say something. 'Raffa is her fiancé. Was. They… split up. He… left her and the child, before the wedding.'

'Ahh!' Dr Blick consulted her notes. 'Yes. We do have that history in our notes. It appears that she is struggling to get over that particular traumatic event. In her delusions, she pleads with him to wait for her. The baby… was born before or after he left?'

'After. A few months after.'

'Is there any chance of them getting back together?'

'Not realistically,' Shekar said, once again restraining Nimmi.

Dr Blick jotted it down in her notes.

'Then, we need to move to the next step.'

'Can she come home?' Nimmi knew she was pushing her luck.

'Not yet. The next step would be to start the bonding process between her and her baby. It is possible that she believes the baby to be the reason why her fiancé left her. Or she is mentally stuck in a period before the baby was born. We have to assess the current risk to the baby, and also build up her confidence in her parenting.'

Minna was frustrated. 'There are lots of families without a father. Fathers leave all the time. Why does she struggle? Why can she not get on with it?'

Amanda Blick fixed the young girl with her blue eyes for a long minute. Minna defiantly held her gaze. 'You are right. Some fathers do walk away. In this case, the combination of childbirth, postnatal depression, and the sudden unexpected loss, just became unbearable for her. It appears she had quite strong feelings for this man.'

Minna bowed her head, guilty that she had not tried to appreciate the depth of her sister's grief.

'This bonding. How will you help with that?' Shekar asked.

'We will try for a place in a mother and baby unit. The mother and her infant are housed together, in supervised accommodation, and assessed. Bonding will be encouraged too. These places are difficult to find. I cannot guarantee it will be nearby.'

Nimmi protested, 'We can take care of her at home. I mean, tell us what to do.'

'Let us not jump the gun yet. We may not get a place at all. In the meantime, I suggest you bring baby along, leave her photos or videos of him, encourage her to feed or clothe him, cuddle… She is not ready to come home yet.'

Dr Blick collected her notes together and tapped them on the table. The meeting was over.

Minna went back to say goodbye to Kals. Her sister smiled wanly at her. 'Enjoying the course, sis?'

'It is interesting. Very demanding though.'

'You must have missed a few lectures.'

'I have missed you too, Kals.'

'Sorry.'

'Don't be. Everything will be alright, you'll see.'

'We will be playing happy families soon,' Kals agreed, 'You, me, mum and dad. Kiran and Raffa too.'

Minna was startled by her sister's words. *'And Raffa too.'* She swallowed the harsh things she was about to say.

She squeezed her sister's hand and said, 'See you soon. Stay safe.'

Even before Minna closed the door to Kalyani's room behind her, her sister snuggled under the sheets and shut her eyes.

*

Kalyani had somehow squeezed herself into a pipe, the ones you see on the roadside, waiting to be installed underground. Spiders with small bodies and long, slender legs had been weaving cobwebs all night across the entrance. Ice crystals had formed on them overnight, and now they were acting as small prisms, breaking white light into bits of rainbow. Because there were so many of them, they turned the entrance to the pipe into a kaleidoscope of bright and intense colours. She could easily spend all day staring happily at it. But someone was standing in the bright light beyond. She held a hand up against the light and squinted at the form. Was it Raffa, hands on hips, grinning at her?

'Joke's over. Come out. Let us go home,' he said.

If she didn't respond, he would go away again. 'I am coming!' she shrieked, and attacked the cobwebs. Swish. Swosh. Bish. Bosh. Yuk. There was a spider in one of them, and now it was crawling up her fingers. She took her hand up to her eye to clear her vision and now the spider was in her eye, hanging on to her lashes, pulling itself up, and spreading its legs around her pupils. Get it off! Hate it. Hate it. Hate it. Get off. Get off.

She pulled at her lids, her lashes, tried to lever the spider out of her eyes. The spider escaped her clutches and crawled over her cheeks and over her lips... Get off. Get off. Get off.

*

Nimmi stared her daughter's face in horror. How had she got all those deep scratch marks? The doctor had attended to her in the middle of the night, and Kalyani's cuts were smeared with brown antiseptic stains and bits of sticky plaster.

'How? What happened?' Nimmi demanded, banging on the table with her palms. She had turned into a force 10 gale since seeing her daughter swaying on her feet, looking like something out of a freak show. She summoned Dr Blick to explain.

'Mrs Sinha, I am not sure how it happened. We will investigate,' Dr Blick tried to pacify Nimmi. 'It may be a reaction to her medication.'

'Or because of her condition. Sometimes, they hallucinate,' one of the junior doctors said.

'The nurse had tried to restrain her...'

'Which explains the bruises on her wrists!'

'... to prevent her from hurting herself further.'

'I want a written explanation of the results of your investigation, or... or I am going to the newspapers. My daughter has been here for many weeks now, and you have not made one iota of difference for her. You don't care! No one does,' Nimmi sobbed. The student nurse knelt beside her, sympathy all over her face, just as she was trained to do. *What do you do with a difficult customer? Good one to add to her portfolio.*

Dr Blick sighed and left the room. On the way out, she glanced at the girl, now sleeping soundly after the hefty dose of sedatives. From time to time, she twitched and jerked, and muttered in her sleep.

The travails of love, she thought to herself. Someone had hurt her and hurt her bad.

Chapter 20

A few weeks later, Nimmi walked into Shahida in an unexpected location. They lived on the same street; they could have bumped into each other several times on the street, at the local Co-op, or in town, but it happened miles away from home.

Nimmi felt hassled that day. When it came to visiting hours, she was punctual, standing outside Kalyani's ward with baby, requisite clean laundry and other knick-knacks, a few seconds before the doors opened for visitors. But on that day, Kiran had needed a nappy change just as she was leaving. Something in his weaning diet had disagreed with him, resulting in copious quantities of mushy stools that escaped the confines of his nappy. He didn't just need a nappy change, he needed a wash. Then, she realised she was running dangerously low on nappies. She stopped at the supermarket to stock up, an exercise that soon extended to formula milk, baby food, vegetables and tea. By the time she reached the hospital car park, it was teeming with cars, relatives and friends in an inordinate hurry.

After fifteen minutes of dodging slow-moving grandmothers in wheelchairs and renegade children, in a bid to find parking, her patience was running short. She huffed and puffed and cursed under her breath at how slow the lifts were, and how crowded the corridors were. Did people have to walk in threes and block the entire corridor? She used her ample derriere to ram the door to Kalyani's room. Dragging the buggy with her, she backed into the room, and into Shahida.

For a long moment, Nimmi stared at her like a rabbit caught in the headlights. What in the blazes was she doing in Kalyani's room? Who had given her permission to visit? How had she even known? Her daughter was not in the room. From the noises coming out of the bathroom, Kalyani was either having a shower… or slashing her wrists.

'I was just leaving,' said Shahida, inching towards the door. Nimmi was furious. She marched up to the nursing station, demanding to speak to the nurse in charge. A plump, pretty nurse looked up from her paperwork. She promised to come over in five minutes to have a word with Nimmi. It took her ten minutes, during which Nimmi worked herself into a frenzy – banging the stuff she had brought into cupboards and muttering to herself.

She launched into a tirade at the plump nurse. 'Do you know what we are going through here? We are trying very hard to get my daughter better. But you let unsuitable visitors in. These are the people who put her in here in the first place! And now, you let them in… in here to upset… everything. Everything we tried so hard to achieve. I… demand an explanation!'

'Mum!' Neither of them had noticed that Kalyani had come out of the bathroom, her powder-blue bathrobe registering areas of damp, from her dripping hair.

The nurse took charge. 'Mrs Sinha, let us all calm down. Take a deep breath and start again. Who are you talking about?'

'That woman! With the green cardigan and blue veil… big brown, fake handbag.' Nimmi felt inadequate that she could not give more details. 'Check your CCTV. You might see her!'

'Mum!' cried Kalyani. 'She came to see me. I… invited her.'

'What? You are lying!'

'No.' Kalyani was calm. 'I phoned her and asked her to come.'

The nurse discreetly escaped and returned to her notes.

'But... why?'

'I wanted to speak to her. To someone other than my immediate family. I wanted to ask her about Raffa.'

Despite herself, Nimmi lost her patience. 'Raffa! Raffa? That useless son of a... After all he has put you through! You want to know about him? Don't you have any self-respect?'

'I think you should leave, Mum.'

'How many times?'

'What?'

'How many times has she visited?'

'Oh! Two, maybe three. What does it matter?'

Nimmi sank into the green sofa that squeaked, speechless, her head in her hands. Her daughter kneeled by her side.

'I can understand you are angry and tired. I am sorry. I think we should all have a break from each other. Maybe two or three days, or even a week?'

Nimmi stared at her, flabbergasted. Kalyani pleaded. 'Please?' She was their little girl again, pretty, jovial, holding up the spangled, expensive doll in the shops. 'Please? Mummy? I will do chores for a whole week. I will share the doll with Minna. Please, please, please.'

'What about your baby? You are supposed to be bonding with him. I am supposed to bring him to you, every day.'

Kalyani glanced at him, lying in the buggy, oblivious, his fat fingers in his pink mouth. He was a beautiful baby, but she felt nothing for him. All this bonding exercise was a waste!

'Mum, I have spoken to Dr Blick. I said I need time to think and she agreed. I just need some space, to get my head around it all. Decide what I should do.'

Nimmi changed tack to what she knew best. To be the practical mother. 'I only brought clothes for one day. How will you manage for a week?'

'Don't worry. There are probably clothes in that suitcase that I have never used. I will ring if I need anything. Promise.'

There was nothing more to be discussed. Nimmi fussed around, collecting the dirty laundry, making sure Kals had enough money (in small notes) for the news vendor and coins for the phone. Did she want anything from the shop downstairs? Did she need her water jug refilled?

Finally, she ran out of things to do and say. She hugged her daughter and said goodbye. On the way out, she stopped at the nurse's desk. The plump nurse was not there, but a Filipino male nurse was.

'Look after her for me.' She pointed to the room. 'Room four. Miss Sinha. If anything happens to her, I will hold you responsible! And please ring me if you need me.'

'Sure. Sure. Don't worry,' the nurse reassured her.

Tears blinded her eyes as she walked back to the car. Tears of helpless anger and frustration.

*

'Look, Nimmi, Shekar. We are all on the same side here,' Shahida addressed them. The families placed themselves on either side of Shahida's coffee table, suspiciously bereft of any items that could be used as a missile. After listening to his wife stewing and ranting for a couple of days about treachery and betrayal, Shekar suggested they meet up with the Mahmoods.

Shahida took one look at their angry faces, and quickly ushered them into her lounge, to avoid a slanging match outside her door. Ignoring their protests, she had insisted on making tea for all of them, thereby giving herself time to think, and her guests time to calm down. She had gotten her husband out of his home office. Ashraf was a man of few words, and hated confrontation. One word about the weather, two about the state of the roads nowadays, three about the dirty tricks of politicians in Parliament. He greeted his potentially explosive guests with the same respect a soldier would pay a hand grenade.

'Hello. *Asalam alaikum*. How is the weather at number thirty-five? It has been raining here, all night. My mother? Yes, she is here. No, not at the house; she is visiting her brother in Manchester. Yes. Bury. Oh? For a couple of weeks. Yes, change of scene will do her good.'

The arrival of Shahida with the tea set Nimmi off. Shahida placed the tea tray out of her reach, and listened as Nimmi accused her of turning Kalyani against her own family, of scheming to send her back into depression. Had she not done enough already? Her son had put them all in this horrible mess! They were the laughing stock amongst their relatives and friends. What more did Shahida wish to bring upon them? Did she want Kalyani to slash her wrists again, this time for good? For all of them to have a mental breakdown?

'My daughter has just started to find her feet. Her medication has just started to work. She is not... a... zombie wreck any more. Why do you have to spoil it all?' she finished, furiously swiping away tears streaming down her face.

'We all want the same thing here,' Shahida repeated. 'Our children to be happy. Kalyani is my grandson's mother. Why would I do the wrong thing by her?'

'How did you know?' Shekar asked, his voice tight with anger. 'How did you know where she was?'

'Come on! We live on the same street. One night, the street is woken up by police cars, ambulances pulling into your house, lights like a beacon. People put two and two together. Word gets around. There was a brief mention in the local news too. I texted Kalyani to make sure she was safe. She didn't reply for weeks. And then, she contacted me. She wanted to talk.'

'About what?'

'Rafik.' Shahida held out her hands in an attempt to pacify Nimmi. 'I know. I know. But hear me out.'

Shekar placed a restraining hand on his wife's arm. She bit back her words.

'Let's drink chai, before it gets cold. It is a special brew, spicy.' Shahida busied herself with pouring the warm tea from a painted teapot into matching cups. Nimmi wondered if she would get away with 'accidentally' dropping her cup, and dismantling the set. Instead, she meekly accepted the tea. It tasted surprisingly good. But Nimmi did not want to discuss tea.

'OK. So… What did she want to discuss with you?'

'Kalyani is not out of the woods, yet. I mean mentally. Is she?'

'So? She is responding to treatment. It is early days.'

'The doctor told us, she is not… psychotic any more,' Shekar confirmed.

'Yes. But she is still delusional,' Shahida said.

'You… you spoke to her psychiatrist?' Nimmi was horrified. She made a mental note to sue the hospital for breach of confidentiality.

'With Kalyani's permission.'

'That girl does not know from which direction the sun rises. You must have wheedled permission out of her.'

Shahida ignored the comment.

'Did you know that she was still cutting herself? Sometimes deeply.'

Nimmi nearly dropped her cup. Shekar watched it rattle in her hands and took it off her, returning it safely to the tray.

'Who told you that?' he asked.

'Her doctor.' Again, Shahida held out her hand. 'They caught her doing it with the metal part of her hair grip. Kalyani confessed to them that she wanted to kill herself, so she could follow Raffa. She still claims Raffa comes to her every night, calling her, asking her to join him.'

Nimmi let out an expletive.

'Excuse me?' Shahida raised an eyebrow.

'There was no need for that, was there?' Ashraf spoke up in his wife's defence. So he *could* string a whole sentence, when he had to.

'I am trying to be helpful here. I didn't have to tell you anything,' Shahida reminded them.

Nimmi apologised. 'Rafik will destroy her.'

'Rafik wasn't there in person, was he? He is in her head. It is all in her head!' Shahida tapped her own head with her index finger.

For a minute, they were all silent, struggling to control their emotions.

'Anyhow, it appears that Kalyani wanted to discuss Raffa. She knew that she couldn't do that with her own family. So she asked to speak to me. She did not want you to know, because she did not want you to feel... betrayed.'

Nimmi rubbed her forehead with her finger. In the face of her daughter's decision, she was helpless. She also felt mildly guilty of excluding Rafik's family. In her childish desire to score points, she had forgotten to consider her daughter's wishes.

As if she read Nimmi's thoughts, Shahida responded. 'You were emotionally too close to her. Your own emotions got in the way.'

'So she just wanted to chat?'

'Yes. We just chatted.'

'Has she told you not to visit for some time too? To give her some space?' Nimmi asked in a small voice.

'I only visit when she calls me. She sends me a text.' Shahida waved her phone in the air.

There was nothing more to say. Shahida had justified her actions. Nimmi and Shekar thanked them and left, feeling less angry, but more confused and alienated. Their daughter was no longer just theirs. She was not their little child, who found her way to the kitchen because she had fallen over, who they could bob up and down on their knees and wipe the tears away with the offer of a lollipop. The world had claimed her.

Chapter 21

Bereft of her routine hospital visits, Nimmi found herself at a loose end. There was only so much housekeeping or watching TV a woman could do; the BBC was broadcasting programmes made two decades ago for the hundredth time, making her wonder why they paid the licence fee, and the freezer was groaning with blended baby meals. Kalyani had not called to request a visit. Every day, Nimmi expected her daughter to run out of clean underwear, or tire of the bland hospital food. She was well prepared for the moment. Her phone was on full charge, her daughter's bag packed with several sets of washed and ironed clothes and other sundries, and her car topped up with fuel.

Kiran, who had been practising rolling over, without his arms getting tangled under him, had fallen into an exhausted sleep on the baby mat. On the wooden deck, outside, fat pigeons fought for the stale bread she had thrown them. Despite herself, she revisited their heartbreak on Kalyani's wedding day. Just as Raeba, their wedding planner had warned, after expressing her shock-horror at the last-minute cancellation, they had not received any refund of expenses. Shekar had not revealed the exact figures to her, and she had been happy to remain ignorant. On the wedding day, they had divided the guest list down the middle and took turns to personally apologise to each of their guests for the inconvenience caused by the last minute cancellation of the wedding. Shekar set the timer for five minutes per call. After repeating the same rhetoric a few times, they started believing it themselves. The youngsters had decided not to go ahead with the wedding. They were too young to get hitched. The groom wished to travel.

Where? Asia mainly, but he wanted to travel all around the world. Oh? Kalyani did not want that. She is more of a home bird. Yes, of course, as parents, they were devastated, but perhaps it was for the best, considering it was an inter-religious alliance.

Up in her room, Kalyani had downed shutters and prepared for a long dark period of hibernation.

Nimmi knew that the jungle drums were beating as soon as they got off the phone. Chinese whispers, rushing along cables, and electromagnetic waves, twitching and tripping over each other in their hurry to get ahead of others, grotesquely altered, coated with fake sympathy. A few of her friends and relatives rang later, some to refresh gossip, and others to genuinely offer their condolences.

Without active encouragement from Nimmi or Shekar, their calls dwindled and ceased; people moved on. Nimmi found this opportune, because she did not want to inadvertently drop the news of her daughter's pregnancy or the arrival of the baby into the conversation.

There was one, however, who knew it all. Nimmi's cousin, Sulu. Sulu had dropped by without warning on the way back from her brother's house in Lincoln. Kalyani was eight months pregnant, big as a beach ball, lounging in the armchair, too lazy to get up to greet her aunt. Sulu was very understanding, once she got over her surprise. For her, the fault was in their stars. The alignment of the planets at any particular time influenced everything that happened to puny earthlings.

Like Nimmi, Sulu had moved to the UK after marriage. Brought up with conservative and traditional views, steeped in superstitions, she believed that a wife's duty was to make a home. She was a great cook, and a model mother, who worked hard to instil good values in her children. She took great pride that all of them now worked for the government, paid their taxes, and were rapidly building their own families. It was Sulu's duty to invoke God's blessings and consult the planets before every important event. Success of a business, interviews, board examinations, marriages and child births were all preceded by a visit to her trusted astrologer. A substantial proportion of her household expenditure was spent on the astrologer's fees, and in following their advice to invest in powders, pastes, magical amulets, pilgrimages, and fasts.

On her advice, when her daughters were born, Nimmi had followed Hindu tradition, and forwarded the date and exact time of their birth to the astrologer, in order that a map of planetary alignment at that point of time is drawn. It was called the horoscope. Simplistically, Nimmi understood that the planets lived in houses represented on paper as nine squares. They wandered in and out of these houses in a pre-ordained manner specific to the child. Their whereabouts influenced health and welfare of the Hindus on Earth. Only an astrologer can predict their movement into each other's houses and foretell if such a movement would cause boom or bust in one's life. The horoscope was a child's celestial ID card to be fished out during events of great importance.

One such event would have been Kalyani's marriage. Sulu had urged Nimmi to get a reading to predict the couple's united future. All she had to do was to send the couple's horoscopes to Gyanji, Sulu's family astrologer. The more the number of matching points between their horoscopes, the better their married life would be. But the horoscope was a Hindu practice. Rafik did not have one. Nimmi didn't know where to start if she had to explain this to his family in the short time they had.

Besides, she had also been fearful of the outcome. What if the planets did not approve? What if they predicted terrible things for the couple after marriage? It wasn't as if she could stop the wedding. Imagine living with a terrible prophecy dangling over their heads, like the sword of Damocles. Nimmi convinced herself that time was short, and there were far too many important things to do, and put Sulu's suggestion on the back burner. Retrospectively, it might have at least saved them some money, if she had paid attention to it.

Now, with time on her hands, and desperate for a resolution to their problems, Nimmi decided to consult the stars again. Before calling Sulu, she had to decide how much information she could safely impart in exchange for her help. From previous conversations she had had with Sulu, she knew she had to endure listening to Sulu's rendition of the long list of blessings, which God and the planets had showered on her family.

As soon as she could get a word edgeways, Nimmi said, 'We haven't commissioned Kiran's horoscope yet, Sulu. What with one thing or the other, it just got delayed. How quickly can we get an appointment with Gyanji?'

Sulu warned her that Gyanji had become very busy of late; he had a lot of customers waiting (no doubt, directed to him by Sulu herself). Nimmi ventured some more juicy details, hoping it would help her jump the queue. 'You know, Sulu, ever since the birth, both mother and baby have been recovering from one illness or another. It is making me and Shekar worried. It will be most helpful if we could meet with Gyanji personally, as soon as possible. Would you be able to put in a good word for us?'

Two white lies. Kiran had been delightfully healthy since birth. Shekar was not even aware of Gyanji's existence. Nimmi could almost hear his response. 'Waste of time. Waste of money. All this mumbo jumbo is not going to solve our problems.'

Nimmi, unlike Sulu, was not a great follower of the planets either. But they were stuck in a rut; going round and round like a conker at the end of a string. Perhaps the Gods were angry and needed to be appeased. Nimmi made a mental note to ratchet up her degree of devotion. Gyanji may suggest some remedial measures.

When Sulu rang back a few hours later with an appointment, Nimmi rectified one of the lies.

'Shekar does not believe in all this... astrology thing. I am not sure if he will approve.'

Sulu was empathetic. 'Don't worry about it. Men don't understand or they pretend not to. Why don't the two of you visit us? We can leave the men at home, watching cricket, and do some "shopping".' Shekar was more of a football fan, Leicester City to be precise. However, Sulu made perfect sense, when she pointed out that both games had balls in them; size didn't matter.

That night, Nimmi waited for Shekar to mellow after a hot dinner, and a second shot of scotch. She cuddled into him, giving him the customary few seconds to softly chuckle to himself, and transfer the goblet of whiskey to his right hand, before putting his left arm tentatively around her shoulders.

'Is there a plan?' he enquired, his eyes twinkling behind his glasses.

'No,' she replied, *if you don't count being abducted to attend a ritual under duress.*

Nevertheless, they decided on retiring to bed early. 'Oh, I nearly forgot to mention. Sulu invited us over to theirs this weekend. They are belatedly celebrating their wedding anniversary. It was postponed due to the birth of their third grandchild.' Nimmi hated lying to Shekar, but she didn't want him to jinx her plan with his *bah humbug* speech. As she simply could not keep a straight face when she lied, she turned her back to him, and busied herself in putting away the baby's clothes. They had moved Kiran's cot into their room to stop Nimmi's paranoid excursions at night to check on him.

'They live in London! That is two hours and forty-five minutes away – on that dreaded M25. I did want to put my feet up this weekend and watch football,' Shekar complained. Nimmi could have taken the train, but she hated taking the tube to Sulu's place, besides it would be cheaper by car.

'I know! But the thing is, I have already said yes. Shekar, I just fancy a change of scene. I am stuck at home with the baby, only making lousy trips to the hospital. Sometimes, I feel I am going mad.'

'God forbid! Not you too!' Shekar swore. 'We will go. But why celebrate an anniversary a month later?'

'How should I know, Shekar! I do not have an analytical brain like yours. I just accepted what she said.'

'OK, OK. Just wondered is all. Can I go to sleep now?'

Nimmi rubbed cream into her hands. 'Forty-eight,' she said.

'What?'

'Two hours, forty-eight minutes according to the AA Route Planner.' She smiled to herself. Shekar would look it up first thing in the morning. He hated being in the wrong.

*

London on a weekend was infinitely quieter than on a weekday. The congestion charge was not applicable. Although the Sat Nav significantly reduced the number of cars that honked at them or their owners sticking their middle fingers up in annoyance, they did have to retrace their route, take detours around roadworks, and circle around a couple of times before finding a parking space – fortunately, before Shekar completely lost his rag. His displeasure, however, evaporated at the warm welcome Sulu and her husband, Arun, gave them, and the sumptuous meal she had cooked. Arun was surprised when Shekar thrust a bottle of Shiraz at him and wished him a happy anniversary. For a moment, he panicked, thinking he had forgotten his wedding anniversary, something that would have serious consequences.

'Oh, he means "belated" wishes,' Nimmi added quickly, while Sulu deftly distracted them. After the meal, the women tucked their men in front of the TV with cans of Stella Artois and crisps, and a sleeping baby. Sulu's son-in-law wandered in with his infant, and the makings of an all lads' club commenced in her lounge. Sulu and Nimmi did not have any problems in slipping out of the house without a fuss, and walking down a couple of streets to Gyanji's house.

Gyanji's son welcomed them warmly, and left them cooling their heels in the lounge, watching Gyanji's grandchildren squabble over crayons, while he alerted his father. He returned just in time to stop the kids from murdering each other, and after restoring order, ushered them into Gyanji's office. Somewhere along the way, Nimmi had conjured up a vision of a small, bald man with glasses, who sat cross-legged on the floor, working with paper and ink. Gyanji wore glasses, but that is where the resemblance ended. He was a fairly big man, with a shock of dyed hair; he sat at a polished, mahogany desk, surrounded by gadgets – PC, laptop, printer, scanner, fax, video cameras, and a couple of phones, and personal effects – shelves of books, a vase of seasonal flowers, family photographs, and his brass name plate – Mr Gyan Bakti. He peeled his eyes off the computer and rose from behind his desk, gesturing to them to sit facing him.

'You want a birth horoscope for your grandson?' he asked Nimmi after the preliminary introductions. 'I need the exact time, date and location of his birth.'

Nimmi nodded and gave him the requisite information. 'There is something more urgent,' she blurted out.

Both Sulu and Gyanji stared at her. Nimmi gathered courage. 'My daughter. I want her stars looked at. Today, if possible. Please.'

Gyanji stared at her for a while longer. 'You are worried about this girl, aren't you?'

Nimmi nodded, her eyes tearing. 'The baby's horoscope can wait.'

'Have you brought her birth horoscope with you?' Nimmi lost no time fishing it out of her handbag. As the astrologer unfolded it, smoothed it out and studied it, Nimmi turned to Sulu. Sulu seemed put-out that Nimmi hadn't been entirely truthful to her.

'Sorry,' Nimmi mouthed.

The older woman patted her arm and mouthed back, 'It is OK. Do you want me to leave?'

'Not at all. Stay. Please.'

After a while, Gyanji, who had been muttering to himself and taking notes, spoke. 'This girl's planets are out of alignment. Venus is retrograde and I see a transiting Neptune. Saturn is entering the seventh house...' He continued for a full five minutes, talking about Lagnas and Dashas and Grahas, until a whole solar system whizzed around chaotically inside Nimmi's head. Sulu, however, was sitting bolt upright, in rapt attention.

'What does it all mean?' Nimmi asked.

'The stars tell us that times are difficult for this girl. She will face obstruction in any path she chooses to take. She has to face her demons.'

Nimmi's heart raced. 'Will she come out of all this? Will her life be better at some stage?'

Gyanji consulted the horoscope again. 'The planets are restless. I see one open door, but it is in a faraway place. The path is treacherous, but it is the path to her salvation. I cannot offer any further detail, with the limited information you have provided.'

'Is there anything else you can do for her to keep her safe?'

'She will require your understanding and your support.' He reached behind him for a cloth bag, and extracted a small package, stained yellow with turmeric paste. 'Tie this on her arm. It will keep her safe.'

After parting with a few hefty notes from her purse to pay the consultation fees, Nimmi and Sulu left Gyanji's office. He promised to post Kiran's horoscope home, when it was complete.

On the way out, a strategically placed, brightly-coloured charity box collecting money for orphanages in India caught their eye. Sulu fished out a handful of change to post into the slot. Nimmi sighed and followed suit. If only their parents had consulted Gyanji before conceiving these unfortunate children, she thought.

As they walked back, Nimmi mulled over the astrologer's prophecy in her mind.

What exactly did he mean? Was Kalyani still in danger? Was she going to attempt suicide again?

'Are you OK? Do you want to talk about it?'

'I was thinking. What Gyanji said… was not entirely reassuring, was it?'

'You really wanted to ask him about Kalyani, didn't you? Kiran was only an excuse. Why didn't you say?'

'I am sorry, Sulu. My mind is always in a state of confusion nowadays. Kalyani has been diagnosed to have postnatal depression, and is on treatment. We have been so worried for her.'

Sulu said appropriately sympathetic things, and added, 'So, that was what the astrologer was implying.

That she is in a poor state of mind. These prophecies sometimes sound frightening – more than they intend it to be. As Gyanji stated, there is a path to salvation. Follow that path, and… get her to a good doctor.'

'What did you buy?' asked Shekar, smiling at his wife.

'Huh?'

'You went shopping, didn't you? What did you buy?' he repeated.

Nimmi had totally forgotten about the excuse she had given her husband.

'Oh. We just window-shopped. I didn't fancy actually buying anything.'

'Just as well, as you left your purse with the credit cards here.'

Nimmi smiled wanly at her husband; it did not reach her pretty eyes.

Chapter 22

'I have been thinking,' Kalyani told her mum.

They were in the small café attached to the rehabilitation centre, enjoying coffee and cake.

Earlier, Nimmi had stood at the glass window, watching Kalyani and a few others working in the small sensory garden outside. They were weeding the vegetable patch. Nimmi found herself holding her breath; what did her daughter know about weeding? Sure enough, it was only a matter of minutes before her supervisor stood over her, shaking her head, vigorously pointing to the chives she had uprooted, mistaking it for grass. She was ordered back to sweeping up dry leaves.

When they were let off, Nimmi took Kalyani to the café. Her daughter was looking better, her cheeks had colour, and the dark circles around the eyes were fading. On her cheek was a smear of wet mud and a few twigs were tangled in her hair. She had also lost the unhealthy weight she had piled on post baby. Nimmi felt proud of her. After eight weeks of waking up with the sole purpose of harming herself, she had miraculously pulled herself together. Enough to graduate towards rehabilitation.

Nimmi had left the baby with Shekar, who was recovering at home from a migraine. Today, they would have some quiet mother and daughter time.

'Coffee tastes good.' Kalyani licked the froth clinging to her upper lip. It brought back memories of the girls enjoying chocolate milkshake outside the Christmas market, years ago, both wearing identical pink, fluffy hats and matching mittens, chasing each other around their parents. It had started to snow, and their squeals of delight filled the air. Happy days. Happy now that her daughter was starting to enjoy life again, she listened patiently to the few short sentences and long silences in her conversation. Her voice no longer had high-pitched, neurotic overtones.

Nimmi scooped a forkful of gooey cake into her mouth, and chewed it slowly, while she waited for Kalyani.

'I know Rafik is gone, and I have been having hallucinations about him for several months.'

Praise the Lord, thought Nimmi, remembering that she was eating in public, and she shouldn't let her jaw drop and drool chocolate. 'Mm hmm,' she said nonchalantly, prodding the food with the plastic fork.

'What is *really* bothering me now,' Kalyani tapped the gold-rimmed cup with her spoon, 'is why.'

'Why?'

'Why he left me and his child. It doesn't make sense. One minute, we are in a full-blown relationship. Next, boom! He is gone!'

'Cold feet?' Nimmi suggested. 'Happens a lot with men.'

'I don't know. Why didn't he say? Why didn't he come and tell me that he wasn't sure?'

'Maybe he was afraid of the way you would react.' Another indifferent scoop of cake.

'Did he not love me enough? Respect me enough? Why leave his job? His parents?'

'I didn't know Rafik well enough to comment, sweetie. He must have had his own reasons.'

Kalyani tapped her head with the tip of her crooked finger. 'It bugs me to not know! Up here. It bugs me.'

Nimmi hoped she wasn't going to work herself up into madness again. Turn the bug in her head into a hungry caterpillar that would gnaw at her sanity. She was wondering if she should change the topic when Kalyani's next sentence hit her right between the eyes.

It made her freeze, her laden fork poised between plate and mouth.

'I *have* to know. I *have* to ask him. I *have* to speak to him.' Kalyani was staring into the ether somewhere behind Nimmi, and rapping her knuckles on the glass table to emphasize her 'haves'.

'Sweetie, you do not know where he is. Has he a forwarding address? Do we even know if he is alive?'

'Yes and no. I know where he is and that he is alive. He did not leave *me* a forwarding address.'

'Then who has his address?' Even as she asked the question, Nimmi knew the answer. 'Shahida?' she spat.

Her daughter shrugged her shoulders, non-committally. 'I asked her and she told me.'

'So? Are you going to call him? Or email him?'

'He doesn't have good phone or Internet connection. He has to travel to the city for that.'

'Okay...'

'It is not something I want to do over the phone or the Internet. I want to see him in person. I have to go to him,' Kalyani said in a matter of fact way. Nimmi used every ounce of self-control to match her daughter's neutral tone.

She pushed her plate away. 'Where – is – Rafik?' she asked through gritted teeth.

'Pakistan. Near the Afghan border.'

Whereas on previous occasions, she looked for reasons to linger, today, Nimmi couldn't wait to leave. She stuffed Kalyani's dirty clothes into large, plastic carry bags, binned the rubbish, and stacked the books and magazines into neat piles several times, before kissing her daughter goodbye.

On the way out, she waylaid the matron in charge and told her to look out for Kalyani Sinha in Room four. 'She may be planning to escape.'

'Aren't we all!' the matron joked, but promised to keep an eye on her. Once back in the car, she gripped the steering wheel with such force that she cut off the blood circulation to her fingers, and her breathing sounded like a train chugging out of the station. If the police had knocked on her door and accused her of dangerous driving because she had rammed into the barriers of the car park and three ambulances on her way home, she wouldn't be surprised.

'She is not even ready to travel home. There is no way she is travelling more than 3,000 miles to a terrorist country!' Nimmi was in panic mode, her eyes as big as dinner plates, her hair escaping the hair grips, her arms flailing so much that Shekar feared she might take off like a bird.

He placed his hand protectively on the right side of his forehead, hoping his migraine wouldn't be triggered off by her. He was feeling vulnerable.

'Look, Nimmi. Calm down. I hope you didn't throw a "wobbly" in the hospital.'

To her credit, Nimmi hadn't. She had calmly returned the dirty plates to the trolley, and walked Kalyani back to her room, telling her the hour granted by her nurse was over.

When she finished relating the conversation with Kalyani, Shekar said, 'I have a lot of acquaintances with relatives in Pakistan. They are not exactly being shot at every day.'

'On the Afghan border, Shekar! Keep up!'

'It may not be as dangerous as we believe.'

'Or more than we know!' Nimmi paced around the kitchen. 'Come to think of it, why is Rafik there, holed up in a place without Facebook or Twitter? Has he joined the Taliban or ISIS?'

'ISIS is in Syria. Look, let us not jump to conclusions. There might be a legitimate reason for him to be there. Do you think his parents know?'

'Of course they do! They probably knew all along. Terrorists, all of them!' Nimmi screamed.

Shekar winced in pain. 'Nimmi sit down and speak quietly. Or this conversation is over. I am going to get some more pain killers.'

He popped a couple of Migraleve tablets on to his palm and swallowed them with water from the tap. He switched the kettle on, intending to make Nimmi a strong cup of tea, but changed his mind. The caffeine could wind her up even more. He poured white wine left over from the weekend into a glass and carried it to her. His wife glugged down half of it and gasped. Shekar wished he could have a glass too, but his migraine and wine were unlikely partners. He made himself some tea and joined Nimmi, who had plonked down on the sofa.

'What do we do?' she moaned.

'I suggest we sleep on it. It is not as though she is going to crawl down the fire escape and stow herself into a ship heading to Pakistan tonight. We need more details. If Rafik's parents know about it, we have to discuss it with them.'

Typical Shekar. He is the type of person who wouldn't start on a jigsaw puzzle until he was sure he had all the pieces, who wouldn't build IKEA flat-pack furniture unless he read the manual three times – not that there was much reading to be done in an IKEA manual. But as usual, he made perfect sense. The details were missing.

Sleep was the last thing on Nimmi's mind that night. A cacophony of random thoughts ricocheted in her skull. She wished she could borrow Shekar's logical thought process and organise them into a flow chart. After another hour of tossing and turning, she got out of bed and crept down to the kitchen. She heated a cup of milk in the microwave, and placed a couple of cookies on the table beside it. She then found a notepad and a pen that worked and did what she did best – write lists.

If Kalyani was speaking rationally, Rafik was alive and well. Rafik was in Pakistan. His parents knew how to contact him. His mother had shared this with Kalyani. *Now, Kalyani wants to meet with Rafik. She wants to travel to a dangerous and unknown territory in order to meet with him. Exactly what Gyanji, the astrologer predicted.*

Logical list done – the unknown, vague questions crowded in like a pack of yelping wolves. How was she going to meet him? What was she going to say? Would her sanity crack, this time for good, if Rafik rejected her again?

She beat the wolves off with a stick – or cookies and hot milk in her case. She did not care about Rafik or his family, but she did not want her daughter to put herself in danger – physically or mentally.

Kalyani must be stopped from going. *Maybe the hospital won't allow it.* Amanda Blick, her psychiatrist, would veto it. Kalyani was safe as long as she was in hospital. If and when she was discharged home, they would have to keep her under lock and key and take turns to stand guard.

Having reached a temporary solution, she finally fell asleep. She dreamt that it was Shahida's turn to guard the prison. Instead of standing guard, she opened the gates and let the prisoners escape. Kalyani was amongst them, running away with the crowds. Nimmi struggled to keep track of her. She threw herself into the melee, pushing and shoving, calling out to her daughter, louder, louder.

She woke up with a jerk to find an irate Shekar defending himself with his pillow.

*

Minna sighed as she read the messages left on her phone. All from her mother, no doubt informing her of the latest drama from her sister. She had sat down to a TV dinner in front of her laptop. The black bean chicken curry with rice smelt better than it tasted, and the BBC iPlayer went into buffer mode. For once, the latest episode in her sister's story was more interesting than her own evening.

'What?' she yelled into the phone, when her mother had finished updating her. 'She wants to go where?'

Her mum yelled back her reply from a hundred miles away.

'That is rubbish. Kals has not even got out of hospital yet! We don't know if she can navigate around the London Road yet.'

'My thoughts exactly!'

'Who told her about Rafik's whereabouts? His mother?'

'The one and only.'

'That woman is out to destroy Kals. I thought the numbskull son of hers had disappeared for good. Nevertheless, Mum, Kals should stop being an idiot. What does it matter why Rafik left her? It only shows his lack of character and his cowardice... To leave a woman standing at the altar. If it was up to me, I would stick him on a dart board and use him for darts practice.'

'Just as well you don't have a boyfriend then. Will you be getting one soon? Or should I ask your aunt to look out for an eligible groom?'

Minna knew her mother was pulling her leg, and she gave her the standard answer. 'Don't you dare!'

Minna always put her career first, and relegated any attraction she felt for the opposite sex to the back of her queue of priorities. All around her, she watched her friends catching the 'lurgy' of love, as if it was an epidemic, and fall – some into a deep, dark abyss like her sister, others into a vat of booze, and yet, others turned into machete-wielding, flesh-eating ogres. She kept well out of their way, not wanting to become the pillar of sanity they clung onto, or the bin they used to declutter their life.

She was aware that the word on the street was that she was – frigid? A lesbian? An alien?

At one point, she had tried to list the guys she was attracted to. Five made the shortlist. They all had a common factor – academic intelligence; they wouldn't be doing a law degree without it.

Number 1 – handsome, but became a nervous wreck on stage.
Number 2 – good showmanship, but an arrogant dick, who got his fix from putting people down with his scathing remarks.
Number 3 – sportsman, all-rounder, too many other girls to compete with.
Number 4 – funny, loud, spendthrift, either spending Daddy's money or in debt.
Number 5 – already had a girlfriend.

Maybe she would end up opting for an arranged marriage. All the necessary vetting done beforehand, one would be assured of meeting a good, healthy male, who has several degrees to his name, good genealogy, rich parents, no pesky sisters or brothers, no obvious flaws in character (at least none he had been arrested for)… the perfect man! Would that make it easier for her to tolerate him breaking wind or shedding dandruff on the pillow?

Her mother was cackling ineffectively over the phone. 'Hello? Are you there? Minakshi? Are you listening?'

Oops, not really. 'Sorry Mum, had to go out of the room and lost signal.'

'Oh, OK. Do you think you can talk to your sister? You used to be close.'

'Used to be, Mum. She doesn't listen to me now.'

'She doesn't listen to anyone, nowadays. Except…'

'Except?'

'That woman! Shahida! Who is using her to bring her son back.'

'So, what are you going to do? Tell her to back off?'

'Yes! And speak to Kalyani's doctor. Tell the doctor that she has gone off her rocker completely and needs to be locked up.'

'Sectioned. It is called sectioned.'

What a bloody mess.

*

Sunday morning. Cloudy, blustery, with rain in the forecast. Cornflakes, baby goo and steaming coffee. And Nimmi's plan.

'We have to go and talk to them.' Shekar knew who she was talking about. He rustled his newspaper, hoping his wife would take the hint and go away. 'Rafik's parents. We need to know what they know.'

Shekar groaned inwardly, a rare Sunday morning watching *Match of the Day* gone to pot. Who wanted to go to the horse-faced, would-have-been-in-laws' house?

'When?'

'Now! I mean in the morning, before they leave for the mosque.'

'Have you checked if it is convenient for them?'

'No. I propose to take them by surprise.' Nimmi walked the breakfast dishes to the sink and left them there. 'I will get ready.'

Shekar brooded over the plan. Although it was tempting, it did not sound fair.

'Phone her first,' he insisted. Nimmi glared at him, but she knew when she had to back off.

'OK. I will give her ten minutes' notice.'

Shekar laid out some rules as they walked up to Shahida's house.

'No shouting. Don't call them terrorists. Don't break her tea cups. Stay focussed. We ask the questions. We get the answers. We walk out. We do not shake hands. If the old grandmother is there, you greet her respectfully.'

'Terrorist grandmother!' Nimmi mumbled.

'… politely.'

'Terrorist old hag!'

'OK. You broke rule number nine. We will have to turn back.'

'No! Sorry, I will behave.'

Nimmi screwed up her face and pouted for the rest of the way.

Shahida opened the door. Her husband had already left for morning prayers. She complained that she wasn't ready for visitors, but with the promise of keeping it brief, Shekar and Nimmi gained access to her house. Grandma was nowhere in sight, but loud snoring emerged from behind the door of the downstairs bedroom.

Lazy, old hag, thought Nimmi, hoping Kiran wouldn't wake her up.

Shahida ushered them into her kitchen diner, and closed the door. Her kitchen table was large enough to seat eight or ten at a squeeze; she sat as far away from them as possible, her hands folded on the table, and waited. Nimmi waited for Shekar to start; Shekar waited for Shahida; then they all spoke at once, and stopped at once. Shekar cleared his throat, and looked at his wife.

'We saw Kalyani, two days ago,' Nimmi started.

'How is she?'

'Recovering.' *No thanks to you.* 'She said that you had visited her and told her that you knew where Rafik is.'

'She told you that?' Shahida frowned.

'Well, she said she knew where he was.'

'So?'

'There is only one way she would have known. And that is from you.'

Shahida played nervously with the salt shaker. 'Rubbish! She is… not well. She must still be hallucinating.'

Shekar interrupted the conversation, his tone irate. He did not tolerate lies.

'Look, Shahida, let us all behave like adults here. There is a young girl's life at stake here and with it, your grandchild's future. You didn't react when we said Kalyani knew where Rafik was. If you are still worried about his whereabouts, you would have held that kitchen knife to my throat, demanding to know the details. The only reason you didn't is because you didn't need the information. You already know.'

Shahida watched her grandson sitting on the table, playing with the sugar bowl. Nimmi glanced at the large kitchen knife with the serrated edges on the chopping board and gulped. She didn't fancy Shahida holding it to Shekar's throat. Shahida's perpetual frown deepened. She rose to open a cupboard and took down a carton of baby rusks. She handed one to the baby, who happily exchanged the sugar bowl for it, and gave her a beguiling grin. A corner of Nimmi's heart began to melt. Shahida had obviously bought the baby biscuits in the hope that someday, she would be able to feed it to her only grandson. But she wasn't ready to back down.

Shahida sighed. 'You are right. I know where Rafik is. I told Kalyani because she kept asking me.'

'You knew all along. When we were all worried about his safety, you knew where he was. All that sobbing and breast beating was an act?' Nimmi cried.

'No!' Shahida shook her head, avoiding eye contact. 'At that time, I didn't know. Four months ago, my brother, Alam, from Pakistan informed me that Rafik was there. He was staying with some distant relatives, Sulaiman Kaka and his family. He was safe and well. He did not want to make contact with any of us. If we tried, he threatened to cut off all ties, and disappear for good.' Shahida paused, thinking back. 'It broke my heart. It made me angry. But I had no choice but to respect his decision, and be patient. I wanted to catch the next plane to Pakistan and plead with him to return. I wanted to tell everyone that he was safe, but I wouldn't have had answers to any of their questions. I still do not have an answer as to why he walked away from everything here: a good life, friends, family… a child. A tiny part of me was also afraid that he had somehow become brainwashed; radicalised by one of the jihadi groups. If he had, how would it affect us? The shame, the guilt, and the accusations that we would have to endure… Until I knew the answers, it was best to keep his whereabouts to myself. It was too late to save Kalyani anyway.'

'Wouldn't put it past him!' Nimmi spat.

Shahida ignored her. 'Ashraf was not as patient. He was angry at Rafik's insolence. He blamed me for bad parenting – for spoiling him from the day he was born. "I will go and drag him back all the way," he said. He flew over to Pakistan, stayed in my brother's house in Peshawar, trying to coax Rafik to return. But the writing on the wall was clear. Rafik refused to meet him or speak to him. He even went to Sulaiman Kaka's place, but Rafik was away at the time. He has set up an IT business and travels a lot. Sulaiman Kaka, concerned at how upset Ashraf was, persuaded Rafik to contact his father.

Rafik sent a message to say he is sorry, and that he will contact us when he is ready. He needed some more time. Finally, Ashraf gave up and returned home.' Shahida's eyes filled with tears. 'Today, Ashraf is a broken man. I try to be strong, to try and understand. But he won't talk about it. He won't acknowledge that he had failed to bring up a child to respect his parents, and honour his promises. I know it is more than that. Ashraf loved his son more than anything else in this world. We both did. It is inconceivable that Rafik did not love us enough to stay.'

In the face of Shahida's distress, Nimmi felt her own eyes sting with tears. She reached forwards and touched Shahida's hands briefly. 'Now, Kalyani is talking of going there. What use is that to anyone? If Rafik did not meet his dad, why would he meet her?'

Shahida sniffed. 'I do not know. I did not ask her to go to him. But I did not discourage her when she said she wanted to. I told myself that Rafik's love for her was stronger; different from the love for his dad. She might persuade him to talk to her… even come back to the life he left.'

Nimmi threw her hands up in the air with frustration. 'You only thought about your son. And I don't blame you for that. But… did you not think that Kalyani is vulnerable? She is a mentally unstable, young girl. Did you not think how challenging it would be physically and mentally for her to pursue this plan?'

'I did not think about the "where" and the "how". I just thought it would be worth a try. Wouldn't you, if it was your child?'

God forbid that a child of mine behaves like yours! Rafik is a pathetic example of a human being.

Kiran was getting fractious. He was arching his back and whinging.

'He needs his milk and his nap,' said Nimmi, excusing herself. A look of longing crossed Shahida's face. But she didn't ask if she could hold her grandchild, and Nimmi didn't offer.

Nimmi walked home with a heavy heart, which ached for herself, her daughter and the woman who now sat desolately in her kitchen.

Chapter 23

Amanda Blick blinked at them behind her glasses, her blue dress complementing the colour of her eyes. If she was overwhelmed by all three of them and a babbling baby, she did not show it. As usual, she jotted down notes on lined hospital paper. She stopped now, intrigued by what the Sinha family was requesting.

'Let me get this right. You want her sectioned?'

The family exchanged looks, as if to confirm the plan, and then nodded.

'Why? I just discussed with you as to how well she has recovered. It is as if she suddenly decided to make an effort to get better. She is starting to show an interest in the world around her. She has been enthusiastic about her rehabilitation. I see no reason to section her. In fact, we will be planning her discharge home.'

'She is plotting something.'

'Plotting something?'

'She is still obsessed with her ex-boyfriend – the one who ditched her.'

'Obsessed?'

Nimmi wished the doctor wouldn't repeat everything they were saying. She sighed. 'Last week, she told me she wanted to find him, to ask why he walked away.'

Dr Blick made a gesture of understanding. 'Ah! We did discuss that. She is looking for closure. The way I see it, she has set herself a goal to work up to, and this is helping with the healing process.'

'Won't it send her back into depression, if he rejects her again?' Minna asked.

'It might do, but this time, she is prepared for it. This time, she is armed and forewarned.'

'But she is planning to travel to Pakistan to meet Rafik.'

'Oh?' Dr Blick was signing reports. 'If you are worried about her health during the travel, we can provide you copies of her relevant medical records and the prescriptions for medication. Ideally, of course, it would be better if she travelled with someone who knows her medical condition.'

'But you don't understand, doctor. Pakistan is not a safe place for her. She has not really travelled in that sort of place. Not like... those backpackers. She could get shot or kidnapped. She does not understand the danger she could be in. Which means she is not thinking straight. She is a danger to herself.' Nimmi spoke rapidly, her words running into each other.

Dr Blick knew people from Pakistan, her colleagues, who regularly visited relatives there. They had come back relaxed and happy. She felt the Sinhas' fears were unnecessarily exaggerated.

'I understand your anxieties for your daughter's safety, but from our assessment of her mental state, she is compos mentis. She is lucidly and clearly able to think through her decisions. We have no reason to keep her here, let alone section her. She is fit to be discharged.'

'What about the bonding thing? The mother and baby unit?' Shekar asked.

Dr Blick sighed. 'We have a long waiting list for these places. Considering your daughter is living with you, in a supportive environment, we can address bonding issues in the community. I will arrange for her to be seen by us regularly.'

'She may not attend. Like before,' Nimmi warned.

Dr Blick sighed some more. 'Well, you are well aware that if that happens, Social Care will have to be informed. I don't think any of us wants that.'

Nimmi fidgeted, ready to launch into another tirade. Shekar laid a restraining hand on her arm. There was nothing more to achieve. Kalyani was fit for discharge, and fit to travel. Dr Blick was not going to offer them tips on how to backpack safely.

*

At the end of June, on a rainy summer's day, three months since she was taken away by the paramedics, Kalyani arrived home in the back of her dad's Volvo, aware that throughout the journey, her mother was anxiously watching her through the vanity mirror on the sun visor. For the first half of the way home, Nimmi had tried to regale her with the changes that had happened to the neighbourhood in her absence.

But Kalyani did not want to know. Outside was the street without Raffa. He would not squeeze into her little, red Clio on Saturday mornings any more. She would no longer hear his voice, powerful and persuasive, over the phone. There was only sadness and silence awaiting her. Kalyani nodded and replied in a monotone, all the while wishing her parents would leave her alone. Nimmi and Shekar exchanged worried glances.

The day before, Shekar had refused to give Nimmi permission to install locks outside Kalyani's door. If Nimmi wished to stand guard outside the door, she could go ahead, as long as she did not expect him to take turns; he made it clear that he would not be sacrificing his sleep for that. He had brought his kids up with freedom and common sense; they were welcome to come and discuss anything openly with him. If Kalyani was mad enough, no pun intended, to creep out of her room and run away, he wouldn't stop her with locks and chains.

'We will discuss your travel plans in a controlled and peaceful way,' he reassured Kalyani.

'Once you find your feet,' Nimmi agreed, hoping it would be a long time before she did.

*

Over the next few days, Nimmi did everything possible to make her daughter feel welcome and comfortable. She cooked her favourite meals, cleaned her room, did her laundry, left glossy magazines and the TV guide on the coffee table, tried hard not to force the baby on to her. She made sure that Kalyani took her prescribed medication by keeping count of the number of pills in the bottle; kept inspecting her kitchen drawers to ensure that none of the sharp knives or breakable objects was missing. She checked her daughter's room regularly, looking out for anything that would suggest regression. When they were together, she kept up an inane chatter, treading on eggshells to avoid controversial topics; all the while, hoping and praying that Kalyani would get too comfortable to want to traipse around the globe in pursuit of Raffa.

For her part, Kalyani did not shut herself up in her room. She came down for her meals, responded to her parents' questions, keeping her answers short and to the point. She volunteered help with chores, and spent time with her son. She attended fortnightly appointments with her shrink, who was pleased with her progress. She enrolled herself into courses recommended by them to enable bonding with her child.

Under Nimmi's watchful eye, she held her son in her arms, took him for short walks down the street, and helped with his care, but they both knew something was lacking. They were both jittery, trying not to overstep the mark, and relieved when Kalyani handed her son over and retreated to her room.

One day, as they sat in the garden, the sun throwing warm, dappled shadows on the stone patio, an angel flew overhead, scattering some long overdue blessings, and Nimmi's patience finally paid off.

Kiran, in the middle of his eighth month, discovered that his feet were not just for chewing. He crawled up to a low chair, trying to work out if he could stand on his feet. He pulled himself up, then realising what he had done, lost his confidence and his balance and plopped back to the floor, scraping his cheek on the chair leg on the way down. His large eyes registered shock; he stuffed a plump finger into his mouth, screwed up his face and burst into tears. His mother leapt out of her chair to scoop him up, her maternal instinct rising like a phoenix out of the ashes. Her soothing voice smoothed out the creases in her baby's face. She blew a raspberry at him, and he responded first with an uncertain smile, which brought dimples on his ample cheeks, followed by a single peal of laughter. It made her laugh too and blow more raspberries. Soon, the two of them were giggling like drunken teenagers.

In a fit of emotion, Kalyani grabbed her son and held him to her bosom. The warmth from his tiny body melted the ice in her heart, her chest swelled, her throat went into spasm, and the tears welled up and out like a fountain that soon turned into a wailing waterfall. She wailed and rocked so hysterically that it frightened her baby, who joined in. Startled, Nimmi ran to them and hugged them tight, making comforting noises. When finally, Kalyani calmed down, her mother brought her some water.

'What's wrong, sweetie? Did you take your pills this morning? Do you want me to call the doctor?'

Kalyani shook her head. 'I am alright.' She hiccupped and sobbed. 'I wish these tears... came when Raffa left me stranded. Jilted. The tears are also for the time I have lost, for missing out on the most important parts of my son's life, and for putting you and Dad, and Minna through all the heartache. I... am sorry... so very sorry.'

Nimmi hugged her again, kissing her head, this time in gratitude that the storm clouds had at last parted and the fog had rolled over the hills. Her daughter was finally on the mend.

But wait: the thunder lingered, growling ominously from somewhere over the horizon. Kalyani was still talking. 'I cannot waste any more time. I need to live again. I mean... not like a zombie. I have my whole life ahead of me and I want to enjoy every minute. But this thing is not letting me. This unresolved mystery, the big question stands in between me and the door to freedom. I need an answer, Mum. I have to go to him. Only then can I move on.'

'Him?' Nimmi's voice quaked. She knew that Kalyani was talking about Rafik, but she didn't want to accept it.

'Raffa. I need to hear it from him. Why he left like he did.'

'What makes you think he will see you? He did not wish to see his dad, you know.'

'Nothing ventured. Nothing gained. Mummy, if I do not go, I will never know!'

Nimmi felt ice in her veins. The fog had not disappeared completely: it was only hiding in the valleys. The wolves in her daughter's brain would return at night to bay at the moon, until she donned her armour and went to battle. But would Kalyani survive? Would she return in one piece, her body and soul intact?

*

Despite her wishes, Nimmi had not managed to stay awake at night to stand guard outside her daughter's door. After a long and hectic day, all she wanted to do was to crawl into bed, and sleep like the dead. On the first few nights, she got up a few times, and paused outside Kalyani's bedroom door, listening for the reassuring sounds that told her she hadn't run away: the creaking of her bed and her talking in her sleep. Her daughter had always talked in her sleep; sometimes, it sounded as if she was urging someone to win a race, 'Go! Go!' Or protesting, 'No, please no!' Or fighting, 'Give it back!' Other times, it was just incoherent mumbling.

Over the weeks, relieved her daughter was not showing signs of wanting to escape, she had relaxed her vigil. That night though, every centimetre of her body begged for her to sleep and heal. Kalyani's words kept revolving in her brain, making her toss and turn, When she did nod off, nightmares of blood, gore, silhouettes of masked men of evil intent, all turning into the vile face of Rafik, jolted her awake, and compelled her to check on her daughter. Frustrated with his wife's perambulations, Shekar carried his pillow to Minna's empty room and spent the rest of the night on her bed. As a result, he woke up like the proverbial daisy, thinking to himself that he could get used to sleeping on his own, while his wife woke up in a foul temper, reflected in the bare breakfast table. Only the baby was being fed that morning.

'Coffee?' he offered. 'Bad night?' he ventured, sipping the brew. 'I made yours extra strong.' He indicated the steaming mug on the counter.

Nimmi glanced at the cup, between spoonfuls of baby goo. 'Not my cup,' she complained.

'Oh? Sorry. Which is your cup? The one that says "Happy Days"? Or the perky pink one with white daisies that says "Good Morning"?'

No response.

Shekar decided that his wife did not deserve a cup saying 'Happy Days', and chose the pink one. He tried to transfer the hot coffee into it, spilling it in the process. He cursed, losing his patience.

'Leave it!' his wife growled. Cold shower, crumpled shirt, continental style breakfast of Cheerios... the day was already ruined. Thank God, he could run away to his office and hide behind the piles of paperwork. But not before his wife told him.

'We have guests for dinner tonight. 7p.m. sharp.' Her tone said *be here, or else.*

'Hope you turn into a princess before then,' Shekar muttered as he let himself out.

Nimmi felt tired and tearful. She just wanted to crawl back into bed and sleep for a hundred years, and then wake up to Prince Charming. She was disappointed that despite all that careful planning, and TLC, Kalyani was still bent on chasing her delusions, and no one but Nimmi appeared to be worried about it. She was disgusted with herself for lying flat on the floor and allowing people to wipe their lazy feet on her. She had given her daughter too much time to sit in comfort and dream about a happy reunion with her lover. From now on, Kalyani would pick up her own laundry, wash up, and start caring for her baby son, all by herself.

Sometime in the early hours of the morning, before leaving her room, Nimmi had arrived at another decision. If her daughter was hell bent on chasing after the runaway groom, there was no point trying to stop her. But she wasn't going to do it on a wing and a prayer. They would meticulously plan every step of the trip together. They would ensure her safe return – with or without Rafik. And for that, they needed Shahida's help. So the Mahmoods were coming to dinner tonight. They would dine on curry and poppadums from the Punjabi Cuisine takeaway menu. She was going to follow her husband's advice to turn into a princess before the guests arrived.

When Kalyani traipsed downstairs, later that morning, she was humming a happy tune. She looked around for breakfast, and not finding any, pointed to the now cold, strong coffee that Shekar had made earlier.

'Is this for me?' she asked.

Nimmi shrugged. 'Have it if you want.'

Kalyani sipped it, made a face. She scooped a spoonful of sugar into it and bunged it into the microwave.

'Any plans?'

'My only plan is to go back to bed. I have a pounding headache,' her mother replied.

'Oh! OK. Do you want some paracetamol?'

'Yes please. In the left-hand drawer.'

Kalyani rummaged through the junk and found some. She brought them to her mother and handed her the coffee. 'Too strong for me. I think you need it more than me.'

'We have guests for dinner tonight. I have ordered a takeaway.' Nimmi chased the pain killers down with the coffee, wincing as the hot liquid stung her. 'Can you look after the baby, while I have a little nap?'

'Ok—aay.' Kalyani was hesitant, but her mother was beyond caring.

With her mother gone, Kalyani looked around, lost. What was she supposed to do?

She carried her bowl of cornflakes to the table and sat watching her son practise his 'pulling to stand' technique, and every time he succeeded, he looked at his mother with a grin, inviting her to applaud. He bounced up and down with joy, his curly, black hair bobbing around his head, when she did. He was still in his onesie, food stuck in his hair, clothes and lips.

'It is just you and me today.' She reverted to baby talk, as she knelt beside him, shaking her head to make her hair swish around her face. He giggled at her, and she did it again. He put out a chubby fist and yanked at her hair. 'I know it is a mess. We need a makeover, don't we? Time to get ready for Daddy.'

Chapter 24

Nimmi would have been mortified to find that she had actually slept though the sounds of Kalyani getting herself and her son ready, putting him in his buggy, reaching for her car keys and driving away in her Clio. Kalyani, on the other hand, was excited, and took pride in getting her son into the bath with her, splashing the water and sending the yellow plastic ducks whirling around, choosing his clothes from the washed laundry, packing his bag with a bottle of milk and a jar of baby food. The bag already had a change of clothes, a couple of nappies, wipes, and a clean bib. Good, old Mummy. So organised, she thought. She helped herself to money from her mother's purse, strapped him into his buggy, and let herself out of the house.

So, the house was quiet, too quiet, when Nimmi woke up. The digital clock on the bedside table said 14:06 in disjointed red dashes. She had slept for four hours. The deepest, longest nap she had had for a very long time. She lay there for a few minutes, getting her bearings.

14:07: Her headache had gone; she had definitely needed that lie down.

14:08: She had a dinner to organise. A light tidy up downstairs; rinse the new plates from IKEA.

14:09: She would wear her tie-dye tunic or the bright, yellow one that went well with her complexion.

14:10: She needed a long soak. But she had to give Kiran a bath too. She had to give him his lunch… *Shite!* It was way past his lunchtime. She had left him alone, with his mother! A mother who was planning to run away! She clambered out of bed in a hurry, listening for noises from downstairs;

> safe, mundane sounds of daily living. She could hear nothing. Her heart urged her to run down, screeching their names, but her brain said walk. She walked down. No one downstairs.

The house leered at her. The front door was locked as well as the back door. Were they upstairs, having a nap like she had done? She walked up the stairs and opened the bedroom door. The bed was empty, the bed covers rolled to the foot of the bed. The bathroom? They must be having a bath… or drowning. Flashes of Kalyani in a blood-stained bath, her hair floating like seaweed, rose into her mind. She rushed to the bathroom, and throwing caution to the wind, threw the door open. Please let them be there, blowing bubbles and playing with the plastic ducks. The bath was empty, the yellow ducks lined up on the windowsill, their red beaks pointing east.

'Kals! Kalyani!' Her voice was piercing, tremulous. In mild panic, she ran down to the garden to peer behind the rhododendrons, ran up to check Minna's room, and ran down again to see if Kiran's buggy was there. Negative.

Deep breath, she told herself – they must have gone for a walk. She looked up at the key stand. The spare house keys strung onto a metal wire and her own set on the 'Love you Mum' keychain remained. Shekar had taken his and Kalyani's car key was missing. Her heart raced, skipped and thudded. Back up in Kalyani's room, relief washed over her, as she found the usual pile of clothes strewn over the floor and in her wardrobe, and the suitcase still wrapped in dustsheets. The bay window in the room overlooked the rows of cars parked on both sides of the two-way street; the absent Clio stood out like a missing tooth in a child's mouth.

Where did she go? How long has she been gone?

The car had more than half a tank of petrol, after Minna had used it over the weekend. Enough gas for a getaway. Enough time to reach Heathrow. Another thought surfaced. Was she even allowed to drive when taking her pills? Nimmi felt weak, as if a slow strain of flu was taking over her body. With trembling fingers, she rang Kalyani's phone, sighing as it went into the answerphone. She sent her a text: 'Where are you?'

No reply in five minutes.

No reply in twenty minutes.

Why oh why had she slept for so long? What should she do? Wait or act? Ring Shekar at his office? Ring Minna during her lecture? Ring the police? When should she start ringing the hospitals to enquire if a mad woman and her baby were brought in? Only the fact that they would laugh at her paranoia prevented her.

She decided to wait for another hour; a long hour spent clearing the breakfast dishes, rinsing the IKEA dinner plates, hoovering, and plumping up the cushions, all the while straining to hear the Clio's purr, and jumping out of her skin every time a car door slammed. Finally, just as she thought she couldn't take it anymore, another car door slammed outside, the fourth one so far, and this time, thankfully, footsteps trod up the path, keys rattled in the door, and Kalyani walked in with her son.

'Hi Mum. Had a good sleep?'

Nimmi's blood pressure plummeted with relief, and rose again as it turned to anger. Her first instinct was to snatch up her grandson and check him to see if he was intact, and then shake her daughter until she unravelled.

'Where did you go? I turn my back for two seconds and you cause trouble. What am I supposed to think?' She stopped shouting when she noticed the change in her daughter. Kalyani was glowing. Her face looked fresh and pretty; her eyebrows were threaded, her hair trimmed and layered, and she had had her nails done.

She was wearing a pretty dress with a floral print that showed off her curves. Her son lay content, in his buggy, sucking his thumb.

'Ta da! Do you like it?' Kalyani gave a twirl.

'Nice. You do realise you gave me a shock? I did not know where you went!'

'Relax. We had a fantastic time, didn't we?' Kalyani shook her hair at the baby, who giggled and babbled. Kiran had traces of an orange meal from the baby jar around his mouth and on his bib, and an empty milk bottle lay beside him on the buggy. He had been taken care of.

Nimmi begrudgingly nodded her approval at her daughter. 'Well done! You do look great! But are you permitted to drive?'

'No one told me I couldn't. It felt good. Now that I know what I am doing, I feel... rejuvenated. How do you feel?'

'Much better. I needed that sleep. Thanks for looking after Kiran.'

'Don't be silly, Mum, he is my son. Now do you mind if I have a nap?'

Shekar was late, by design. By the time he walked in, the others were sat around the table, sipping their soft drinks, chosen in deference to the Mahmoods' teetotaller lifestyle.

The takeaway arrived just as he was about to close the door. He signed for it and brought the oil-stained, brown paper bags to the dining table, avoiding eye contact with Nimmi, who was shooting imaginary daggers at him for being late.

He nodded in greeting at the rest of them, sitting in various stages of discomfort around the table. Minna had been summoned from her university and Romy had innocuously wandered in to say hello to Kals, and was trapped. Nimmi had decided he would play the role of a peacekeeper, if necessary.

'Drink, anyone?' Shekar offered. The girls and Ashraf turned down the offer, and Shekar poured himself and Romy a stiff cognac. 'Food smells great!' he remarked, as he handed the glass to Romy.

'Can I top up your juice or water?' he asked Ashraf and Shahida.

Both declined.

Minna and her mother busied themselves with opening the takeaway containers and distributing the oily saturates onto Nimmi's white, ceramic plates and bowls. Kalyani played with her son's pink toes, oblivious. Romesh was the only one making polite conversation. Shekar took his drink upstairs, while he changed into something more comfortable. He could almost hear his wife warning him not to dawdle.

Exactly eight minutes later, the families dipped their bread into the spicy curries, and broke poppadums. Nimmi had prepared a lettuce and sweetcorn salad, which was quickly passed around the table to provide the requisite antioxidants. Either the people around the table had starved themselves all day, or they were trying to hasten their departure, because very soon, the foil containers were empty. After unenthusiastically offering them ice cream and coffee, Nimmi got on with the real reason for the meeting.

'OK. There is no point pretending that everything is back to normal, because it isn't. Kalyani is still keen to go and meet with Rafik. I don't think that is going to go away.' She now looked at her older daughter. 'Is it?'

Kalyani squared her shoulders and tossed her hair back. 'No...' softly, then louder, perhaps a touch too loud, 'Yes. I have decided that we should meet with Raffa.'

Shekar looked up startled. 'Hang on! Who is "we"?'

'Me and Kiran.'

Several voices were raised in protest. 'No blooming way!' cried Nimmi.

'What?' cried Shekar.

'Are you mad?' cried Minna, regretting her choice of words almost immediately.

'That is no place for a little baby,' said Shahida.

Ashraf got up, desperate for a cigarette, but Shahida pulled him back.

'But… People over there have babies too. Surely they survive,' Kalyani fought back.

'Look. Let us get some facts right. You want to make a foolhardy trip into terr… land, it is up to you. The baby stays here.' Nimmi had nearly said 'terrorist land'. If Shahida deduced it, she did not react.

Nimmi held the defiant gaze of her daughter. 'I mean it. I will not hesitate to bring the authorities in to safeguard the baby.' She sighed with relief when the younger woman dropped her gaze and accepted defeat.

Nimmi turned to the tense group around the table. 'I am asking this, because it needs to be asked. Is there any way we can avoid Kalyani travelling so far?'

'Like what?'

'Well. How about Rafik and her meeting somewhere nearer and safer – on neutral ground?'

Shahida squirmed and her seat squeaked. Ashraf came to her rescue.

'Not going to happen. My son… refuses to meet with any of us. Don't ask me why!'

Shekar shot him an empathetic glance and hoped Nimmi did not have a go at the man.

'So… you are not even sure he will agree to meet with Kals?' Minna shot her question before her mother could react to Ashraf.

'We… don't know that he will. We can only try,' Ashraf conceded.

'He will,' Kalyani affirmed, in a quiet but assertive voice. 'I know he will.'

Nimmi suddenly felt that too. Rafik would agree to meet with Kalyani, if not because he still held a torch for her, but because his ego would not allow him to hide away from her questions. He would not wish to be seen as someone who could not justify his actions, especially to his former lover. But she needed some more assurance, before allowing her daughter to go on a reckless chase.

Shahida jumped into the fray. 'Look. The past is done. I cannot undo it. What we should concentrate on is how to get the girl there and bring her back safely.'

The girl has a name, thought Kalyani grumpily.

The group around the table agreed to Shahida's proposal. They turned towards her, waiting for her to go on. Shahida listed the facts.

'Rafik is staying with one of my distant relatives, Sulaiman Kaka, in a village near Muzaffarabad. He travels away frequently for his work. Muzaffarabad is a few hours' travel from Peshawar by road. My brother, Alam, and his family live in Peshawar, our family home.'

'Where are all these places?' Minna asked.

Romesh, who had been a silent spectator, fished out his laptop from its bag. Romy and his laptop were seldom apart. Shekar and Minna pranced around, clearing a space for the laptop, and the group adjusted their chairs to face the screen. Soon, the map of Pakistan flashed up. Wikipedia, Google Maps, and Ashraf provided them with abundant information. Peshawar was an ancient capital city, known for its culture, economy, universities, and the Taliban.

'It is easy to fly to Peshawar from here, with connecting flights from the Middle East. Muzaffarabad is somewhere in the middle of the route between Peshawar and Chitral.' Ashraf traced his finger over the map. 'You can either take the coach to Muzaffarabad from Peshawar or fly to Chitral Airport and travel down. Roughly five hours' travel either way. From Muzaffarabad, there are local buses to Sulaiman Kaka's village. The small village is tucked away amongst the hills, a scenic place. It could easily be a tourist attraction if it was more accessible.'

'Local buses!' cried Nimmi. 'Kalyani does not know the language. How on earth is she supposed to get the right one?'

'I am sure Alam will arrange someone to pick her up,' Shahida said.

'Why can't this someone be Raffa? He should take some responsibility,' Minna said.

Shahida made a frustrated noise and flapped her hand. 'Look, I am trying my best. I cannot answer everything from here. Rafik is not easy to contact due to poor phone and Internet access. Don't ask me why or what he is doing in such a place. I do not know.'

Nimmi gulped down her opinion with a mouthful of water, but Minna, who sat next to her, heard her utter the word 'terrorism'.

Kalyani, stuck in her own world, thought only of meeting up with Raffa. The details of the journey were proving to be tedious. Surely, Raffa would arrange for her to be safe. *How much harder can it be than travelling in England anyway?*

'How safe is it?' Nimmi was continuing her interrogation.

'The road to Chitral is a national highway. Well maintained. The roads to the village itself may not be good, but are passable in good weather,' Ashraf replied.

'Kalyani can stay with my brother, Alam, in Peshawar. He will make all the arrangements for her to travel to the village. Alam is in a top position in the Peshawar government. He has a lot of political contacts too. He will keep the girl safe,' Shahida said. 'In fact, I will personally guarantee that my brother will do everything in his power to keep her safe.'

Nimmi did not have a lot of confidence in Shahida's assurance. But she had the common sense to realise that they had no other choice. She could take it or leave it.

For the next hour, the group planned the trip. They were on a tight schedule. If Kalyani wanted to travel that year, she had to do it before the weather turned cold and the roads up in the hills become icy and dangerous. The minimum time required would be two nights in Peshawar, and one night with Rafik in his village, before returning to Peshawar and heading home. Everybody agreed that the end of August would be perfect – it would leave them enough time to process visas, and avoid inclement weather in the hills.

August was also the first anniversary of Kalyani being jilted. If anyone other than Kalyani realised this, they did not voice it.

All that remained was to book the tickets. Two tickets.

'Two?' Kalyani queried.

'Yes, you didn't think I was going to let you travel alone, did you?' Nimmi glared at her.

Shekar started, 'You are going with her? You know nothing about travelling! You get lost on the way to the town centre!' That was an exaggeration, but it was true that Nimmi was hopeless at directions.

'So? What do you suggest? Can you go?'

Shekar clearly hadn't considered this part of the plan. August was a time when a lot of his colleagues went away on a much deserved holiday. Shekar was covering for them, and it would be bad form for him to take time off, what with back-to-back meetings and deadlines. Minna? No one voted for her. The Sinhas were not about to sacrifice both their daughters.

'I will go.' They all turned towards Romy. 'I mean, I *can* go.'

Romesh worked freelance, which meant he could be flexible, as long as a Wi-Fi connection was available. 'I sort of wanted to visit that ancient city of Peshawar someday.'

Nimmi hesitated. Romesh was a close family friend. She had known him since he was knee high. He was a good lad. But was it wise to send Kalyani off with an unrelated man, to meet with a nearly related one?

Shahida's frown deepened, but Kalyani did not care. 'I am happy with that,' she said. Romy's easy going and non-judgemental attitude would make him an ideal travel buddy.

'It is decided, then. Romy will go with Kals.' Shekar rubbed his hands together, wishing that the visitors would hurry up and leave. No doubt, there will be many more conversations to fine tune the plan, but for now, he wanted to reclaim his lounge.

Nimmi bade the Mahmoods goodbye, thinking to herself that they were holding a tiger by its tail.

Momentarily, Kals and Romy found themselves alone in the lounge. 'Hope you have been taking notes, Romy. All those names of strange places make me want to go to sleep.'

'Thank your stars, Kals, that I love travelling. I can already think of writing a travelogue, with gorgeous photographs.'

'You don't mind, do you? I mean, I don't want to force you to drop everything for me.'

'For you, Kals, I would drop a lot more.'

Kals blushed. She knew Romy was not joking.

'Even if it means reuniting you with Raffa,' Romy thought sadly, as he packed his laptop away.

Part 2

Chapter 1

The house in Peshawar that the driver brought her to took Kalyani's breath away. It was big, it was beautiful, it was antiquated. It stretched on either side of a gabled porch. To arrive at its gates, the driver had skilfully negotiated a path through the narrow roads of the old town of Peshawar, littered with craters, avid shoppers, motor vehicles of various shapes and sizes, and ones without a motor – bicycles and carts laden with goods. The residential buildings lining the narrow roads had scalloped arches over doors and the windows opened out onto balconies adorned with lacy fretwork. *Havelis*, the driver called them; most were in a state of dilapidation, and appeared to lean on each other for support.

Earlier, when she stepped out of the air-conditioned airport with her luggage, the oven-like heat rushed at her, dust scratched her throat and eyes, and noise erupted all around her. Overwhelmed, she joined the exodus of people moving towards the exit. She soon learnt to use the trolley to plough through the crowds, marvelling at how deftly the individuals in her path escaped being run over. Relief flooded over her when she spotted Alam's driver standing in the aisle, holding up a placard with 'Alam' written on it.

'Sahib?' he enquired, looking past her for Romy. Kalyani shook her head. Romy was not with her. The driver, with a pragmatic nod of his head, took control of her trolley, and she scurried behind him like a panicked rodent as he led her to the car.

Sahib. Romy would have been chuffed to hear himself being called a sahib. Their travel had stopped being uneventful at the Middle Eastern transit airport. While she whizzed through without any problems, Romy was scrutinised by a very suspicious official. Things escalated when they found some equipment used for reporting in his hand baggage. The official held the device and the laptop up and requested an explanation.

'I carry it everywhere. I am a journalist,' Romy protested. It was the wrong thing to say, especially when he did not have any papers to prove this, because he was on holiday. Another official arrived, and Romy and his baggage were politely but firmly whisked away.

Two hours later, barely minutes before boarding the connecting flight, Romy had called her on her mobile. It was obvious that he was not alone. 'Kals. Listen,' he had said, cutting through her frantic jabber. 'There is some confusion here. The authorities want to check ID, the rest of my luggage etc. I won't be able to board the connecting flight until they have sorted it. You have to get the flight and go ahead. I had rather you went to Peshawar and stayed amongst friends, and not in the airport. I will keep you informed. And don't worry.'

Out of her depth, and at a loss as to how she could help, she called her dad. Shekar waited for her to calm down and agreed with Romy's advice. 'You cannot do much by staying at the airport. I will see what I can do, but you should carry on as planned. These things happen. Don't worry.'

Nimmi called later, very worried. Kalyani ended up reassuring her in the few minutes they had, before she had to switch her phone off on the flight. She texted Nimmi from the car to say she had been picked up, and was on the way to Alam's house.

The driver pulled up at the tall, imposing iron gates of Alam's house. He honked impatiently and muttered abuse at the stooped watchman in uniform, when he finally opened the gates. As the gates closed behind them, the hustle and bustle of the streets receded; she was transported into an oasis of greenery surrounding the grand house. The tiled path, flanked by symmetrically planted flower beds and lush lawn, led her to the ornate front door, on either side of which, decorative palms in massive earthenware pots and rattan chairs were arranged.

She almost expected the door to be opened by a butler in uniform. Instead, the driver urged her to ring the doorbell, while he collected her bags. When there was no response, he tucked the bags under one arm and rang the bell a few more times with the other. Kalyani could hear its shrill sound, echoing inside the house. Finally, with a tinkling sound of bells, the door opened to reveal a tiny servant girl, wearing a neon-green veil, who ardently delivered a lecture on the virtue of patience to the driver, which did not go down very well with him. After a short skirmish of wills, they appeared to remember her existence and ushered her in.

Kalyani blinked to adjust to the comparative darkness inside. Then, she blinked some more as she took in the splendour of its interior. Pink-tinged marble floors and pillars, with bluish veins, surrounded a sunken courtyard, in the middle of which stood an indoor fountain – dry at that time of the day. Kalyani's eyes were drawn to the domed and tinted glass roof high above the fountain. The first storey of the house was built as a mezzanine, looking down at the central courtyard from all sides. Almost as if the architect had built a solid house, and then cored a square chunk out of its middle, and replaced it with the courtyard and the fountain.

The servant gestured for her to enter the living room, which was equally impressive. Tasselled, silk curtains, held strategically aside with jewelled bands, majestic, gilt sofas, covered with dark velvet, around a marble coffee table, gold-framed paintings and portraits of important-looking people, made her feel like she was visiting royalty. She wondered if she would be expected to bow to Alam's family.

All of a sudden, the silence was broken by excited speech. Three veiled women and a teenage girl hurried in, talking all at once. One of them stepped forward smiling, and introduced herself as Begum Alam. 'You can call me Fawzia,' she said, before introducing the others – her mother, Nanima, her daughter, Aliya, and her sister-in-law, Hamida. They greeted her warmly with *Asalam-alaikum*.

Kalyani was invited to sit, and the ladies quickly arranged themselves around her; tea was ordered, and questions tumbled out from all sides. How was the flight? Had her baggage arrived safely in one piece? How was the food? Was she hungry? Praise to Allah for keeping her safe. What was the weather like in England? How are Shahida and her family? Was Shahida eating better? She was always too thin. All this affair with Rafik... Not good. May Allah give her strength to bear it. And to you too. Kalyani nodded or shook her head and smiled through the conversation, barely answering one question before another was shot at her.

They had already heard about Romesh from Shahida, who had rung them. Fawzia assured her that Alam was already on the case, and was contacting people with connections, and Shekar had contacted the Embassy. 'Allah willing, he will join us soon.'

'Those authorities are very strict. Once their suspicion is raised, they are like a dog looking for a bone,' Hamida warned, shaking her head. Whereas Fawzia and her mother had a pleasant, welcoming face, and a warm smile, Hamida's closely-set features and her dark, piercing eyes, made her look less endearing.

As the maid served tea, and the ladies fussed over how they wanted their brew, she excused herself and dragged in the suitcase with the gifts that Shahida had sent. Excited exclamations filled the air. Chocolates, perfumes and trinkets were all met with gratitude to Allah. Aliya squealed with delighted as she unpacked her bracelet.

'Aliya loves jewellery – trinkets to wear to school.' Her mother smiled her approval.

'College now, Ammi! Not school!' Aliya protested.

Conversation revolved around Aliya's college for a short while. Kalyani sipped her second cup of the sweet and minty tea, which she had accepted out of politeness, and picked up the courage to decline the offer of yet another refill. At last, they seemed to have run out of topics.

'Dinner will be ready in about an hour. Would you like to rest?' Fawzia asked. Aliya jumped up, keen to show Kalyani to her room.

The maid brought her bags up. In comparison to the grandeur downstairs, her room seemed almost stark. The floor was still made of marble, and the bed covers were silk. Elegant, but simple, table lamps were placed on either side of the bed, and a fan with four wings dangled from the ceiling. A mahogany wardrobe stood against one wall.

Young Aliya seemed to have no intention of leaving. She made herself comfortable at the foot of the bed. 'Ammi said if you sleep now, you would find it difficult to sleep at night. Besides, I was hoping to hear everything about London.'

'London or England?'

'I mean England. Somehow, we think London is England,' Aliya giggled. 'But I have been looking at the map. I know where Shahida aunty and you live.'

Kalyani smiled at the eagerness on her pretty face. 'Have you visited England?' she asked.

The girl sighed. 'I would like to come to England to study. Do my MBA. But first, I must get into university here. I want to be a business woman. Open my own chain of boutiques. Daddy says I can sell ice to the Eskimos.'

All Kalyani had to do was nod and grunt, as Aliya kept up her prattle. Her enthusiasm and simple approach to life was refreshing.

It seemed that Aliya had already made plans to entertain her visitor the next day, and resting was not on the agenda.

'We are taking you shopping. Unless you want to do something else.' Aliya listed the tourist spots, but it was clear she herself was not interested in them.

'Shopping sounds good!' Kalyani agreed, and Aliya's face lit up.

Dinner that night was a blur. Fawzia and Aliya made her feel at ease. The food was delicious and plentiful and spicy. However, Fawzia apologised for the simple meal. 'We thought you wouldn't be able to eat much, what with the jet lag and everything.' Kalyani assured her that there were more dishes than she was used to back home. She wondered if Alam Sahib was due to join them later.

'Oh, Daddy is always busy. He is always in one meeting or the other,' Aliya replied. Hamida's husband was also travelling.

'They will all be here tomorrow,' Fawzia promised. 'We will have a party.'

After dinner, Kalyani requested Fawzia's permission to phone her parents. Fawzia led her into another room, tucked into the western corner of the corridor running around the fountain. 'Alamji's den,' she teased.

The décor here was different – westernised. Carpeted floor, flock wallpaper, furniture imported from England, deep, comfortable, leather sofas, a massive polished oak desk, with a silver snuff box and a green bankers' lamp. The den obviously doubled up as an office. On the desk perched a cream-coloured retro phone with an old-fashioned dial.

'I can dial Shahida's number for you. I might have a brief chat with her too.' Fawzia fished out an old-fashioned phone book, with entries made by hand with ink, in alphabetical order.

From the way Fawzia greeted Shahida, it was obvious that the two of them got on very well, and they would have had a good, old natter if Kalyani was not fidgeting nearby. After thanking Shahida for her thoughtful gifts, Fawzia handed the phone to Kalyani.

Shahida didn't say much, but what she said, in a low voice, was disconcerting. 'Fawzia… does not know about the… baby. Only Alam knows,' she said. 'Hope you can keep it that way.' Then, she conveniently finished the call.

Fawzia next dialled Nimmi's number and gave them some privacy by leaving the room. Nimmi expressed bucket loads of concern that Romesh had not accompanied her to Peshawar.

'He called us. It appears that they think he is some sort of spy. He has been badgering the authorities, and they give him the same answer. They are checking his credentials.'

Nimmi advised her to wait for Romesh before going to meet Rafik, which was in direct contrast to Romy's counsel.

'Kals, a lot of plans and negotiations have been made,' Romy reminded her, when she called him. 'If they fall apart, we may not have another chance this year or… any year. Just use your common sense and gut instinct. I will join you as soon as I can. Believe me, I will give these guys a headache until they release my passport.'

She knew it hadn't been an easy decision for Romy. He was responsible for keeping her safe. His mother and her parents would come down on him like a ton of bricks if anything adverse happened to her. Also, Romy cared deeply for her, and would never forgive himself if anything happened to her.

There was nothing to it but to go to bed and mull over what Shahida had told her. Why had she kept Kiran's birth a secret? No doubt, she wanted to preserve her son's character. A man may walk out on his girlfriend, and still be honourable, but what kind of man walks out on his son?

Raffa's behaviour seemed to be in sharp contrast to that of the rest of his family. Despite being aware that she had been abandoned, his family were going out of their way to make her feel welcome. She would soon be able to ask him why. The sleep that followed was restless, beneath the four-bladed fan.

*

The five-hour time difference between the two countries meant that by the time Kalyani came down the next day, the sun was high in the sky; breakfast had been cleared away and Aliya was pacing impatiently. 'At last! We were wondering if you would ever wake up!' she exclaimed.

'Aliya!' her mother cautioned. 'That girl is always hyper.'

'Sorry. I didn't realise the time.'

'Don't worry. We have saved some breakfast for you.'

Under Aliya's scrutiny, Kalyani tried to eat as quickly as possible. And then, it was shopping time.

The driver brought the more luxurious family car around – it smelt of leather polish and incense. A miniature replica of the Pakistani flag adorned the dashboard. Aliya, her mother, Kalyani and Hamida sat at the back. Aliya's grandmother had excused herself.

Outside, sunlight blazed, and reflected off glass, metal, silica in the pavement, and the tar on the roads.

Following instructions from Fawzia, the driver, with generous help from an eager Aliya, gave a running commentary on the famous buildings they passed. It transpired that the driver had briefly been a tour guide in the past. The Alam family lived more or less in the centre of Peshawar, and they passed some of these national treasures every day.

Kalyani was impressed by the sprawling buildings, built in Islamic and colonial styles. The majestic Peshawar University, founded in 1950, built over a thousand acres of lush, green gardens. The domes, minarets, arches of mosques and public offices competed with colonial style and more modern buildings. Kalyani was surprised to hear that relics of Buddhist stupas and monuments existed too. The driver reminded her that more than half a century ago, Pakistan and India were one and the same. Kanishka, the emperor of pre-British era, had been an ardent Buddhist in his later life. There were also churches, a reminder of Peshawar's ethnicity. Romy would have been delighted with the tour, she thought regretfully.

Old Peshawar's town centre overwhelmed her with a cacophony of colour, noise, smells and dust. Kalyani had a hard time just keeping up with the ladies, as they confidently strode through the maze of shops, and alleys, skilfully avoiding rubbish, dogs and children. Brightly coloured and decorated, three - wheeled horrors called auto rickshaws, and foreign cars, honked their way through the narrow roads, competing with the more traditional cycle rickshaws and bullock carts. Two wheelers weaved in and out, most carrying an entire family and their kitchen sinks on them, like acrobats in a circus. How they avoided plucking out an eye here or a limb there or driving over bare feet, was an enigma.

The atmosphere inside the shops was only marginally better. When she did get to the counter, helped by a giggling Aliya and a mocking Hamida, she was dazzled by yards of rippling silk fabric on display. Under the harsh fluorescent lights, chunky, gold ornaments, the likes of which she had never seen, made her fish out her shades from her bag. Another store specialised in kitchenware: steel and brass pots, large enough to hold three ample adults in them, and some tiny enough to fit into a child's palm. The fragrance of fried food from the street vendors, ripe fruit and freshly ground spices clashed with that of sweat and sewers. She heaved a sigh of relief when the next stage of the shopping took them to a much quieter, air-conditioned mall. Here, she was able to admire the wares, without the risk of being pushed and shoved or having her purse stolen. She openly gawked at the intricate embroidered silk dresses, dotted with bits of mirror, beads and sequins, displayed in the windows. The family ignored the men entreating them to visit their shop with the promise of a discount or a soft drink. They seemed to know what they wanted, and made their way to the back of the mall, where the true artisans worked. Here, the light was poor, the conditions cramped, and the artisans sat cross-legged on low stools or on the floors. Many were family concerns; the grumpy artisan worked on the goods, while his son-in-law, the crafty salesman, sold and bargained at the till.

Dictated by Aliya, Kalyani chose a toy lorry made of wood, painted with pink and green flowers, like the ones dashing around on the roads, and a spinning top for her son, a set of embroidered, silk cushion covers for Nimmi and Shahida, a pretty silver bangle inlaid with semi-precious stones for Minna, and a beautifully carved letter opener for her dad. She watched tersely as the Alams bargained fiercely to get a fair price. Their shopping trip ended with a snack of spicy mint pakoras, washed down with cold lassi, a sweet and delicately spiced buttermilk.

Tea was waiting for them at home - made from loose tea leaves, simmered in water for just the right time, and mixed with boiled milk. The cook had gone overboard with the sugar, making Kalyani wince. Aliya's grandmother joined them, listening patiently as grandmothers do at her incessant chatter, describing the highlights of their trip.

Fawzia smiled at Kalyani's intolerance of the excessively sweet tea. 'Musa, our cook, always gets excited when guests arrive, especially young and pretty women. He adds extra sweetness and fat to everything. Daddy always tells him off, threatening to take the extra expense out of his wages.'

'Aliya!' her mother cautioned again. 'Why don't you go freshen up?'

'She is a lovely girl. Daddy's pet?' commented Kalyani, when Aliya reluctantly obeyed.

'She is, but she can also be quite a handful.' Her mother sighed. 'Teenage years can be so difficult. Her daddy spoils her rotten.'

'Well, what do you expect? She is his only daughter, and the only child from this marriage,' Hamida said.

'*This* marriage?' Kalyani asked, immediately apologising for being nosy.

'Oh, it is no secret. Alam was married before. Has two grown-up sons from his first wife, both settled abroad now. He is divorced from his first wife.'

'Divorced? Is that allowed in a traditional family like yours?'

'Nowadays, everything is allowed. Divorce is getting more common. Almost everybody knows somebody who has been through a divorce. The youngsters expect so much more from marriage nowadays. A ready-made life - like in the movies. Everlasting love, guaranteed riches, unfading beauty...'

'And if they have everything, they get bored and want to search for adventure. Like your Rafik,' Nanima observed.

Fortunately, Aliya's return with considerably cleaner hands interrupted the conversation.

When the tea was drunk, the older women retired for a siesta, before getting ready for the night's dinner party. Aliya suggested they went up to the terrace.

The midday sun was too hot to stand in, but they sat in a shaded area under the awning and watched doves flying around the branches of trees hanging over the balustrade.

'Aziz Kaka, the old gardener, keeps a dovecote at the north end of the garden. At one time, he had more than forty of them. They made such a mess that Daddy put his foot down and made him sell half of them.'

Kalyani laughed with the young girl at the plight of the gardener.

'And what about you? What are your plans, Aliya? Have you any boyfriends?' Kalyani probed.

'Well... yes and no. I don't know,' she said, suddenly shy.

'Someone going to your college?'

'No.' Aliya made a great show of examining the sequins on her dress, before resuming. 'There is this guy I met at a cousin's wedding. We have a lot of cousins and a lot of weddings. He is older than me. He said I was the most beautiful girl he had ever seen!'

'Oh? Is he in college or university?'

'I think... he is working. I can't remember where.' Aliya was clearly talking about someone much older than her.

'Do you meet or talk on the phone?'

'He called me once on the house phone, but my mother took the call first. He didn't say much, but told me that it would be better if I had a mobile phone.'

'Oh. Was your mother OK with you talking to him?'

Aliya hesitated. 'I told her it was my French tutor calling to rearrange lessons.'

'Do you know if he has a girlfriend or if he is married?'

'It is not that type of relationship. I mean, he just makes me feel good. He says nice things,' Aliya shrugged.

'Maybe you should ask your cousin about this person. Best to know everything about someone, before being his girlfriend. That way, you are not at a disadvantage.' Something that she herself should have practised before preaching, Kalyani thought bitterly.

Aliya pouted stubbornly, but Kalyani knew she had sown the seeds of doubt in her mind. She changed the subject.

'Now, can you help me ring this travel agent and ask him to bring home my tickets for the coach tomorrow?'

Aliya, only too happy to stop discussing this uncomfortable subject, called the company and insisted that they deliver the pre-paid tickets within the hour. Kalyani did not cancel Romy's ticket, despite the fact that he was still stranded in that godforsaken Middle Eastern airport, venting his frustration by threatening the officials with the wrath of the British Embassy, and making regular tours of the duty-free shops.

That morning, when she rang him, he had joked that while he waited for his papers to be cleared, he was practicing his negotiating skills on the Arab shopkeepers, from whom he had bought umpteen packs of chocolates and dried dates, an overpriced watch, and a gadget to reduce double chins. He had sampled the perfume testers and free food, and sat in the glittering Rolls Royce on display so many times that security had trained their CCTV cameras on him.

'Stick to the plan. Whatever happens. Whatever Rafik says. One night only. Come back to Peshawar to think through any future plans,' he had made her promise. 'You will manage. Trust your instincts.'

Romy seemed to trust her instincts more than she herself did. But she had come so far. She had sacrificed so much. Raffa was only a few hours away. There was no way she was chickening out. Romy or no Romy, she was going. She needed answers to the questions gnawing at her brain like a cancer.

Aliya was regarding her thoughtfully, her head cocked to one side, eyes unfocussed. The girl had something on her mind.

'I was just thinking about your advice. You said I had to find out more about someone before becoming their girlfriend. Did you know all about your Rafik, before becoming his girlfriend?' Aliya blushed, mortified at herself for speaking outright.

Good question, Kalyani thought to herself. If she had spent a lifetime collecting an encyclopaedia of useless facts on Raffa, would things be different? What would she wish to be different?

Could she say she wished she had never fallen in love, when she had enjoyed every moment with Raffa? Never had a baby, when she could not imagine a life without Kiran? Waited till she was older and understood things better, when it had felt so right with Raffa? Everything she had known about her boyfriend hadn't amounted to much; it certainly hadn't stopped him from leaving. Could anyone know another person fully, ever?

The conversation with Aliya brought back memories of happy days with Minna. Minna had a way of subtly pointing out the obvious, as Aliya had done.

Chapter 2

'Is it going to be a big party tonight?' Kalyani asked Aliya, who looked elegant in a silk *lehanga*, her hair piled high on her head in a messy bun, secured by pearly pins, eyes lined with kohl and lips glossed. She was now sifting through Kalyani's limited wardrobe, rejecting every outfit.

'I suppose no one warned you to come prepared for our impromptu parties,' Aliya shrugged dismissively. 'Everything is big in the Alam family. The smallest party involves upwards of thirty people and caterers. But tonight, Ammi has kept it exceptionally small and has invited only half that number. I am sure there will be lots of disgruntled friends and relatives, complaining that they have been left out. Our family is one of the oldest in Peshawar; several generations have held important positions within the government, the justice system, hospitals and schools. Daddy calls himself "Peshawadi Alam". He has always worked as a civil servant for the Government, but I think he would be much happier if he was an entertainer.'

'Oh? What sort of an entertainer?' asked Kalyani, while she watched the young girl hold up the garments from her suitcase, her face showing dissatisfaction.

'Daddy used to write plays. He is very good at satire. Satirical comedy. Sometimes, he is so funny and intelligent at the same time. He would have made a great politician. But he sticks to poking fun at them.'

'I think comedians are very intelligent,' Kalyani agreed.

'Why don't you borrow something from here?' Aliya said, throwing open the mahogany wardrobe, revealing rows of beautiful garments. 'There must be one that fits you. Visiting relatives from abroad buy these expensive clothes for weddings or engagements, then decide that they will not have any opportunity to wear them at home. So, they leave them here, for when they visit next time. By the time they come again, they have put on a few extra pounds, and the clothes don't fit.'

Kalyani laughed with her. When Aliya assured her that no one would mind if she borrowed the outfits, she chose as modestly as she could get away with. Aliya fetched some of her own fancy jewellery, and took great pride in adorning her ward.

'You look gorgeous!' She clapped her hands at the result. Before Kalyani could ponder on the fact that she may be overdressed, Aliya jumped up, the skirts of her *lehanga* swirling around her.

'Come on or we will be late!'

The 'small' party comprising family, close friends and others who had casually dropped by, bustled around the living area. Dominating them all was Alam. She couldn't have missed him, even if she tried; he was easily the largest in the crowd. At five feet, nine inches, he was only slightly taller than the average Pakistani, but considerably wider. His flab appeared to be held together by a broad, ornate belt, tied around his saffron and gold jacket.

'Daddy!' Aliya cried, as she ran into his arms, as though she hadn't seen him for a year. Her mother rolled her eyes at her daughter's immature behaviour amidst company.

Aliya excitedly introduced Kalyani to him. 'Pleasure to meet you, Kalyani.' His voice was smooth and sincere, like pure honey. He was not the most handsome man in the room, but he was certainly the most charming.

'You too. I have heard a lot about you!' Kalyani replied.

'Aliya!' he roared with mock anger. 'What have you been telling our guest about me?'

Kalyani jumped out of her skin, but Aliya giggled like a five year old. Alam asked her the customary questions about her flight, and if she liked the markets of Peshawar. Despite his ready smile and happy demeanour, Kalyani recognised him as a man who paid careful attention to detail, and didn't miss a trick.

'We should discuss your travel arrangements later. And about your friend,' he said, before his attention was sought by someone else.

The party might have been small by Peshawar standards, but everyone had taken great care to look their best. Every shade of the rainbow was represented in their costumes and veils, and their jewellery twinkled like a mini disco as it reflected the light from the chandelier. Fawzia had left few stones unturned to create a party atmosphere. The chandeliers gleamed, the marble floors glittered, the fountain gushed, and the extra palm trees made the space look a million dollars. Soon after, Musa, who was promoted from cook to the master of ceremony, summoned them to dinner.

'Today, we dine Peshawari style. Do you know anything about our food, apart from the Peshawari naan in your supermarket?' Alam joked, turning to Kalyani.

His jokes continued to punctuate the party, some of which his guests had obviously heard before, but nevertheless, they laughed politely; some were a subtle dig at them, making them squirm and protest, but they were all definitely entertained.

He held up a goblet of fruit juice and tinkled it with a silver spoon, to gain everybody's attention, before delivering a pre-dinner speech. He welcomed them all into his humble home, and introduced Kalyani as a friend of Shahida's from the UK, who wanted to see how the Peshawaris live. The people around the table raised their glasses to welcome her, before resuming their conversations.

Kalyani bridled. *A family friend!* As the mother of Raffa's child, she was practically part of the family! Damn Raffa for leaving her at the altar and damn him for leaving her holding the baby. Yet, he was not even mentioned in the same breath as her. Alam, with silky smooth ease, had glossed over the past, as if it didn't exist. She watched him glibly carry on with his hosting duties, her respect for him diminishing.

The dishes, prepared by Musa and co. smelt divine and looked delectable. Some of them, Kalyani learnt, were national specialities, some were local fare from Peshawar, and some had been invented by the Alam family and passed down through generations.

'You must give me the recipe for this vegetable biriyani!' Kalyani exclaimed to Fawzia.

'Begum will have to kill you, if you learnt the recipe. You might end up on the table like that poor lamb,' Alam joked, pleased that the guests laughed with him.

After dinner, the hookahs were brought out, the conversation turned to politics, and it was time for the women to withdraw. Fawzia led them into a different room, to discuss more feminine topics, and munch on *paan* – betel leaves, wrapped around spicy- sweet coconut, and fruit. The feminine topics did not entirely exclude politics, but brought it closer to home and gave a humane touch. Did they know that so and so's son was arrested last week? Suspected association with the Taliban. Or that a friend's cousin was killed two weeks ago in the hills, someone else was reported missing, or a servant had not turned up for work, likely recruited by some terrorist gang or the other. Of course, the jihadi groups made their lives difficult – the cost of living had gone up and they feared for their children. But they could hardly sit at home and refuse to go out. What sort of life would that be? A living death. After all, there was no guarantee that they would not be bombed in their homes while they ate their mughlai lamb curry, and slept on their silk pillows.

The women had automatically gravitated to cliques in accordance with their age and interests. The older women compared notes on their aches and pains. The younger mothers bragged and complained about their children. The teenagers exclaimed and giggled as they browsed through magazines featuring movie stars, and gossiped about their Pathani cousins and handsome, eligible boys.

Aliya rescued Kalyani from a peevish woman who was grilling her about how she became acquainted with Shahida when she did not attend the same mosque as her, and dragged her to join her friends. The girls badgered her with questions about London fashion.

'Tell us about the hats they wear. We heard they have very long legs. Do they really look like they do in the magazines? Is their hair made of real gold? Do you see movie stars in London?' Torn between disillusioning them and feeding their delusions, Kalyani built up a series of images, based on Barbie and Ken, which seemed to satisfy them.

She watched the little children playing with dolls and dice, and on the PlayStation, squabbling and rolling on the floor with laughter. She could picture Kiran amongst them, and her heart ached for what might never be. How different her world would have been, if Raffa had done the honourable thing and made her an honest woman.

How many of these people would have welcomed her into their houses, if they knew she was an unmarried, single mother? Heavy clouds descended over her, and she knew from experience that the tears would follow. Wondering if she could slip away quietly, she rose. Her skirt caught on the edge of a table, causing her to trip. Enough to gain Hamida's attention. She beckoned Kalyani over, and chirped excitedly, 'Kalyani is visiting Tasneen tomorrow!'

Fawzia looked like a mother whose five-year-old had just revealed the whereabouts of the family jewels to a burglar. Hamida had obviously been groomed to say nothing about Kalyani's plans to meet Rafik, but no one had told her not to mention Tasneen. She obviously wanted to conjure up some gossip. The group collectively exchanged knowing glances, and sighed.

'Ah, Tasneen!' Hamida leaned back, satisfied with the damage she had done.

Her curiosity piqued, Kalyani decided to stay a while longer. Who was Tasneen? Shahida had not mentioned her. Fawzia noted her confusion and took a deep breath.

'Tasneen is the only daughter of Sulaiman Kaka, with whom you will be staying.' She explained. 'Her mother passed away in childbirth, and she was brought up by her father. She married a Christian boy, Harry. Unfortunately, the marriage ended tragically with the death of her husband. The poor girl is left with a little son.' To the others, she said, 'Kalyani wanted to see the beauty of some of the villages. Sulaiman Kaka kindly invited her to stay with him for a couple of days.'

The ladies in the group were only too happy to carry on with this topic. 'Poor Sulaiman Kaka. All these problems with Tasneen proved too much for him to bear. Gave him a stroke, and left him paralysed.'

'What Allah gives, Allah takes.'

'Something was not right about that marriage. Doomed from the start.'

'Something was not right about how it all ended, either.'

A sharp cry from one of the children, who had fallen over, distracted the ladies and put a stop to the conversation. A kindred spirit, thought Kalyani. A widow and a single mother; a societal outcast. Maybe she and Tasneen would get on like a house on fire.

As she excused herself, Fawzia whispered in her ear. 'Alam wants to speak to you later.'

What a bunch of gossip mongers! Kalyani understood why Alam had not introduced her as family. That lot would have had her for breakfast.

Once in her room, she slipped into more comfortable clothes, and lay staring at the whirring fan. Scattered around her were the contents of her suitcase and the tickets to Muzaffarabad. Due to time constraints, and limited flights to Chitral, the plan was to travel from Peshawar by coach to Muzaffarabad, and return by flight from Chitral.

She would have to leave Romy's ticket here. She felt sorry for Romy, who had been looking forward to visiting Peshawar. He had collected umpteen brochures, trawled the Internet, making notes on the places he wanted to visit, and spent a sizeable portion of his savings on accessorising his Canon camera.

How different the two men in her life were. Romy was a bosom friend, who she had grown up with, and had few secrets from; Raffa was her lover, whose entire life appeared to be full of secrets. Romy knew her mind like the back of his own hand, while Raffa knew her body like even she didn't. Funny how both were a night's travel away from her when she needed them.

With a sigh, she started packing for her one-night only trip to see Raffa. Her mother had made a list of what she should take in her overnight bag. Nimmi had lists for everything, even if she needed three things from the shop: bread, milk and eggs. Passport, tickets, Dr Blick's happy pills, list of addresses and phone numbers, phone charger and extra battery, cosmetics, toileteries, money... The bulky envelope Shahida had sent for her son caught her eye. As she slid it into her bag, something escaped from the envelope and fluttered to the floor. A couple of photo prints. Kalyani picked them up, and held them to the light of the table lamp. They were selfies of Shahida holding Kiran. In the first one, Kiran was sucking on a rattle, peering into the camera, his curls framing his face, and in the second, he had turned towards Shahida, his eyes large with uncertainty. Shahida's face was not familiar to him. Kalyani envisaged the sequence of events that would have followed – the trembling of her baby's wet, slobbery lips, crumpling of his face, and his robust cry of protest, which would have brought Nimmi rushing to his aid. Oh how she missed his little, warm body and his baby smell. Her breasts swelled as if they were engorged with milk.

Kalyani was not aware that Shahida had taken these photos. No doubt, she wished to tempt her son back home with the baby pictures. With the same intention, Kalyani had brought her own album full of Kiran's photos. She put the loose photos back in the envelope and slipped a rubber band over it. She wondered what Shahida had written to her son.

Last to go into her bag was the carefully chosen outfit for the reunion with Raffa. Despite herself, her heart pounded with anticipation. 'Raffa, here I come,' she whispered.

The banging of car doors and fond goodbyes – '*Insha Allah*', and 'Come again' drifted up. The guests were leaving. She waited until the last of them left and the front door was shut and bolted. The heat and the excessively rich food she had eaten made her thirsty; she crept down to get a drink of water. Fawzia was overseeing the servants as they packed away the leftover food. She looked up as Kalyani walked into the kitchen.

'Ah, there you are. Alamji was looking for you. He is in the den, the room where you used the phone.' Kalyani filled a glass with water from the water filter, and assured Fawzia that she could find the den on her own.

The chandeliers were turned off, and the now silent fountain and the palm fronds gleamed in the moonlight. A sliver of light shone from under the door of the den. Alam invited her in when she knocked. He had exchanged his jacket for a silk dressing gown, and was relaxing on the sofa with his feet up. He looked like an enormous, beached whale.

'May I join you?' she asked, smiling.

'Please.' He gestured to an adjoining chair.

'It is not your bedtime yet?' she asked.

'Me? I never sleep at this time. I don't seem to need much sleep anyway. Never did. You, on the other hand, must be jet lagged.'

'Yes. I have another couple of hours before sleep time. Is that a hookah?' She indicated the smoking pipe connected to the gurgling container.

'This? Yes. One of the Mussalman's guilty pleasures. Me, my castle and my pipe.' The curtains fluttered in the gentle breeze from an open window, and the distant noise of traffic filtered through. A nearly full moon shone high in the sky. 'Helps with the stress.'

'You are... stressed?'

'All Pakistanis are stressed. Everything stresses them: the traffic, the servants, the wife, the children, work. They eat to reduce the stress – they get high blood pressure, sugar, cholesterol... and more stress.'

Kalyani giggled. Alam added a hint of sarcasm to everything. A glint in his eye and a dimple in his cheek turned it into a joke.

'You have to get up early to catch that coach. Would you like a shot of brandy to help you sleep?' he offered.

'No, thank you. It might give me a migraine. Do you drink? I mean Islam says you can't, right?'

'True. I keep some for my *Angrezi* guests.' Alam tapped the side of his nose.

'You have a lot of *Angrezi* visitors?'

'On and off. Friends from a different era. I studied in England, you know. At the University of Leeds, for three years, and worked in the Embassy. Made a few friends then. I tempt them to visit, by sending them photoshopped postcards of Peshawar.'

'Oh! I didn't realise. That is why you speak such good English.'

'Oh no! I always spoke good English. In fact, some of us speak the Queen's English. Just with a variable degree of Pakistani accent. Our dad sent us to the best schools here.'

He sucked on the hookah, making soft, gurgling noises, and fixed her with his bulging eyes. 'By the way, my contacts tell me your friend has been cleared at the transit airport. They are always suspicious of journalists, especially those with Indian connections.'

'That is good news indeed! Thank you.' Kalyani clapped her hands. 'When will he arrive?'

'There are no flights tonight, so I doubt he would arrive in time to accompany you tomorrow.'

'I understand.'

'So! You are meeting your *pyari jaan*, your lover, tomorrow?'

'I am hoping to. Except, I am not sure what to expect.'

'As long as you remain open to any possibility, you will not be disappointed.' He nodded at her, his jowls wobbling like jelly. 'Also, be careful. I know how a man's brain works. It is always me. Me. Me, first. Rafik is like that too. Always has been. Looks after number one – himself.' Kalyani bowed her head, not knowing how to respond. Alam continued. 'You have one night.

After that, I will have to send a search party for you. Any decision you feel you have to make, any decision he is forcing you to make, listen for Alam's alarm bells. Withdraw. You come back here to think about it.'

Alam was serious, she could tell. He was leaning towards her in a paternal way, his mildly bloodshot eyes demanded her attention. 'I know that you are vulnerable.'

Kalyani's head shot up. How much did he know? As if in answer to her unspoken query, Alam said, 'Shahida told me. She will demand my head on a plate, if I don't put you back on the plane to Heathrow safe and sound.'

'Oh!' Kalyani felt emotional, 'I didn't realise Shahida felt... protective towards me.'

Alam stared at her for an entire minute, as if making up his mind about something. Then he gave himself permission to continue. 'Don't judge a book by its cover. Don't judge Shahida by her outward moods. She... had a hard childhood.' The hookah gurgled, louder, as Alam sucked harder. Kalyani waited, hoping he would continue with the story. He did, fixing his gaze on the fluttering curtains.

'I was about seven years old when Shahida was born, the third child of five. Shahida was the youngest. Our mother, for some reason, never liked her. She never held her, or fed her. The baby almost starved to death, until the rest of the family took over her care. Our mother slowly withdrew from all of us after Shahida was born, went into a shell. Prior to that, although she was never very demonstrative with her affection, she had been there for us. She became confined to her room, up in the attic. Our father brought in doctors, priests, and Shamans to treat her. I don't know if she was ever completely cured, but she was not allowed near the children without supervision, especially near the baby.

'Everybody blamed Shahida. They used to call her names when they fell out with her, portraying her as evil. Our father was never a "hands-on" parent, so he employed nannies to look after us. He stayed well away from his youngest daughter. Later, he put our mother in an asylum, and married another woman – polygamy, by the way, is allowed in Islam.' A sarcastic note crept in at the end of his story. Disturbed and saddened, Kalyani did not smile.

'Could she have had postnatal depression? Like me?'

'Retrospectively, it is possible that she had something like that. In those days, people were quick to believe in demonic possessions, rather than scientific explanations. Shahida was a demon who put her mother in an asylum. She never lacked food or clothing or jewellery, but what she really needed was love. She learned quickly to fend for herself – to fight her corner. Only I tried to stand up for her, as much as I could.

'After her marriage with Ashraf, Shahida moved to England. She couldn't wait to move away from this house where she had experienced so much pain and distress. She was initially not keen to have children. I think all of us were a bit scared of having children, lest we suffered the same fate as our mother. But Shahida had a mental block, and for a long time, despite not identifying any medical problems with either of them, they remained childless. When she finally had Rafik, she overcompensated. She poured love on him. She gave him everything a child would want and more. I would say she spoilt him rotten. And she knows it.' The hookah gurgled, nearly empty.

'Anyhow, she was happy in her marriage, proud of her son – until he walked away, leaving her life and your life in shambles. All the painful emotions she had once suffered and packed away must have resurfaced: the guilt, anger and, above all, the feeling of rejection. She is as much a victim here as you are.'

For a long time, Kalyani and Alam sat silently, watching the last of the smoke curling from the pipe. Somewhere in the house, a cuckoo clock sounded the hour.

'I am sorry if I upset you even more. You did not really need to hear more sob stories.'

'No. But thank you for explaining this to me. Now I know how badly she must be hurting.' Kalyani felt tears prickling her eyes. 'I think I will go to bed now.'

Alam nodded his agreement. 'You have set your alarm? The coach to Chitral leaves early in the morning. It reaches Muzaffarabad in six hours. I have arranged for Biran to pick you up at Muzaffarabad, and take you to Sulaiman Kaka's house. He will also drop you at Chitral airport, for your flight back to Peshawar. Biran used to work for me. Very reliable, fiercely loyal. It was he who persuaded Rafik to contact me in the beginning. I have sent word through him to Rafik, about your arrival. Biran would have informed me if he had been unable to contact Rafik.'

'Is there anything you want me to convey to Sulaiman Kaka?'

'Sulaiman is a good man. He may be a distant relative, but he is more a friend. When my boys were little, we used to spend our holidays with his family. Those were the "hey-days". Their business: they had a monopoly on pony riding clubs in the region – was booming because of tourists, and everybody was carefree and happy. Please, give him my regards.'

'Will do. Thank you once again for all your help.' She smiled gratefully at him.

At the entrance to the den, she turned around. 'One more question, if I may. Is the place as dangerous as people say?'

Alam struggled to turn to face her, and gave up. 'It is the people who make it dangerous, not the place.

Don't worry about it. There is more chance of your coach toppling over a cliff than a group of terrorists on horseback, wielding machetes, cutting you down. We don't hear about the road traffic accidents, but a terrorist attack on foreigners becomes international news. Everybody gets tarnished with the same brush – we are all "terrorists". The frequency of these attacks is something like once in two years or so. Quite rare.'

As she returned to her room, she wondered if it was two years since the last attack.

Just as Shahida promised, Alam had kept his side of the bargain. He had sent word to Rafik; arranged for her to stay at his relative, Sulaiman's house. One of Fawzia's cousins, Rehman, had volunteered to take her to the coach station in the morning, and make sure she got on the correct coach. He would also have a word with the driver to ensure she got off at the right stop. Biran, Alam's trusted worker, would pick her up and take her to Sulaiman's house, where Raffa would meet her.

Above all, her mother had tied a magic amulet from an astrologer on her wrist. 'To keep you safe,' she had told her.

With such detailed planning, what could go wrong!

Chapter 3.

As promised, Fawzia's cousin, Rehman, arrived promptly the next morning, clad smartly in white, a matching white turban worn like a Pathan, on his head. He nodded in greeting, and held the door open for her. His driver loaded her suitcase in the boot. The maid, who woke her up in the morning with Musa, the cook's uber - sweet coffee, handed her a packet of food in a cloth bag. The rest of the family was obviously still asleep.

Despite the odds, she wished for Romy to screech to a stop in a taxi, shouting 'Surprise!' But it was not to be.

Rehman's driver weaved expertly through the 8a.m. traffic, which was already hectic. Vehicles loomed from seemingly nowhere around them, and just as she expected to end up as roadkill under the wheels of one of these juggernauts, they passed her by like a scene from a 3D movie. If there was a rule, it would need Stephen Hawking to decipher it. Road rage, verbal abuse, honking buses, crafty auto rickshaws, and bikes with precariously perched school children carrying school bags twice the size of their bodies, and buses pulled to one side by the sheer weight of travellers hanging from the windows and doors by their fingertips, made her hold her breath in horror. Rehman's driver, however, remained cool as a cucumber, and Rehman spent most of the time on his phone to his business clients, oblivious to the near- miss incidents they were having.

The coach station was no better. At least the coach numbers were displayed digitally over the stands. The people swarming around them with their oversized luggage resembled flotsam and jetsam tossed in stormy waves. Everything from battered suitcases to baskets of fruit, chicken and even snakes passed her by, most carried on heads. Excited cries heralded the arrival of her coach, and the waiting crowd surged forward, carrying her in their midst. Her feet hardly touched the ground as she clutched her handbag close to her chest, and wondered where the rest of her luggage was. As if by magic, Rehman appeared at her side. A path opened in front of him, where a minute ago, there had been none.

'Ticket,' he shouted in her ear, waiting patiently for her to fish it out of her handbag. He took it and waved it in front of the harassed ticket checker in khaki uniform, who punched it and returned it to her. Rehman helped her up the steps into the bus, and squeezed behind her, ignoring the ticket checker's protests. He found her seat and heaved her suitcase to the rack above her head.

'Biran will be there. I have informed him,' he told her, before pushing his way to where the driver sat, and knocked on the partition grille, separating him from the passengers. Money was exchanged, and the driver turned around to glance at her – a small man with an anxious face and quivering whiskers. Rehman could not make his way back to her as the aisles were by now piled with luggage, and travellers searching for their seats. He held up a hand to say goodbye. She waved back, wishing she had thanked him earlier.

Alone, she took a deep breath, and for the first time that morning, dared to relax a little. The scenes outside were no less tense than the drama inside. But while she could hear the travellers squabbling inside, the milling crowd outside seemed surreal, even comical, like a silent pantomime in which actors mimed their lines. There were a couple of men wearing traditional turbans trying to load luggage on top of an adjacent bus, shouting and gesturing to each other; the man on the ground not quite lifting the bag high enough, and the man on the roof, not reaching down far enough. The queue behind them was getting irate with people giving advice and abuse. Judging by the thumps from above, luggage was being loaded to the roof of her coach as well. Vendors swarmed around, persuading the travellers to stock up on last-minute provisions. They did not bother with her air - conditioned coach, because the windows were closed and tinted. At one point, she thought she saw Rehman outside the window, his phone stuck to his ear, but he soon disappeared. Finally, her fellow travellers settled in their seats, rising periodically to check that their bags had made it into the bus with them, and to catch a glimpse of their relatives one last time.

In front of her, peeking over the top of her seat, was a young child with large, inquisitive eyes. Beside her was an old couple, dressed traditionally. The man looked frail and leant heavily on his walking stick; the woman was plump, and sweated profusely. Mr and Mrs Khan, they introduced themselves as.

'Kalyani,' she smiled. 'Speak English?' she asked.

'Little. Urdu? Hindi?'

'Little,' Kalyani replied, wishing she had paid more attention to learning the language at home.

Until the bus reached the highway, the ride was jerky and slow, and Kalyani was starting to feel queasy. Like the others, she relaxed when the coach picked up speed and the ride became smoother. Around her, her fellow travellers opened their food packets and struck up conversations with their temporary neighbours. Soon, most discovered common acquaintances, distant relatives and college mates, and within the hour, some were already tossing opinions on politics, wives and movies.

Mr and Mrs Khan were travelling all the way to Chitral, to visit their son and his family. 'What about you?' Mr Khan asked. 'Are you married?'

'Er… no. Not yet.'

'Visiting someone?' Mr Khan persisted.

Only my boyfriend who jilted me at the altar, left me with a baby and severe postnatal depression. I figured the only way to get out of overdosing on the twenty different bottles of pills in my cupboard and ending it all was to go after him. Ask him 'Why'. Bring it all out in the open and put a lid on the whole thing.

Aloud, she said, 'Friends.'

Kalyani was stunned at how easy it was to sum up her ordeal – a whole year of excruciating suffering into a few lines.

Munching on the food Fawzia had given her, Kalyani texted her mother to say she was on her way. Nimmi rang back immediately, wanting to know details. Kalyani reassured her that the coach was comfortable, and the people friendly.

'Romy rang us. He is trying to get a connecting flight to you. August is holiday time. Most flights are packed. Oh, and Helen rang to enquire if you are alright.'

Kalyani remembered making up with her friend. Helen had visited her in hospital, very apologetic for how the last visit with Lola had gone. It wasn't the joyous reunion Helen had hoped for, but they re-established the bond of friendship between them.

When Helen heard about her plan to chase after Raffa, she organised a coup. She roped in Romy and Minna, and the four of them met at the café. The evening was warm, and the lazy notes of a busker's violin floated in the breeze.

'You have thought this through, Kals?' Helen queried.

Kals munched on a raisin from her sticky bun. 'Have thought of nothing else for days.'

'I can confirm that to be the case.' Romy held his hand up solemnly.

'Not the logistics. I mean the real reason you want to meet your ex.'

'I dunno…'

'What do you mean?' Helen persisted, trying to ignore Minna rolling her eyes.

'I mean, I am not sure he is my "ex". He hasn't officially broken up with me, has he?'

Minna hastily stuffed her bun into her mouth. Helen chose her words carefully. 'Do you still carry a torch for him?'

'I think I always will. There is no denying he is my first love.'

'Are you thinking you can lure him back then?'

Kals twiddled her spoon between her fingers. 'Well… if that is the way it goes, I wouldn't say no.'

'I thought you only wanted this "closure" thing,' Minna exclaimed.

'I do want closure,' Kals replied.

'Okay. Sis, let me put this bluntly,' Minna waved her hands impatiently. 'Have you considered this closure might mean he officially dumps you? Do you want to hurt all over again?'

'Of course I have. But at least I will know for sure.'

'And… you will not do anything silly?' Helen asked.

'Silly?'

'I mean top yourself or something. Tell me to shut up, if you want.'

'Ah! Been there, got the T- shirt. Frightened the bejesus out of the family. I do not feel suicidal anymore; besides, I have a son to look after. I have to return to him. Hopefully, healed and wholesome.'

Minna and Helen still looked unconvinced. Romy felt sorry for Kals, who he felt was being unfairly grilled. 'You know we are only looking out for you,' he said.

Kals held her hand up. 'I promise I will be strong and not be swayed by Raffa.'

She smiled, recalling their relief.

Lulled by the swaying of the coach and a full stomach, most of the passengers had nodded off. The Khans slept too, their heads lolling on each other's shoulder. Mrs Khan was snoring softly, and Mr Khan had loosened his grip on his walking stick. It tipped towards Kalyani. The handle of the walking stick was beautifully carved into a roaring tiger's head. Did it symbolise something? Maybe he was a successful businessman, or a brave soldier. Beside him was his tigress – flabby and grey with age. Maybe she used to be pretty, and had borne him bonny babies. Did they have ups and downs in their marriage? Had he walked away, and had she chased after him, into a strange land?

Kalyani leaned her head on the tinted glass of the window and thought about her family back home – safe in their beds. They seemed so far away, they could be on a different planet. Her sweet, kind mother. And her sturdy, reassuring father, who reminded her of Alam in many ways. Both loved their jobs, took uncensored pride in their family, and did not worry about being judged by society. Minna, who fiercely chased her dreams, at the expense of life itself, and her little son, embroiled unwittingly in this great, big drama between his mummy and daddy. She also realised that in the last couple of days, she had not been besotted with Raffa as much as she used to. She had not carried him around like a lead weight in her chest. Raffa was now a destination, a point on the map where her journey would end. That is *if* he met with her. It was possible that despite Alam's efforts, he had not received the message. Or he simply changed his mind. Would she accept his decision and go back home, or lose her sanity again? A vision of herself, roaming around the barren hills in tattered clothes, and matted hair, shouting out his name, and despairing when only the echo replied, loomed before her.

Of course, at the back of her mind, she harboured hopes of winning him back. Everyone in the family did. She was expected to tempt him back with memories of the good life.

The good times - their morning courtship within the confines of her red Clio. Hot, melting flesh, lips Velcro-ed together, while she drowned helplessly in the depths of his grey-brown eyes... They had belonged to each other; the world had stopped for them – at least, it had stopped for her.

Chapter 4

The bus stopped at the foot of the hills to refuel.

'Tea and toilet break!' the Khans announced. Kalyani wanted neither, but she got out to stretch her legs.

'There may not be another one for hours. Once we are climbing upwards through those narrow roads, there will be no stopping,' Mrs Khan warned her, as they hobbled towards the toilets.

The scenery had changed completely. Gone was the hustle and bustle of the city. Here, the sky was the clearest blue, and the air tasted pure. Hills flanked the road for as long as she could see. Her fellow travellers jostled for space outside the roadside teashop, which was no more than a tin shack with a stained canvas roof. The chai wallah pouring the scalding tea from one mug to another, held at arm's length with the practised precision of a juggler, mesmerised her, as did the flies buzzing around the rows of green bottles of flavoured soda, plugged with a marble in their narrow necks. Baskets of green lemons and yellow bananas hung from the roof. Other vendors selling charms and packets of peanuts swarmed around them.

Kalyani decided to take a short stroll down the road. She found a fairly large rock with a flat area for a seat. The rock angled upwards and outwards, overhanging a deep abyss. If she craned her neck, she could see the hairpin bends winding up the hillside, miniature vehicles crawling on them. Half an hour, the driver had given them. She sat down and took her phone out to check for messages. There were none. Using the phone camera, she took a few photos, including selfies. Romy would love them. A brightly decorated local bus drove past, honking in camaraderie, its passengers hooting and waving at her. She waved back.

Another hour to Muzaffarabad; she had checked with the whiskered driver. She ought to make herself presentable. Placing the phone on the rock, she rummaged in her handbag for her hand mirror and lip-gloss. Sod's law – she found everything but what she wanted – her pill bottle, pens, her mother's list of phone numbers, loose change, tissues, spare acrylic nails, hand gel, mint... A shadow fell over her. Still muttering to herself, she looked up and squinted, a half smile on her lips, thinking one of the passengers must have come over to remind her that time was up. She stared at the man standing over her. He was blocking the sun, and she couldn't see his features, but she could smell him. A mixture of stale sweat and fried onions. He moved closer and bent over her. A mild sweat sprouted under her arms, which had little to do with the heat emanating from the rock. She could now see the yellows of his eyes, streaked with blood vessels. His lips parted to show stained, rotten teeth as he grinned at her. Kalyani gave a short scream, scrambled back up the rock face, her feet dislodging loose gravel. The sudden movement upended her handbag, its contents spilling over her bosom. She realised she was now hanging precariously over the rock edge. A dislodged stone hurtled over the rock face and plunged into the abyss, hundreds of miles below. A similar fate would befall her if she moved any further or lost her balance.

To her horror, the man only moved closer; she could feel the rough cloth of his shirt against her skin, and see the dirt caked in their folds. He drove his knee between her legs. His fingers travelled towards her breasts, his nails broken and soiled. Using one hand to steady herself, she flapped ineffectively at his fingers with the other. Her neck ached at the effort of holding her head up, and her voice caught in her throat. Her hand slipped on the rock, and her feet searched frantically for a purchase. She wondered where her bag was; if she could reach it, she could use it as a weapon. But all she could feel was grit and rubble. She was caught between the abyss and this wretch. Should she yield to him or fling herself over the edge?

Something flashed in front of her eyes. For a moment, she wondered if it was her life flashing before her eyes prior to death. Girl falls in love. Girl gets jilted. Girl loses life chasing after her lover...

Blood-curdling yells jolted her out of her reverie. The pressure on her body eased, and sunlight blinded her once again. The wretch was moving away, holding his bleeding ear and yelling. She was free. Hands were reaching out to her, pulling her away from the abyss. As she sat, trembling and panting, she saw Mr Khan trying to sheath a thin, pointed sword into his walking stick with his shaky hands. 'Never know when it may come handy,' he winked at her.

Someone gave her water to wash away the grit from her skin, and someone else brought her some tea. They helped collect the spilled contents of her handbag, and led her back to the coach. She could hear them grumble – some against the wretch, and some against her. '*The man should be locked up. Women should not wander off by themselves. Now, they were all late.*'

They were well on their way by the time she stopped shaking. She thanked Mr Khan for saving her. He waved dismissively at her. 'I was in the right place at the right time.'

'Only because you couldn't queue for the toilets and wanted to take a leak in the bushes,' his wife teased.

'Do you always carry that sword with you?' Kalyani asked.

A shadow passed his eyes.

'Only since our daughter's death,' Mrs Khan said softly.

'I am so sorry. May I ask what happened to your daughter?'

'Oh. It was years ago, dear. She was taken, dragged away at gunpoint in front of our eyes – for listening to music on the way to school.'

Mr Khan's eyes filled with tears. 'I couldn't help her then. I had no weapon.'

'Oh my God! Who killed her?'

'They were never caught. The Taliban or someone radicalised by them. She was pushed from a bridge and died from an injury to her head.'

Kalyani apologised again for dredging up their tragic experiences. Mr Khan described how he had come up with the idea of a weapon hidden in his walking stick after watching a fencing match in a movie. 'Allah be praised that I could save you today,' he said. Kalyani could not agree more.

Chapter 5.

Thanks to the drama at the tea shack, they would be an hour late arriving at Muzaffarabad. She hoped Biran hadn't lost his patience and left. She ought to give him a call and warn him. Where was her phone? She scratched at the contents of her bag like a hen hunting for worms in the dirt. No phone. It must have fallen off the rock when the wretch attacked her. Panic gripped her. Without her phone she would be lost, severed from the world she knew. The Khans were sympathetic, but it was too late now to turn back. Even if they did, it was unlikely her phone was where she had last seen it. Either it had fallen over the edge or someone would have stolen it by now. Her pill-box was missing too, and perhaps some of the loose change.

In comparison to the bus stop at Peshawar, the one she arrived at was deserted. Mr Khan and the driver got down with her and helped her with her bag. A stocky man with dark glasses and a silver bracelet, leaning against a jeep, raised his hand to greet her, before approaching.

'Kalyani?' his voice was deep.

'Biran?'

The driver and Mr Khan conversed quickly in their own language with Biran, updating him of events at the tea shack. Biran's face clouded with anger. He thanked the two men who returned to their coach.

'Alright?' Biran enquired, taking charge of her bag. 'Where your friend?'

Kalyani was not in the mood to launch into a lengthy explanation. 'I am alright, Biran. Romy is arriving later.'

Biran led her to his vehicle – a hybrid between a souped - up jeep and a truck. He helped her into the jeep and tucked her suitcase under the tarpaulin stretched over the boot. There were two other people in the jeep, apart from the driver. When she hesitated at the entrance, Biran told her not to worry. 'Farm workers. We pick up some building material – they help. When we travel two hours to Muzaffarabad, we have big shopping list. Two for one. Save time, diesel etcetera.' Biran spoke in heavily-accented, broken English.

The farm workers did not speak at all. One of them was a middle-aged woman, her skin, dark and weathered, adorned with silver jewellery, tarnished and dull, and the other, a young boy, in his late teens. Both looked bored, barely gave her a second glance, and kept to their side of the vehicle. Biran poured water from a bottle over a towel and handed it to her, before climbing in beside the driver.

As they pulled away from the bus stop, she did her best to wipe off the dirt from her hands and her face. Her palms were grazed and she must have hurt her chin, because it was starting to throb. At least she had made it to her destination. Relief flooded over her. Tears threatened to fall; she pressed the wet cloth into her eyes to stop them. The boy was staring at her with a mixture of concern and terror, lest she started crying. He was growing a beard; she could tell from the few wispy and tentative hairs on his chin. When he realised she was looking at him, he glanced away, embarrassed. The woman muttered to herself, stretched herself on the seat and went off to sleep.

'We stop at market,' Biran called out from the front. He had not forced her to have a conversation, for which she was grateful, but she was desperate to ask him if he had managed to contact Raffa. It didn't seem appropriate to shout out the question in front of the others. Besides, he had the car radio on loud, and wouldn't have heard her.

The market was closing down for the day; the last few vendors were packing up their wares, covering their trolleys or baskets with plastic or sacks. Kalyani wondered what Biran intended to buy from an empty market, but he drove past the empty stalls into the dark, narrow alleys in the back. In contrast to the makeshift shops in the front, these were more permanent structures, made out of brick and mortar, in various stages of disrepair – crumbling plaster on the walls, broken tiles on the roof, and faded tin signs hanging lopsided above their entrances. There was barely enough room for people to walk between the shops, let alone for a big jeep to drive through. Biran gestured for the driver to stop outside a particularly narrow street.

A row of ramshackle buildings flanked the alley. One sharpened knives, another melted tin to solder cracked metal pots, welded broken bikes, and yet another mended raggedy clothes. Across the road, a man worked on a typewriter, his glasses perched on the tip of his nose, and outside a shop that painted signs, its owner sat on his haunches, smoking handmade cigarettes and gossiping with his mates. Apart from greeting Biran, they showed no further interest in them.

The men and the woman left the vehicle and disappeared into the alleyway, leaving the boy in charge. He promptly stepped off the jeep and borrowed a cigarette from the sign painter. Kalyani wished she could get some fresh air too. The evening was still warm, and she felt cramped and dirty. She wondered if the boy had a mobile phone she could borrow, but he pretended not to notice her, until she swung her legs out of the jeep. He moved quickly to block her, gesturing that she should stay inside.

She felt annoyed. She wasn't exactly a puny Pakistani woman who should neither be seen nor heard, but before she could protest, the men returned, carrying between them a sack of something long and heavy. The boy rushed to lift the tarpaulin on the boot. The bundle hit the floor of the boot with a metallic clatter. The boy pulled the tarpaulin over and replaced her bag over it. They made a few more trips, fetching a couple of bamboo poles and wooden planks, baskets of vegetables and fruit, spilling over with herbs and spinach leaves, and finally, a third basket was delivered, covered with frayed blue plastic. A faint stench of decay emerged from it, making her want to gag. This was placed right on top of everything else. She fervently hoped that the smell did not soak into her clothes. She did not want to smell like a corpse when she met up with Raffa!

Finally, satisfied with their day's shopping, they pulled and fastened the tarpaulin down, and got back into the jeep. As the driver reversed out of the alley, the men distributed cans of lemonade. She would have given one of her expensive acrylic nails in return for a hot cup of sweet tea and one of those mint pakoras she had eaten with Aliya yesterday, but no one thrust an à la carte menu at her. The cold, tangy, chemical - laden drink, however, quenched her thirst and gave her some much needed calories. She rolled the sweating can over her neck to cool herself and thought of her cosy home in England, her soft bed, goose down white duvet, and the soft chink of ceramic as her mother laid the table for supper. A lump rose in her throat. She chased it down with another swig from the can.

Her dream of sleeping on cloud-soft pillows flew out of the window as the jeep jerked to a stop and she nearly fell off her seat. She was still clutching her drink, but some of it had spilled out and soaked into her clothes, leaving a sticky residue. How long had she slept?

The jeep had stopped at a police checkpost. The farm workers, who sat in the back with her, were talking rapidly to each other in a low voice. The woman pulled out a long piece of red chiffon from under her seat; it was woven with silver and gold thread, mirrors and tassels – a bridal veil. She leant towards Kalyani and shoved it into her free hand, gesturing that she should wear it. Kalyani hesitated, but under the woman's glare, placed her drink on the floor and fumbled with the veil. She could hear pleading voices and footsteps approaching the vehicle from the direction of the checkpost. Cursing, the woman snatched the veil from her hands, unfolded it and wrapped it over her head, pulling it forward to hide her face completely. The teen boy with wispy beard leapt to her side, the side of his thigh lightly touching hers. The woman once again stretched out on the opposite seat, pretending to sleep.

Before Kalyani could say anything, the door of the jeep was wrenched open by a uniformed man. Behind him, Biran stood with his arms folded in supplication. The woman, who had been pretending to sleep, sat up, looking aptly confused.

The uniformed guard let his gaze linger on the veiled bride and her lovestruck young groom, trying to protect her from being ogled at by strange men. He tapped his baton on the side of the boot, urging Biran to open it. Without further ado, Biran unfastened the tarpaulin. The guard let out an expletive as the smell of the rotting meat hit him; he winced and wrinkled his nose. Cursing under his breath, he hastily poked his baton between the baskets of vegetables and planks of wood, and then into the baskets, pushing the carrots and marrows around. Kalyani recognised the word 'Nikah' bandied around a few times and guessed that Biran was pretending they were going to attend the wedding party for her and Wispy Beard. The groceries and the meat were being delivered for the meal.

'That meat – you take for dog? Not fit for human consumption by the time you take it home,' the guard cautioned in a mixture of broken English and Hindi before moving away.

'Yes sir. We try to go fast, sir,' Biran mumbled, with great humility, as he closed the boot.

Five agonising minutes later, Biran boarded the jeep with the signed and stamped papers in his hand. '*Chalo*. Let us go.' The teen groom sprang away from her, as if she had suddenly become contagious. Kalyani undid the veil from around her head, and returned it to the older woman, who tucked it back under the seat. She had played her part well.

They drove in silence for a while, and then broke into celebratory laughter. '*Saale*,' Biran cursed. 'He bought it!' They laughed and clapped each other on their backs. 'Guards – always stop and check,' Biran explained for her benefit. 'No take this. No take that! Want bribe all time. Give money... they let you go.' Though she felt used, their mood rubbed off on her and she smiled with them.

Half an hour later, minutes before reaching their destination, they threw the basket of rotting meat into a ditch. They had successfully smuggled whatever it was they were trying to hide past the checkpost.

*

By the time Biran directed the jeep into Sulaiman Kaka's yard, it was the dark side of twilight. The skies were the colour of a purple bruise from a love bite. The place glowed with an eerie light; the house, built on a slope, silhouetted crookedly against the darkening sky. The jeep swayed from side to side as it negotiated the uneven path.

There were no streetlights and the moon was yet to appear. On the drive up, Kalyani had not seen another house for miles. This was truly the middle of nowhere.

In response to Biran banging on the door of the house, it was opened from inside by a woman who was in no hurry to let them in. The woman was stooped and old; she held a lantern in her hand as high as her arthritic shoulder would allow. Biran shouted something to the woman, and the woman shouted back, her speech slurred and unclear. Following Biran's instructions, she retreated into the house with the lamp, leaving them in the dark.

'Huma. No teeth. No hear. Bird brain,' Biran grumbled.

The men laughed amongst themselves and cursed, until she returned with a bunch of keys, which she handed to Biran. Biran inspected the keyring to choose the ones he wanted, simultaneously holding a conversation with the woman. Finally, he isolated a couple of keys and handed them to one of the other men. He then unloaded Kalyani's case from the back of the jeep and gestured to her to enter the house.

Kalyani felt a frisson of excitement. The place was an ideal romantic backdrop for her reunion with Raffa. Hopefully, romance was on the cards. She followed Biran's example and left her shoes outside. The house was warm, and the floor cool underfoot; the air smelt of spices and burning oil. Judging from the smoking wood burning stove, over which a cauldron of food was bubbling and spitting, and the dull gleam of copper and stainless steel pans, they must have entered through the kitchen. Biran led her upstairs, and placed her bag in the room she would stay in, and showed her the tiny washroom in the landing outside. 'Food. Down.' He pointed downstairs, before leaving her with the lantern.

Kalyani tackled him with the question she was dying to ask. When was Raffa arriving?

'Tomorrow. Lunchtime,' Biran told her.

Music to her ears. Kalyani requested him to send a text to Alam to let them know she had arrived safely. 'My phone needs charging.' She wasn't sure why she hadn't told him she had lost her phone.

Any expectation of a long soak in a hot bath was dissipated when she looked around the tiny bathroom. It had a loo and a tiny sink with a small, mottled mirror over it, but no bath or shower. She cleaned up as much as possible with the thin trickle of water spurting from the tap and a sliver of soap.

The men had already started eating, and did not pay much attention to her when she entered the dining area. Biran rose to welcome her, and old Huma gave her a toothless grin and handed her a stainless steel plate, pointing to an empty place at the table. What Kalyani really wanted, other than a bath, was a good sleep, but the enticing smell of spicy lentils reminded her that she hadn't eaten anything since breakfast. She made some headway into the meal, before realising that sitting at the head of the polished, wooden table laden with supper and candles, around which Huma hovered as she waited on the diners, was Tasneen.

First impressions? There wasn't much to see, not only because of the lack of light, but because she was wearing the hijab, covering her from top to toe, including the lower half of her face. Only her kohl - lined eyes were visible, fluid and deep in the reflected light of the candles. She wasn't big, but her presence seemed to fill the room. The people around the table looked up to her, included her in their conversation, and did not seem to mind that she did not say much. When she did, her tone was hushed and 'breathy', as if every word had been weighed and thought through before it left her mouth. The men hung on her every word.

Amidst the noise of clinking cutlery, slurping and chewing, the men conversed in their own language, a mixture of Urdu and Pashtun. From occasional words thrown in by Biran in a familiar language, and the glances that the group directed at her, she guessed that they were discussing her ordeal at the tea shack. Tasneen's eyes appraised her. If her mouth expressed anything, it was hidden behind the veil. The bread was passed around, and the men bragged about their conquest at the police checkpoint. This time, Tasneen's eyes smiled at them. 'Allah be thanked,' she said.

Kalyani could have fallen asleep into her food and not be noticed. She soon became invisible to the host and the diners, until the men rose in unison from the table and, except for Biran, headed off to their sleeping quarters in one of the outbuildings.

While Huma and Tasneen cleared the table and blew the candles out, she asked Biran where Sulaiman Kaka was.

'Kaka leave this morning. Family emergency. He say Tasneen look after you.'

'Sorry to hear that,' Kalyani said. 'Please thank Tasneen for this delicious meal. I would like to go to bed.' If Biran wondered why she couldn't do it herself, he did not say, but agreed.

There were only three rooms on that floor – hers and, presumably, Tasneen's and her son's bedrooms. Her own room wasn't big; it was long and narrow, and the flickering light from the lantern picked up the irregular bumps on the whitewashed walls. Her bed was between the door and a wardrobe, either of which she could reach in a few strides. On one of the smaller side walls, a window opened out onto the front of the house, and the other wall adjoined the neighbouring room. Apart from a trio of identically framed photographs hanging on that wall, the room was sparsely decorated. Ignoring her tiredness, Kalyani carried the lantern over to examine the photographs.

The one at the top was of the stables. 'Sulaiman Pony Riding Club' it said in italics. Posing in front of it was a pretty, young girl, holding the reins of a chestnut pony. Her hair was blowing in her face and she was squinting into the sun. Beside her was an older man. Judging by the doting and proprietary way he was watching over the girl, he could only be her father. And the girl was most likely a much younger Tasneen. Beneath the photo, somebody had used a slanting handwriting to write 'T & darling D'. Tasneen and darling daddy?

The second one had three people in it. An older Tasneen, her father, and a man holding her around the waist, who Kalyani deduced to be Harry, her husband. Sure enough, the script confirmed it. 'T & D & darling H.'

The third was of children posing with their ponies – memories of a bygone era of Sulaiman's business. A successful enterprise that had put his family on the tourist attraction map in the region, and allowed them a sufficiently lavish lifestyle.

She peered again at the photo of Tasneen – innocent, carefree, like any other girl of her age. Yet, this was the girl who had stirred up so much interest at Fawzia's party – the girl who has always been hounded by bad luck. Lost her mother at such a young age, lost her husband, Harry, so soon after marriage, lost the business...

'She is a brave girl,' they had said, in a tone that suggested she was anything but brave. They had exchanged looks with each other. Tasneen did not sit comfortably within their idealistic society, but they could not resist talking about her either.

Having met Tasneen, Kalyani could not blame them. Tasneen was playing host that night, as her father was not there. Yet, she had not greeted Kalyani or introduced herself. But she hadn't indicated that Kalyani was not welcome either. She had not shouted from the rooftops that she was lady of the manor, but she was clearly in control. There was something disconcerting about her. She seemed to fit into the picture people painted of her – a mixture of despondency and courage, tragedy and mystery.

Chapter 6

Kalyani slipped into her pyjamas. Huma had placed a bottle of water in her room. Having been brought up with the basic mod cons using electricity, she knew very little about lanterns. Uncertain as to how long the flame would last, she decided to use the toilet now. Her room was just opposite the stairs, and from where she stood, leaning on the curved, wooden balustrade, she could see the entrance from the kitchen into the dining hall. The dining table itself was tucked out of sight under the landing. Downstairs was dark and silent.

The door to her room intrigued her; it had two separate halves, a right and a left half, which opened outwards. She could pull them shut by using piece of string that was threaded through a hole in one of them, but there was no latch. Correction – there was no longer a latch. Someone had taken a screwdriver to it and removed it. She felt uneasy; anyone of the servants could come in while she slept. To be on the safe side, she dragged her suitcase away from the door and placed her handbag and her valuables on the bedside table between her bed and the wardrobe. She would have to sleep with one eye open.

The bed creaked as she lay back, and sagged in the middle from years of use. She wondered whose bedroom she was in. Who had slept on the sagging mattress? Had Harry and Tasneen spent passionate nights together on it? Did Raffa sleep here when he stayed over? Despite herself, the thought of sleeping in Raffa's bed gave her pleasure.

What would tomorrow bring? More sorrow? Was she ready for closure? Was there a chance that love could blossom again? Could she forgive him for all the hurt he had caused her and her family?

Only time would tell.

*

Deep and dreamless her sleep was, but long it wasn't. A sharp thud woke her up. The man with yellow eyes was tearing at her flesh with dirty nails, fork- tongued serpents emerged from his open mouth, hissing. They twisted and turned into a sharp, pointed sword and plunged into her heart. Death was in the room. She rolled out of bed in panic, pulling the sheets down with her. The lamp had run out of oil and the flame had died down, but the room was lit by silvery moonlight, seeping through the slats of the reed screen at the window, casting strange, fluttering shadows on the wall. And was that a spider? Crawling a little to the left, an inch upwards, with long, hairy feet? Kalyani detested spiders, especially the ones with hairy legs. From years of maintaining a vigil for the creatures, she knew that some moved slowly, creeping cautiously, while others ran like athletes after a gold medal. She had no idea what the spiders living in the remote hills of Pakistan looked like. As long as she kept the spot within sight, she could move quickly if it targeted her. If she could commandeer her aching body to move at all.

But what had disturbed her sleep? She had heard something. A door slamming. She twisted around to look at the door to her room. The left half was wide open, swinging slightly on its hinges. She gathered the sheets up to her neck and backed into the bedpost, frantically searching the unfamiliar shadows for a hiding trespasser. A whole minute ticked by with nothing happening. Her valuables and the suitcase were exactly where she had left them, but her handbag wasn't. She had definitely placed the bag on the inside bedside table, and now, it wasn't there. Had she moved it herself in the night, or pushed it down when she scrambled out of her bed? She peered into the darkness around the bed, using her hands to feel around it. The Prada lookalike bag she had bought from the Leicester market had all her worldly belongings in it – the return tickets to Peshawar, money, and most importantly, her make -up! Without her Mac foundation and Bobbi Brown lipstick, Raffa would take one look at her and congratulate himself on having made the right decision to run away, a year ago. Already, she had lost her phone and her pills to that wretch.

Unbidden, the events from earlier in the day (or was it the day before?), flooded into her brain. How close to death had she been! One false move and she would have ended at the bottom of that abyss. The authorities would still be fishing for the pieces. The reality of it all hit her. Her body shook like a leaf, cold with delayed shock, then hot with terror. Only the fear of waking Tasneen next door kept her from having a sobbing and screaming meltdown.

With shaking hands, she unscrewed the bottle of water and drank deeply. Feeling calmer, she threw off her blanket and stood up, wincing at the cold stone underfoot. Unsteadily, she tiptoed to the window. A nearly full moon sat right outside, like a happy Buddha, unperturbed by the threat of dark clouds. The moonlight bounced off every reflective surface – the metal of the jeep, rocky shale, and smooth bark of the tall deodars. Steamy, green mist swirled in the valleys beyond, too dense to float upwards. An owl, which was resting on the windowsill, watched her warily, with big, round eyes. When she made a sharp move, it shrieked and took off, its strong wings slapping against the wind. The clouds swallowed the moon, and darkness swept into the room.

She tried to think calmly. The half-open door suggested that someone had entered the room. They must have taken her handbag. Should she raise the alarm immediately, or wait until Tasneen was awake? She walked to the door and peered into the dark corridor. Empty, as far as eye could see. Holding her own breath, she strained to hear sounds from anyone hiding nearby. Either there was no one hiding or they were holding their breath too. She considered stepping out of the safety of her room to check the landing, but didn't fancy the prospect of being hit on the head with a saucepan. She pulled the door shut. It made a sharp noise. On the way back to her bed, she picked up the sheets off the floor; something heavy fell out. With a mixture of relief and joy, she realised it was her handbag. Maybe she hadn't left it on the side table after all. She must have left it on the bed, where it had become entangled in the sheets, as she pulled them off in a hurry.

The wind rustled the reed screen at the window. She sighed. The wind must have thrown the door open. She jumped back into the bed, which creaked loudly. The noise of a child whimpering in its sleep, and the soft comforting voice of the mother, drifted through the thin walls. Feeling guilty for waking up the child, Kalyani slid back between the sheets. Strangely, her last thought before she drifted back into a restless sleep was of the comparatively benign, foraging spider.

*

When she next woke, the room was bathed in warm, yellow sunlight. The sun turned the window into an orb of white light that stung her eyes as she parted the slats. Outside, the mist had lifted out of the low-lying valleys, and invaded the village. Far away, the peaks of the Hindu Kush poked out of the mist, glowing like soft gold. Joy and hope filled her. This was the morning of the day she could be reunited with Raffa. There was no time to waste.

Her fingers ran over the scabbed over abrasion on her chin. She must restore order before she faced anyone. Gingerly, she stepped onto the landing, hoping she wouldn't run into Tasneen and her mocking eyes, and tiptoed to the tiny bathroom. When she returned, she revelled in the fresh air and birdsong that filled her room. The blankets were now neatly folded, and sitting in the middle of the bed like butter wouldn't melt was her Prada lookalike handbag. Huma must have come up and tidied the room while she was in the loo.

It was time she checked the contents of her bag properly. She emptied it on the bed, and sorted the contents into neat piles. The pills and the phone were definitely missing, maybe some loose change, but nothing else. But something had been added. A tightly wrapped bundle of paper, held together with a yellow rubber band. Had Shahida sneaked something else into her bag for her son without her knowledge? Pocket money for the local tuck shop? She slipped the rubber band off and unrolled the bundle. It wasn't money, but newspaper cuttings. Did Shahida want her son to keep in touch with the news in *The Guardian*?

The cuttings were from a local newspaper dated from five years ago, fragile, yellowing and creased; some were in English and others in a language she could not read. She unfolded a full - page report, and smoothed the creases, along which the print was starting to fade, and took it over to the window to read.

'Sulaiman in court,' the headline said.

Chapter 7

Tasneen's father, Sulaiman's ancestors, were rich. As the firstborn, he inherited a lot of wealth, land, and the house with which he built a successful business. Tourism was starting to flourish; the beauty of Narran and Chitral, and the Swat Valley, was legendary, and well known to the rich aristocracy. But now, a new breed of middle-class Pakistanis residing overseas could afford the holiday packages. Sulaiman Pony Riding Clubs were part of these packages. His family wined and dined with the rich and the influential people. But, though his business flourished and his wealth increased, his personal life was tragic. When Tasneen was five years old, his wife and his unborn second child were killed in a road accident. Everybody who knew Sulaiman's love for his wife understood his disinterest in marrying again. Instead, he devoted all his energy and love to bringing up his daughter. She lacked nothing but a mother's love. She attended one of the best schools; her holidays were with rising movie stars; her parties were lavish – no expenses spared affairs. She had servants at her beck and call, expensive cars and horses and a whole wing of the house to herself. He entertained her every whim and fancy. She went to a reputed drama school in the city.

When she came of age, Sulaiman arranged a line of suitors for her; she rejected them all. Just when her father was starting to think she would be left on the shelf as an old maid, she brought Harry home. Harry was her college mate and a Christian. She wasn't sure if she was in love with him, but the more her father tried to discourage the relationship, the more she became determined to marry him. Sulaiman finally gave in, like he always did. At her request, he gave Harry a major role in running the business.

Harry did not have the same business acumen as Sulaiman did. Besides, he was regarded a foreigner, as he did not belong to their community or religion. People did not trust him. Five years into the marriage, when they had a two-year-old son, the business started to buckle. Instead of going to his father-in-law for help, Harry borrowed heavily from unscrupulous lenders. He gambled. He lost. Tasneen begged, pleaded, and fought with her father on Harry's behalf, demanding that he pump more money into the failing business. Blinded by his love for his daughter, he did. By the time he realised his mistake, Sulaiman and his family stood to lose everything.

Days before the bailiffs were due to move in, Harry was dead. They found him in the main hall of the new riding club he had started – Harry's Riding Club. Stabbed several times. He had been entertaining, and judging by the level of alcohol in his bloodstream at his post mortem, he had been very drunk. The word on the street was that his debtors, some of them from the Taliban, had finally lost their patience, and had come to collect their dues.

The business never recovered. Sulaiman was forced to sell his land, his horses, and his business to pay off his debtors. He held on to his ancestral home by the skin of his teeth. But all this stress and strain took a heavy toll on him. The shock of seeing his daughter dressed in a widow's robe, and facing a lifetime of comparative poverty, gave him a stroke, which although didn't kill him, left him paralysed.

Eager to learn more, Kalyani smoothed out the smaller cut - outs, which were in English.

'Sulaiman Syed's daughter weds a foreigner.'

'Sulaiman Riding Club closes its doors for the last time.'

'Businessman found dead.' This one had a mug shot of Harry. He was a handsome bloke, a lazy smile on his fleshy lips, and a shock of dark, curly hair falling over his forehead.

'Sulaiman files for bankruptcy.'

The smallest cutting was tucked away inside one of the bigger ones: 'Who killed Harry?' The cutting itself was heavily creased, as if it had been crumpled into a ball and discarded, and someone had salvaged it and ironed it out. It outlined the graphic details of the wounds on Harry's body. Five on his arms, one to his abdomen, one to his neck. Harry had been entertaining women that night; women who were later identified to be of 'ill repute'. He was very drunk, and therefore unable to defend himself effectively. The stab wounds had not been deep and had not killed him outright; the likelihood was that he had bled to death. The murder weapon was thought to be one of the hunting knives that hung over the fireplace. The weapon had never been found. Kalyani sat back on her haunches and had an OMG moment. *Major gossip!* But who had put these paper cuttings into her bag, and why?

She dug her fingertips into her eyes, until she saw stars. Her eyes felt gritty. A bath was what she needed. She had to concentrate on Raffa's impending arrival, not Tasneen's forgotten past. She gathered the cuttings back into the handbag and grabbed her wash bag, towel and a change of clothes. This time, before leaving, she locked her handbag in her suitcase.

The kitchen was deserted. She found her trainers where she had left them last night, amongst several other pairs of footwear. Tasneen must have a lot of visitors. The mountain air was crisp, pine - scented, tinged with... motor oil. As if to emphasise the point, the birdsong was interrupted by the start of a motor. If anyone had plans for a lie-in that morning, they would be sorely disappointed. It was coming from the direction of the stables on the west side of the property.

The main house she had spent the night in was clearly an older building – the family home. Adjoining it was a smaller, new build – a bungalow with a tiled roof, and modified ramp for a wheelchair. It must have been built for Sulaiman Kaka after he suffered a stroke. A few yards further away were the stables. Behind the buildings stretched what seemed to be acres of farmland, flanked by hilly terrain and woodland. She walked towards the stables, certain that if there were any ponies left, they were stone deaf.

The stables were spacious enough to house three or four horses, but had none. Instead, parked haphazardly, were a couple of bikes, the jeep they arrived in last night, and a car.

The rest of the space was occupied by DIY equipment, piles of wood, broken furniture, and a fierce, black dog, which bared its fangs at her and growled. Warned by the beast, Biran rose from behind the generator he was working on. He wiped his greasy hands on a rag and greeted her.

'Oh. Kalyaniji. Good morning. Hope noise not wake you?'

'Good morning, Biran. No, I was awake. I thought I would take a walk. Would that be OK?'

'Yes. Yes. You want guide?'

'If you have time.'

Biran gave his hands an extra wipe, and joined her.

'Sorry, I don't want to disturb you.'

'Don't worry.' He waved his hand dismissively. 'I have to fix pump, on other side.'

The dog reluctantly got off the floor and hobbled after them, but every time Kalyani made an attempt to befriend it, it growled and barked.

'Not a friendly dog!' she complained.

Biran nodded sagely. 'Guard dog. Only loyal to master.'

'You get robbers here?'

'Robbers, vandals, wild animals...'

'Wild animals? Which ones?'

'Oh. Foxes mainly. Out there, wolf, wild dogs, maybe black bear, snakes...' He pointed towards the woods and the hills beyond.

Kalyani cast a sidelong glance at him. Was he pulling her leg? But the small, muscular man looked deadly serious. She wondered if one guard dog was enough to drive all these unwanted visitors away.

As if he had read her thoughts, he added, pointing his chin at the dog, 'Snake bite – lost foot.'

'Oh? Poisonous snake bit one of his legs?'

'Not poison. Infection.'

'Oh. Poor dog.' The dog snarled at her.

Biran carefully chose the paths between the lush, green fields, to avoid wrecking her shoes.

'They are only cheap trainers,' she assured him.

But he shook his head and said, 'Here, in the *pahaad*, hills, people keep things for long time. No throw away if see small hole.'

Suitably admonished, she followed in his footsteps, flushing out white storks and cormorants fishing in the water around golden brown fields ready for harvest. She wished she could have taken some photographs.

She asked him if he had managed to send a message of her safe arrival to Alam Sahib. Biran confirmed that he had. Kalyani told him how highly Alam Sahib had spoken of him.

'Alam Sahib and family like God to us. Sahib save us from danger many times.'

'Danger?'

'My parents... they die when I was little boy. Alam Sahib and Begum take me, feed me, give me job. He teach me horse riding. I take him hunting.' He smiled. The picture of Alam trying to camouflage his not too small body behind a bush on a hunting trip made her smile too. She liked Biran. He seemed an honest and good man. Alam trusted him, and that was good enough for her.

'Does all this land belong to Sulaiman Kaka?' Kalyani was awed.

'Had more land before. Now sold. Horses sold. No one look after. This is – ancestral property.' Biran gestured with his hands to emphasise the many generations of ancestors.

'So, their riding clubs were here?'

'Only first one. Kaka then spread business in other areas – tourist places. Harry bought one place few miles away to build own company. By then, Taliban stop tourists. His company go bust.'

Kalyani paused to digest this information. 'Sulaiman Kaka seems like an interesting man.'

'Kaka and Alam Sahib. Real gentleman, both. They lay down life for family and country, any day.'

'How did you know Rafik?' she continued to quiz him.

'Met him two times in Alam Sahib's house. I take him sightseeing in open jeep.'

The day was getting hotter as they walked down to the pumphouse. Meandering rivulets of sweat ran down her back. The heat and the lack of breakfast took its toll and she yawned.

'No sleep well?' he asked, concerned.

'Not really. Something or someone woke me in the middle of the night. I… thought someone came into my room,' she told him, trying not to moan.

'Huma!' he said crossly. 'Walk in sleep, Huma does. She walk in Harry's room.'

'Harry's room?'

In his accented, broken English, Biran described how Huma, taken in by his small gifts and flattery, had become close to Harry. Harry could be charming when he wanted, and Huma responded by being at his beck and call, often making him food in the middle of the night, when he rolled in drunk. When he died, Huma was heartbroken. She mourned for him for a long time, and even today, she wanders around his room most nights, bringing morsels of food for him.

The fact that she had slept in Harry's room and in his bed last night made Kalyani uncomfortable. And Huma had walked there in her sleep? Was it Huma who had placed the news cuttings in her handbag? A shiver went down her spine.

*

Twenty minutes later, Biran stopped at what appeared to be a wooden building on stilts. The pumphouse. Biran unlocked the wooden door and put his shoulder to it. Years of damp and heat had made it swell up and stick. His muscles bulged as the wooden door moved slowly, creaking all the way. The pump occupied the entire area downstairs.

'Pumphouse,' Biran confirmed. 'Main water supply to all house, field and orchard. Very old. All time breaking down, like everything here.' Beside the pump was a spiral staircase.

'Where do the stairs go?' Kalyani asked, as Biran poked around the machinery.

'Hmm? To room upstairs. Sulaiman Kaka tell stories about brothers and him playing soldiers there. They pretend room is fort, fighting Afghans, Alexander Great. Good fun, eh? You go up. I check funny noise in pump.'

Kalyani left him to tinker with the pump, and ascended the rickety stairs. What a fascinating time the children must have had, pretending to defend their fort. She could see how it would have served as a fort. The water was pumped from a well and fed into an open canal. The room upstairs was built across the canal, like a bridge. The view from the narrow window fairly high up on the wall was marred by overgrown vegetation, but she could see a grassy knoll, leading to a copse of trees, with a backdrop of gentle, sloping hills. If a child stood on a chair and peered out, their eyes could just see above the edge of the knoll. Anything approaching from the woods walked straight into an ambush, as the children showered them with pretend gunfire and blood-curdling howls. The enemy who was shot would simply fall head first into the canal with a plop, and get swept away by the gushing water, flowing under the room.

She could hear the water flowing gently beneath the room. It could be noisy when the pump worked, but for now, it was quiet and cool. A couple of deep cane chairs with cushions and throws were strategically placed on either side of the window. Perhaps Harry and Tasneen had spent romantic evenings together, drinking tea, and making love in the moonlight. A tea chest between the chairs served as a coffee table – strewn with magazines and a brass table lamp. She wondered if the toy guns Sulaiman and his brothers had played with were stored in the chest. Carefully, she moved the magazines and the lamp, and opened the lid a little to peek. Old blankets, colourful scarves, a party mask, a set of opera glasses, gramophone records, cassette and CD collections. She switched on the table lamp and examined the CDs – Neil Diamond, The Carpenters, Pink Floyd. Timeless classics that could have belonged to Harry or Tasneen. There was a convent school leaver's yearbook from nearly fifteen years ago. Kalyani paged through it, and soon found the photo of a much younger Tasneen; beautiful, confident, her eyes mocking the cameraman. Under it was the comment – 'Most likely to be a famous actress'.

A prophecy that Tasneen had tried to fulfil by attending drama school. If she had been educated in a convent, and exposed to more liberal Western culture, why was she pretending to hide behind the hijab and not speak a word of English? A consummate actress. What else was she hiding?

With a loud rumble, the pump downstairs came alive, startling her. Quickly, she closed the chest and replaced the magazines on top of it. She gathered her wash bag and towel and went down, trying not to look guilty.

Biran was too busy to notice anyhow. He apologised for keeping her.

'I go back to work.' He pointed to the towel in her hand. 'You want bath?'

'Yes… yes. Where is bath?'

'I show,' he said, leading her back towards the house through a different path.

As she followed him, something struck her. She had switched on the lamp in the pumphouse. The place had electricity connection. Biran was also working on a generator in the stables. Why then had they dined by candlelight last night?

'Was there a… power cut last night?' she asked him.

'Sometimes we have power cut. No last night,' Biran replied in a matter of fact tone.

Having a conversation was getting difficult, because they were walking down a muddy slope in single file.

The land around the house was certainly not even, a reflection on the fact that they were in hilly terrain. Biran pointed to a tin shack a few feet behind the main house. 'Bath.'

As she thanked him for his time, his phone rang. He answered it and with a wave of his hand, he walked towards the stables.

Chapter 8

The tin shack bath was hardly a five-star affair. There was no bath she could get into. It was more like a wet room sans a shower. Along one wall, large, metal drums held tepid water, heated by the sun. The stone floor felt smooth underfoot, and there was no roof. Only clear, blue sky. If she couldn't see over the tall, corrugated sides, Kalyani told herself, it was unlikely that anybody else could look in. Nevertheless, she kept her towel wrapped around her, as she scooped water with a small, brass vessel and washed herself. It was not the long, refreshing soak she longed for, but at least she wasn't covered in sweat and grime.

As she walked back, her things bundled into her very wet towel, a myriad of thoughts ran through her brain. She wondered if Romy had got his connecting flight, and Alam had conveyed the news of her safe arrival to her parents. She mulled over what Biran had said. Yesterday, when they arrived, the house was lit by oil lanterns. She had assumed that the property either did not have electricity supply or they had a power cut, which happened all the time in Pakistan. If neither was true, why were they all wandering around in the dark? Was Tasneen saving money on electricity bills, or had she lost her mind after her husband's cruel death?

Stop brooding over Tasneen, Kals, she told herself. Raffa was coming, and that is what mattered. She should get ready for him. Look her best. Think about what she should wear. She had carefully chosen the colours that had merited a second glance from Raffa in the past. The tangerine orange dress she had bought from one of the small and unique boutiques on the high street that he had relished unzipping; the vibrant-green scarf, he had slowly pulled off her, all the while gazing into her eyes...

She stopped in her tracks, confused. Busy with her thoughts, she must have taken a wrong turn from the tin shack bath and now she couldn't recognise her surroundings. Rugged rocks, dry tufts of long grass, and loose gravel underfoot were unfamiliar. Black crows and small, brown sparrows flitted in and out of the crevices, fishing for worms. Over the rocks, washed clothes, pinned down to dry with heavy stones, fluttered in the hot breeze, and on reed mats covered with fine netting to keep away the birds, red chillies and salted mangoes shrivelled into pickles. She perched on a flat piece of rock to gather her bearings. It must be well over an hour since she left her room. The mid - morning sun was scorching everything in its path. In a few minutes, it would burn her skin, and frazzle her hair, and make her sweat. The towel bundle had stopped dripping, and dry patches felt rough against her skin.

She realised she had been walking uphill, along a path lined with tall oleander bushes, bearing pink and white flowers and other thorny shrubs. Peering through them, she had a view of the sloping roof and the back of Sulaiman Kaka's bungalow. Even from where she sat, she could see the cobwebs hanging in thick shreds from the rafters. No one had walked out of the back door for a very long time. In fact, the backyard had become a dumping ground for broken furniture, rusting metal and forgotten toys. On the west side of the bungalow, separated from it by a small alleyway was a small outbuilding.

She searched for a path down to the house to avoid walking all the way back. There was a dirt trail a few feet away from her, but just as she made a move towards it, she spotted the small group of three men, standing in the shadows between the bungalow and the outbuilding, conversing in low tones. She was too far away to hear what they were saying, but she recognised Wispy Beard boy. She was about to call out to them, but there was something suspicious in the way they huddled together, and cast furtive glances around them. They lit their cigarettes, cupping their palms around the flame, taking great care to extinguish the match by grinding it into the dirt. Wispy Beard picked up the spent match and put it in his pocket. If they had looked up in her direction, they wouldn't have missed her crouching by the rocks. But they didn't. Instead, they walked off around the corner of the bungalow, and disappeared from her view. In a few minutes, she heard jeep doors open and shut, the engine starting, and the vehicle driving away from the house. She waited until the noise of the jeep faded to a faint burr, before she rose from the rocks and found the path leading down. She walked to the place where the men had stood. The smoke from their cigarettes still lingered, and tickled her throat. The outbuilding was no more than a small, white - washed shed, built in such a way that it was not visible from the front of the property. Although its plaster was crumbling and the paint on the door was peeling, there were no cobwebs framing the doorway, or layers of dust on the ledge outside the door. The door was latched on the outside, but wasn't locked.

Curiosity killed the cat, a voice in her head warned. Ignoring it, she quickly unfastened the latch and let herself into the shed. She was only going to take a harmless peek, while she sheltered from the sun. Despite the sunlight streaming in through the open door, it took her eyes a few seconds to adjust to the comparatively dim light inside. The windowless shed was only about eight by ten feet, offering standing space for two, maybe three, small people in the centre. Lined along the walls were several long packages wrapped in sackcloth or hideous turquoise plastic. Probably building materials. Most of the floor was occupied by a large, open wooden crate, its lid askew. The contents of the crate were covered with old, faded blankets. A faint smell of something familiar reached her, the scent of decayed rotting meat. *These must be the blankets they used to cover the rotting meat in the boot of the jeep last night.*

She lifted the blankets and peeped inside the crate. What she saw made blood rush to her head and throb in her ears; she heard herself gasp. In the crate were rows and rows of guns of various shapes and sizes. Rifles, machine guns, pistols... Kalyani knew nothing about weapons, but even she could see that these were not toys built for children to shoot water out of. A small, sealed box nestled amongst them. Ammunition. This was what they were smuggling past the check post last night. Were the packages lining the walls guns too? This meant smuggling operations had been going on for a while and the shed was being used as a storehouse for the weapons. Who were they smuggling them for and what were they using them for?

Suddenly, she realised she was in danger. Surely, she was not meant to stumble upon the firearms. The men wouldn't have left the shed unlocked unless they were expecting to return soon. She did not want to dwell on her fate, if they caught her snooping. Hastily replacing the blankets over the crate, she scrambled to her feet, gathered her things, remembering not to leave any evidence of her presence, and rushed to the door.

Too late. For above, the noise of panic in her ears, she heard footsteps.

Please let them pass by, Kalyani pleaded silently to the Gods. 'Please let them collect their clothes and pickles and leave.'

But the footsteps continued up the gravel path outside the shed. Crunch, crunch. CRUNCH. She looked around the room for somewhere to hide. She could climb into the crate and curl up under the smelly blankets. The crate was not long enough; either her head or her feet would stick out. She imagined the conversation between her captor and Tasneen.

'What would you like for tea, Memsahib Tasneen? The lovely, long legs connected to her bottom, well acclaimed at her college, or her head that keeps thinking of Raffa? Or would you rather savour the tid bits – candied lips, or pickled tits…?'

Or she could shuffle between the layers of rifles propped up against the walls, and hope to blend into the shadows. Before she could decide, she heard something that turned her blood cold. The panting of an animal. The hobbling dog that only responded to its master. The dog would pick up her scent, and flush her out of whichever hiding place she chose. Cold sweat ran down her spine.

The Gods had not heeded her prayers. The footsteps and the panting stopped outside the door to the shed. Her heart was beating so fast that it was ineffective in keeping her circulation going. Her hands were turning cold and clammy, and her mouth was dry. She fervently hoped that whoever it was would not look in; they might just pull the door shut and leave.

The thought stopped her in her tracks. If someone did lock the door from outside, she would have no way out. She would either run out of air and suffocate slowly, or die of dehydration. How long would she last, before she turned into a desiccated mummy, like the pickles on the reed mat? How long before the spiders find her, and the scorpions and the snakes crawl over her, their scales scratching her, their feet scuttling…

The dog was growling softly now. They knew there was someone in the shed, whom the dog considered an enemy. Kalyani made up her mind; she would throw herself at the mercy of humans, rather than insects. If she surprised them at the door, she may be able to run as fast as her legs carried her, out to the road, all the way to the nearest neighbour, miles away.

The door was being opened from outside. It swung on its hinges with a whine and hit the wall behind it with a gentle thud. Tasneen, in her hijab, stood outside, her hands on the dog's collar. The dog bared its teeth, its hackles stood up, and saliva drooled out of its mouth as it waited for its master's command. Mistress, in this case. Tasneen's eyes, the only visible part of her face, registered surprise. For a disconcerting moment, the women stared at each other, each deciding on the next step.

'Sorry, I... lost my way. I... was looking for the... er... washing machine,' Kalyani blurted out, lamely shoving the bundle of clothes in front of her, as she inched around the dog and its mistress.

Tasneen's eyes spoke volumes. She was deciding what to do with her. Let the dog loose on her. Push her back into the room and leave her to die slowly, and dispose of her body later, like they did the basket of rotten meat. And put out a story that Kalyani never arrived on that bus.

To her surprise, Tasneen meekly stepped aside and let her go. As she walked away, she expected to be attacked from behind. Any moment now, Tasneen would order her to stop and point one of those guns at her. Any moment now, the mongrel will bury its fangs into her ankles

Trying not to show fear, Kalyani walked stiffly on trembling legs, all the while feeling Tasneen's kohl-rimmed eyes and the mongrel's yellow ones boring a hole into her back. Once around the corner of the house, she leant against the wall and slid down, her legs no longer supporting her.

What was she supposed to do now?

She contemplated running. But where would she go? To the barn in search of Biran, or to a neighbour's house, begging for protection? All the way to the police station? Not that she knew where it was. No prizes for guessing whose side they would choose to take. The whole village could be involved in the gun trade. What then?

Besides, if she was going to be killed, she would rather it was in the house, where she would leave plenty of evidence for her parents to find, if and when they persuaded the police to investigate her disappearance. She ran to the house, panting like the mongrel she had left behind. The bundle of clothes she had been carrying had ripped open, and its contents were spilling out. Sweat poured out of every pore, drenching the clothes she wore. So much for the wash in the tin shack.

She took off her trainers and carried them as she hurried through the kitchen. Past the shelves stacked with metal pots, their bottoms covered with years of soot from the wood-burning stove, past sacks of rice and lentils, baskets of onions and garlic, and jars of homemade spice blends, past Huma, who had her back to her. Huma was frying something in a large pan of oil, filling the kitchen with smoke and the smell of fried food. She was too deaf to hear Kalyani above the hiss and splutter of oil. On the kitchen counter was a large knife that she had been using to cut vegetables. Instinctively, Kalyani grabbed the knife, and ran through the dining room, up the stairs, her heart thudding against her ribs. That was close. So very close.

She slammed the door to her room, wishing it had a latch, and collapsed on the bed, trying to catch her breath. Clutching the knife and her trainers in her trembling hands, she drew her knees up and faced the door. She would die fighting, if necessary.

After fifteen minutes, her hands were starting to cramp, and her thoughts were beginning to wander.

Why had Tasneen let her go? Or had she let her go? For all she knew, Tasneen might be planning her next move. The disappearance of a foreign national could prove too messy, unless carefully planned and performed in a controlled manner. Or perhaps, she believed that this infatuated girl with frizzy hair was indeed searching for a washing machine, and was too stupid to notice the stacks of guns in the shed.

Her hand was starting to shake with the strain. She put the knife down on the bedside table, its handle facing her, so she could grab it if needed, and massaged her wrist to coax the blood supply back. It was a butcher's knife, with a serrated edge, its wooden handle dark and smooth with use. She could inflict some serious wounds with it.

What had she walked into? An Ali Baba's cave of smuggled treasure? She didn't even have to say 'open sesame' because no one had locked the door. The guns were not a secret to the residents of the house. Tasneen, Biran, the other men in the jeep, knew. Did Sulaiman Kaka know? From what she had heard, Sulaiman was an old man, an invalid after his stroke; was he in a fit state to comprehend what was going on? Was he turning a blind eye, or had he been coerced into it?

Was her Raffa involved too? She put her head in her hands and groaned. *Get a grip*. She could be over-dramatising the situation. After all, it could be a legal trade. The family might be trading or storing the weapons for the Pakistani army. But why would they smuggle them in, if that was the case? The gun trade must be illegal, meant to be sold to the terrorists. The family was in debt, their business was non-existent, there was a lack of strong men to work in the fields; they had to keep the wolf from the door.

Now that she had stumbled on it, what should she do? Go to the police? Ask Raffa if he was aware of this? Tell Alam? What if they already knew?

Somewhere downstairs, a door slammed. Kalyani froze. Tasneen was back! What was she planning to do? This was her house. She could walk up the stairs, kick open the door, point the gun at her and pull the trigger. She wouldn't even need a silencer. There was nobody within hearing range, except for deaf Huma. Then she could drag her body down, load it into the jeep and dump it in the mountains – another Taliban killing. Or she could call the Taliban and hand her over to them. What fun they would have with the poor, stupid girl from England who wanted to play James Bond.

Kalyani strained to listen for footsteps on the stairs. She heard none. The woman was not in a hurry to finish her off. Perhaps she was phoning Terrorist HQ for further instructions. Jeez, her imagination was working overtime.

She looked around the room, thinking of ways to barricade herself. The bed was made of iron, too heavy for her to move. The bedside tables on the other hand were too flimsy. Nevertheless, she piled them on top of each other in front of the door. Not much of a barricade, but it would at least warn her. Was there any way to attract attention to her plight from a passerby? The window looked out onto the front of the property – the view was spectacular, but there was no other house in sight, and no one passed by. She had no phone. The only choice she had was to wait for Raffa. He would know what to do.

Raffa! She had wanted to look like a fresh - faced, happy bride for him, not like a tramp who had been dragged backwards through the hedge. Her long hair was knotted and snarled. Her skin was probably starting to peel in charred sheets. A film of red mud coated her arms and legs where they were exposed. She needed make-up, hair straighteners, deodorant and perfume – lots of it. A girl had the right to look pretty, even if she was going to be slaughtered. Carrying the knife with her, she rummaged in her suitcase for the hair tongs, and searched for a plug point, before she recalled the lack of electricity. But the room had light switches. There was one right beside the door, and a lampshade dangled from the ceiling over her bed. Nothing happened when she flicked the switch on. Off and on; off and on. No flicker, no glow. She walked over and stood under the dusty lampshade – white plastic, yellow with age. She would have to stand on the bed to reach the bulb – only there was no bulb; the brass holder in the shade was empty. Someone had deliberately removed the bulb, or they had not replaced the last one that had fused. There were no other electrical gadgets in the room. No table lamp, no fan or music player. Caught up in the mood for snooping into other people's things, Kalyani opened the wardrobe, and gawked, fascinated at the lines of expensive jackets, silk kurtas, riding boots, hats, and designer underwear. Harry's forlorn and expensive wardrobe. His collar size and shoe size suggested he had a thick neck and large feet; yet, he had been killed without much resistance.

She remembered the framed photograph of Harry on the wall. Lifting it off the wall, she carried it to the window. Harry was slimmer in the photograph than his clothes in the wardrobe suggested. He must have acquired the flab later, the result of a lavish lifestyle. Something fluttered to the floor from behind the frame. A smaller photograph. This one had two adults and a child. An older Tasneen, holding her baby, and a much plumper looking Harry. The three of them were standing before the fireplace, smiling casually at the photographer. Over the fireplace, on the faux yellow brick wall, hung a stuffed stag head, its antlers reaching the roof, and below it, a pair of hunting knives, their blades crossing each other. One of them would be used later, to kill Harry, the one that would go missing. Inscribed at the back of the photograph was 'Harry's Riding Club'. The one he had set up on his own.

There was something odd about the photo. It wasn't one exuding happiness like the others.

Harry seemed to twist his body sideways to avoid touching his wife, and Tasneen's smile seemed plastered on. Obviously, this wasn't one of Tasneen's favourite photographs, which was why it was tucked out of sight, but why had she kept it?

Kalyani's head was starting to ache with all this thinking. The lack of sleep and food, and the constant flow of adrenaline, were taking its toll; she was running on empty. She was desperate for a drink of water. She did what she always did when everything became overwhelming, wriggled under the sheets and curled up. She promised herself that she wouldn't sleep; she would just lie there, holding the knife, until Raffa arrived. Everything would work out, when Raffa arrived, she told herself. He would have a sane explanation for everything. All will be well... He would be her saviour... or her murderer.

Half an hour later, she woke with a jolt. Despite her promise to herself, she had drifted off. Her hands were stiff from clutching the knife and the handbag. Drool coated her chin, but at least she was alive. No one had crept up the stairs and shot her in her sleep. Only you can sleep through danger, Kals, she berated herself.

From the courtyard came the noise of a vehicle pulling in, revving up the horsepower as it negotiated the rugged slope. The dog barked and human voices hushed it. Doors slammed, and the voice she had travelled thousands of miles to hear floated up to her. She rolled out of bed and rushed to the window. Gleaming in the now harsh sun was a red four-wheel drive SUV. Though she couldn't see anyone, she felt his presence.

With the help of her handheld pocket mirror, she fastened her hair with a clip, and cleaned up as much as possible with a packet of wet wipes, dowsed herself with perfume and squirted mouth freshener into her mouth until she gagged. She applied some lipstick and rubbed some on to her cheeks, and smoothed her clothes down. It would have to do for now.

Only the fear that someone might be waiting outside the door with a sack to trap her in prevented her from throwing the door open and running out. Cautiously, she checked either side of the corridor before she crept to the head of the stairs.

From there, she could not see anyone, but she could hear voices. The soft sighing one that belonged to Tasneen, and the more familiar one, the one that was music to her ears – Raffa's. Like butter in a hot pan, her resolve melted. Suddenly, it wasn't 'closure' she wanted. Not anymore. She wanted Raffa. She ran to the stairs for her first glimpse of him.

She closed her eyes, picked up her skirts and flew down the remaining stairs, her feet hardly touching the cold stone. 'Raffa!' she screamed as she tripped over the last stair. She was going to land on the floor in an ungainly heap, but her lover sprang to her rescue. He leaped forwards with hands outstretched. Her momentum sent him reeling backwards and they ended up on the floor with her landing on top of him. He laughed; his slightly crooked left canine and the dimple in his left cheek made him look like the boy who had stolen the last biscuit from the cookie jar. She laughed with him, the sound echoing through the rafters of this old house, waking up its slumbering ghosts. Their eyes met, his grey and soft, and hers deep and dark, reigniting the spark of love. With a twist of his body, he held her in the crook of his arm and kissed her. The passion made her shiver like a naked Eskimo on an iceberg; then made her sweat like a nomad in the desert. I missed you. So much. I do not know how I existed without you in my life, he said…

Except… except none of that happened. She froze on the stairs, her left leg hanging in mid-air. Something was off – unbalanced, like the twang from a broken guitar string. The man was holding Tasneen around her waist, listening to her soft voice, hanging on her every word, gazing into her beautiful, kohl-lined eyes as if nothing else existed in the world around them. She wished fervently that the man wearing Pathani costume, his skin dark as burnt sugar, with a shaggy mane and beard, was not Raffa. Please let it be Tasneen's long-lost husband, Harry, who would lay claim to his dusty clothes and bed tonight, she prayed.

In vain. His posture, the shape of his head, his husky voice, all told her that he was none other than her own Raffa. Except, he may not be hers anymore.

Biran walked into the kitchen, carrying Raffa's bag, talking loudly on the phone, and caught sight of her on the stairs. He looked up at her; Raffa and Tasneen followed suit.

Her insides screamed. Unpleasant words tripped on her tongue. She itched to rush at them, to scratch and gouge their faces. She wished she had brought the knife down with her. Instead, she took a deep breath and descended the rest of the stairs, on wobbly legs, and crossed the floor, purposefully, towards him.

'Hi Raffa!' She wished her voice could be steadier, but there was nothing she could do about it.

He smiled at her. 'Hi Kals.'

If there was one word to describe the mood, 'awkward' would be it. At least he unhanded Tasneen.

'You… look great! Even better than how I remember you.'

Despite everything you put me through, you bastard, she thought to herself, but she was not going to wash her dirty laundry in front of Tasneen.

'You look fit too.'

Raffa did a twirl. 'Glad you think so! At first, I missed my gym routine. You know, climbing these hills here is better than the gym. They are beautiful. I should take you sightseeing.'

Tasneen said something softly to him, her voice sing-songy.

'Yes. Tasneen here is right. Lunch first,' he said. 'I must have a wash though. See you in a few minutes.'

'Oh, I will get ready too.' Kalyani excused herself. She had no intention of being left alone with her host. Back in her room, she fumed. Oh boy! She hadn't seen that coming! She was told Raffa stayed in Sulaiman Kaka's house, but travelled away frequently. She had visualised Tasneen as an old widow, with a son: a woman who was not well-liked – not someone Raffa had fallen for.

There were two voices in her head now. One that sowed the seeds of dissent and another that reasoned with her.

Sightseeing, he had said! Like she was a bloody tourist! How dare he! Why was his hand around Tasneen's waist? In honour of his visit, Tasneen had discarded her hijab. In different circumstances, Kalyani would have gawked at her too. The woman was beautiful! Like the pale moon in stormy skies. The years had been kind to her, and the few fine wrinkles around her eyes, and the slight expansion of her waist, only added character to her appearance.

The voice of reason told her she was reading too much into how Raffa had greeted Tasneen. It was just a hug between familiar people, who are fond of each other.

Dissent: *Why had he not even touched you in greeting? Or asked about his son?*

Reason: *It has been a while, Kals. There is bound to be some awkwardness. Give him time. Maybe he is terrified of being sucked back into the past! One touch might make him fall head over heels with you again. Maybe he* wishes *to keep Kiran a secret from Tasneen. Don't lose heart, Kals.*

Dissent: *It is well and truly over, Kals. You have your closure now. You should pack your bags and go home.*

Reason: *The Fat Lady has not even started singing. Today is your debut. Get on that stage and play the role of the temptress. Play it right, so Tasneen wouldn't compare. The man will be yours by tonight. Yours to punish or to forgive.*

The voice of Reason won over. How should she look? The demure bride who would lead him back to the altar, or the sultry temptress who would steal him away from Tasneen?

The silk garment she pulled over her head, felt hot against her skin. Almost immediately, she felt her sweat glands wake up. By the time lunch was over, she might end up looking like a pig on the barbie. She could imagine Tasneen's eyes smiling sarcastically. Poor, lost lamb, they would say, and Raffa would squirm with embarrassment.

The spangles scratched her arms as she wriggled out of it. Temptress she would be, in the comfort of cotton. With the help of her compact mirror, she brushed her hair, but gave up on the foundation as it was leaving streaks on her sweaty skin.

As she collected her handbag, her eyes fell on the knife. Not wanting snooping Huma to find it in her room, she dropped it into her handbag.

By the time she was satisfied and summoned the courage to go down, the put together family, consisting of Tasneen, Biran, Raffa, and a couple of farm hands, had already gathered around the scarred, wooden table. The odours from the dishes on the table stirred her gastric juices. It did not compare with Fawzia's feast but the food was plentiful. There were no place cards suggesting where they should seat themselves, but it was pretty obvious that she was expected to sit in the empty chair opposite Raffa. Tasneen herself had chosen to sit at the head of the table, from where she could survey them all.

As she made her way to her seat, Kalyani felt Tasneen's eyes follow her. It made her hair stand on end. Had Tasneen smeared her plate with deadly poison? If she had, it would be a slow-acting poison, because Tasneen would not miss the drama of the 'jilted bride meets the groom' episode for the world. From where she sat, she would be able to study her and Raffa. Every move they made or didn't make would be registered. Raffa, on the other hand, was grinning at her.

'Come on, Kals. I am famished.'

'Sorry to keep you waiting,' Kalyani said, as she took her seat. The group mumbled, accepting her apology. All except Tasneen. She merely nodded at Huma and her daughter, who had been roped in to help with the cooking, signalling for them to start serving. Before the food reached her, Kalyani 'accidentally' pushed her plate down. The stainless steel plate clattered loudly, as it bounced off the stone floor.

'Oops, sorry.' Out of the corner of her eye, she could see Huma's daughter rushing to help; she reached the plate at the same time Kalyani did. Kalyani grabbed the plate from her. 'No. Let me. It is my fault.'

Much to Tasneen's consternation, and Huma's embarrassment, Kalyani insisted that she carry the plate to the kitchen sink to wash it, as thoroughly as possible. When she was satisfied that she had at least diluted any possible poison smeared on it, she brought it back to the table. The group tucked into the food, making appreciative gestures and noises. On high vigil, Kalyani refused any food that wasn't served to anyone else, and as if by accident, drank from her neighbour's glass, in case her own drink was poisoned. She was on an emotional roller coaster anyway, and was content with nibbling on the food. If anyone had noticed her bizarre behaviour, they did not comment on it.

'So!' Raffa said. 'Did you have a pleasant journey?' Kalyani wondered which part of her long journey he was referring to. 'Biran told me you had a scare on the bus.'

As Kalyani described her ordeal, she was aware of Tasneen's eyes flashing with impatience.

'It was scary! I wonder if the authorities have caught him,' she finished.

'Most likely not, unless you filed a complaint with that police station,' Raffa commented, and the men agreed. 'Tasneen had a similar experience a few months ago, didn't you, Tasneen?'

Tasneen nodded; her eloquent eyes blazed triumphantly at Kalyani. The scores were even. Between mouthfuls, Raffa told the story of how Tasneen was accosted by three men, who wanted her purse. She had pretended she had a gun in her bag, and the men hadn't waited to find out.

Tasneen's stooges around the table made appreciative noises to declare their admiration for her valour. Tasneen must have a fetish for guns, though Kalyani. She changed the topic.

'Was there a power cut yesterday?' she asked.

'Don't know. Was there, Tasneen? Quite common, these power cuts.'

A lively discussion about how frequent power cuts were, how the new government did nothing to make it better, and how the grid needed revamping anyway – currently anything from rock fall, heavy rain, a dead crow, or a broken tree branch could damage the electricity lines. But yesterday had not been one of those days.

'We didn't have lights. I mean, Tasneen had lit oil lamps. I thought maybe there was a power cut,' Kalyani insisted.

'Oh!' said Raffa. 'Tasneen prefers it that way.'

Only Kalyani seemed surprised by this revelation. The others continued eating with gusto, their plates rattled, bowls chinked and spoons scraped. Obviously, no one thought the practice to be odd enough to comment upon. It was simply a lifestyle choice. Like choosing a particular brand of shampoo or having a siesta mid-morning. I prefer to be groping around in the dark with oil lanterns – like Florence Nightingale in the Crimea.

Drama queen!

After lunch, Kalyani pinched herself at regular intervals to see if she was still alive, and wasn't succumbing to slow poison.

'Kals. Would you like me to show you around?' Raffa offered. Pinch.

'In my jeep.' Pinch.

'Just you and me.' Pinch. He was waiting for her answer.

Her spirit soared. At last! The moment she waited for. Raffa and her alone! Shamelessly, despite her own joy, she wanted to see Tasneen's reaction. Nothing would satisfy her more than seeing bitterness, envy, and anger in those eyes. But she was disappointed, because Tasneen was, at the moment, busy greeting her son who was home from school, and had run into her open arms. She was kneeling beside him, unburdening him of his school bag, tucking a curly lock of hair behind his little ear, all the while talking softly to him. She was no longer a gun-toting man-stealer. Somehow, Tasneen's love for her son made Kalyani feel wretched. Her heart ached for her own child, Kiran, whom she had abandoned in pursuit of her own selfish quest.

At his mother's bidding, the boy smiled shyly at Kalyani, and greeted her. '*Asalaam Alaikkum*.'

'*Wa Alaikkum Aslaam*,' said Kalyani, wishing she had brought him a gift. 'What is your name? Were you at school?'

The little boy nodded, his hair escaping from behind his ears again, 'Perez. My name.'

'Hi Perez. Nice to meet you. You remind me of my son, Kiran.'

Tasneen's eyes sparkled. Surprise, kinship or hostility? Before anymore was said, little Perez spotted Raffa standing behind her, and his eyes lit up.

'Rafik Kaka!' he shouted, running up to him. Raffa lifted him and swirled him around. He fished a sweet from his pocket and held it out to the child. The boy squealed in delight and put his arms around Raffa's neck. It should be his own son, Kiran, in his arms, clutching his father's gift, she thought bitterly.

When Perez peeled away to eat his candy, Raffa turned towards her.

'Ready?'

She had been ready and waiting for months.

Chapter 9

It did not matter to her where Raffa took her. It sufficed that they were alone together. There had been no more overt signs of fondness between Tasneen and Raffa, but Tasneen spoke with her eyes, and Raffa seemed to understand.

He led Kalyani to his jeep.

'Kiran? You called him Kiran.'

'Yes. It means "ray of sunshine". He is the sunshine in my life.'

Raffa gave her a small smile, and was about to say something, when Biran called him back into the house. The moment slipped away.

Raffa's jeep looked fairly new, where the splattered, dried mud did not coat it. The numerous dials and knobs suggested that it was equipped with every mod con a man would ever need to drive through the rough terrain. When Raffa returned a minute later, he bent over the hood to inspect a hairline scratch on the bonnet, before opening the passenger door for her.

'Yours?' she enquired, as he climbed beside her and started the engine.

Raffa had a twinkle in his eye. 'Every inch of her is mine. Like it? Cost me a bundle. But she is a beast and a beauty.' Raffa spent the next few minutes waxing lyrical about the 4x4 Wrangler's nine-speed transmission, traction management systems, Xenon fog lights, leather seats, and its ability to crawl over rocks, plough through sand, and wade through rivers in spate.

All Kalyani could think of was how spacious the interior was and how much more upmarket it was compared to her tiny, red, second-hand Clio back home with faded fabric seats. She remembered their cramped frolicking in the back of her car on Saturday mornings.

'Get a bigger car,' he had told her then. Now, there was enough room for a mini football team in his car, but would there be any frolicking?

When the one-sided topic extolling the virtues of the jeep was exhausted, they indulged in meaningless banter, awkwardly avoiding skin and eye contact, steering clear of grey areas in conversation. As they passed the stables, where the three-legged dog sprawled lazily, Raffa told her how much Sulaiman Kaka valued his ponies.

'Kaka commissioned a painting of every pony he owned. He also had the head of his first pony mounted on his wall, when it died.'

'Not sure I spotted that,' Kalyani said.

'You wouldn't have. Kaka lives separately in the bungalow. Tasneen and Harry moved into the family home – the east wing. When Harry died, she preferred to continue to live there.' The word 'preferred' kept cropping up in conjunction with Tasneen. Tasneen's preferences were starting to sound like the Constitution.

As they drove past the empty grain silo, and the redundant farmhouse, Raffa told her about how the silo had once been over-flowing with grain, and the farmhouse provided an ample supply of milk and eggs. Now, only a blind goat that relished charging at anyone she heard approach, and barren chickens too old for the pot, lived there. He then turned sharply onto the road that led them out of the estate. The sharp turn made her slide along the seat towards him.

'You need to hold on to that leather bit,' he warned her, pointing to the leather thong over the door. Not like old times, when they first met, she recalled sadly. Then, they had driven roughshod over bumps with the express intent of being thrown against each other, causing electricity to fizzle and fry the air between them, and burn the parts of their body that touched with flames of passion. She watched as he manoeuvred his machine with tender loving care around the potholes in the road, cursing whoever should have maintained it.

The comparatively smooth ride ended abruptly when Raffa turned the jeep into an unmarked dirt road strewn with pebbles, rocks, boulders and craters, which grew in dimension as they ventured further. She hung on to the leather thong for dear life, not to avoid being thrown against Raffa, but to avoid being thrown out altogether. The revving of the jeep and the crunching of gravel made enough noise to drown any conversation. With a final shudder, the jeep climbed a ridge and found a much smoother path.

'Phew! That was tricky,' she exclaimed.

Raffa grinned, his eyes shining with excitement, his forehead dotted with sweat.

'That route always gets me going!'

'You mean there are other routes to get here?'

'A much smoother one; a private one the family had built decades ago.'

'So why not take that one?'

Raffa shrugged. 'This is more exciting, is it not?'

'You are lucky I didn't throw up my lunch. Where are we going?'

'Tasneen knows a lot of secret spots. This is my favourite.'

Tasneen again! Involuntarily, she turned around to see if Tasneen had accompanied them and was sitting in the backseat.

They stopped beside a tall, rusty, metal gate – its bottom had rotted away, leaving jagged edges. On top was a rusted motif of a star and a half moon. The big padlock and chain on the gate were not a deterrent, because Raffa found another way through the fence where rust had eaten away at the iron supports and the barbed wire lay tangled up in the unkempt grass.

The ragged path only allowed them to walk in single file, and Raffa strode ahead, while she stopped several times to disentangle her clothes from the brambles and entwining roots. To her left, grey tombstones jutted out of the swaying, long, dry grass. A mangy dog shamelessly cocked a leg up against one of them.

Tasneen's favourite spot was a graveyard? Was this where Tasneen shot pesky people who spied on her stash of guns, and buried them? Was Raffa her partner in crime who was following her instructions to get rid of the spy? A shiver went down her spine. She looked around frantically. Apart from the gravestones and Raffa, there were no other signs of human habitation – dead or alive. If Raffa wanted, he could cut her up into teeny-weeny pieces and invite Queen Tasneen to admire his handiwork later. Suddenly, the man she thought she knew so well faded into uncertainty. Was this man a clone of Raffa, brainwashed by Tasneen? Or a zombie, who no longer remembered their past together? Or was this strange land playing tricks on her mind?

She fingered the kitchen knife in her handbag, grateful she had brought it with her. Smiling wanly, she heeded to Raffa, beckoning to her from an arched doorway of a brick building. The steps leading to it were irregular, crumbling. The bricks were black with age and moss, miniature trees and bird nests filled the crevices, teal-blue windows hung off their hinges, and the roof had lost several tiles. A crow cawed desolately from a nearby tree as if to warn her of impending death. Feeling confused and helpless, she climbed towards him. *Hope you die gracefully, Kals. Not crapping your pants.* For some insane reason, she remembered her friend, Helen. So far away. Everybody she knew and loved was so far away. A lump as big as a boulder formed in her throat.

Her future life with them was at the hands of this man she had stupidly pursued.

'Are you alright?' he asked, irritated at how long she was taking. He gestured impatiently to her. 'Come on!' He was already crossing under the archway to reach the back of the building. Smiling, he took her hand. 'Close your eyes!' he commanded.

Here it was. This is where the guillotine fell. Her bloody, chopped head with unseeing eyes would soon join a sea of rotting bodies at the foot of the stairs on the other side of the archway. But she obeyed. Raffa led her forward a few steps and released her hand.

'Now!' he said triumphantly. She flinched, expecting the cold, sharp metal to slice the skin of her neck. 'Open your eyes. Now!'

For a moment, she blinked. Instead of grinning skulls or bloody carcasses being eaten by vultures, the emerald waters of a lake glistened in the late afternoon sun. Water lilies and lotuses, their leaves spreading like bronze dinner plates, floated on the surface. A lone white egret stood on one leg, fishing amongst the floating stems, and dragonflies darted in and out, rippling the water, and breaking sunlight into the colours of the rainbow with their wings. On the horizon, the mountain peaks stood white and silent.

Raffa was waiting for her reaction.

'Beautiful!' she exclaimed. 'Never expected this.'

Giddy with relief, she lowered herself onto the crumbling step. He sat beside her, smelling of the sun and mountain air. Jasmine straggled over the balustrade, its creamy white buds waiting to open, and below them, black fish swam amongst the long stems of the lilies. Raffa took a packet of breadcrumbs from his pocket and tipped some into the water. The placid water churned up white as yoghurt, as the fish splashed around, fighting for a bite. He held the packet out to her and shook the crumbs onto her palm. Cautiously, she crept forward and placed her palm just beneath the water. Soon, one brave fish attempted a nibble, followed by others. She giggled as she felt their slimy bodies bumping against her fingertips. Slimy, green deposits of algae clung to their ankles as they sat dangling their feet in the cool water. Raffa told her the story of the place.

Tasneen's great-grandfather had a harem. A small one – only three wives. He loved them all, but there was no love between them. Each of them accused him of loving the others more. In the end, the romantic man built this place, for the three of them, as a monument of his love. He brought one wife at a time to this place. 'For a bit of one to one attention.'

'Like Shah Jahan, who built the Taj Mahal for his wife?'

'The Taj Mahal is a mausoleum. These wives were alive to enjoy this place.'

'Did the wives live happily after that?'

'They must have, because they are all buried here together.'

'Those graves?'

'This is the family's ancient burial ground.'

'Is Tasneen's husband here too?' She didn't want to pry, but she was curious.

'No. He wasn't a Mussalman,' said Raffa. 'But neither will Sulaiman Kaka be here, when his time comes.'

'Oh?'

'This land doesn't belong to them anymore. It is under dispute. Kaka claims that this is his ancestral land, as his forefathers are buried here. His nephew has challenged this claim. The case has been in the court arena for several years now. Unfortunately, in the meantime, neither party has been maintaining the place.'

That explained why it was overgrown, the gate padlocked, and why they had to take the hazardous back routes to get here.

Something scuttled into the bushes, disturbing her from the trance she had fallen into. She wasn't as lost in the beauty of this place as she was in the chaos of her own thoughts. *How many lovers had Raffa brought to this place? How many times had Raffa and Tasneen sat side by side while the black fish nibbled on their bread? Had romance between them blossomed here amongst the broken brick and water lilies?* She started to ask the question just as Raffa said something. They both stopped, waited politely for the other to continue, and then talked at once again.

'You first,' Kalyani conceded, with an awkward chuckle.

'Oh! I was just trying to show you those mountain peaks, far away.'

'Yes, they are beautiful.'

'There are lakes up there in which the waters are like mirrors, reflecting the glaciers. Terrains left undisturbed, older than any civilisation; cold, aloof, beautiful. There are so many fairy tales told by the simple folk living up there. Most are dismissed as folklore, but if you visit those lakes on a misty morning, the silence wraps around you and whispers in your ears, and you have your own fairy tale.'

'Nice.'

'Do you have time to visit?'

'No. I am on a short schedule. Your uncle Alam is expecting me back by tomorrow.'

'Ah! Peshawadi Alam! How is he? If you let him, he will soon convince you that he is somehow related to the iconic Bollywood actors who have ruled the Indian film industry for decades. A little before our time, but they are still legendry in these parts.'

'Is there a movie theatre in these parts?'

'Oh yes, in the village; wooden seats and a screen stretched between two poles. The good ones are in the cities. The Taliban are not great fans of them. They destroy them.'

'Like they destroyed Sulaiman Kaka's business?'

Raffa was taken aback slightly by the change of conversation. 'Many businesses were destroyed by them, and many never recovered.'

'Men lost their lives in the process? Like Harry,' Kalyani probed ruthlessly.

Rafik stared into the distance. 'Harry had other problems too. He… had vices. And enemies. The Taliban issue did not help. It was all before I knew the family well.'

'When did you meet them?' Kalyani maintained a neutral tone.

'We used to come down to Pakistan, during school holidays. We stayed with Uncle Alam. I remember wandering in and out of any house on the street with the other kids, climbing trees to steal mangoes, and being constantly fed. Alam and Biran took me and my cousins sightseeing or on hunting trips for little birds and beasts; we sat around fires in the middle of abandoned fields, roasting the meat, nursing scratches on every part of our limbs, beating mosquitoes off, listening to tall stories, dirty, happy… But we all got lost in our busy schedules, and these visits tailed off. The last time we visited was for a wedding. It was magical. Everybody dressed up like princes and princesses; the venue was like a palace, with swaying curtains, fairy lights and bling everywhere. Music from the lone flute wove romance into the incense-filled air. Food and drama transported us to a different era altogether.'

'And you met Tasneen?'

'Tasneen and Harry. She was already married, yet there was something alluring about her. She was quiet, mysterious, waif-like; as wispy as the chiffon curtains. She was not the most beautiful face there; in fact, she was not even pretty, but she moved with such faultless grace that she stood out. For me, she stood out.

'We have been "friends" on social media ever since. I messaged her when Harry died, Skyped her a year later. Her family was in deep financial shit. Her dad had a stroke, and the business was dead. She seemed to be both lost and found; bravely holding everything together, while chunks of the life she knew drifted away. Not everybody was kind or sympathetic. When she married Harry, many believed that she had let her family name down, by marrying out of religion and community. She was really alone, but she was too proud to beg for scraps from her extended family. She isolated herself in her childhood home with her disabled father and her son, like a queen in her fortress, fighting for her rightful kingdom.'

Despite herself, Kalyani was as fascinated by Tasneen as Rafik was, and would have happily spent the afternoon gossiping about her, but she could hear her sister Minna sighing and rolling her eyes. '*Kals, you haven't travelled thousands of miles of terrorist-infested mountainside to listen to Tasneen's life history. Get on with your mission.*'

Couldn't agree more, sis.

Aloud, she said, 'Raffa, much as I would like to listen to Tasneen's story and your fascination for her, that is not really what I came for.'

Raffa reached into the waters and yanked at a lotus bud. The stem broke – pale and watery where the cut was made. He chewed absently on it. 'Why did you come, Kals?'

'To ask. Why?'

'Why what?'

'Why did you leave? Why did you leave when you did? Why did you leave the way you did?'

Raffa lifted his feet out of the water and lay on his back, staring at geese flying in formation in the sky.

'I asked myself the same question, many times, on many sleepless nights.'

Kalyani liked the fact that he had spent sleepless nights thinking of her. 'And? Is there an answer?'

'Yes. I think so. At least, possible answers. I guess I wanted a meaning to my life. A reason to get up in the morning, a reason for my existence.'

'You had a life back home! Parents who loved you, a great job that many would have killed to get, friends, me, and most importantly... your son. Was that not meaning enough?'

Raffa grinned at her. 'Looks good from the outside, doesn't it? I had "made it". Made it in accordance with the expectation of society. The good child, the good student, the good husband, the good father. Got the grades, got a job, got a wife, got everything for a content life. Doesn't end there – you are expected to beget healthy, intelligent, beautiful kids, wait for them to grow up and do the same. Every morning, you mount the hamster wheel, scrambling madly, thinking that you are getting somewhere. Thinking you are in control over your life. In reality, you never get off that wheel – you spend your life doing mundane, insipid work to fill the world with metal and concrete and digital noise. You are always someone's underdog, slaving away to keep everyone around you happy.'

'But, Raffa, you were so passionate about your job. It was anything but mundane to you.'

'I was. But I got tired of sucking dicks to get to the top.' Didn't mind the tits though, he thought to himself.

'Everybody sucks some dick, don't they?'

'You don't get it, do you, Kals? Look at us. We are dark-skinned foreigners from British colonies. We are always second-rate citizens there. If we are offered an interview, it is because of their equality and diversity stats; if we get the job, it is because the locals do not want to slog day and night analysing data for the government. I must admit, the pay was good. But after a while, I ran out of toys to buy. I wanted something else, something more... fulfilling.'

'So... did you find what you wanted, here?'

'That and more. Everything is simple and pure in these mountains. The river water is clear, the mountain breeze filled with apricot blossom and fresh snow, and birdsong. I can do what I want – not waste time in traffic queues, breathing polluted air. My skills are valued here. I also teach children in *madrasas*, schools to you, their faces filled with the joy of learning. People are grateful for everything you do for them, you know. I matter here. People know me by name. Rafik Sahib, they call me. With due respect.'

'So why didn't you speak to me? Tell me how you felt. Did you not think I would understand?'

'Would you have understood, Kals? You were caught up in the flurry of wedding preparations – pleasing yourself, recruiting everybody into your dream. You wanted to play happy families, roses around the front door, coffee mornings, and gossip at the school gates. Suddenly, I didn't. Would you have understood that? Would you have let me leave? Without tears and tantrums, and emotional blackmail? Once in, I could see no way out. A never-ending trap.'

'So, you left me without any explanation! Pregnant. Jilted. Disgraced, and in financial ruin. Worrying that horrendous things had happened to you.'

'Kals. Thank God for opening our eyes to the mistake we would have made, if we had married.'

'And which God would that be?'

'To the Almighty Allah. The only true God for me.'

'To think I was willing to sacrifice my Gods to accept yours. Because of my love for you. You sat back and let me do that! How foolish of me.'

'I am sorry you feel that way, Kals. At the end of the day, if you felt strongly about your beliefs and your religion, you would never have let human love dictate your choice.'

'Did you ever feel any "human" love for me, Raffa? Or was it just lust?'

Raffa sighed. 'What we had was good, Kals – it was.' His eyes were soft and tender. 'But now, it belongs to a world I do not live in, that I can never live in again. I have moved on. I wish you can too.'

'Does my presence here with you not evoke memories? Touch me, hold me, Raffa, and tell me you do not feel anything.' Kalyani placed her hand on his arm. He turned to her. There was no love in his grey eyes, not even lust. The corner of his mouth curled slightly in annoyance. With deliberation, he removed her hand, and sat up.

'Look, Kals, of course I had feelings for you. In the past. This is my life now, and I cannot take you with me.'

Kalyani felt a flash of rage at how easily he was dismissing her.

'Is this about Tasneen? She is your "thing on the side", isn't she?' She was beside him now, snarling into his face, no longer in control of her emotions.

Raffa clicked his tongue and pretended to look amused. 'Talking dirty doesn't become you, Kals. Tasneen saw that I was lost, spiritually defeated. She saw a kindred spirit in me and invited me over. She has been good and kind to me. And to you too. I think respect would be more apt.'

'I can only go by what I see, Raffa. And what I see is the chemistry between the two of you. If you haven't yet explored the physics and the biology, maybe you should get onto it, pronto.'

'You are just jealous. She is a survivor. A strong woman.'

Kalyani was transported into the black oily waters of depression, whirling around her, its current, moving faster and faster, sucking her into its depths, drowning... gasping... her brain exploding... Her anger bubbled over and an orange-red mist enveloped her. She grabbed the kitchen knife out of her bag and lunged at him. The unexpected action pushed him over. As he lay on his back, she held the knife tip to his throat. She could see the indentation the tip was making on the skin of his neck.

'You have a thing for strong women, Raffa?' she growled. 'You didn't have to travel thousands of miles to find a strong woman. Could you not see them all around you? Your mother who survived her own loveless, difficult childhood, but dug deep from within to find so much love to shower you with. And me? So strong was my love for you that my whole world collapsed when you left. I could not bring myself to believe what we had together was a lie from which you simply walked away. I believed you were dead and I tried to die with you, over and over again. I was in a perpetual nightmare, wherein I was trapped in the deepest, darkest pit with no escape. Yet, I pulled myself together because I had a duty to be there for the baby we created between us – the one you abandoned, and to the people who love me. That makes me a survivor too.'

She drove the tip of the knife further. It punctured his skin and a tiny bead of blood emerged, wobbled uncertainly for a second before mingling with the sweat gathered in the creases and trickling away. His pupils dilated with the pain. The muscles of his arms rippled.

If he wished, he could flick her off, as if she was an annoying insect.

'But I will tell you who isn't a survivor, Raffa. You! You had everything given to you on a plate. You lacked nothing; and you got bored. Like a spoilt child, you just turned the page, forgot the mess you made, and changed the scenery to suit you. Now, you want to die on someone else's cross. Have you no responsibility for your son? To provide a stable and happy life for him? Oh no! You had to run away to look after someone else's son!'

Anger flashed in his eyes, making them dark and dull. His jaw clenched. He grabbed her wrist and wrenched it away from his neck. The pain made her drop the knife. With a swift motion, he twisted around, and grabbed her neck, suffocating her. Her face turned purple and tears sprang to her eyes as she tugged at his hands. Just as she thought she was going to black out, he released her. Choking and spluttering, she scrambled to her knees and crawled away. Like a predator, a wounded animal, he watched her from afar.

'Are you accusing me of being a shirker?' His voice was dangerously low. 'I will do everything right by my son. He will lack nothing, Kals.'

'What would you know about his needs, Raffa? You lost the rights to your son when you walked away. He will soon have spent a year of his life without a father. Can you make that right?'

Raffa looked away, biting his lip. 'Well. I cannot undo the past, Kals. I do hope you will bring him up to have the courage to break the mould, do what he wants to do, not what society expects him to. To fight for himself and his beliefs.'

Fire burned in her throat. Her voice was hoarse, fractured. 'My son will be brought up to have the courage of his convictions – not run away in cowardice. He will be brought up to love and accept, not hate and hurt. He may not have a father in his life, but he will not lack love.'

Raffa sat still, staring at the ripples in the pond made by tiny feet of insects surfing the water.

'Look, Kals, let us not fight. Don't waste the time we do have together, with all this drama.'

'Oh? Don't worry. I would never win. Tasneen takes the biscuit for being the drama queen!' Kalyani said bitterly. 'High drama! She has it to a T. And you have fallen for it: hook – line – sinker!'

'What do you mean?'

'The dark nights where she wanders around in the light of oil lamps, the exaggerated hush in her voice, the Mona Lisa smiles... Is she good in bed too?'

'Don't know. Never slept with Mona Lisa. You are just jealous.'

'And what about the bloody guns she trades in?'

'What bloody guns?'

For a moment, Kalyani wavered. Did he not know about the guns? Was he just the naïve idiot who got drawn by the beauty of this place?

'I... saw them. Lots of them in her storage shed.'

'How did you...?'

'I walked into the open shed. Just like that.'

'Tasneen just keeps them... for a friend.'

'The Taliban?'

'No! Look, don't involve yourself with things you don't understand! This is Pashtun territory. Guns are everywhere. Both the good and bad guys need them. It is not just the Taliban; the soldiers need them too. Not a big deal!'

'Some of those guns travelled with me from the city. They were smuggled through the checkpoint, which means they are illegal. Which means they are meant to be used by the bad guys.'

Raffa held up his hands to pacify her. 'Calm down.'

'You are in it too. Aren't you? Gun smuggling. Terrorism.' Kalyani was concerned. She frowned, remembering Mr Khan's daughter. 'Guns that kill and destroy the lives of innocent people!'

Raffa shrugged his shoulders indifferently. 'Every war has its casualties.'

'Is this what Tasneen has brainwashed you into? How does she do that, Raffa? How does she convert an intelligent, educated, well-adjusted person like you into a gun smuggler? She must be very good in bed.' She regretted the last sentence as soon as she uttered it.

'Petty, Kals.' He shook his head. 'I am disappointed in you! What Tasneen and I have in common is beyond petty restricting boundaries. Our goal is not restricted to individual needs and wants of the common man, *my* spouse, *my* child, *my* house, *my* bed... Look beyond all that. We are protecting the interests of our community, our religion and our country. Anyone with similar interests is welcome to join us. In fact, we urge them to join us in our noble cause.'

'Is that what you are doing through your *madrasas*, Raffa? Teaching children to become terrorists; to train them to shoot and kill? Filling their tiny brains with hatred and despondency?' If she thought Raffa was going to explode in anger, she was mistaken. He didn't bat an eyelid. It was as if he relished these arguments. Inadvertently, she had put him on the soapbox.

'Aren't all schools places where children are brainwashed? Schools are society's institutes, where children are moulded to fit in. Be quiet, sit down, do not run, do not, do not, do not. Until everything that comes naturally to the child is crushed, bruised, soured. They are turned into automatons trained to work for the upkeep of the society, like ants in a colony – each with a specific role. Anyone with a different agenda is a naughty child, a rebel, a terrorist. The Western media, the Western culture shouts the loudest, and by default, they are deemed to be right. The rest of the world – those that protest against their invasion – are labelled as terrorists. It is you who is brainwashed, Kals.'

'Such patriotism, Raffa,' she mocked. She shook her head sadly. 'I am sorry, Raffa, but all I see is a brat, having an adventure in which he is the super hero who saves his empire. As for Tasneen, she will stop at nothing to build up the lost fortunes of her family. I would suggest you guard your own back, so you are not thrown out into the cold when the adventure ends.'

She felt his anger before she saw it. With a bound, he was upon her, pinning her against a pillar, his snarling face inches away from hers. She winced as her elbows grazed against the rough stone, and her head snapped back and crunched on the concrete. Ignoring the pain, she held his gaze.

There she stood; defiance and righteousness flaming out of her eyes, her long hair flying around her in the evening breeze, dark as the flowing river at night. It flowed right at him, trapping him in its scent. Like tentacles, it drew him into her femininity. He became aware of her body under him, her soft breasts blooming like the water lilies around them. His own body buzzed like a hoard of hungry bees.

His fingers brushed her face, leaving a burning scar in their wake; his hungry lips sought hers. His breath mingled with hers, scorching hot. He tasted earthy. She yearned for him to crush her lips, drive his tongue into her mouth, for his hands to find her tingling nipples.

But he pushed himself away from her, panting. She slid to the floor, her legs no longer capable of holding her upright. Around them, the dragonflies danced in frenzy, and the pungent smell of lotus mixed with the heady jasmine infused the air.

'Temptress!' he accused hoarsely, glancing at her out of the corner of his eye. She smiled, half in triumph, half in mockery, but her eyes held sadness for what would now never be. She watched him wade into the lake, and splash cool water on his face. Then, as if he made a decision, he took his shirt off and plunged into the water. With strong strokes of his arms, he swam away from her. The displaced fronds of water lilies floated back into place behind him, and silence returned.

Still, the tears that stung her eyes and throbbed at the root of her nose wouldn't flow; instead, they lodged in her heart, like shrapnel that no amount of crying would wash away. The pain cloaked her brain, and dragged her into a black hole of oblivion.

Chapter 10

When she became conscious of the world again, she was staring into the bulging compound eye of a giant dragonfly, hovering with aerodynamic precision over her face, as if it was investigating an alien species. Startled by her open eyes, the dragonfly reversed and, with angular movements, buzzed away.

Behind it, Raffa's face reflecting the late afternoon sun, golden drops of water dripping off his hair, drifted into focus. He was leaning over her, splashing wet drops on her skin. Obviously in a better mood than when he swam away, he grinned at her.

'Time to wake up, sleeping beauty. Time to go.'

He held out a bunch of pink lotus flowers, their heads flopping on weak green stems, their hearts golden yellow, towards her. 'Don't say I never gave you flowers,' he smirked.

She sat up and held the flowers on her knees. They made damp patches on her clothes. Raffa sat down beside her. She could sense the change in him; he was in a reflective mood.

'Kiran,' he said. 'Your ray of sunshine.'

'He truly is one.'

He nodded. 'Who does he look like? You or me?'

'Both of us. You when he smiles, and me when he pouts. Here, I have some photos.'

For a while, Raffa turned the pages of the album she handed him. When he returned it to her, he had tears in his eyes.

'I guess he will never know me now.'

Kalyani had tears of her own. 'Come back, Raffa. For all our sakes and for yours.'

Raffa shook his head. 'I have made my decision, Kals.'

'What compelled you to make such a drastic decision, Raffa? Do not tell me to mind my own business. I travelled thousands of miles to understand this decision of yours. I deserve to know.'

After what seemed an aeon, Raffa nodded. 'I am not the man you think I am, Kals. Not any longer. I… couldn't take the pressure any more. The pressure to perform. I felt trapped. I made some bad decisions.'

'What bad decisions?'

Raffa turned to her. There was pain and shame in his eyes. 'There is really no need for you to know. But I will tell you. I… made a pass at one of my clients in Finland. She was gorgeous – all legs and tits. I suppose I wanted to have one last fling before the marriage. But she complained. I was given a choice to resign or get sacked. I left. I was too ashamed to come home to my parents. Tasneen was sympathetic. She understood. Her husband was a womaniser. She wanted to save me, before it was too late. Give me a cause to fight for, for which I am grateful.'

'I wish you had told me. I would have…'

'Understood? It took me nearly a year to come to terms with it myself. Bringing it raw into the marriage would have destroyed us.'

They sat quietly for a long time, thinking thoughts that remained unsaid. The sun was descending towards the horizon. The air was cooling down sharply. She shivered.

'We have to leave before the dark. Or the road will be impassable, and we will be trapped in this voodoo forever,' he said, breaking the silence.

'Is that a problem?' she mumbled as she rose.

'Not for me. I only live across the road. But for the princess who has to travel thousands of miles – big problem.'

She nodded, not trusting her voice. 'You are letting me go? After I have seen the guns? Are you not afraid that I will tell?'

Raffa looked bewildered for a minute, before throwing his head back and guffawing. 'Poor Kals! You were always a naïve dreamer. Who are you planning to tell? The village headman sends his grandson to my *madrasa*. The police commissioner plays chess with Sulaiman Kaka on the weekends. Besides, Tasneen has probably got rid of those guns, or at least arranged for them to be removed. They may even be travelling on the same transport as you, Kals. If you get searched by the authorities and they find the guns on you, you will be dragged to the police station and a hundred questions fired at you. Do you know, we Paks hate interfering Indians – especially British Indians? Your passport will be taken away and you will spend the night on the tiles in the Pak jail, before your Embassy comes to your aid. Or maybe the Embassy will refuse to help you, if you are accused of "gun smuggling". Or Tasneen can arrange for you to disappear. Poof.'

'Would Tasneen do that? Frame me? Or arrange for me to disappear? Would you let her?' Tears wobbled in her voice. This was a different Raffa, a cold, calculating, ruthless man. The mask was back on, and nothing would touch him.

He knelt beside her, caressed her hair, and kissed her on her forehead.

'Goodbye, Kals.' He took a gold ring off his little finger, and slipped it on to her ring finger. 'Give this to our son. You are a better parent to him than I will ever be. I have chosen my destiny. Tell him or don't tell him about me, you decide. I only request that you do not paint me as the coward you think I am.'

She looked up at him, tears clouding her vision. She would never remember for certain if there were tears in his eyes too, but she would remember the smell of lotus blossoms crushed between their bodies as they hugged goodbye.

As he drove back, she brought the subject up once again. 'Raffa, do you have to get involved in all this dangerous stuff? It doesn't make you a hero, you know. Could Alam or your parents help you stop?'

Raffa spat out of his side of the jeep.

'Kals, this game is way beyond you and me. It involves big politics, tyrant countries that are always poking their noses into our business. No one is a hero in this game. The small man's happiness will always get sacrificed in their grand scheme of things. Go home safely, Kals. May Allah be with you.'

May Allah be with you. A phrase that was repeated by several others, including little Perez, as they bade her goodbye.

Raffa and Tasneen were conversing in a low voice, when she dragged her bags down the stairs. Maybe he was putting in a good word for her. She gave him the package from Shahida, and conveyed Alam's regards to Sulaiman Kaka. Finally, she thanked Tasneen for her hospitality. Then it was time to leave. Biran placed her bags in the jeep, and Huma handed her some fruit and a bottle of water for the journey.

Up in her room, as she packed, she had thought long and hard about what she should do with the paper cuttings outlining the story of Tasneen. She could use them as leverage, if Tasneen created trouble for her, though a story published years ago may not interest anyone. Nevertheless, she put the bundle in her handbag, and left some money on the bedside table for Huma to show her gratitude.

Little Perez asked her if she could bring Kiran to play with him when she next visited. She kneeled down to hug him and promised that she would. 'And he will send you a toy plane. Would you like that?'

Perez nodded happily. 'A red one?'

Tasneen knelt beside her son, and for a brief moment, the women's eyes locked. Tasneen's fluid eyes seemed to say something, but it was lost in the urgency to leave. Biran started the engine and it was time to go. She waved to the small group – man, woman, child, their house, their servants, and the three-legged dog, until the jeep turned around the corner and they disappeared from her view.

Kalyani felt a strange mixture of deep sadness and freedom – sadness for what would now never be, and freedom from living in uncertainty, and doubt. Relieved that she had been allowed to leave the house, but apprehensive that she could still be in danger. Had Tasneen stashed some guns in the boot of the jeep, just as Raffa warned? If they were caught, she would be in hot water.

Heeding her request earlier, Biran had texted a message to Alam to say that she was on her way to Chitral airport. In a few minutes, they would reach the highway, and Biran would hit the accelerator. Outside, the setting sun bathed everything in a luminous yellow. She leaned into the soft leather, and wished she did not feel so alone. Tears threatened. She also wished she still had her prescription happy pills on her. Opening her handbag, she rummaged for a tissue. Her fingers rustled against a polythene bag wrapped tightly around something. It didn't belong in her bag. She unwound the polythene, and pulled out a rectangular box. It was made of transparent plastic and was sealed. She held it to the fading light filtering through the window. Inside the box was a knife, the type used for hunting. The handle was elegantly carved and engraved, in a language she could not read, but the tip of the blade was missing. Even in the poor light, she could discern dark, rust-coloured stains on the blade and the handle. Instinctively, she knew she was holding the missing knife from the display at Harry's Riding Club. The missing weapon used to murder Tasneen's wayward husband, Harry. Out of the blue, she knew whose fingerprints were on the hilt.

She closed her eyes and pictured the scene. A drunken Harry, who had ruined her father's business, and didn't give a damn, now cavorting shamelessly with women of ill repute in the riding club. The women leave when they see her, but he was too drunk to notice his wife standing at the entrance. She shouts at him, trying to drill into his thick head the shame he had brought upon them. But he laughs at her. He tells her to lighten up. '*Here. Have some of this excellent imported wine, and join these women. You will fit right in.*'

With tears of shame and anger, she walks to the hunting knives displayed on the mantelpiece. She pulls one out and approaches him. He doesn't notice until she is right on top of him. She plunges the knife into his flesh, flaccid with years of sloth-like inactivity, again and again and again, until her rage is spent... then she carries the knife home and hides it in his wardrobe. In a secret compartment. The police never found the murder weapon. But Huma did, when she was cleaning Harry's room. Huma liked Harry, and wanted his murderer brought to justice, but as long as Huma was employed by Tasneen, she didn't dare to try and expose her. Until Kalyani arrived. Huma deduced rivalry between Kalyani and Tasneen, and concluded that Kalyani would not hesitate to bring Tasneen to justice. So she had placed the murder weapon in Kalyani's bag, just as she had placed the paper cuttings.

With a gentle jerk, Biran braked and pulled the jeep over. He tapped the window for her attention. She hid the box under her handbag before winding the window down.

'Prayers,' he told her. She watched him carry the prayer mat to a ledge by the side of the road and prepare to say his evening prayers. His back was turned towards her. They had stopped by a brook, its current swift and strong as it meandered through the black rocks. She got out of the vehicle and knelt beside the brook. Cupping her hands under the cold water, she splashed it on her face and her eyes to clear her thoughts. What was she supposed to do with the evidence Huma had entrusted her with? This was her trump card. If she submitted the weapon to the authorities, Tasneen would be apprehended. Her gun business would be exposed. She and possibly Raffa would go to prison for a very long time. If Raffa escaped going to prison, he would come back home to his family and her. To the loveless, trapped existence that he ran away from. All she had to do was walk up to the authorities at the airport.

The box felt heavy in her hands, and her eyes drooped with fatigue. Her brain was playing tricks on her. *She was standing at the entrance to the riding club. Raffa lay on the gilt sofa, naked women clawing at him. They pointed to her and jeered; their laughter echoed around the room, reminding her of a pack of hyenas. Raffa joined them. 'Do not destroy my life,' he shouted at her. Black, oily waters were rushing towards her. Soon, they would surround her and drag her into the sludge. Her breath caught in her throat. She slammed the box on the rocks until it cracked open. Reaching in, she gripped the hilt of the knife; the pattern of the carving dug into her palm. She felt the wind rush past her hand as she brought the blade down; she felt the shudder travel up her arms as it sliced through bone and sinew. Again and again and again. She watched in horror as the blood gushed out of the limp body, warm, sticky, and smelling of metal. And then she thought of her own survival.*

In a cold, clammy sweat, Kalyani sat back on her haunches, and stared at the knife gripped in her hand. She would have done exactly what Tasneen did on that fateful night to rid the world of vermin like Harry and to protect her son. In Kalyani's court of law, Tasneen would be acquitted. She understood what Tasneen's eyes were trying to convey to her as she prepared to leave – the power of a scorned woman, and the love of a mother.

She replaced the dagger in the box and held it under the water. When the box was full, she released it. The package swirled in the current, knocked against obstacles in its path, as it was carried downstream for a few feet before it gurgled and sank to the murky depths. She then threw the newspaper cuttings and finally, the lotus flowers Raffa had picked for her into the water. With her eyes, she followed their path as they twisted and turned, lingered briefly as they snagged amongst rocks and debris in their path, before disappearing under the veil of gathering darkness.

'With this water, I wash my hands of you all,' she murmured. 'Raffa, Tasneen, Huma, and their crooked house at the foothills of the Hindu Kush.'

The plaintive cry of prayer from the nearby mosque floated through the dark skies. May Allah be with us. Tasneen's eyes stopped talking.

Biran arrived just as she got back in the jeep, his rolled-up prayer mat under his arm. As he started the engine, she unscrewed the bottle of water Huma had given her and drank deeply.

Nothing that Raffa decided to do would matter to her. Not anymore. He had nothing more to offer. His memory would only be extra baggage, which she wasn't going to carry for the rest of her life. She knew that the strange prickle in her back meant her new wings were growing. Soon she would fly, so alone and so high – no one would spot her scars or her tears.

The water left an odd aftertaste in her mouth. She held it up to the passing lights of a busy street. Bits of an insoluble powder floated in it. Too late.

Her brain was shutting down, and a wave of extinction broke over her.

Chapter 11

When Kalyani woke, she knew she was dead and floating on a cloud. The cloud was soft as Egyptian cotton sheets on an expensive bed. All around her, the most pastel of the multiple shades of sunlight glowed. A shadow loomed in front of her face, and she involuntarily shirked away, anticipating water droplets from the lake to drip on her.

'Breakfast, Memsahib.'

She glanced at the tray of soft rotis, fresh, churned butter melting over them, and the inevitably sweet tea, and realised she was ravenous. Her head spun around and her hand trembled as she reached for the food. The servant helped prop her up on the pillows, and poured the tea for her. The sugar in the tea revived her.

'Where am I?' she croaked.

'In Alam Sahib's house, *ji*,' said the maid. Kalyani chewed laboriously on a piece of roti, her jaw aching with the effort, and tried to remember how she had reached here.

As painful as it was, she remembered Raffa had given her the closure she wanted and Biran was driving her back, and she had drunk water from the bottle Huma had given her. She remembered nothing more of the journey, until she was shaken awake by Biran. He had pulled up at the side of the road and was gesturing to her to get out. He pointed to a long queue of vehicles, beeping angrily at each other.

'Where are we?' she muttered, her words thick and slurred.

'Airport. Police check. Better walk,' he hissed. The unflappable Biran appeared to unravel at the seams. He helped her out, paying no heed to her swaying on her feet, and carried her suitcase up to within a few feet from the entrance. They could see the police cordons and the uniforms checking the vehicles. He thrust the suitcase into her hand, and pointed her in the direction of the lights. Her legs felt like jelly, sweat poured off her, the lights shattered into multi-coloured shards that pierced her eyes, and the noise rushed at her like the surf. She stumbled past the police cordon, where her ticket and Nimmi's list of contact numbers that she held out to them were scrutinised, before she was waved into the waiting area. She chose a row of empty plastic seats and curled up on them. All she wanted was to sleep...

'Kals! Kals.' She recognised the voice, the same one she had heard at the airport before everything went black.

'Romy! You are here,' she croaked.

He rushed to her bedside. 'Kals. Thank God you are OK. We were all so worried about you.'

While Kalyani fed herself spoonfuls of honeyed yoghurt, he explained how as soon his papers were cleared at the transit airport, he had flown to Chitral, intending to hire a taxi to Sulaiman's house. But Alam had texted him to say that Kalyani was on her way back. So, he decided to wait for her at the airport.

'We were all worried that we could not reach you. Your mobile appeared to be switched off. Thankfully, Alam messaged us with updates from Biran. Nimmi and Shahida have been on the phone 24/7.'

Kalyani asked him what happened at the airport. 'Bet you don't remember,' Romy grinned. 'You were out for the count. I had to tell the officials you were drunk.'

'No! You didn't!'

'OK. I didn't. I told them you were pregnant and I had to rush you to the hospital in Peshawar to avoid complications.' He smiled at the horrified expression on her face. 'They gave me a wheelchair for you, and leg space on the plane, and didn't bat an eyelid when I finished your dinner as well.'

Kalyani was shocked to hear she had slept for a whole day. Fawzia and Aliya fussed endlessly over her, insisting she saw their family doctor, ate plenty of food and had fresh air. They made sure the calls to Nimmi and Shahida were kept short and did not tire her. No one plagued her with questions about her ordeal or the outcome of her trip. In fact, they were stepping on eggshells around her, in case she was one step away from losing her sanity. She hadn't told her mother that she had lost her happy pills.

In the evening, Romy sat with her on the terrace, chuckling at the newspaper. The setting sun turned everything pink. The smell of jasmine drifted up from the garden below, and Kalyani drifted back to the lotus pond and Raffa.

A sharp pain tugged at her heart, making her gasp. Romy looked up, alarmed. He leaned over and pulled the woollen blanket around her. This tiny gesture proved her undoing; her emotions finally bubbled over the cauldron, unbidden and uncontrolled. She sobbed and wailed and shook and trembled. Romy held her in his arms, until her delicate shoulders stopped shuddering. She clung to him, relishing the human touch and compassion. She had expected the same from her lover, Raffa, the man who knew her body intimately, every dip and curve and taste of her, yet had given her no solace. Instead, he had revelled in her shameless desire for him. She had walked over thorns for him, and had only her scars to show for it.

'Thank you,' she sobbed. 'For being there for me.'

Romy regarded her tenderly. He reached out and tucked a damp strand of hair behind her ears. 'You are welcome.'

Kalyani felt something she hadn't done for a very long time. She felt like a lost sailor who had spotted land.

*

Aliya was happy when Kalyani came down to breakfast.

'Glad you are well,' she cried, hugging Kalyani.

'How is your boyfriend?' she asked Aliya, when they were alone.

'Oh. He is not my boyfriend. Mum tells me that I will find much better friends at college, and I think she is right, for once.'

'Cool.'

'How is our dear niece, Tasneen?' asked Fawzia, when Aliya left to do some errands. Kalyani described her strange rituals, neglecting the part about the guns. She wanted to be safely out of Pakistan before she discussed it with anyone. Heaven only knew who was involved in what!

'She was always a drama queen, that one. A tragic one,' Fawzia mused. 'She was always one step away from drowning in a well or falling over a cliff. The electrician who had come to fix her television and accidently touched her had "raped" her, or the woman next door who glanced at her was a witch, who was planning to turn her into a rat.'

'Raffa is happy with her, I think,' Kalyani said, a disappointed note in her voice.

'So he is not planning to return?'

Kalyani shook her head.

Fawzia patted her arm tenderly. 'Poor Shahida,' she said.

*

Fawzia and Alam bid a fond farewell to Kalyani and Romesh. They had begged them to postpone their return trip until Kalyani had recovered completely, but Kalyani insisted it was better to keep to the plan. That morning, Romesh had a guided tour around Peshawar with Alam's driver, and Aliya made a pact with Kalyani to keep in touch.

Alam apologised for the unsavoury experience Kalyani had. 'I will never hear the end of it from Shahida,' he moaned. In return, Kalyani assured him that they were eternally grateful for all his help.

When their flight to Heathrow finally took off and the seatbelt sign disappeared, she heaved a sigh of relief. She smiled at Romy fidgeting beside her, reached up and planted a kiss on his cheek. He raised his eyebrow at her. 'You only have to ask if you wanted a sip of my Bloody Mary,' he joked, but she could see that he was chuffed to bits.

'You never asked me about my trip.'

'I reckoned you would tell me when you are ready. Did you get what you wanted?'

'From Raffa? I got closure. Yes.'

'Was that not what you wanted? I am sorry.'

'It is what it is. I will heal. But that is not what I wanted you to ask.' Romy sipped his Bloody Mary and waited. She lowered her voice. 'You did not ask me why I was so drowsy when you picked me up at the Chitral Airport.'

'I was only thinking of getting you back to Peshawar.'

'I was drugged.'

'You didn't... OD on your pills?'

'Not mine, you idiot. Someone drugged my water bottle.'

Kalyani told him about all about the guns and Tasneen's story, keeping her voice low. She didn't want to alarm their fellow passengers.

'Why didn't you say something to the authorities there? Or to Alam?'

'Because of what Raffa told me. He told me that this "game is way beyond small people. It involves big politics, tyrant countries". I didn't know who was involved. Raffa and Tasneen, for whatever reason, let me go. But Alam is a powerful man. If he is involved and we got on the wrong side of him, we would not be on this plane home. Or on any plane to anywhere.'

Romy downed his second drink in one gulp and ogled her.

'So why drug you?'

'They wanted to keep me quiet until I left their borders. They must have also loaded guns in the boot of the jeep, so if I called attention to myself, I would be the first to be implicated, and no one would believe my story. It explains why Biran panicked when he realised he had to pass through a police check post at the airport.'

'OMG girl, who says you cannot look after yourself? I... we should all bow down to you.' He raised his drink in a toast to her.

After a few minutes of ruminating, Romy asked. 'I am still intrigued as to why they let you go.'

'Too many people knew where I was; getting rid of me would get messy. Easier to drug me while they shifted the weapons to another hiding place. I would like to think there was also something deeper than that. Tasneen could see something of herself in me: we are both survivors, who have taken the reins of life into our own hands and ridden the storm.'

'Amen to that!' Romy tossed another dose of Smirnoff into his mouth.

'The only person who lost out in all this is poor Huma. She wanted justice for Harry.'

This time, she stopped Romy from carrying the drink to his mouth.

'Hey, go easy with the booze. Do you want to be detained again?' she hissed.

*

Forty-eight hours after she reached home, Kalyani walked over to Shahida's house. When Shahida found that Rafik hadn't returned with Kalyani, she had been in no hurry to meet.

Shahida led her into the kitchen, and half-heartedly offered tea. Kalyani opted for a glass of water.

'So you couldn't persuade him to come back?' Shahida raised an eyebrow, as she slid the glass towards her. Kalyani sipped her water, and decided to ignore the remark. 'Did he tell you why he left?' There was bitterness in Shahida's voice. She wasn't relishing the fact that she was at the mercy of the younger woman.

Kalyani nodded. 'He told me he wanted a change of scene.'

'Obviously,' Shahida spat.

Kalyani observed her over the rim of her tumbler. She owed this woman nothing; she could rise from her chair right now and simply leave.

Two days ago, when she arrived home, tired and sleep deprived, she had made several promises.

'I promise never to put you through this ordeal again,' she told her parents. To Minna, 'I will never forget you are my dearest sister and my closest friend.' She texted 'Love and Peace' to Helen. Above all, as she held his tiny body so close she could feel his heart beat, she promised her son she would never leave him, to be by his side no matter what, to protect him from all that hurts in this world, and to help him pick up the pieces when things go wrong.

Shahida was a mother too. In this very kitchen, she would have made umpteen promises to her own son, Raffa. For her, there would be no closure. She could not walk away, like Kalyani had. Her unconditional love for Raffa would not allow her to.

When she realised Kalyani was not forthcoming with any more information, Shahida asked in a small voice, 'How is he?'

'Happy. He is teaching children. He looks well.'

Despite herself, Shahida burst into tears. Hesitantly, Kalyani moved to her side, expecting the older woman to resist any offer of sympathy, but Shahida clung to her, sobbing.

'Let me make us some tea,' Kalyani said when finally, Shahida released her.

'You don't know where the teabags are,' Shahida sniffed.

'Show me?'

The women worked together to make the tea, awkwardly shuffling around each other. They carried the cups and a plate of biscuits into the garden, where the last remnants of summer glowed warmly. They watched the blackbirds hopping and pecking the crumbs around the bird table.

'I wasn't the only reason why he moved away,' Kalyani said, inclining her head and squinting into the sunlight.

Shahida nodded tearfully, reached out and squeezed Kalyani's hand. 'My son has hurt you so much. I am so sorry.'

Kalyani felt her own tears starting. Choosing her words carefully, she said, 'You are hurting too. Raffa has hurt us all, with his thoughtless deeds. But, I think deep down, he is suffering too. I think one day, he will regret the choices he has made, and he will want you in his life – more than ever. He needs to know you will be there for him, whatever happens. Your love alone will steer him home – wherever home is. You have to speak to him, and to Alam and Tasneen and Sulaiman Kaka. Very soon.'

She could see the confusion in Shahida's eyes. Kalyani had spent two whole days agonising on how much to reveal to Raffa's parents. She concluded that they would never believe her story, and accept that their son could get involved in such wrong doing. They would accuse her of making it all up. Besides, by revealing how much she knew, she would be putting herself and Kiran at risk. Better to allow them to find out for themselves.

'You are talking in riddles,' Shahida accused.

'I am sorry. All I can say is that Raffa is involved in things that could cause more harm than good. And you have to stop him before it is too late.' Shahida frowned and fiddled with her cup, lost for words.

'There is something else,' Kalyani continued – she had rehearsed this part of her speech. 'It is obvious that Raffa is no longer in my life or Kiran's. Kiran is your grandson. I would like you to be part of his life, but for reasons that you will understand later on, I do not wish Raffa to have contact with his son – not directly or through you. I do not expect anything from you. As his mother, I will have sole responsibility for his upbringing. If you can accept this, you are welcome in our lives. If not, I will understand.'

Shahida took a moment to process what she had heard. She recognised the benevolence of the proposal. Kalyani could have forced her to choose between her son and her grandson. Fresh tears of gratitude welled up in her eyes. Leaning across, she patted Kalyani's arm. 'You are a good girl, Kalyani. May Allah be with you.'

*

Heeding Kalyani's warning, Shahida and Ashraf made several trips to Peshawar. They also rejoiced in the progress Kiran was making – his first words, his first tooth, his first steps, his simple joy over the little things in life; a stone, a flower, butterflies and birdsong.

A year later, Ashraf accepted a job at an international concern based at Peshawar. They sold their house and left the UK. Shahida hinted that marriage and grandchildren might be on the cards.

That same year, Romy went down on one knee and proposed to Kals in the middle of his band performance. He gave her a ring he had made out of a broken guitar string. Soon after, Kalyani rang Raeba the wedding planner. This time, she was prepared and armed with lists for her impending wedding.

About the Author

Su dedicated most of her adult years to a successful medical career. One day, when an old school friend asked her when she was going to write a book, she heard the muses calling. Her debut novel, Jilted has blood, sweat and tears smeared all over it. But she has also cherished every minute she spent telling the story of Kalyani and Rafik.

Su spends any available spare time on writing poetry, abstract art, gardening, and looking after the family – in no particular order.

Her published book of Poetry – A Poetry Pit Stop is available on Amazon. She is currently writing her second novel, and compiling a new collection of Poetry.

Connect with me on Facebook at
www.facebook.com/sumattiewrites

37448269R00202

Printed in Great Britain
by Amazon